GOD, HOW SHE WANTED HIM.

His lips were soft. And hard. And demanding.

His tongue sought entrance bit by bit, and Cathleen surrendered it gladly.

Her body moved by itself . . . closer to him . . . and she knew instinctively it was because she wanted, needed, to feel him against her. His tongue danced with hers as his upper torso moved in combination with his lips on her mouth. Back and forth. Against her lips. Against her breasts.

Mesmerized by the energetic lethargy she felt, she moved away, raised her head and looked at him.

His eyes were molten earth, blazing from the passion that burned bright and hot.

Oh, how she wanted Matthew, this man who was not what he seemed.

"Saints and angels help me," she whispered into the wind.

The wind did not hear. Matthew did.

He smiled crookedly . . . and fatally.

"There is no help for this, Cathleen. There is only more. I can give you more . . . if you want it."

BARBARA CUMMINGS

FORTUNE'S FIRE

Kensington Publishing Corp.
850 Third Avenue
New York, NY 10022

ZEBRA BOOKS
KENSINGTON PUBLISHING CORP.

ZEBRA BOOKS are published by

Kensington Publishing Corp.
850 Third Avenue
New York, NY 10022

First Printing: October, 1994

Printed in the United States of America

There are men too gentle to live among wolves. I have had the privilege to live with and love one of them for forty years. I have also had the pleasure of giving birth to another.

To the two *B*s in my life: Bill, my husband. Bob, my son.

Hang in there, guys! God's not finished with me yet.

Prologue

Ireland, 1771

Her cheek was softer than satin. The back of his knuckles could still feel the texture.

Her breath was sweet. It lingered in his brain, overpowering the pungent smoke from the fireplace. Why could he not forget that she was a thief?

Her skin was translucent. He smiled, remembering how her temple would throb when he approached; but he quickly turned the smile into a frown when his body heated and hardened.

Her nose was small and straight and lightly dusted with cinnamon-colored specks, as if the fairies which peopled her land wanted her to forever remain young.

In all the world ... no smile compared ... not only because of her full, generous lips and straight, white teeth, but because she smiled often and joyously. Certainly she did. She had the world, and him, fooled into believing she was more and less than she was—a thief.

He gritted his teeth and gripped the arms of his chair to will away these contradictory thoughts. By all that was holy, because of all she had done to him, he should be over her! Why then could he not think of anything other than what was wonderful about her?

He slammed his hand on the desk top, sending the ink pot into the books and rattling the glass stopper so it clanged, and jarred, and matched his new mood. Bah! This traipse through memory lane led nowhere, to naught but confusion. He must keep that in mind, else he would lose far more than Cathleen Cochran's family had taken from him already.

So Matthew Forrest, the Earl of Dunswell, picked up his quill pen and with a flourish appended his new title to a complaint which would produce a writ and send the magistrate's guards to arrest those responsible for looting Dunswell Manor and Dunswell Stables.

The damnable thing was, she would not be one of them!

The point bent and broke, and Matthew swore loudly and long. But he sanded the ink nonetheless, blew it off, folded the paper, held a mahogany-colored candle over the edge until there dripped down sufficient sealing wax to hold the flap securely. Then, using his new signet for the first time, he pressed it firmly into the wax.

Done.

He called for Fenwick, his estate steward, who was attempting to fill the servant shortage with reluctant village people—and having a damnable time in the attempt—and ordered him to deliver it to the magistrate, "Posthaste, Fenwick. Before they know we know where they are."

"Aye, my lord. And about time, I do say, sire. Terrible lot, these Irish. Terrible lazy louts. And cunning. All of them. Cunning and sly."

"Aye, man. Now be off with you."

Fenwick returned quickly from his errand and reported that the magistrate would serve the writ on the morrow.

The next night, as Matthew tossed and turned in his bed, disturbed by his nightly dream of her, the magistrate's guards swooped down on the Cochran enclave, confiscated the property delineated in the writ of seizure, and—after tying their arms behind them with leather thongs—arrested all the Cochrans who had been responsible for stealing property which was claimed by Matthew Forrest, the Earl of Dunswell.

Cathleen—the paragon of virtue, the angel, the devil—screamed the house down and cursed the land the Earl walked upon, the very air he breathed.

1769

Deception

Chapter One

Ireland.

The green isle.

Matthew Forrest loved the land and people but was sick to death of the landed gentry—the English who had wrested great chunks of the delicate island from the original owners and were now in seemingly complete dominion, especially here in Ulster and neighboring Leinster. The English had settled in either place because it was only a few miles over the Irish Sea or St. George's Channel to England's snug winter homes. The municipal districts of Connaught and Munster—to the west and south—were still too untamed to garner attention of folk who liked as many comforts as they could get.

And there were many of the English gentry chasing their comforts that evening late in April. Late, but early in the season for many English families. There were enough, however, of the gentlemen and ladies in residence to occasion the first of the spring and summer "at homes."

Matthew had positioned himself behind heavy draperies, the better to see the assemblage which represented the best of the best of the new England—the monied class which had risen through fealty and bribery to titled status. He did not particularly want to be there, but a promise to a father was a promise not lightly given.

On his death bed Robert Forrest had begged a boon: *Get that title, Matthew. It is our due. We have paid for it with our bread, if not our lives. Foreswear it, my son. Foreswear it.*

Robert had been right and generous. He had paid off many of the King's and parliament's war debts, asking "only for that which lesser men had gotten." They came, tricorn and bills of lading in hand, bills long overdue, bills for armaments and food for the Army in the Colonies. Ah, for a time he was feted by any minister who had debts to pay.

The French and Indians have us in a screwpress, Master Forrest. We need Swiss arms; but the mercenary Swiss refuse our orders until these paltry sums are settled. The King tears his hair out, what little he has, and worries that the people will suffer because of the scarcity of currency. Please, only this small favor, my good man. The treasury is near bankrupt. The country will pay dear for our losses in the Colonies. Give but this boon and I shall be

*your champion at court. A title and lands I will
barter for you. It is only right and just for such
a generous man.*

But Robert Forrest had been wrong to trust base
ministers, some who had earned their own titles
merely for introducing their King to a young lady,
who quickly became the newest mistress to the
crown. Robert's life had been vainly spent searching
for that which had been always promised and never
delivered.

Night after night, day after day, year after year,
Robert Forrest waited and wondered why the title—
such a simple thing—had ne'er been delivered. He
thought of many reasons; but he was so good within
himself he could not see behind false smiles and still
falser hearts. Matthew had keener vision. He knew no
Catholic would be welcome in the peerage, unless
forced to be put there. And Robert Forrest could not
do that. He could not demand to go where he was not
wanted, nor could he refuse to help his King. Where
the King's ministers and their sovereigns fell short,
Robert Forrest had, by example, taught his son honor
and duty and loyalty to family and country.

So Matthew foreswore to his dying father and
knew that in doing so he sealed his life to his father's
quest.

He had but to wait until this latest uprising in the
Colonies, these rumblings of independence and repre-
sentative rule. As he had expected, the ministers once
again came to Forrest and son, Mercantile.

"Your father was more than generous, my good man, more than loyal to his King. If you could see your way clear to double his last gift to George . . ."

By their manner, Matthew guessed they thought "like father, like son." But Matthew was not so naive as his father. And he had spent the last year of Robert's life watching this good man die by degrees because these men could not be trusted to keep their word.

"Ah, gentlemen . . . we have a small problem. I am, of course, most grateful that the King has singled me out in this manner. It shows great trust and great good sense. But I must be honest, my lords. I am afraid I cannot see my way clear to forward half the sum requested. Nay, not even a quarter of it . . . without due recompense."

The men answered, "But of course there will be recompense as soon as the conflict is completed satisfactorily and the country is at peace once again."

"Nay, my lords, you do not understand. My coffers are also on the dry side. I could, however, wet them a bit if there were a gesture of goodwill from the King prior to my donation for the cause. I do recall mention being made to my father of a title and lands? Now, if one . . . preferably both . . . were to arrive within the fortnight, I believe I could find sufficient funds in the company to satisfy each of you."

They left, hemming and hawing, perplexed that the interview had not gone as previous ones had, flummoxed that they had had to deal with an upstart half their age. Matthew smiled to himself, and stood firm.

So, it took Matthew only one month to accomplish what his father had not in ten futile years. When the next honor's list had been published, Matthew's name was on it.

As he stood behind the draperies in one of the grander drawing rooms in Enniskillen, set beside Lough Erne, Matthew was well aware that some men in that room had routinely scoffed at the Forrest name, snickered at his father and himself. For ten years, they had snubbed them on the street, ignored invitations to dinner, denied the Forrests' very existence. To them, the Forrests were not *English* since Matthew's mother and grandmother had not come from a European nobility. No, they had been born and raised among those ruffian Irish hordes across the channel. The Forrests, therefore, were not only un-English—they were barbarians.

Now, however, these men and their families fought to acquire estates in this barbaric country. Worst of all in their estimation, they had to swallow, bow, and pray to have the pleasure of Matthew's company, and offer rich wine and richer foods.

Though Matthew sometimes delighted in the outcome; he did not delight in the result. For he, too, was forced to swallow them and their ways, as he had learned to swallow so many things. But he kept his council; for he trusted few men until tested. Most had not weathered his exacting standards. And that was just as well ... Matthew liked his privacy ... but he had more on his mind that night than the perfidy of ambitious men. Yet it was not the ambition of

men which had him cosseted in a corner. It was the
ambition of women.

Mothers. Aunts. Sisters. Guardians.

Ambitious women. A pox on them.

He leaned nonchalantly—yet vigilantly—against a
post and surveyed the company that night. He kept
his eyes and ears sharp, lest he be accosted by one
such woman set on making him her son-in-law. That
would never do. He did not fit the strictures of
these . . . these folk who fought to bring the perqui-
sites of rank to a rankless land.

Silks and laces. Creped hair with spiral curls.
White powdered wigs. *Petit pointelle* waistcoats. Delicate jewelled fans. Satin slippers. Elegant gold watch
fobs. Pearls. Rubies. Emeralds. Sapphires. Diamonds.
And not all of the jewellery bedecking women. The
men wore their share in the shape of heraldic
brooches. Some of them may even have belonged in
their families; but Matthew doubted that most did. As
he would someday soon, these men had most likely
designed their own heraldic arms. Unlike Matthew,
however, who didn't give a sou for the new King, his
fellow Irish usurpers would have made their arms
conform as closely to the King's as was possible.
Judging from the number of red grounds in the
brooches, everyone, it seemed, was a sixth cousin
once or twice removed from royal blood. It was ludi-
crous.

But understandable.

For it was that these English landowners, like
him, had been granted an estate—not because it was

theirs through inheritance or through blood—but because of some honor or favor they had done King George. They had worked hard, or paid dearly, or, more probably, married a sixteen-year-old daughter to a licentious—but well-born—octogenarian.

Matthew eyed the number of young girls who fluttered around older men with steely, rheumy eyes, and shook his head at the baseness of the English barter system. These English Protestant landowners would sell their daughters' souls to gain her a title and them admittance to court. They were already about their business with Matthew. And suddenly it mattered not that Matthew was Catholic and half Irish. What mattered was that he was the new Earl of . . .

Matthew chuckled. He had no earldom yet, since he had no estate or land. He had only the silly sobriquet he had heard recently.

The Mad Earl.

He perked his ears at an indignant interchange on the other side of his leaning post—an interchange which most assuredly described himself.

". . . watching, always watching. And him near thirty and no wife in sight! Why, my dears, if he had not bedded his share of eligible widows, I should wonder whence his inclinations bent."

"But you would have him take notice of your Sarah, Felicity."

"Of course, Annabelle. Don't be a ninny. He is an Earl and Sarah would be an ideal Countess."

"They say he's mad, you know."

"Why? Because he has not yet settled on an estate?"

"Well, it does make it difficult to introduce him properly."

"He is an Earl. What more do we need to know?"

"The Mad Earl," Annabelle spat, and her skirts swished as they moved away.

So, there was talk tonight, too. What did it matter? Matthew cared not what others thought of him. Let them call him mad because he wandered alone among the common folk in the countryside. Drank in their coffee and ale houses. Scoured the hills and dells for an estate worthy of his father's and his own hard work. Was he mad because he crawled on hands and knees when necessary in cellars and attics to seek out the elusive difference which—when he found it, he would know it—set one estate higher than any other? Was he mad because he took no notice of eligible, marriageable girls, but set himself apart as he did tonight?

Then he would be mad and get on with his life.

"Forrest, my good man! There you are."

A tall, grey-haired gentleman with a smiling face but anxious eyes took Matthew's elbow and leaned closer in a confidential stance. Alan Cook had been one of the few English-Irish who had been more than merely civil to Matthew. He had been helpful in Matthew's quest to find the right estate.

The man looked as if he had forgotten something in his toilette; and Matthew was amused to see that his waistcoat was stained with gravy and his lace shirt sleeves grimy with soot. "How have you been, Alan?" Matthew asked. The next words out of Alan's mouth gave evidence of the reason for his anxiety and *deshabille*.

"Harried. Margaret is in her ninth month and I must hurry back or she threatens to play Salome and have my head. But I wondered ... in your quest to find the perfect domain have you heard about the Dunswell estate in Donegal?"

"Only that it has been on the ministers' foreclosed list for three years."

"Almost four, now. And empty the last two because it sits in the hills a four-day ride from Dublin or Dundalk. No one who has seen it has wanted it."

"Because of its isolation?"

"That, and because it has only twelve rooms ... with an additional few servant quarters."

"Sounds small for the likes of this crowd."

"Aye. But I thought you might not need so much space since you seem determined to go to your grave unwived."

"St. Paul admonished that wives were only to be taken if men must. Thus far no woman has forced the bindings on me."

"Ah, but you do not know the joys of marriage, Matthew," Alan said with a sigh.

"Do I not?" Matthew cocked his head and nodded toward a particularly fetching figure, surrounded by a coterie of admiring men. "Widow Flemming would argue that point."

"Ah, Matthew! 'Tis not the pleasures of the flesh which matter. 'Tis more to life than that."

"If so, I have not found it."

"You have merely not found the right woman."

"Mayhap you are right, Alan. But, pray, tell me about this Dunswell."

"They say the rooms are large and airy . . . and . . ." He winked. "And I have discovered lately that it has one remarkable saving grace . . . its stables."

"Ah!" Matthew laughed. "You do love your horses."

"If you had seen the ones from Dunswell Stables, you would love them, too. They produced sixteen winners at the Bellinaugh Stakes, Matthew. Sixteen!"

Though they had only known each other a short time, Alan knew Matthew well. Race horses doing what they did best were Matthew's passion. He did not wager, instead he watched their symmetry; their vigor, their undulating muscles. He admired their will to win—their heart. Aye, that was all that separated true champions from come-laters.

Heart.

But sixteen winners from one stable? To accomplish that kind of feat, there had to be more than merely horses with heart.

"Irish bred racers are particularly swift—if they are well trained. But they have been known to be unpredictable. I have lost many wagers when a steed with seemingly impeccable ancestry should have swept the field."

"Aye, Irish bred have been unpredictable in the past. But these that I saw were not merely Irish bred. They were taller, longer, and had the unmistakable dark ears and tail of the Arabian or Turk."

"A mixed breed?"

"Aye. It appears so. And better than all the others at the Stakes, I vow."

Matthew had always envisioned himself with the kind of horses that not only could run like the wind but were the embodiment of the wind herself. Purpose. Pride. Valor. Devotion. Freedom. Those, he found in horses. Most he found in himself, for Robert had bred them into him just as surely as they had been bred into horseflesh.

But freedom? True freedom? This, he did not find in himself.

He wanted it . . . craved it. Yet found it only when he allowed his tightly reined spirit to soar with the horses on whom he placed a tiny portion of his fortune.

Ah, what irony. He could not leave Forrest and Son, Mercantile. His father and grandfather had spent their lives building it. Matthew was bound to it as fiercely as he was bound to his family name. In truth, he did not want to leave it; he merely wanted a measure of his life to be different from what he had. To be more spontaneous . . . more tuned to the vagaries of nature, not the stultifying columns of figures which were his daily fare.

And here—in this isolated Dunswell estate—Alan had found a step in the direction Matthew wished to go. A strain of horses to rival Arabians and Turks. If he had a stable with this breed, he would find a capable manager for the business and devote his energies to a pursuit of that which had eluded him thus far.

"But if the house is empty, Alan . . . how, then, do the stables thrive?"

"The Cochrans. They have been hired by the estate agents to manage the grounds and stables until a buyer can be found."

"The Cochrans? The breeders and trainers from the Donegal Stakes?"

"The very same." Alan grinned. He dug into his waistcoat pocket and brought out a square of paper. "I have the estate agent's name and location. He would be delighted to show you the place . . ." He withdrew the square and held it above his head. "Unless, of course, you are no longer interested?"

Matthew laughed and made a grab for the paper. "You know damned well I am!" He waved his arm around the walking finery. "It will give me good excuse to leave this folderol far behind." He grasped Alan's hand. "Wish me luck."

"You shall need it," Alan said. "You go into the northernmost section of Ireland, Matthew. 'Tis wild and icy. Take warm clothing."

Matthew had taken abundant warm clothing. But he cursed himself for having abandoned his coach and four, his heated bricks, his upholstered seats, his myriad lap rugs, his pewter tankards of brandy, and taken to horseback. He laughed to himself. Surely he *was* mad. Yet, he wanted to see the country he would settle in as it was, not as the gentry forced it to be. He wanted to evaluate this Dunswell estate as a stranger, not as a prospective buyer. And he wanted to assess any villagers who could become servants, groundskeepers, and stable hands. Most especially, he wanted to take the measure of these Cochrans, the people who would manage the estate should he buy it. He wanted a staff as feisty as mongrels, fighting for scraps; not fawning like pampered lap dogs, licking their master's hand for treats.

In truth, he wanted what he believed was the reality of Ireland, not the facade the English had erected.

But reality did not make for a pleasant ride. And the pursuit of freedom had damnable drawbacks. Matthew groaned and gritted his teeth against the ever present mist which would have been called rain in England. The first week in May, and still teeth-rattling cold. No wonder the island was as green as agates. The grass sucked up the mist, as thirsty as the people were hungry. But Matthew was becoming accustomed to the cold, wet mornings and the warm, dry, sun-sparkling afternoons.

Matthew pulled his cloak around him and clicked to the horse he had hired in the village. The directions the estate agent had given should put Dunswell Manor just around the next bend. Which meant the land for one hundred acres before and behind him, and over the hills and down to the river and Dunswell

Draw—"Where you shall find the best trout and salmon fishing in all of Donegal," according to the estate agent—was part of Dunswell Estate.

"An earldom and an Irish estate, Father. What you always wanted," he whispered into shadows already dappled with a sun which struggled to escape its cloak of clouds. Oaks and elms grew beside the single-laned road. Their strong branches reached high, some bending across the lane, all studded with lime-colored half-open buds. They would make a fine canopy when once full leafed, a twisting tunnel marking the entrance to the estate.

The house kept sentry on a slight rise, where the bricked carriageway curved in a half-circle. The house itself was faced with weathered dun-colored brick, but its sides and what he could see of the back were white-painted wooden clapboards. Central double doors. Three windows to either side of them. Eight windows above. Center and two end fireplaces. The agent had said the house and outbuildings were timbered from oaks grown on the estate. They were also shaded by them. Dozens of oaks, elms, and sycamores rimmed the hill on which the manor house stood.

"Cool in the summer from all that, I doubt not." He chuckled again and chided himself for talking aloud when alone. "The Mad Earl will earn his sobriquet if you keep that up, old boy!"

Matthew alighted at the hitching post and dug into his waistcoat pocket to consult the written description the agent had given him. He read it over carefully, then tethered his horse and strode purposefully up onto the front portico. The double doors gave inward. He almost knocked, but decided against it. He wanted to see it without the intrusiveness of a local caretaker breathing down his neck.

Inside, Matthew found that Dunswell Manor was empty of caretakers ... and of most of the previous owners' furniture. Auctioned to pay off creditors, the agent had said. Only a harp stood silently in one corner of the righthand drawing room. He strummed the strings and was amazed that they thrummed clear and on-key. Who cared enough to keep it in tune? More likely the agent had sent a tunesmith, hoping to put in order whatever was left, to make a good impression. A fervent hope, born out of desperation to sell a house which had been on the lists for almost four years. If not Matthew, there might be no buyer at all.

For an hour, Matthew prowled the twelve family rooms and additional servant quarters. On the first floor—on either side of the central hall—were two front drawing rooms. Behind one drawing room was a large dining room which looked as if it would comfortably seat twenty. Behind the other drawing room, a library whose walls were lined by carved oak bookcases. On the second floor, three bedrooms took up the front of the house. A large master suite and an accompanying nursery and sick room rimmed the back. The ground level held two kitchens. A summer kitchen in the back, opening onto a square which must have once been used for a kitchen garden. The winter kitchen was tucked into the front to keep out drafts during the bitter months. Between the two were storage and scullery rooms. Two suites for butler and housekeeper in the attic. According to his list, the other, much smaller, servant quarters could be found above the stables.

As Matthew left by the back door, he noted that the sun had finally burned away the grey and rain. The rolling hills around the manor house sparkled with raindrops, looking as if a million fairies had dropped their dust. He smiled. A grand house this was. It was huge for this part of Ireland. Not as large as others he had seen; but he did not need monstrous meandering corridors and useless turrets. He saw no need to advertise his wealth. He had it. That was enough.

As he skirted a wide-open field which held remnants of many previous seasons' rye harvest, he marveled at the order and symmetry of the stables. Here was a horse-breeding station worthy of its name.

Beyond the rye field lay a training oval, where three men and several boys put a half dozen horses through their paces. Matthew sucked in his breath at the spectacle. The horses were not of one color, as in most stables. Instead, these were variegated. Greys. Pied browns. Roans. Russets. Dun yellows. All with unmistakable dark tails and ears. And all running as if trying to catch the tail of a comet.

Good God, they were magnificent!

But he did not get much chance to enjoy the spectacle because the peace of the estate was shattered by a loud voice laced with impatience and a touch of a woman's laughter.

"Stand still, you monster, or I shall sic the night fairies on you, I shall. I'll not have you prancing like a prince when there's exercising to be done. Now stand still."

A stamping and great gulps of breath, then one wicked whoosh of air gave rise to whoops of laughter.

"And who this day has sprinkled mischief dust into your oats? I'll not be able to sit on my backside for weeks if you keep this up, I won't. Here ..." a clanging sound interrupted the teasing voice, "... smell. 'Tis only a new bridle, Firebrand. And not the first you've seen. That's right. Only a little leather and iron. Naught to cause you injury. Not here would that be done, you Arab devil ... else how will you satisfy the mares awaiting you? Aye. That's it, that's right ... now I'll just slide this on, easy as sin ..."

Matthew crept quietly to see the Arab devil who might be the sire of those four-legged wild beasts in the training oval.

"Nay, I'll not force you to try the new saddle, too, One new thing is quite enough this day, my prince. And aren't you the good boy, standing there quiet as churches? Drat it, where is that stool?"

Matthew peered into the stall and staggered back at the sight of the horse and its master.

Good God, she was magnificent!

The sun shone in through the door of the stables on

hair streaming down her back. Red hair. No, more
like the mahogany chest he had in his bedroom.

God, the woman did remind a man of bedrooms.
And beds. What the hell was she doing? Kicking off
her boots and climbing on a stool beside the tallest,
darkest horse Matthew had ever seen. And he paid it
no mind because she bent, reached behind her to
scoop up her skirts, brought them through her stockinged legs, and stuffed them into her skirt band.

Good God, her legs were magnificent!

The bunched up skirt barely covered her backside
and left all else revealed. Before he could let out his
breath, she hopped up and down on the stool to give
herself spring, then vaulted onto the stallion's back.
He sucked in his breath as her skirt escaped its prison
in her hand and settled in two pools of cloth behind
and atop the saddle. Her bare thighs and knees encircled the horse as she tucked her feet firmly under his
heaving chest, closed her eyes and smiled, patting the
stallion with small, dirty gloved hands. Her eyes were
closed so he could not see what color they were. He
imagined green or blue. The half-moon of her lashes
rested on cheeks reddened by the cold. Her nose was
small, her face a perfect oval. And when she smiled
her full lips curved deliciously, and a dimple appeared near her right cheek.

He had been to court many times and spent countless hours in the company of beautiful women who
powdered and rouged to achieve what this one had
without artifice. A more sensuous vision Matthew
had never seen.

She could have been dressed in queenly garb and not looked more beautiful. As it was, she wore a heavy green wool corset over a white woolen chemise. Those legs—he had to take more deep breaths and noticed that he no longer felt the bone-chilling cold—were encased in green and brown tweed woolen stockings that ended just above her knees and left a good twenty inches of thigh exposed . . . to be savored. But only for an instant, because when she raised her head, she gasped, then reached to a hook on the wall for a dark brown cloak. But the stallion danced away and her hand grasped air. She threw an anxious glance over her shoulder and from somewhere near the cloak she produced a fine musket. Faster than he could blink, she dropped in firing powder and leveled the damned thing directly at him, but too low to do much good.

He grinned and stepped forward.

She cocked the musket.

"Nay, sire. 'Tis not what you think, so close up your mouth and wipe it dry. Cathleen Cochran is not for the taking, by you nor any other. Nay, stand firm! This musket is fully loaded and I am Donegal's best shot. Take one more step into this stall and 'tis gelded you'll be."

Chapter Two

"Whoa, now, Mistress Cochran . . ." Matthew held up his hands as if to ward off the ball and sucked in his breath. "I mean you no harm."

"Creeping up on a girl unawares, and you mean her no harm? You would have had a laugh and a half in the pub this night, once you had pulled your way with me, I vow." She began to slip from Firebrand's back, but a tightening of her thigh muscles kept her upright. "Thank the saints and angels I listened to my da's warning about roaming men and what they do if given the chance. Now I keep a musket near to hand with fresh balls full loaded."

She looked him over, squinting to bring his silhouette out of the stream of sunlight and realized she could see naught but that he was wider in the shoulders than any of the Cochrans—and taller. For a woman, she was the best shot in the district—and could beat most of the men, besides. But she had dumped so much powder into the breech she was afraid to fire the blasted thing. She'd like to put her own eye out if she did. So what in the world was she going to do with him until her da and her brothers got back?

The ropes coiled on the wall gave the answer.

Tie him up, of course! Then let the Cochran men deal with him. If he had an explanation for creeping up on her, he could well give it when she was safe from his reach and ruin.

"Back out of here, now, and perch yourself down on the barrel, there, against the wall."

She made another grab for the cape but missed. She cursed and tugged her skirt down as best she could. She pulled so hard the tie in the rear gave and she stopped quickly else she lost it completely. "Blast!" Since she had to hold her skirt on, she could only urge Firebrand forward using the pressure she applied with her knees. It was enough. The man backed up . . . but his eyes . . .

His dark, dark eyes . . .

What was happening? She had all she could do to keep her seat on the large stallion—still skittish because of stomach gas from the week before—and here she was, swimming in a chocolate gaze so potent it threatened to pull her under . . . and off . . . and away from the tight hold she had on the trigger. "Blast!" She shook her head and tried to keep her aim. Tried to ignore those glistening brown eyes and the message they held. Nay. She had to hold to the message. Had to remember the danger she was in. But how to keep those thoughts uppermost, steady

Firebrand, hold the musket to her eye, and keep her skirt round her legs too . . . it was impossible. Suddenly, the skirt caught on the edge of the stall door and swept out as Firebrand clomped past the opening of her hand.

And the foolish man stood there, gaping for more than a few heartbeats before he up and grinned crookedly at her exposed thighs. Well, for the love of the fairies! She had a musket trained on him and he acted as if . . . as if . . .

Oh, Fergus and Oisen, she was in for it for certain, she was, now! She dared not move, else he strike.

Then, with one long, sweeping, heart-pounding look, he unabashedly took as thorough an inventory of her as ever she had seen. "God in heaven," he said.

And they called women brazen, did they? *God in heaven,* aye.

Such a look he gave her that her hands began to shake. Her mouth went dry.

"Sit," she ordered.

"Aye, Mistress Cochran."

"I'm no man's mistress, sire." She glared when the left side of his mouth once again popped up crookedly. She could imagine what had flashed through his mind at her words. Best now to set straight this man thing before his imagination curled round twice over. "I am called Cathleen, or my friends may call me Cat."

"I think I shall call you Cathleen. 'Tis soft as your voice and hair."

She rolled her eyes. "Foolish flattery."

"Aye. Once I crossed the borders of your fair country I caught it."

"Like a pox?" She asked with an arched brow.

"Nay. Like a melody. After tramping the countryside, spending my days and nights with your people, I could not help but pick up the winsome ways they have with their tongues."

He looked at her expectantly, and she knew he wondered if she found him winsome. Well, she would not fall for that trap. *Sure and the fairies are muddling your mind, Cathleen.* She knew she did find him winsome, regardless of the situation in which they now found themselves. The man was handsome, veering on charming. For some reason, she found herself inexplicably, powerfully, attracted to him. She dare not allow him to ken her true thoughts concerning him, the sly devil, else who knew what might arise from such knowledge.

"And why would you be tramping the countryside?"

By her blush, he knew she fought to bring ordinariness to their conversation. Well, if that was how she wished to play it, he would give in—this time. He would have other chances to bring her round to his way of thinking, *if* he did naught to bring her suspicions to the boil. "I tramp, trying to find a place for myself."

And, indeed, that was exactly what Matthew was trying to do—trying to find a place for himself. A manor house, not a hut or cottage. But he did not want this woman—this beauty of the first order—to know exactly who he was and what he was doing there. He did not want the gentry to discover he was here and extend their interminable invitations. He could not bear one more mother pushing her daughter forward and the vile girl vying to be the next countess of . . .

He perked up and cocked an eyebrow around the stables, then focused fully on that gorgeous stallion and the more gorgeous rider. If things worked out as he hoped—that is, if the stables were as they had been advertised—then he quite possibly could be known as the Earl of *Dunswell.* But if this lass suspicioned it, it would spoil things, put up a wall between them. And, damn him, he did not want that to happen. He would, in fact, like to get to know this woman. He sighed. It was the first time he'd had any interest in any woman, young or no. But there was one way to ingratiate himself to her *and* to learn all he could about the estate, the stables, and the content—especially the female portion of it.

"I've been seeking a situation," he said.

"Well, there's plenty of places around, and all. But not much in the way of work. This is a poor land, but harbors proud people."

"Aye. So I have noticed." He winked, smiled once again, put out his hands, and gave way to the broad chest of the horse she kept inching forward.

Oh, she did like his smile, she did. It caused his square, almost stony face, to soften—but only a dram.

When his knees finally reached the barrel and he plopped down on it, he crossed his legs and nonchalantly leaned back against the wall. Saints and angels, he was a fine eyeful. Dark brown hair, darker eyes under thick brows. A chiseled nose above a pleasant mouth. And that crooked smile, which settled in to stay above a square chin and firm jaw.

His clothes were coarse, but better made than those her da and brothers wore on a Sunday. Fine wool, they were, with good, sturdy boots hardly scuffed at all, and wasn't that strange? The dark brown of his weatherproofed cape matched perfectly his trousers and coat. On neither coat nor cape was there intricate needlework or embellishments; but his corded vest was overworked with tiny fleurs like those on the Norman flag.

He surely had not been tramping the countryside.

"And exactly what kind of situation are you seeking hereabouts?"

He hoped his lies wouldn't earn him a place in hell, but he had no choice if he were to remain *incognito*. "I've worked as a stable hand and trainer."

She whooped with laughter. "You? Mucking up stalls with those boots and those clothes?"

Clever, she was, damn her. And damn himself for thinking these would pass as proper garments of the working folk in this area. He had been too long away from the docks and ensconced in his office. His father had always said he needed to get down in the muck once in a while, to put a proper perspective on his life.

" 'Tis not forever that we have had this good fortune, my son. And unless we know what the true working man does to earn his bread, we'll not know how to get it again if we lose it."

With taxes rising—every hour, it seemed—it was getting harder and harder to turn a decent profit. Oh, it would take a major catastrophe to wipe him out; but he could become circumscribed if he wasn't careful. Which was why he was being so cautious in his selection of estates. He did not want to mortgage his future. Dunswell Manor was large enough for him, yet small enough to keep the tax collectors at bay for several years. He could easily pay the bankers the entire mortgage on the estate and have enough left over to increase the size of the stables. A good fifteen horses coming into foal next Spring would exactly fit the dreams his father had once had. Matthew had achieved the title, found an estate worthy of his father's life and death. Now he had his own dreams to pursue.

"I must admit I've had a spot of luck; but good things don't always last. So I'll take whatever I can get for now. I'm a strong man and a good worker. I'll once more work my way forward."

She began to laugh and with each soft giggle her fear of him vanished as quickly as treacle pudding set before her brothers. "Aye. I've no fear you'll work your way forward. Forward seems to be the only way to go. Unless there's a horse pushing you backwards and a musket trained on your breeches."

He grinned, liking the thrilling whoosh of her laughter's sounds and the dimple next her chin. She was that perfect part of Ireland, like the story of the rose of the rood—a piece of heaven dropped from the sky to bloom in the warm sun of Saint Patrick's isle.

"I have had many backward days, and better ones beside. But not many better views."

She looked at the sparkle in his eyes and the angle at which he viewed her and her heart near dropped out of her breast. She had donned only one underskirt that morning, though it was quilted. Why, he could see right up past her stockinged legs and under to the skin of her thighs . . . and more besides!

"Cathleen! By the blessed mother, what are ye doin' sitting astride with not a coverin' on your legs? And who is that there at the end o' your musket?" Maeve Cochran whipped the skirt from the floor and threw it over her daughter's lap. "He didna . . . did he, Cathleen?"

"Nay, Mama. He mere surprised me, he did." Though the weight of the blasted musket had her shoulders in knots, she dared not lower the thing. Her mother had asked the one question she could not answer. With a proud snap of her head, she asked the blasted intruder, in imitation of her indignant mother, "Who is this here at the end of my musket?"

Matthew tipped a salute to the fortyish woman who looked not at all like her daughter. She was squat where Cathleen was tall, grey to Cathleen's mahogany, blue eyes to Cathleen's green ones. Mrs. Cochran had a round face with puffy cheeks, small nose, pointed chin. She looked worn and weary, painted not with powder and rouge but with a haunted look which spoke sad secrets. But if there was a sadness there, she seemed to visibly force it down as she conversed with her daughter. Though obviously not at all amused by the situation in which she had found Cathleen, she had not been able to put a tough, harsh edge to the soft, musical cadences of her voice. It was so much like her daughter's—and surprisingly the only trait of hers which had been passed along to Cathleen.

She seemed like a nice woman who was forced to face something dreadfully unpleasant, and was braving it out for the sake of her family. He hated like hell to do what he must.

"My name is Matthew . . . Dunn."

Of course it was. And wasn't. But when he became the Earl of Dunswell, he would not be lying. He was certain that then he could explain the reasons for this momentary and quite innocent deception.

"He says he's looking for work," Cathleen explained.

"Here? When we're barely able to support ourselves? He must be daft."

"Nay, Mistress Cochran. I'm neither fool, nor daft. I scouted out the situation and know the land is poor and the estate in the hands of creditors. But I'm more than a fair hand in the stables and fields. I'll work for food and lodging until there's money enough to pay me."

"Would you, now?" Maeve's face screwed up and she squinted into the sun and out, across the fields which surrounded the house. She thought quickly, then decided even more quickly. "I could use a good man in the fields. They've ne'er been planted yet and spring near done." Maeve ignored the astonished expression on Cathleen's face. "The men and women . . ." she glared at Cathleen, ". . . all in this family are besotted with those halfbreeds of theirs. My men are too busy to put shoulder to spade and Cathleen is needed in the training oval with this monster she sits, since none can tame him but her. But I don't ken where you could settle. The estate manager willna' allow us to lodge in the house, the wicked beast. So only the four rooms over the stables do we have."

Once she realized her mother truly meant to give this stranger shelter and bread in exchange for the work *Maeve* wanted done, Cathleen breathed easier. Her mother was overworked and Cathleen often felt guilty that she could not help do those things Maeve felt important. But Cathleen knew that training the horses—especially the reluctant ones like Firebrand,—was the family's only true way to survive. Knowing this, Cathleen ventured, "There's the tack room, Mama. 'Tis snug and backs up against the fireplace so 'twill be warm at night."

"Aye, daughter. Well . . . that's that, then." Maeve turned and retraced her steps to the stable door, giving instructions as she went. "Bring out your gear, Matthew Dunn, and settle in quick. We've no time to be awasting." When she got into full sunlight, she turned around and stood there with her hands bunched on her hips, her head cocked to one side. "Well? Are you deaf as well as daft? Put your legs to the floor, your body to standin', and hop to it."

Matthew grinned at the disparity between what this woman was and what she pretended to be. Though she tried mightily, she could not put that gruff, sharp edge to her voice which commanded. But if he wished to discover the true nature of this stable and the new breed it housed, he had best pretend she had as much presence as a regimental watch commander.

"Aye, mistress!" He hopped to his feet and looked at Cathleen. "You can lower that musket now, Cathleen. And I suggest a hot, wet poultice of horse ointment for your arms and shoulders or they will ache for a week."

Now where, Matthew wondered, as he rode away from the frowning Cathleen, would he get his "gear," as Mistress Cochran had put it? He could hardly ride into town and buy a workman's change of clothes. There was no such thing. A workman's garb was stitched by his wife or mother, of homespun and yard goods. *That*, at least, Matthew knew because of his merchant business. Nor could he command his own tailor to make him up a tramp's costume. It was over three weeks to London, and he needed good, solid workclothes *today*.

He thought of knocking on doors and offering to buy what he needed from a farmer's wife. But from long experience with the gossipy goodwives in all those drawing rooms and salons, that gesture would certainly occasion talk among the natives. If Cathleen were to hear that he was not what he pretended to be . . .

He shuddered. Naught would go well if that . . . he smiled . . . that *firebrand* were to start asking the right questions in the wrong places. And Matthew did not doubt for a moment that Cathleen was more than capable of ferreting out information if she wanted and needed to do it. She had the look of the she-tiger about her. She would protect her territory and family . . . mayhap more than her mother would.

So . . . he couldn't buy the things he needed. And he needed more than clothes. He also needed tools and a kit bag with all the essentials in it, else how explain that he had been tramping the countryside with naught but a horse and a rolled-up blanket? No, he would have to show wooden or tin plate, cup and spoon; and basic tools such as a short-handled ax, small hammer with a few nails, a flint for starting fires, and a handgun and rifle for shooting game.

He growled in frustration.

It had seemed so simple. Merely pretend to be a worker and learn all he could about the people . . . *Hah!* He had been lying so much that day, now he thought to lie to himself . . .

And another lie, or at least a half-lie. Cathleen came into the dilemma into which he had snared himself good and proper. Or, hardly proper, the thoughts he had about that firebrand. The way she looked on the back of that stallion was like a queen on her throne. A half-naked Irish changling-eyed queen; but that only made it all the better.

Damn your eyes, Matthew Forrest! You should be scaring up some clothes and tools, not wasting your time on the most beautiful woman in Ireland.

Especially since it was getting damned hard to sit comfortably in his saddle with thoughts of her cluttering up his head.

Her stockings. He laughed aloud. They had been two colors. The one on her right leg, a neutral knit wool with a delicate rope pattern knit up the sides. The one on her left, a darker shade, as if dyed with onion skins. The pattern the same. But he guessed she had dressed in haste, and had given no heed to the color of things.

Ah, the color of things. At least he knew her hair was not artifice, brought to that unusual shade with a rinse of henna or red onion skins. No, he had had a good enough angle up those mismatched stockings to the dark at their apex to know that what was on her head was real.

Damnation! Were these breeches not tight enough, fool?

He reined in his horse at the top of a hill and eased himself from the saddle. He had to stop thinking about the woman and start finding a solution to his problems.

There must be something he could do to appear to be Matthew Dunn. . . .

He leaned against a tree and surveyed the land around him . . . land which might be his in a few weeks or months. The rolling hills went on for miles. It was not miles that caught his attention, however, but a nearby cluster of buildings on the edge of a stream . . . and the clothes spread out on the surrounding stone wall.

The woman of the house had obviously been doing her washing. There were men's things, sheets, aprons, even underskirts. And hanging on pegs at the side door were trousers, shirts, capes. He scanned the rest of the yard and saw tools scattered on the ground and several small outbuildings which could house others. A cache of treasure, surely. But to get it meant he must take from those who looked as if they had but little.

Take, hell . . . steal.

But not if he left coins in exchange. Technically, he would be buying. And if he left more than enough . . . his conscience might allow that.

Another half-lie, and this one more than a prick of the thumb.

But there was naught for it. He needed what was there. He mounted quickly and rode hellbent for leather over the hills toward the house and its booty. He only hoped he would not have to face down the owners.

When he entered the enclosure he slowed, fully expecting the same kind of greeting he had received from Cathleen. Save for two yapping dogs, however, the household was silent. He tethered his horse to a tree and crept up to the window to look in. He saw poverty and cleanliness; but not a man or woman, boy or girl. The outbuildings and barn yielded naught. But Matthew's keen eye spotted a group of people along the river, about two leagues away. Two men and two boys were in the water, fishing. One woman and a girl on the bank, gutting fish.

He might have time. . . .

When he left the house a sheet was tied onto his saddle. Inside were two pairs of trousers, two shirts, a pair of boots which were snug but not too long, three pair of stockings, a carpenter's apron, a wooden cup and bowl, a tin cup and plate, two spoons, one fork, one knife, an old chipped ax, and a flint box. On the settle table in the kitchen of the house he had piled up several pence, topped by two half-crowns.

At least Matthew Forrest, the new Earl, was not a thief.

Chapter Three

When Matthew returned to Dunswell Manor he found Maeve Cochran in the fields, hoeing a row of potato hills. She wore a soft-brimmed straw hat tied under her chin with black ribands and a homespun blue linen skirt and shirt, with an apron pinned to the front bodice and tied around her ample figure. She shaded her eyes, took a quick peek at Matthew and grinned.

"Well-a-day, is this the same man who left us an hour ago, now?"

Matthew could understand her surprise and amusement. He had abandoned his wool suit and harmonizing accoutrements for the mismatched costume he now wore. Black boots with rusty iron tips and heels. Knitted linen stockings. Too-large brown homespun breeches with tied front panel and side bands—and thank goodness for the ties, else the breeches would have cascaded over his hips at each step. The last of his clothes was a pale yellow homespun linen shirt, the sleeves rolled above his elbows because they were too long.

He felt uncomfortable and hoped he did not look it. He had to appear an ordinary workman if he hoped to mislead these Cochrans. From what he had seen of Cathleen and her mother, they were an unusual type—educated beyond the norm for this region. They would not take too kindly to his subterfuge; but he hoped they understood why he had thought it necessary to deceive, when once they learned the reason he had done it.

"I thought it best to begin today to earn my keep," he said.

"Aye. Though the day is almost over, working together should give us a good beginning." She handed him a hoe from a bundle of tools in a barrow. "You'd best start on the row behind me. I've already planted the potatoes. Now we must keep down the weeds." She spread her arms round the place and indicated fields fading off to the right, far away from the training oval. "All this must be hoed and planted if we're to get a crop at all."

"And you thought to do it yourself?"

"Nay. I hoped for Silent Sean's help."

"Silent Sean?"

"Our muck-out. He works in the stalls for the morning and helps me in the afternoon. But he's almost useless away from his precious horses. He can't speak, you see; but somehow he communicates with those four-legged beasties."

Matthew attacked the hill as vigorously as Maeve

did. When he chopped a few leaves off the plants in his unfamiliarity with the hoe, he pushed them into the dirt and aimed better next time. "Why, then, is Sean not here now?"

"Ah, there's one of those mares about to foal and he and Cathleen are keeping watch."

"Isn't it late in the year for birthing?"

"Aye, but Sidhe always drops late. Doesn't seem to hurt the foal. Her other two have kept pace with their cousins well enough and they are about their masters' business . . . running out on the flats."

With that, she clamped her mouth shut and did naught but dig at the base of hundreds of hillocks of potatoes. She worked hard and quickly and by imitating her actions, Matthew soon had an easy-going rhythm of his own. It was hot, dusty, back-breaking work; but Maeve did not complain. She worked for another three hours, until the sun began to set and a cool breeze crept over the hills around them. Then she surveyed what they had done, nodded and threw her hoe into the barrow.

"Supper in ten minutes, Mister Dunn. Wash first at the washing well behind the stables."

He strode up to a gathering of men and two boys . . . and Cathleen who pumped the handle for two young men with hair lighter than hers, but with faces and features which proclaimed them as Cochrans. She cocked an eyebrow at him and smothered a smile as she took him in from toe to head and back again.

He was dusty with the dirt of the potato fields. Sweat had run light-colored rivulets against dark dirt.

Oil from his skin and hands left dark spots against his shirt and trousers. His knuckles were grimier than the boys'. Yet there was something about him which made her pause and assess him closer. His hair had come out of its riband and hung around his shoulders. But it was cut clean and straight, not chopped off the way women, mothers, or betrotheds did for their men folks in these parts. Behind the grim, his face was unmarked. No cuts. No scars. No blemishes. Not one man in the village could claim the same. Hard work in the fields or on horseback produced accidents. Accidents left their mark. But not on this man.

And why were his fingernails not broken and split? Why, instead, were they cut straight across ... as if ....

She frowned and did not like the thoughts which brought on that frown. She had seen fingernails similarly cut but always on propertied gentlemen. If this man were working to get back to a position he had once had, he had lost it recently. Within the week, she'd warrant.

Why, then, had he come there? Certainly not to be a muck-out like Sean, nor a field laborer like Taddy Weeks. Although, from what he and her mother had accomplished, this Matthew Dunn was a good worker. Uncomplaining. Tireless. And able to take direction from a woman. Unusual, that. The men hereabouts ... the men in her own family ... were not of a mind to take orders from mother or daughter. Oh, they did as she and Maeve bid, but not *when* bid, not until they were of a mind to do it, if not of a dis-

position. And unlike Matthew, they made certain all
and sundry knew their displeasure. Matthew, had not
lashed out, nor denigrated, nor joked about his place
in the pecking order at Dunswell. Still, there was
something about him she could not name. She took
great care to listen to her misgivings. She had instances of second sight and now it niggled enough
that she vowed to keep careful watch on this Matthew Dunn.

"And who might you be?" one of the brothers
asked as Matthew toweled his face dry.

Matthew got a shock when Cathleen said, "He
calls himself Matthew Dunn and *says* he's had experience in field and stable." Could she have guessed?

"He's to be Mama's field hand. Though I warrant
he's more interested in horseflesh than potatoes, oats,
and rye."

"Donal Cochran," the young man said, giving Matthew his hand. "And that's my older brother, Paul.
And our da, coming round the corner of the stables.
These here are our stable lads and handlers. And that
stumble foot over there is Silent Sean, the muck-out."

All the men washed quickly with lye soap. Each
used the same towel to dry themselves and by the
time Matthew had need of it, it was grimy with six
men's leavings. Never in his life had he used a dirty
towel; but Cathleen kept a steady eye on him and he
did not want to give her pause to doubt his identity.
So he tucked in and used the blasted thing, scrubbing
away as if his life depended on it.

"You'll take off a layer of skin, Mister Dunn,"

Cathleen warned, with a wry lilt in her voice which nearly matched one of the barn wrens.

" 'Tis Matthew, Mis . . . Cathleen."

"Oh, aye. I know what 'tis." With a toss of her head and a saucy flip to her skirts as she pranced away, Cathleen trilled, "Come along, *Matthew*. Mama has supper on the table."

He stood rooted to the spot, shocked to the roots of his hair by the sensuous way her voice had caressed the syllables of his name. *Math . . . thew.* Good God, her mouth had pursed on the ending of it like a kiss. Damn, this was not working out as he had hoped. Or it was and he was in more hot water than he had envisioned in his grand plan. To distract himself—and his body—Matthew hurried to Cathleen's side and jerked his head back to indicate Silent Sean. "Is he not coming?"

"Nay. He'll keep watch on Sidhe and warn me when she's about to foal."

"How? Your mother said he doesn't speak."

"Why, Mister Dunn . . . here and you tell us you're familiar with breeding horses and have been around stables for years and years . . . you don't know about the stable bell?" She laughed when he stopped dead and stared at her. "Caught you out, did I? Ah, don't worry, Matthew Dunn. If 'tis a secret you've got, 'tis safe with me. I'll not tell that you may be more or less what you say. And don't you worry about the mare. Sean will ring the bell when 'tis her time."

If 'tis a secret you've got. The woman was uncanny. He was beginning to believe in this extra sense the Irish claimed their women had. This one, now, saw through . . . wait! What if it were merely guessing that she did. Or teasing. Women liked to do that. It gave them some silly sense of power. But did Cathleen Cochran appear that kind of woman? Nay. He wondered, though, why, if she had some true inkling he wasn't who he said he was, why she did not tell her mother. Cathleen Cochran was a mystery to be solved, an enigma to be broken, a woman to be watched.

Indeed, as Cathleen had said, the bell sounded halfway into the simple meal of back-of-the-oven mutton stew and solid molasses and oat bread, all washed down with home brewed ale. Cathleen swallowed a mouthful, then bolted for the stables. Her father and brothers more leisurely finished up.

"Are you not going to help with the birthing?" Matthew asked them.

"Och, but Cathleen is the best there is in training oval and birthing stall," John Cochran said. The tall, slim man with grey flecked hair and those sky-sea-and-earth eyes so much like his daughter's pushed back his chair. "She's been tending to the new foals since she was fourteen . . ."

"Nine years, now," Paul said, sidling a glance to see if this news about Cathleen's age had any import to Matthew. The family had been trying for years to get Cathleen well and married. Was this man the one to overlook her spinsterhood to take her? He did not look as if he could be choosy. But looks never gave an indication of all a man was. If they did, he and

Donal would be in their proper sphere, not stuck here still doing their father's bidding, still playing at life instead of actually living it. If he and his brother were ever to have the life they deserved they had to marry off their sister. He didn't know how, but by craggy this man might be their last hope. He had to do something . . . and soon. He decided that throwing the two together—whether or no they wanted it—was the only way to accomplish his goal. But he needed to have Donal's help, so he nudged his younger brother to leave the table.

As they rose, Donal said sardonically, and just a mite bitterly, Matthew thought, "We never worry about Cathleen when she's around horses. She's always done just fine without us."

The Cochrans might be able to ignore the plaintive horse sounds coming from the stables, but Matthew tensed at each upward note. When he nearly snapped his tin spoon at one particularly mournful cry, Maeve gave him a lopsided smile and jerked her head in the direction of the sound. "Get on with you. You've been itching to have a go at those animals since you first set foot on this land. Like all the men on this place, you're besotted with horseflesh." The bitterness in her voice was unmistakable and she sighed, then waved him away. "Go chase the dream. I won't stop you. But 'tis work for me, you'll do, 'til I say aught. That was the bargain, Matthew Dunn."

"Aye!" Matthew flung over his shoulder as he pelted for the stable. "And never let it be said that Matthew Forre . . . forfeited his bond in a bargain."

By God that was close! He had to be more careful, less excited around this new breed, else he'd stumble his way into revealing the half-truths he'd bandied about this place.

The birthing pen was bathed in candlelight from several lanterns hung from pegs on the wall—a testament to just how many mares decided to drop their foals in the middle of the night. Matthew expected to see Sidhe laying on the clean straw. He did not expect to see Sean tugging on her legs and Cathleen behind the mare, writhing on the floor, her skirts soaked with birthing fluids and once again wrapped around her waist. Such a position exposed her legs and all together, but she paid it no mind as she groped with both arms elbow high inside the mare.

His body jolted at the sight of Cathleen's long legs, rounded bottom and shadowy secret place. He threw a wicked look at Silent Sean, who did not seem to notice the condition of Cathleen, he was that much more concerned with the mare. Thank goodness.

Matthew entered the stall and asked Cathleen, "What are you doing ... ?"

"She's presenting hind legs first," was all Cathleen had time to grind out before Sidhe tossed her head as her belly rippled like giant waves at Dover. The mare screamed. Cathleen struggled in the straw, bracing her feet against a huge beam nailed into the floor. She pulled with all her might. "I can't ... 'tis too slippery." She took out her hands and shook them to get the muck off.

Suddenly, she realized the position she had gotten

herself into and quickly rolled away, tugging at her skirts in the process. She jumped to her feet and stamped to unroll the damnable things. She couldn't look at Matthew. Twice, he had seen what was not his to see. Twice was once too many. "Sean, you take over," she bit out angrily, but more at herself than at their helper.

But the young man backed away and shook his head. His mouth worked like a fish out of water and his hands trembled.

By God, Matthew could not allow this! He could not lose one of the horses because of a frightened young man who could not stand to see or take part in giving pain to a mare during a breech birth. He shouldered Sean out of the way. His own hands were clean, his shirtsleeves rolled up. "Tell me what to do," he demanded of Cathleen.

Though she was embarrassed at what Matthew had seen, the condition of Sidhe and her foal was far more important than a little flash of skin. "You have to grope inside, Matthew. Catch *both* legs. Not one! If you pull one leg without the other, you're likely to break it and the poor thing will be finished before he has a chance to start."

"He?"

" 'Tis not difficult to tell what kind to expect, when your hands move all over the rump." Though her hair was plastered to her head from exertion, her green eyes twinkled at him. "Be sure you have a hold on a leg, mind."

"Oh, aye. I think I can tell the difference. Though how a maiden like you could . . ."

She blushed and turned her back, ostensibly to help Sidhe when the next contraction took the mare. "Been around horses and sheep all my life. Couldn't hardly not notice, now could I?"

With Matthew working on the legs and Cathleen leaning all her weight on Sidhe's bulging stomach, they managed to help the tired mare complete the birth.

While Sidhe cleaned her new colt and Silent Sean cleaned up the mucked straw, Cathleen and Matthew hung over the top of the stall gate.

"Cuchulain," Cathleen breathed. "Your name shall be Cuchulain. You did fight to be born. Now you must fight to catch up with your cousins. And mayhap with the name of the ancient great king who tamed the sea and ne'er lost a fight he wanted mightily to win, you will be strong and swift and sure on the flats."

She sighed and her weary body slipped toward Matthew. "Thank you, Matthew. You gave life tonight."

"I only did what you asked, Cathleen."

"You did wonderfully well, you did." She looked up into his handsome face and smiled. "We almost lost them."

"Nay. You would have finished the birth the proper way."

She shook her head and sadness suffused her face. "I was tiring fast. My arms are strong, as is my body.

But sometimes nay strong enough, Matthew. And to lose this one ..." Tears crowded behind her lashes. "You'll not ever know the pain that would have caused."

"Because to lose the foal, means losing the mare."

"Aye. A brood mare who drops the imps on this place. We don't have enough imps here or any-where."

Imps like yourself, I warrant. Matthew put his arm around her and gave her a gentle hug. "We did not lose them."

"Aye." She beamed with joy.

They had not lost them. Mare and colt were safe. *She* was safe. Safe here in the stables, one place she felt truly alive and useful. And the closeness of the man beside her was all she needed. Sleep was just around the corner; but not yet. She leaned her head on Matthew's shoulder and without thought to the fact that he was virtually a stranger—and a strange stranger at that—she snuggled against his shoulder. "Uhmm. I dearly want to go to bed. . . ."

Matthew stiffened in more ways than one. He put his arm around Cathleen and whispered, "A pleasure . . ."

Cathleen's head snapped up. She leaned back to see his hooded eyes and found what she thought his tone of voice had implied. "Angels and saints, con-ceited as the gentry you are!" She pushed away from him and whirled for the door. "A bath, I need. As do you."

"And where do you find the comforts of a bath at this time of night?"

"Who said aught of comfort?" She ran from the stable, him following, and plucked up the soap from the washing well. She threw it and a large towel into a small pail. " 'Tis a cold bath you need, to shock those devilish thoughts from your head. You'll find it in the river."

Holding the pail out, her hips swayed as she darted away. Damnation! She did it so innocently—and it was innocent, Matthew felt certain—but as aware of her as he was, a mere flick of her hips was provocative. Any man would think it so. He dare not let her wander away at night. Yet she knew the lay of this land better than the previous owners, he had no doubt. One thing was certain . . . he was dirtier than he'd been since the days he'd worked on the docks for his father. A good scrubbing in a river sounded like heaven, regardless of the cold.

He grabbed up a length of sacking towel and stumbled after her, dodging overhanging branches that he was convinced she deliberately let snap back to vex him. Games, was it? Well, when they got to the river he would show her who was more adept at games.

Of all kinds.

But when he reached the bend below the hill where Dunswell Draw was located, Cathleen was not to be found. "Cathleen?" Only rustling bushes gave away her location. "Cathleen, are you in trouble?"

"Nay. Turn your head, Matthew Dunn. I mean to give my whole self a good scrub."

"Cathleen . . . you're not stripping down to your skin, are you? I don't want your father or brothers to come after me with a rifle, a priest, and a ring."

She laughed merrily. "Then go back up the trail and wait until I'm finished."

"Cathleen, you are more stubborn than a mule and more dangerous than a stallion in the mating season."

He had no choice but to obey her orders. He was not in season for a mate at the end of a rifle . . . not even one as beautiful as this tantalizing woman. He reached a comfortable distance where there was a hiding place in the scrub. He could glimpse the river from his location and decided to keep an eye on the bedeviling witch so she could take her bath in peace and safety. Never knew who was tramping the woods. *He* had been, hadn't he? Aye, it was good for him to watch out for lustful layabouts.

Yet it seemed all around them conspired to lustful acts. Insects flitted in and out of the bushes, flashing their mating ritual. Bullfrogs garrumphed, calling ladies to their den. Dragonflies darted, then swooped down to ride the backs of the larger females. And in the background were the unmistakable sounds of one or more stallions neighing loudly for the mares.

Matthew, however, had no mating call to give, and thought it a shame. He had no doubt that Cathleen was as worthy a woman as any he'd seen; and he anticipated her emergence with great eagerness. In fact, it was imperative he get out of his trousers, his eagerness was so great.

But when she came from behind the bushes and

streaked for the river with the pail in her hand, Matthew silently cursed a storm. The minx still had her chemise and underskirt on! By the time he stripped to his own linen undershirt and breeches lining, she was submerged up to her waist in the water, soaping herself—chemise, underskirt, and all.

He got to the edge of the river and took two steps in, then froze. Literally. "Mother of God!"

" 'Tis cold, as I told you."

" 'Tis an ice bath."

"Quite invigorating, it is." She watched his slow, teeth-rattling progress and laughed. "Run or you'll ne'er make it, Matthew Dunn! The cold numbs quick as ever you please, and you'll soon be able to stand it. But only if you run."

He contemplated the icy tongues of the river as it lapped around his calves. Below that, he could no longer feel where his ankles or feet were. He could well imagine what it would feel like if he walked into the river slowly. Inch by inch, up his calves, past his knees, up his thighs to his . . . no! Only a mad man would do it that way. Yet Cathleen had plunged right in, hadn't she? If she—a snip of a woman—could, then he . . .

He held in his breath and with a wild yelp, dove shallowly into the water. He came up sputtering, flaying his arms like a Dutch windmill.

He stopped dead, his eyes riveted on Cathleen. Her underskirt floated on the top of the water, moving with the waves she made, undulating back and forth, up and down. With the moon overhead in a three-quarter sliver resembling a thumbnail, she shimmered, bathed in white from above and below. *Venus.* He had seen a sketch of the famous statue. That goddess—that was what Cathleen appeared as she hummed merrily and took down her hair. The wind whipped it round her face and she pushed it back. Then, taking a breath as deep as his had been, she dumped a full pail of water over it.

"Blessed be God!" Matthew praised as the water cascaded in sheets all over her shoulders and arms, giving her a silvered sheen. His fingers knew her skin would be silky and sleek. His tongue knew it would taste like the sweet grasses that grew in the river. But for now his eyes feasted on a woman so pure and natural she was not even aware of her sensuality—or if she was, paid no attention nor care.

She let the pail bob on the water and attacked her hair with the soap, working it in. No bubbles, the water was so cold. She worked quickly with her eyes closed as she scrubbed her scalp and the long, wavy strands. With his heart thumping madly in his chest, Matthew audaciously came up behind her and took the soap out of her hands. It was like some dream or an erotic episode from a French narrative. The feel of the slick soap in her long hair made the pads of his fingers tingle, sending shafts like Franklin's electrical current coursing through his body. As he scrubbed, he moved around her until they were face to face, and still his hands wound through her curls. He soaped them, combed his fingers through them, wound individual curls around his thumb, let the strands tickle down his arm.

Suddenly, he was no longer cold, but warm throughout and beyond to the shaft that he kept inches away from her lest she bolt and run, denying him this consuming pleasure.

God, such pleasure!

Such freedom. It had been freedom he sought, and thought it could be found only in acquiring the stables. Yet, here in this river with Cathleen he felt an emancipation from worries and pressures that not many sovereigns enjoyed. Merely washing her hair had done that. Merely washing her hair.

Ah, saints and angels, don't make him stop! Cathleen was transfixed by Matthew's quiet, powerful ministration. When he had first taken the soap from her, she had thought to sweep his legs from under him and dart away. But the first touch of his fingers in her hair sent shivers up and down her spine, then a great warmth spread through her body. As a child she had loved to have her hair washed and brushed; and Matthew's touch evoked memories of those occasions. But his touch was nothing like her mother's and this midnight toilette did not take place in her nursery.

She was well aware that they were isolated here in the river. She was here with a man, with naught between them save a linen chemise. Her floating underskirt could do little to protect her, she was that vulnerable to his touch below the waist. Yet, he did not touch her there. And because he did not, she relaxed, allowing herself the pleasure of his gentle movements.

As the river lapped around her, she moved occasionally to keep her balance. When she took another toe-hold on the slick bottom, she brushed against . . .

Oh, angels and saints!

She held her breath and moved a fraction away, but the knowledge that he was not unaffected by simply washing her hair was overwhelming. They were alone. No man had ever touched her so tenderly, no man had ever been so much in her thoughts. As his hands moved through her hair, she did not mind his secrets. She did not care who he was or where he came from. There was only one thing she wanted to know. She bit her tongue to get her mind focused. For the first time in her life she wanted to know a man, as a man.

There was too much about Matthew Dunn which was held back. That mystery, and the quick sensual response she had had to him, made him dangerous. He had walked into their stables and imperiled everything she thought, everything she felt. She had listened to her misgivings but had foolishly thought she could control her own reactions. But she had walked into something she could not have foreseen, nor understood. For both their sakes, she had to find some way to give them an easy way to disentangle themselves from . . . whatever these delicious, dangerous feelings were.

"Matthew," she whispered, afraid to break the spell he created with the gentle massage of his fingers. "I cannot keep my eyes closed one more minute, I vow. Please rinse with the pail."

"Aye," he croaked. He filled the pail and poured it on her head slowly, making sure all the soap was out. "One more rinse should do it."

The water poured over her and he thought he had never seen a lovelier sight. Daft, was he, because when she arched her back and flipped her head to send her hair flying over her shoulders, lovely was too coarse a description. *Dear God!* Her breasts broke the surface of the river, breasts so magnificent in their lush fullness that his mouth went dry and his body throbbed. Her nipples were large, taut from the cold. He wanted to reach out, let his fingers feather over them, feel them against the palms of his hands. He nearly did, until her eyes popped open and she took a step back.

"Matthew!"

Why was she calling him? He wasn't finished looking at her, wanting her.

Cathleen knew the look in his eyes and knew she should bolt and run; but Matthew might come after her and she was not at all sure if she would fight him off. She did not want to fight him. But she could not join with him the way his eyes told her he wanted. There was only one thing for it—she must try to keep him at bay, but as a friend, not as an enemy. If she could only think of him and treat him like a brother, then all would be possible and these *feelings* would stop.

She hoped.

"Matthew . . . hand me the soap. The soap, *now*, Matthew."

Reeling from feelings raw and primeval, feelings he had never had while in the company of London's best widows, he obeyed this Irish country lass, so lost was he in the soft appeal of her eyes and voice, the wild appeal of her body. She held him captive with those eyes as she casually ran the cold, wet soap down his arm, working it into the muscles at his shoulder, then massaging it deep into his flesh . . . all the way to his fingertips. One finished, she worked on the other.

"Will you clean my legs, too?"

"Not on your life . . . you're much too much man for that kind of soaping, Matthew Dunn. But for helping me in the birthing, I will do your back and your hair, *if* you keep silent and make no move to touch me."

"Ah, 'tis a hard bargain you drive, Cathleen."

"Aye or nay, Matthew?"

"I'd like to say aye to the first part and nay to the second."

"All or neither, Matthew Dunn. All or neither."

"All." But he meant far more with that word than she could ever dream.

Chapter Four

By God, it was not easy for Matthew, standing still under her touch. It was torture not being able to reach out and feel those globes of flesh which his hands already knew and his brain already savored. It was hell watching every movement, anticipating each contraction of muscle, bracing his body for the assault which was a barrage of caresses.

Cathleen gave a final swipe to Matthew's neck and craned her head to look at him. His eyes were closed, his face screwed up in ... saints and angels, he looked to be in ecstasy. How stupid of her! She had thought to treat him like a friend and had only increased his passions. Daft she was, and all.

She flipped the soap into the pail. "Finished, you are, Matthew Dunn."

He opened his eyes, reached out and snaked his hand on her wrist. "Nay. We are not near done."

His head swooped down and he captured her lips in a kiss that rocked her into the soft bottom of the river. She fought to keep her balance—inside of herself and out. Fought to keep some semblance of order and ordinariness.

But it did not come.

It could not. Matthew had irrevocably changed her world from what she knew.

Oh, her mother had warned her. Six years ago, when she was seventeen and young men flocked to the suppers her mother gave for their friends and relatives, Maeve had whispered of secrets and strange yearnings which would come unaware when young ladies were in company with young gentlemen. Then, when the awful family troubles began and the young men's flock had trickled to naught more than an aged peacock or two—bullies all—Maeve had described too graphically what these kinds of "gentlemen" had in mind. So graphically, Cathleen had expected that when once a man made more than a fuss over her, but actually seized the opportunity of "bringing her round to his point of view"—her mother's words— then something dastardly would happen.

Certainly, she had not expected *this!*

This tingling that started at the sweet friction of Matthew's lips teasingly tasting hers. This warmth that quickly flamed to heat and settled where, for her, only the backs of horses ever touched. This startling excitement—not fear or repulsion—which had her fingertips all pins and needles, her toes curling under of their own free will, and the scalp on her head apparently able to feel her hair grow.

Surely, she had not expected this craving which, it

seemed, left every inch of her body parched and aching.

"Oh!"

Her mother had warned her, but not near enough.

"Oh!" she said again, confused and exhilarated, happy and desperately melancholy. This was so much less frightening—and so very much more wonderful—than anything in her life. And for many reasons . . . for many God-awful reasons . . . she knew it could not be.

Matthew drew away and studied the startled expression which had turned Cathleen's usually smiling face into a morose mask.

"Oh, dear. The lady didn't like it."

At the use of the word *lady*, Cathleen sucked in her breath and pushed him away. She took two steps backward and glared at him across the expanse of the river. " 'Tis no English lady you have here. 'Tis only a lowly Irish lass . . . who liked it well enough." *Too well.* "But do not preen, Matthew Dunn. She has liked other kisses as well, don't you know."

How trippingly the lie tumbled off her tongue.

She whirled and eddies of water swirled in her path as she hastily made for the shore. She heard splashing behind her as he started to come after her, but she called back as she had done that first day, "Not one step closer, Matthew Dunn. I'll not have it, I won't. What's done is done . . . and won't be repeated. Stay wherever you are, or the consequences this night and ever more will be dire, I vow."

She did not stop to gather her clothes; she could

come back for them in the morning. She merely plucked up a large piece of sacking towel and draped it over her, then in her bare feet, streaked down the well-used lane to the stables and made for the stairs to the dimly lit family quarters above.

She took the stairs two at a time and—plucking up the lit candle lantern her mother had left for her— Cathleen rushed through the front room which served as both parlor and her father's office. Papers were scattered on table tops and over the surface of the small settee placed in front of the only window. They were testaments both to her father's preoccupation with the business of horse breeding, and her mother's inability to coordinate even a minimal amount of housekeeping. How could she? She was too busy being cook and serving maid, farmhand and tailor, keeper of the books and estate overseer.

Cathleen's thoughts of the kiss faded as she sighed as she passed the closed door of her parents' bedroom and the small open area where long pallet beds attested to the fact that here, Paul shared sleeping arrangements with Donal. The cots were empty; her brothers were probably at one of their friends' houses, liberally sampling the first fruits of the home brewing which had gone on in the fall.

As she always did, she slowed as she passed their room, a room that was no bigger than a horse stall. It amazed her still, the sight of a tall combination desk, bookcase, and dresser made of cherry and inlaid with maple and walnut. Such a magnificent piece, it was, carved with care and creativity. It was so large, it took up the entire west wall next to Paul's cot. It was so tall, it looked as if it held up the ceiling. Its surface glistened from the weekly waxing Paul gave the beastly thing.

Why did he keep it? As with Matthew's use of the word *lady,* this manor house piece was a constant reminder of what Dunswell Manor had once been and was no more. How could Paul stand to look at it, never mind tend it with more care than he gave the Cochrans' winning race horses? Such loving devotion to an object which bespoke of other times and other lives, often brought tears to Maeve's eyes, though she never let them drip over their tightly maintained dam.

Cathleen sighed again. There were so many anomalies, so many contradictions in their lives these days that she had all she could do to keep straight who she was and what was her own purpose. She could do naught more than shrug away the perplexity of her brother's actions. He was a morose and tight-lipped man who did not let anyone breech his barriers, not even Donal. That there were barriers was unavoidable. He was a Cochran. All Cochrans had barriers.

Even she.

But Matthew had managed to breech hers . . . and all too easily.

Well, she had ways of dealing with some of the problems he had handed her. Once in her garret room under the east eave, Cathleen quickly donned a long, soft, woolen nightshirt and sought out two sacks of bits and pieces of leather, suede, and yard goods. When she had what she needed, she lit several candles and grouped them on her small bedside table. Although she knew she would be needed in the stables and paddocks the next morning, what had happened between her and Matthew took up most of her thoughts. The little drama in the stables and at the river had occasioned the need. Now the erotic feelings Matthew had pulled out of her demanded the use. To counteract any repetition, to stave off the feelings she could not completely tamp down, she sewed late into the night.

Weeks passed, yet Cathleen's physical discomfort did not abate. Holding that musket up to keep Matthew at bay had only been made worse by the birthing of Cuchulain. Add to that the fact that only she seemed to be able to handle Firebrand and had spent almost every hour of every day training him, and it was no wonder her arms and shoulders ached as if from a thousand pricks of a needle. Each morning she struggled into her shirt. Three weeks from the day Matthew had sneaked into the stable, it was too much. She stifled a moan, but her mother heard and came quickly to her room.

"Oh your arms, Cathleen! Do they still pain you, now?"

"Aye, Mama. I thought cold river baths and heated bricks wrapped in flannel would help; but they seem to have done it worse."

Maeve sniffed. " 'Twas no the river bath nor the bricks. 'Twas the sewing each and every night that was no help at all."

Through her pain, Cathleen giggled. She and her brothers had never been able to hide things from her mother. Her father was another matter. He was always too wrapped up in what were his troubles to keep an eye out for his children's parade of woes, bundles of mischief. "The fairies whispered in your ear again, did they, Mama?"

"Aye." She held out a piece of oiled paper on which a glob of greyish ointment lay. "That Matthew Dunn ... he sent you this ... said your movements have been tight and slow lately. Thought it might be needed."

Cathleen took it; but the odor singed her nose. "Nay, I'll not use *that*."

"You will, Cathleen. You've much to do this day." Maeve left, then quickly returned with a green glass bottle with a tall stopper. "You may use this."

Cathleen shook her head. She knew how precious the expensive scent was to her mother. "If I must use the damned ointment, then I shall stuff lavender blooms and wild mint into my chemise to ward off the devilish smell.

"I'll have Donal pick them for you."

By the time Maeve returned, Cathleen had liberally slathered the vile stuff on her shoulders and arms— which amazingly gave her immediate relief—then donned the garments she had spent her precious sleep hours to sew. She smiled. Though she hated to admit it, Matthew's foul-smelling ointment at once put her at ease physically. As soon as she dressed, she began—for the first time since Matthew had stepped

foot into the stable—to feel freer mentally. Finally
she would be able to perform her tasks without worry
about what, if anything, Matthew Dunn could see of
those private places upon which no other man had set
eyes.

But when Maeve caught sight of her daughter's
costume, Cathleen cringed. A white hot anger took
away her mother's normally pleasant, ruddy complexion and left spots of pale pink on Maeve's
cheeks, while her neck suffused with blood and
turned beet red.

Cathleen had modified one of Maeve's oversized
homespun shirts so from the neckline began a jabot
of pleats, making a waterfall from neck to breasts. A
wide leather belt held the shirt inside her skirt. And
what a skirt! She had stitched together bits and pieces
of leather and suede into a crazy quilt pattern. But as
if that were not enough, she had cut and stitched the
front and back up the middle so the skirt looked like
a wide set of breeches. Maeve studied it. Obviously
there were underskirts made in the same fashion. No
wonder it had taken Cathleen so long to finish this
new kind of trouser. She could well see how this
would help Cathleen. With it, her daughter could sit
a horse comfortably and not reveal her legs—or anything else.

Maeve's heart felt as if it were deflating into a
shriveled up lump. Had they not had enough of trouble? Must there be ever more to crowd out the glory
and joy of the past? And now Cathleen intended to

become a man thing, an object of ridicule, of all that was changed. . . .

"No. I'll not have it. Have I . . . we . . . not suffered enough that you make yourself a mocking thing? No, Cathleen. I cannot bear any more . . ."

Cathleen put her arms around her mother's trembling shoulder. "Oh, Mama. 'Tis not mocking. 'Tis practical. You saw what happened that first day in the stables with Matthew. It happens all the time. No matter how careful I am, my skirts ride up when I'm in the saddle. The training boys know me . . . have known me from birth. They do not pay it any mind; but now that there's Matthew Dunn . . ."

Cathleen implored with hands and words; and Maeve shook her head as she realized her daughter did not intend to ridicule or change. Of them all, Cathleen was practical and ingenious. She had the intelligence her brothers lacked and the fortitude they sorely needed.

Though she hated the look of it, Maeve had to admit that the proof was in the clothing Cathleen had fashioned during the last fortnight's sewing spree.

"Well-a-day . . . 'tis inventive you are, I will give you that." She picked up the scrap bags from the corner where Cathleen had carefully repacked them. "You will need more than one shirt and skirt, I vow. I shall begin to sew a whole new ensemble this night."

"Thank you, Mama."

Cathleen tucked the lavender blooms and wild mint into her chemise, where they itched until she thought of wrapping them in a soft cloth. When she was ready, she went down to help her mother for breakfast, wondering what Matthew would say when *he* discovered what she had done.

But she was not to discover his reaction now, since he had already eaten and was busy in the fields beside the training oval. For reasons she couldn't explain, his not being there was most vexing.

Matthew whistled happily in the fields near the horse training track. Though he hoed and spaded, his attention was on the horses and the Cochrans. They worked hard. Starting with a tether on the younger colts and fillies, Paul and Donal instructed the hands to put them through the entire litany of paces: walk, trot, and a gentle canter. When they were satisfied that the horses were in shape, only then did they allow the beasts to be saddled. They chose carefully among the small, but strong, boys to determine who seemed to have an affinity for a particular horse and rode best ... who brought in the fastest time in the wild gallop from red stick to white and back again. Round and round and round.

Sweet Mother of God, those halfbreeds ran like the wind was chasing them. These were no dainty pacers nor trotters. These were muscular full-out flat race horses. He could imagine them in the oval, outdistancing every competitor. Or on the measured flat, streaking from one end of a field to the other, breaking records, winning silver plate or cups.

All of them wearing the Earl of Dunswell's insignia.

At midmorning he fetched water to the table Maeve had laid outside near the brick ovens which now held that morning's share of molasses bread and oatmeal currant buns.

Like each morning for the past three weeks, before Maeve allowed him to sit at table for second breakfast, she craned her neck to check the fields just beyond the kitchen garden. As he had come to expect, she said ne'er a word, but nodded once, satisfied to see he had weeded the entire section and watered it liberally. It had taken him ninety-seven trips to the well and back with two full pails, and he was of a mind that he'd need some of Cathleen's ointment that night; but he had accomplished in one morning what Maeve had calculated would take two days.

It felt damned good to use his body like this again. It was also good for his soul. Digging and trenching. Planting and weeding. Watering and liming. Staking and sheltering the delicate plants. He even liked picking the leaves of their harmful insects and inspecting the ground for worms which in less than an hour could eat away a whole day's work. Maeve Cochran was a hard taskmistress but he knew she would wrest a crop of oats and rye and corn from the land or kill him in the trying.

She poured him a large cup of hot, dark tea and laced it the way she had learned he liked to drink it, with honey and a crushed clover blossom. "A hard worker, you are, Matthew Dunn. And a good one."

"Not good enough for you Cochrans, or your good husband would let me help with the training."

"Well, now, I may have a wee surprise for you." She shaded her eyes and studied her menfolk as they led the horses from the training oval. "John and the boys have been reining them in this day. The half-breeds ran hard all week and today is their day of half-work. The men will be in soon for their tea."

Matthew gaped. Half-work? If that exercise he had seen was half-work, then by God these must be the fastest horses in all Donegal. Why had not some other petitioner taken over this manor house and stables? Could the distance away from London be that important? For a man with a family, Matthew supposed it would be. But for himself, a man with no wife or child, the appeal of these horses more than compensated for the wildness of the terrain, the back-breaking work it would take to bring the manor house into proper order, and the long distance he would have to travel to get to his mercantile in London. But with the competent Cochrans here to oversee the place he should have no worries when he was away on business.

While he had been musing, Maeve had propped open the oven door. Now she took a long-handled bread board in each hand, pushed them into the hot interior, and slid out the first batch of bread. She tested the surface with her index finger and nodded.

"Cathleen, darlin'. The bread is ready!"

Matthew swiveled to the sounds of Cathleen's pounding feet. Dear God! What did she have on her back ... nay, over her *backside*. "What the hell is that?"

With pursed mouth and averted eye, Cathleen ignored Matthew's words and glare and hurried with clean cloths to loosely wrap the fresh-baked loaves. She pointedly gave Matthew her back as she put the bread in the shade to cool. She did not owe him an explanation. Why, it must be plain as the nose on his very handsome, very angry and perplexed face what her new clothes were, and the purpose for which she intended them. Suddenly, she gave a faint giggle. Aye, he knew what she had intended. That was why he was so angry. Hurrah and well-a-day, her plan had worked!

For the next few minutes, she and her mother moved as a team, neither speaking, both knowing their jobs and doing them without incident or accident.

For Matthew, it was maddening—for more than one reason.

Though he dearly wanted to upbraid the brazen minx for manning herself, he pushed that to one side for a later confrontation with her, and concentrated instead on the "wee surprise" Maeve had mentioned so casually.

"Mistress Cochran, for the love of all that's holy, what wee surprise do you mean?"

Cathleen and Maeve exchanged one of those "women's glances" and laughter spilled out of them.

"When once I heard the plan, I warned you he

would not sit still for more than a blink," Cathleen said.

"Two blinks, I gave you," Matthew muttered. "Now, what . . . ?"

"John likens as how you have not complained once over the chores I've piled on you—and I've pushed you like a mule for these past weeks, I must admit. We think, then, that you have earned the right to work with them on the training track." When he gulped down his tea and made to bolt from the table, Maeve bonked him on the head with one of the bread shovels. "You've time and more, boyo. The lads'll water and feed the horses while my men folks have their tea. After they nap, then 'tis your turn to help train the two-year-olds."

As she had said, the men returned. But they deliberately—and maddeningly—paid him no mind and would not answer his questions. They merely grinned, bolted down their currant buns and tea, and propped themselves in the shade for their daily hour's nap.

Matthew growled and went in search of the stable lads, who were, indeed, watering and rubbing down the horses which had been out in the oval that morning. While the animals drank, the lads rubbed the sweat which hard exercise in hot sun had brought out on the stallions' and mares' backs and sides. He was about to offer his help when Cathleen stumbled through the door carrying a pail filled with water. From the pain etched in her face he knew her shoulders still ached.

"Here, let me carry that," Matthew said, coming up beside her and easily taking the wooden pail from her hands.

"I can manage."

"I know you can. But I want to earn my bread and board."

She giggled. "Working for Mama, you've done that and more, though my brothers won't credit it and will work you as hard as the horses."

"Where do you want this?"

"Just inside the door."

Cathleen hung over the rail on the stall, offering Firebrand the leavings from the oatmeal currant buns. Matthew climbed up and sat next to her.

"What do you call that contraption you've stitched up for yourself?"

"Comfortable."

They eyed each other, and as had happened every time they were together, very quickly their gazes locked into a blaze of passion and need, something Cathleen had thought her new skirt and shirt would avert. What was happening? Why this man? Why this feeling that if she did not lean into him and feel his arms around her, she would not, ever again, see the sky as blue as it was ... hear the birds trill their sweet music ... or, quite simply, breathe normally. Saints and angels, had she thought she could treat him as a friend or brother? This was not friendship and it was certainly not sisterly devotion. This was that other thing, that secret thing which bound men and women together, a thing she had never thought to have for herself.

It frightened her, and made her heart full with a pleasure she could not name—and needed desperately to break away from, for his good as well as hers.

"Tis a boon they're not lathered, you know," she said.

For one moment Matthew thought she meant *them,* Matthew and Cathleen. And why not? They were putting out such singing heat merely from looking into each other's eyes . . . and being close enough to touch, but not touching, that lathering was the least of what could happen to them. "What boon? Who is lathered?"

"The horses, Matthew."

There it was again, the lilting way she said his name. Her lips pursed each time and he wanted desperately to lean over only a fraction and taste the tempting moue of her mouth, that seductive circle of flesh. And there were other circles of flesh which needed his attention, other places to taste, nibble, suck.

"Ah, God . . ."

"Ah, aye. You should not leave horseflesh hot and wet. Could render them useless for racing."

By God, you should not leave a man hot and wet, nor a woman. Made them useless for near everything. But this woman did not know that. Though her green eyes were filled with a wanting and a deep desire, they also revealed her inexperience and wonder at what was happening. If he wanted her he would not get her by swift pursuit, like those eager English entrees he had been served in Ireland. Cathleen was a prize worth being awarded. He could not frighten her off if they were to experience the kind of pleasure he could imagine with her . . . and it would, indeed, be pure pleasure.

"We can't have them hot and wet and useless, now, can we?"

"Nay," she said seriously, ignoring—because she didn't understand what had occasioned it—the underlying sensual tone to his voice. But she could not ignore the way his eyes seemed to drink her in. Instead, she backed away from it . . . and wished she did not have to. "If you're to help Da and the boys, you'd best learn the signs of real problems."

He did not pretend to know them already. She was too prespicacious for that. "Tell me about them." Anything to keep her here, beside him, her elbow touching his knee, her shoulder brushing against his ankle.

"Rattling chests. Constant snorting. Difficulty breathing. Hot sweats. Stiff muscles. Heaves. Limps. Refusing to rise. If you see or hear any of these, call Da or me right away."

She could have been describing him after a close encounter with her. His chest rattled because he could hardly breathe. He sometimes snorted to clear his thoughts of the erotic image of her in that river. He sweated more in her company than he did in the fields. As for the rest . . . stiffness was so much a

problem he often limped away from her. Or refused
to rise in fear that she or her men folk would see the
problems her nearness occasioned.

God, what was he going to do about this mad lust-
ing? He was no boy in the schoolroom—though
sometimes she made him feel like one. He wanted
this woman. Pure. Simple. Awful and wonderful and
damned complicated. And she was worried only
about horses?

Well, if that was the way to accomplish his goal,
he would play her game and later find an opening to
her heart.

"Aye, I'll be on the lookout for the signs," he said
lazily, his attention more on her eyes and the heat of
her body than on her words.

"Matthew! Mind what I say, now. If you treat this
lightly, you will forget. And if one or another gets
sick and we don't catch whatever has attacked them
in time, whoever is ailing could die."

"It's that serious."

"Aye."

"You really care about these animals, don't you?"

"Oh, aye! They're the Cochrans' life work, don't
you know? See that black mark on their ears?"

"Where?"

"There, near the tip."

She clucked to Firebrand and he came closer, nuz-
zling her outstretched hand. She scratched him under
the chin as she pulled his ear forward. The black
mark looked burned into the skin. It was small, but
he could easily see that the mark was an outline of a

C topped by a turban. Of course! C for Cochran. And a turban for the offspring of the Black Turk. Ingenious.

"How did you do that?"

"The blacksmith forged an iron into the shape Da chose. We heat it red hot, then press it on the horse's ears. I wish it didn't hurt; but Da said it must be done. And the scar does soon heal."

"So you can always tell which horse is yours and none can steal them from you."

"Aye. But 'tis more than that, don't you know. We want all to know that each Dunswell . . . uh, *Cochran* . . . racer wears our mark of care. Anyone can tell you that a Cochran horse is the best there is. Why since Black Turk came to Dunswell, there's never been a horse for miles to compare. And now, with these halfbreeds as Mama calls them, we have something which no other stables in all Donegal can claim." She flung her arm out and her hazel eyes glistened with pride and love. "Winners, all."

She slipped smoothly away from him, down to the last stalls in the stables, where she hung over the boards to look at the latest addition to their growing stock.

"They're fairy blest, they are."

From Maeve he had learned that the spring foals had recently been separated from their mothers for a few hours each day. Two hours in the morning, one in the afternoon. They played together, now, in clean straw. One young colt, the offspring of the grey and the Turk, nipped at the leg of a roan colt, while nearby the colt they had helped birth—Cuchulain—slept fitfully, his forelegs pawing at the straw.

"Have you learned their names yet, Matthew?"

"I know Cuchulain. And the grey is Coltie."

Cathleen giggled. " 'Tis pronounced kilt-eh, like the Scots skirt."

"But 'tis spelled abominably."

"Nay. 'Tis spelled C-A-O-I-L-T-E. 'Tis an old Irish name, Matthew. Some day I'll tell you the story of Caoilte and Cuchulain. And Fergus, the wandering poet priest. And the Rose of the rood. And the whispers of the fairy folk that come in the night to bring fair warning to heedful souls." She skipped away from the stall and reached for three rope halters. "But not now. Now I take these offspring and their mothers to the field. Then, I am going fishing for supper at Dunswell Draw."

"The best salmon and trout in all of Donegal . . ." He caught himself as she looked quizzically up at him. "Something I heard in the coffee house."

"Ah, don't credit all that the locals say. Though . . ." she laughed, delighted and delightfully, ". . . unless you fill it with soap from washing your hair, you must admit the water is the clearest in these parts, and I will tell you, the fish the very sweetest."

She had the stall gate open and the halters over the foals' heads before they knew what she was about. She led them out into the stable aisle. When he followed, she stopped and cocked her head at him. Her eyes twinkled with suppressed laughter . . . or was it excitement.

"What? Are you for the fish ... giving up your first afternoon in the training oval?"

"If I were to go with you, 'tis not for the fish I'd be going," he growled. "And you know it."

"And what is it that I'm supposed to be knowing?"

He thrust up his face close to hers and talked between clenched teeth. "Don't fence with me, Cathleen. You know ..."

She sucked in her breath. "Nay."

"Aye." His right hand encircled the flesh of her upper arm. "Ever since the first time we laid eyes on each other there has been an ember building to a flame. And that night in the river is not to be ignored, though you seem to have managed over the weeks. Now, me ... I am a man. I cannot forget the way you leapt onto the back of that stallion when I came up on you suddenly. How your skirts rode up to reveal every inch of your long, shapely legs. How the shadows at their apex hinted of things delightful and more. How you braved it out when I frightened you.

"And I have seen you working with the horses and your mother. The sun glints off your hair like a million sparks of light. When you bend over in the fields, you have the most luscious curves, exactly where they should be. And when you splash yourself with water to chase away the blasting heat of the day, you always dribble half the damn ladle down your front.

"And that night in the river ... God, how can I describe it? Your chemise clung to you like a second skin. Your hair felt like satin against my palms. The moonlight glistened off your wet skin like diamond dust on velvet.

"Now, when you tell me you're going to go fishing, I have to fight away flashes of what you would once again look like in the water up to your waist, letting the eddies lap at your legs. I have to fight back what I have already seen . . . your shirt damned near transparent, until 'tis plastered to your skin all the way up to your breasts and I can see the outline of your ni—"

She sucked in her breath and quickly slapped her hand over his mouth—then quickly snatched it away again when he trailed his tongue over her palm.

She was thoroughly shocked—not only at him and what he had said and did, but also at herself for allowing . . . nay, *wanting* him to say it and do it. And liking the fact that he did both with suppressed heat, that that heat aroused a corresponding heat in her which made her tremble all over—even in forbidden, secret places.

And by the cunning, satisfied look in his eyes, once she realized that she had responded to his honied words exactly as he hoped she would, she punched him in the stomach and kicked him in the shins.

"We'll have naught of that, Matthew Dunn. Fight away your damned flashes . . ."

"Oh, I do, Cathleen. I fight many things. But if I tell you about them, most of them would get me another punch in the gut or kick in the shins and I've had just about enough today and for the past weeks of pain from merely watching you."

He turned on his heel and began to stride away.

But she could not get the implication of his words out of her mind—nor her own reactions to them. She forgot the mares and dragged the foals after her as she ran to catch up to him. Without thinking—or mayhap thinking too much, and being embarrassed by her own flashes—she kicked out again—and found a warm pile the horses had left in their path back to the stables. Her foot overshot its mark and caught Matthew dead center in his backside. He whirled.

"Oh, saints and angels!" She had no chance. With her weight off balance, she fought to keep upright. "Bother the beasts!"

She plopped down in a heap.

The foals bolted.

Matthew lunged for their trailing leads.

And found the same warm mound.

"Damn it to hell!"

"And back," she muttered. She looked up at him, aware that the stable lads had seen the whole sorry mess, broken into gales of laughter, and gone quickly to round up the foals before they did themselves some mischief. She peeked into Matthew's melted chocolate eyes and saw dangerous glints in them. Offering her hands in appeal, she whispered, "I did not mean for this to happen."

He ground out in a hoarse whisper, "Aye, I'm sure you did not. But the consequences are dire when you play with a man like me; because I do mean for *this* to happen."

When he put his face in front of hers, she flinched, expecting a tongue lashing which she fully deserved.

Instead, his lips brushed softly back and forth against hers.

Softly.

Slowly.

Back and forth. Back and forth.

Ah, God and all the hosts of heaven!

She was lost.

Chapter Five

His lips were soft.

And hard.

And demanding, as his tongue sought entrance bit by bit and she surrendered it gladly.

Her body moved by itself . . . closer to him . . . and she knew instinctively it was because she wanted . . . needed . . . to feel his chest against her breasts. Closer. Closer. And then the contact. Glorious. Shivery. Electric. Her breasts swelled. Her nipples hardened. And his tongue danced with hers as his upper torso moved in combination with his lips on her mouth. Back and forth. Back and forth. Against her lips. Against her breasts.

Mesmerized . . . and puzzled . . . by the energetic lethargy she felt, she moved away, raised her head and looked at him.

His eyes were as molten earth, from the passion which blazed bright and hot.

"Ah, saints and angels help me," she whispered into the wind.

She wanted Matthew Dunn, this man who was not what he seemed.

God, how she wanted him.

The wind did not hear. Matthew did.

He smiled crookedly . . . and fatally. "There is no help for this, Cathleen. There is only more. I can give you more. If you want it."

They sat there in the middle of the stable yard, surrounded by horses ready for breeding, left to themselves in a swirling blaze of passion so deep and all consuming that she did not know how it happened, did not care, only wanted that "more" which Matthew promised.

Left to themselves, they were a dangerous combination. She smiled. They fought mightily, as cosmic elements did. Drinking each other in like the parched earth did the rain. His touch . . . his very gaze . . . lit their way like lightening, while her insides thundered to a rhythm he set up. And like the river current against the banks, he eroded her restraints, wresting a submission she did not have the fortitude to fight. She was twenty-three years old and had never known a man. Her mother had borne both Paul and her by that age. Maeve had known her John physically, emotionally, and spiritually; and welcomed him even now . . . even when she was so angry at him, so disappointed in him. At night Cathleen could hear them and their loving sounds.

Saints and angels, what was that like?

She knew from the way she responded to Matthew that this whirlwind of desire drew her to him the way the mares raced to get to Black Turk during breeding season.

Breeding season.

She knew all there was to know about horses, and the way of them.

She knew all there was to know and she knew naught.

She had seen Black Turk nip at Sidhe's flanks to keep her in line, and the mare whicker with pain . . . but not move. Then, after their mating Sidhe would rub her neck against the stallion. Was that her way of thanking him, or of showing her allegiance, her respect? Pain and pleasure. Sparks and submission.

Well-a-day, combustion and sparks always seemed to ignite into red hot flame when Matthew and she were alone, left to themselves as now. Left to themselves to test their desire, to savor it, to push it to limits she did not understand. Left to themselves . . .

To themselves?

Her head swiveled and she saw what she dreaded, yet was not at all surprised to discover—her brothers leaning against the paddock fence, watching her and Matthew the same way they oversaw Black Turk's breeding ritual. Paul's satisfied smirk sent shivers of a different kind up her spine. Any other brothers would be storming over, separating Matthew and her. But not these two. They wished . . . nay, probably prayed . . . for it to happen, to escalate, for her and Matthew to . . .

But a shadowy figure in the door gave terrible meaning to the consequences of what had happened. Maeve moved slowly forward as if she were the walking dead. Her hands groped for support but there was naught and she staggered once. Her hand swiped across her eyes. She brought it forward in silent supplication.

Cathleen knew what it meant . . . the loss, pity, and terror her mother felt every day and sometimes keened about long into the night . . . what Cathleen herself had forgotten each and every time she was with Matthew. As her mother continued to move step by faltering step, Cathleen groaned. "No, Mama. By saints and angels, *nooo!*"

She jumped to her feet and dashed for the paddock where Firebrand munched grass. He was already saddled, awaiting their daily afternoon ride. He snickered and reared; but she put out her hand and quickly quieted him. Then, using the fence rail for support, she boosted herself onto his back. She whipped him with her hand as her heart exploded from the shame and degradation her mother felt.

What bit of Cathleen's heart that was left, kept rhythm with Firebrand's feet as she licked him into a gallop. Left hind leg thundered down. *No!* Left fore leg. *NO!* Right hind leg. *NO!* Right fore leg. *NO!* All four feet sailed for a moment in mid air. *NOOO!*

She had left the stables far behind when she dimly heard a shout and thundering hooves behind her. She looked back and saw Matthew—on Black Turk. Of all the horses on the manor grounds, he had somehow known the only one which could outdistance Firebrand. He meant to catch her. She meant not to get caught.

Matthew swore at the top of his voice. Cathleen cut up the terrain as if she had the devil himself chasing her. Damnation! What had spooked her? It had started out innocently and had not progressed to anything which should have shamed her. He was a man. She, a woman. What they did was purely natural.

But not purely natural to be doing it in front of her brothers. No, that did not bode well . . . and spoke of things unscrupulous in their manner.

But Cathleen was not unscrupulous. Mayhap she had too many scruples. Too many rules. Man skirts and high-necked shirts four sizes too large! Did she think that would stop his cravings? Probably. By God, she did not know enough about what drove a man, what drove him. *She* drove him. Drove him to distraction. Luckily, he had the means to do something about it. Luckily, he had the foresight to pen his bid for Dunswell Manor after the first week when he and the brothers had gone to the public coffee house to down a few raw, dark ales. He had received the reply from the estate agent three days ago and had been biding his time until . . .

Biding his time until Cathleen was well and truly his.

That was it. The reason he had not told the Cochrans his plans and what they had to do with them. Because he knew that once Cathleen discovered he was to be master here, he had less of a chance with her than a Hottentot did with an Esquimau.

Matthew Dunn might woo Cathleen Cochran and win her. Matthew Forrest, the Earl of Dunswell, could not.

So, then. He would be Matthew Dunn today, for the last time. And he would ... they would ...

Damnation!

He leaned over Black Turk's neck and slapped the reins against the horse's flank urging him to the beat of Matthew's heart. The great thoroughbred ate up the ground, never breaking stride, never faltering over the uneven hillocks. He drew up to the rear of Firebrand and the other stallion seemed to sense that this was a race with his sire. Firebrand put on a burst of speed and Black Turk whickered, then with a great grunt he thundered forward inch by inch.

"That's it! Go for it, Black Turk. Go for the prize, you great black beast, you!"

And the prize, when he reached over with one arm and wrapped it tightly around her waist to tug her into his own saddle, was Cathleen. She didn't come willingly and her tight grip on Firebrand's middle nearly unseated them both. But Matthew and Black Turk were the stronger team. He kept his grip. Black Turk stayed in perfect stride with his offspring.

"Let loose of the reins, Cathleen!" Matthew shouted over the drumlike pounding of two exhausted horses's hooves. "Let loose! You're wringing Fire-brand's neck!"

Cathleen would rather die than hurt her precious horse. "Damn you, Matthew Dunn!" She let loose of the reins and felt herself being lifted from the saddle by a man whose strength was unnerving. It seemed effortless for him to pull her up and over the edge so she faced him full. Looping the reins over Black Turk's neck, Matthew allowed the horse to slow into a graceful trot. When the riding was easier, he wrapped both arms around her waist and tugged her close to him, until her head rested under his chin and she could feel and hear the thunderous, uneven beat of his heart.

"Ah, Cathleen. Where are you going, lass? You cannot hide from me, you know. And you cannot hide from the way we make each other feel."

"You don't understand. And I can't explain."

"I understand this."

His hands caressed her back, her sides, her shoulders. Black Turk walked now as Matthew learned her body. His palms ran over her bottom and along her thighs, then back up to her waist. They did not stop there but continued until what she had dreamed about, thought about, from the night at the river, finally happened. It was as if she had been made to fit into his hands, and her heart soared at the wondrous feeling he evoked merely from cupping her breasts.

"Matthew . . . we can't . . ."

"Ah, Cathleen . . . there is so much that we can . . ."

His fingers kneaded her flesh and she gasped when tingling shafts of pleasure radiated from her hardened nipples. His thumb found the tiny buds and he played with them like a local named Billy Weeks played on the fiddle, thrumming back and forth, flicking over them, making her breasts harden and throb, and sing to his tune.

"Matthew!"

"Say it again, Cathleen. I love the way you say my name. With a cadence that is uniquely yours."

She smiled. "Matthew."

He abandoned her delightful breasts to cup her face in his palms. "Again."

"Matthew."

When her lips puckered on the second syllable Matthew held her head captive and kissed her. He took delicate nibbles on her lips at first, tasting the sweetness that came from the mint and honey she used in her tea, tasting the spice from the molasses bread, the tang from the currants, the salt from her tears as they dripped.

"Cathleen, darling, this does not occasion tears. Unless, of course, they're tears of joy."

She hiccuped and shook her head, but she said—as if knowing what would happen when she did—"Aye, Matth . . . thew."

His mouth covered hers; and Cathleen believed he was truly a field hand, or a man parched from weeks of tramping in the wild, wide desert. As he drank from her and made her completely giddy, he untied the laces at the front of her shirt and opened it fully, exposing her delicate lace-edged chemise. It, too, gave with a tug to the neckline tie and he worked it over her shoulders and let it and the shirt puddle around her hips. His eyes locked onto her breasts; but though she held her breath in anticipation, he did not touch them. Instead, he reached up and pulled the riband which held up her hair, letting the curls cascade over her breasts and bare shoulders.

The sun was warm and his eyes were hot with desire, shining with delight.

"Untie my shirt, Cathleen."

Fumbling like a child reaching for a treat on a top shelf—the forbidden fruit which was so delectable—she pulled on the tie which held his shirt closed. It gave too slowly and she tugged, nearly tearing it from its loops. Finally, she had it done . . . and off . . . and pulled it down around his shoulders as he had done to hers.

They sat on the swaying horse as Black Turk took them far from the manor house and deeper into the woods. Sat and faced each other, naked to the waist.

For the first time she feasted on the delights of his body. His neck was solid and thick, the cords standing out in relief, his pulse beating strong and fast. His shoulders knotted with muscles so firm they looked like rocks. But when she poked them with her fingers, they gave.

Oh! that this too, too solid flesh would melt . . . did melt, at her touch. She smiled to see it ripple as her palms splayed over it and for the first time in her life she knew what a man felt like.

She drew in her breath when her fingers found his sparse, curly chest hair and traced its route where it began just below his shoulders. He sucked in his breath and began to breathe raggedly when she delved into the silky strands ... allowing them to wind themselves around her fingers as she feathered her palms over his chest ... down and around his own tiny buds of flesh ... and continued exploring his hair in an arrowed path to his waist and the pool of coarse homespun which was his shirt and trousers.

"Stop, Cathleen."

"Why? Does the gentleman not like it?"

"The gentleman likes it all too well." He took her hands and drew them up, putting them around his neck. "There, that's enough for now."

"But ..." She looked down to his lap and then up, grinning. "Oh."

From the rhythm which Black Turk set, her breasts glided over his chest ... up and down ... back and forth.

"Oh, aye," she whispered. "Aye."

He kissed her and allowed the horse to set a gait which sensitized them both until they were breathless. The saddle was hard; but he was harder, still. When he decided they were far enough from the house he found the trailing reins and stopped Black Turk.

They were surrounded by centuries old oaks and walnuts and scrubby pines. Last year's needles and leaves muffled the sounds around them in a deep layer which left an odor of musk and wild mint. It was as if they existed in a world of their own, without time, without half-truths and troubles.

Matthew leaned his forehead against Cathleen's. "Darling ... we ... I ..."

"I ken, Matthew."

"Do you want to go back?"

"Aye, I do." At the stricken look in his eyes, she laughed delightedly. "But not yet," she teased. She kissed him fiercely, her arms a vice to hold him close. "Nay. Not yet will we turn for home. For here ... for now ... this is our home." She pushed away from him, and holding to his proferred arm, she slid down from the saddle and waited below him.

She was perfection, itself.

Venus could not be so beautiful. No one could pull off her shirt and chemise and be shy and seductive at the same time. Not like Cathleen.

He had been with other women. Not very many, but enough to know the differences when he saw them—the innocence and natural instincts which few had and he cherished in her. She stood there now, not as a coquette with a sly gleam in her eye pretending not to know what to do next. She did not cover her breasts; but neither did she hold them in her own hands as a gift for him. That would be contrary to her nature. Her standing there was gift enough. Her standing there without averting her gaze from the all too obvious evidence that he was a man and fully aroused, was more than he expected to get in this life.

He touched the man-skirt. "What do we do with this?"

"One tie. Here, tucked into the waist in the front." She allowed him to find it and when his knuckles skimmed along her midsection, she sucked in her breath and her skin rippled and warmed to his touch. "Tickles," she whispered.

The riband tie gave easily and her man-skirt floated over her hips, dropping to the ground in two pieces. Clever," he said, grinning. "And I will remember there is an entrance without undressing. For next time."

"Wilt there be a next time?"

"Oh, aye. There will be forever times for us."

She sighed, wrapped her arms around him and leaned her cheek against his chest. "I dreamed of it. Of this."

"Did you now?" Matthew asked with a grin.

"Aye."

"And is this as good as your dreams?" he whispered into her ear.

She shook her head and a dreamy expression lit her eyes. "Nay. 'Tis better."

"Glad I am of that. And gladder, still, will I make you."

Her palms seemed to feather down his back to his own wasitband and he knew the tickle feeling she had felt. His ties were not so easy; but with his hands over hers, guiding her, she managed to open the side flaps and push them over his hips. They snagged on his manhood and she hid a smile as she tugged the trousers over, then pulled them down his legs.

"Your boots."

Though he knew he didn't need to have them off to make love to her, he stood obediently as she tugged them off. "Now yours."

God, he wanted to pick her up and ride her to completion, he was that ready for her. But she wanted the dream and more. He wanted to give it to her. And more. So much more. Would she want it as much as he did? Would she accept it, the limits of it, and still be as eager as he was now? *Ah, please. Let it be so.*

When they were finally Adam and Eve together, he took her hand and held it gently but firmly. "I take thee, Cathleen . . ."

"When?"

He laughed at her audacity. "I thought you wanted the words."

A momentary sadness eclipsed the brightness in her eyes and she shook her head. "The Irish know that words are only words. I want you."

"Then we will have no more words. Only the touch of our lips." He kissed her, exploring the inner softness of her mouth, her honied taste, her warmth and eagerness. "Our hands and mouth."

He touched her breasts, filling his palms with them. Then bending his head, he laved them with his tongue, circling the peach-tinted bud with tender care. She sighed and pulled his head closer and he took her into his mouth, sucking gently, then harder until she stiffened, arched her back and moaned.

His mouth trailed down, down to the soft place underneath her breasts where he nibbled and left wet kisses. Down to the sensitive area of her waist and the tantalizing indentation about her belly. Down to the right, where he found her hip and thigh and knee. Then up the same trail, wetting it this time, until he repeated his ministrations to her left side. As his head rose slowly, he felt her legs tremble and he held her bottom, gently lowering her to the carpet of leaves and pine needles. With his fingers, he spread out her mahogany-colored curls in a fan around her head and over her shoulders. He covered her breasts with them and tickled her nipples with a strand.

Her eyes closed and she arched her back. He groaned as her full breasts broke through their satiny prison. He wrapped her hair around them like a nest and sucked on the creamy globes, drawing in as much of her as he could. Wanting more. Wanting so much more, it was agony.

As she clasped his head to her and cradled him with her arms, he skimmed his hands down to the fiery heat her twisting movements proclaimed. He delved between moist folds and touched the most sensitive part of her. Though she stiffened and would have drawn away, he did not stop. Soon—almost immediately—she sighed and her body relaxed, her thighs opened slightly and he knew such joy it was indescribable.

Pleasure was only the beginning.

Cathleen could not believe the journey to bliss which Matthew prepared for them both. His touched enflamed. His kisses propelled. His mouth, his tongue, his hands, his body. Each was an instrument.

The bow to her violin. The pluck to her harp. She *felt* music in his touch.

But she also felt the ride . . . the rhythm . . . of the journey. Her skin contracted and undulated and a tiny ripple of fire burst from each nibble or kiss, spun along some inner roadway she had never known existed, raced to a central core which throbbed—not from pain, but from a pleasure so beautiful, so breathtaking, tears dripped of their own accord. She was hot and wet where his fingers delved, and there was an insistent ache which had to be assuaged, filled, brought to completion.

Her hand went to touch his, to tell him without words what she needed; but he was so gentle, so loving, she cried out, "Matthew, please! Ah, saints and angels, I want you. All of you."

"You don't know what you ask," he ground out.

"But I do," she whispered and kissed the top of his head. She felt it on her leg, that pulsating, powerful part of him which she knew . . . and didn't know at all. She put her arms around Matthew and pulled him up so his chest was lying against her shoulder. "For this, I ask."

She touched him and found silk covering a pulsating shaft of iron. Such disparity was so profoundly male, she sucked in her breath at the thought of what God had wrought . . . for her. Her fingers encircled it and learned the length and breadth and workings of it. She smiled when it fluttered beneath her fingers, pleased that she, and her touch, held dominion over this man. But her mind knew what her fingers taught her—that there was a domain awaiting them to which only this man could take her. She swept her hand up his shaft and opened her legs in a silent invitation to guide her where they were meant to go.

Her body opened as he slid slowly inside, filling her. He stopped and she arched up; but he held her down.

"Shhh . . . we have to go slow, Cathleen, darling. It can be painful . . ."

"Oh. Aye. Mama said . . ."

Far too much about the pain. And far too little about the joy and pleasure. "Is it not best to make the pain the tiniest part of the journey? Do not go too slow, Matthew, else I ken the pain will eclipse the pleasure."

"We can't have that, me darlin'," he teased in the brogue of the villagers.

And that lightness took them through the worst part and into the best. She bit her lip when it hurt, then opened her mouth in awe at the glory of having Matthew deep inside her. 'Twas only the beginning, she realized, when he began to move within her in a rhythm which drew her breath away.

"Oh, Matthew . . . 'tis so beautiful."

"*You* are beautiful." He matched his movement to his words. "This is passion."

She knew such joy, she mimicked him, moving her hips up to capture his thrusting stroke. "And fire."

They moved apart, then joined madly, wondrously, together.

"Exquisite pleasure."

She rode over terrain she had only dreamt about, below, not atop, an animal so loving she experienced every wondrous inch of the way. The pleasures inside her body multiplied until they were one great bursting ecstasy of dreams indulged, fantasies fulfilled, imagination satisfied. And still he took her upward. Her body pulsed with a million sparks. Her mind spun in to a space and a time that were endless, enduring . . . theirs. Explosions began at their coupling and rippled through her body. She arched her back. She searched for and found what she was feeling in his eyes, which locked with hers as the breath whooshed out of her and she could no longer feel where she ended and he began.

They were one flesh. One body. One pleasure. One joy.

With his arms around her waist, Matthew guided Cathleen to the waiting stallion. He could not remember how they separated after that perfect mating. He only knew that somehow he had helped her into her damnable man clothes, and she had helped him into his. He stumbled over sticks and stones. Looking down, he snickered, then laughed until the bower rang with his crazed whoops.

"Matthew, what's wrong?"

"My boots . . ."

She could not see the problem. The boots were on his feet. She shrugged and kept walking while he plopped on the ground and switched the long black things. It wasn't until they were in the saddle, Matthew seated behind her on Black Turk's flanks, that he explained.

"I could not stand the other boots I wore. They gave me blisters and pained so much, even soaking did not help. So I had these made to my specifications in town. They bend with the curve of my feet. And in our haste, we got the right one on the left and the left one on the right."

" 'Tis a fairy story, aye?"

"Nay. 'Tis true, my love."

"I ne'er heard of such a thing. Boots come as they are, both the same. Right boot and left boot. What a lark!"

"Nevertheless . . ."

He stuck his right leg up and she saw the slight curve on the outside which wasn't on the inside. Suddenly, she realized these were not merely *boots.* They were not of coarse, home-cured leather. These were shiny, soft things which must have cost the moon. How could he, a field hand who worked for room and board, afford such luxuries?

"Where did you have them made?"

"Clarkson's in . . ."

"I know where Clarkson's is," she snapped.

The most expensive leather goods came from Clarkson's tannery. Writing boxes. Hats. Gloves. Boots. Saddles. But only the gentry could afford them.

She eased her body slightly away from him as an unnamed fear washed away in the glory in the grove.

"Matthew Dunn, how could you afford Clarkson boots?"

"Ah . . . well . . . that is . . ."

"Spit it out, Matthew; or 'twill choke you." *If I do not do it first.*

"Ah . . ." He cleared his throat and tightened his hold on her, afraid she might jump off as soon as she knew the truth. "I haven't been completely honest with you, Cathleen."

"Aye. So it seems."

He inhaled deeply then began. "First, my name is not Matthew Dunn."

"Nay? I could not have guessed."

So she would not make this easy, the little minx. He'd play it all out and then reel her in. After all, what they had finally shared should show her that he meant the best for them both. And telling her the truth would show her that he was not one to toy with her affections, that he could be trusted.

"My real name is Matthew . . ."

"Oh, grand. I thought I would have to learn a whole new title for our field hand."

"You will."

"Oh, aye?"

"Matthew Forrest. The Earl of Dunswell." Her body slumped forward as if she were curling herself in a ball and Matthew knew he had to get it all out quickly else he would have an hysterical woman on his hands. "And so I took the position . . ."

"You begged for it," she moaned.

"Aye, I did that. And for good reason, as I've explained. But now I've made my bid and it has been accepted. I'll take up residence as soon as the manor house is repaired and furnished. Of course, since the Cochrans have served here several years, I will expect your family to continue in its present capacity . . . training the Dunswell breed. There is one exception, however. I would like your mother to be my housekeeper. I will hire an estate overseer and several hands to do the hard work in the fields that she had done until now. And a full servant staff for her to oversee, of course."

"Why, we could expect naught less," she said with a snort.

"You, Cathleen, will get much more."

Just before they arrived at the stables he explained what else he had in mind. Though she wanted to scream from frustration, shame, and rage, she held her tongue. She also held herself steady, never allowing her body to give away the turmoil of her mind.

"It sounds a good proposition from your point of view."

"It is one."

"Aye. But I will need time to think on it."

"Take all the time you need. I will be patient, but persistent. As you must know by now, that is my nature."

It was also the nature of a snake; and though the legend had it that there was none in Ireland, she knew them well enough to know that they hid in the grass, slithered their way into the open, then pounced on unsuspecting prey.

Matthew Dunn.

Matthew Forrest.

The Earl of Dunswell.

And she had given herself over to him as Eve had given herself over to the serpent in the Garden. With almost the same results. Cathleen Cochran was now naked before him, and there were no leaves large enough or strong enough to clothe and protect her. Even from herself.

"Will you tell your parents that I wish to speak with them about the new arrangements?"

"Nay, Matthew . . . 'twould be best if I told them. It would lessen the shock that way."

"Shock? They had to expect someone to purchase the manor house and estate."

"Aye. But not their field hand."

"Ah. I see. Your way will be best, I suppose."

She could also be persistent. That, he did not know yet; but he would. "Aye. 'Twill be best, I promise."

"I will be gone two days to get the papers signed and the money to the mortgage bankers. When I return we will discuss the new arrangements . . . all of them."

"Aye. When you return."

Though she seemed distracted while he spoke of his plans for the estate and for her, Matthew paid it little mind. It was a surprise, that was all, he thought. She would get used to it . . . used to his being called *my lord* . . . used to the manor house being occupied, the fields filled with laborers. Used to many things, not the least of which was their loving each other as often as possible under the circumstances. That, he assured her, would not change.

He kissed her passionately and left her at the entrance to her family quarters. She stood staring pensively after him as he hastened to the stables to saddle and mount his horse. From over his head he heard loud noises, raised voices, and one quiet, stubborn, insistent murmur. Cathleen seemed the calm in the storm as she must be pleading his case, allaying her family's fears.

He smiled as he rode out of the estate. He stopped and reversed in the saddle to take one last look at the house which would soon be his home. It was perfect. It held Cathleen, did it not?

And those wonderful horses.

When he returned two days later, the Cochrans were not in the training oval. Maeve's oven was cold. The tables and chairs which had been neatly spread around the grounds were gone.

And so were the horses.

The stable echoed hollowly as he walked through it. Each stall held fresh straw but was empty of everything else. In the tack room one set of tack, a hoof pick, and a hoof file hung on the wall. The feeding trough held fresh water for . . . what? . . . ghost horses?

He contained his anger . . . his doubts . . . his questions . . . and stormed through the door to the quarters above.

"Cathleen! Cathleen!"

Indentations in a soiled rug with so many holes it was fit for naught more than a washing rag bore mute evidence that once furniture had been in place and people had lived here. One, two days previous. Two days ago these stall rooms had held five Cochrans. Now field mice skittered in front of his feet as he stomped his way back to the room where he knew Cathleen had slept. There, pinned to the wall was a large piece of folded and sealed paper. *For the new Earl* was written in a good, bold hand on it. The seal resembled the mark Cathleen had showed him on the halfbreed's ear.

Trepidation turned to anger. Anger, to rage, as he read the few words.

Matthew Forrest, The Earl
   My lord and master
   We Cochrans are a proud people. We do not suffer liars kindly. And we do NOT serve this manor house. Not for the previous owners. Most assuredly not for someone who would gull us, then gut us. We have taken only that which is—by God, and in His sight—ours. We leave behind only the empty manor house and out-buildings. May you find in them more than the proposition you offered us.

She did not sign it; but he knew it was Cathleen's work.

Damn her.

Matthew Forrest, the Earl, was it?

The Earl of Dunswell, it was!

She would know that name soon. She would have it shoved down her throat until she used it properly. He was the Earl of Dunswell now. And the Earl of Dunswell would scour this country until he found his property.

The horses.

And the woman.

1771

Betrayal

Chapter Six

Matthew Forrest, the Earl of Dunswell, scanned the May racing crowd at the Rood Running in Donegal. "There are more here than in previous years, I vow," he said to his estate overseer, Rodney Fenwick.

"Aye, my lord. And not what I would call a change for the better," the tall, spare, dark man said with a sneer.

Matthew chuckled. "Ah, Fenwick . . . where do you get your aversion to the female sex?"

The other man did not answer, merely snorted and gaped at the next woman to sway towards them. Matthew concurred with Fenwick's assessment of this particular woman. Matthew's head swiveled and another, then more, came into his purview. Good God! Where the track had once been a man's world, this race had drawn out human fillies of all types. Did they not know that racing was hot, dirty work? Had no one warned them they would be walking where horses had left unpleasant reminders of their passing?

Where were their brains . . . if they had any at all to begin with. By God, they looked as if they were going to the magistrate's ball!

Startling hair topped their attire, piles of white curls festooned with feathers, bows, and jewels. Their gowns—not dresses or riding habits, which would have been more reasonable—were of quilted satin or silks, embroidered and laced until they looked like towering pastries served by the King's ministers. They carried matching sunshade parasols. And their feet were shod in dancing slippers.

No wonder he nor Fenwick had ever married.

He paused and looked out over the flat where the first race was due to go off in a few minutes. He saw the grand parade, but let it pass unnoted. His thoughts were on the only woman who had ever captured his attention for more than five minutes. The only woman whom he had considered for wife. A woman who would have known what to wear, how to wear it, and what the horses could or would do.

She would have been able to talk about more than the King's new mistress or the last ball she had attended. In fact, she probably had never attended a ball in her whole life. But she had never ceased to have something to say, if only a diatribe directed towards him.

Damnation!

She was like no other of her race.

Her cheek was softer than satin. The back of his knuckles could still feel the texture. The texture of a thief.

Damn her! Damn her whole family.

He did not know how, but after they had stripped him naked two years previous, he had gone on with his life. Not easily, but in necessity. Two years ago he had ridden into that isolated estate and discovered that along with the entire contents of the stables, Cathleen and her family had even stolen the harp from the manor house drawing room. The harp, he could forgive mayhap. But the horses, never! For two years he held his head high ... and hired three men from London to find the thieving Cochrans. He grunted. He had been forced to go to London to get them. There was not an Irishman who would take his money, no matter that it came from a nobleman.

A nobleman. Damnation!

He had heard them laugh behind his back when he had gone to hire them to work his fields. They called him the *bought-me-a-title-earl*. He, who had worked for everything he had, was now a laughingstock in the village which was part and parcel of his largesse. Because of her, that devious, proud-as-a-peacock Cathleen and her thieving menfolk, he had scoured the land to find servants, and in the end, had to settle for a series of barely qualified drudges from a London agency. To a man and woman these English layabouts had found Donegal unfriendly, unwelcoming, *unEnglish*. He couldn't remember their names, there had been so many in the last two years. Only Fenwick had stayed on. He seemed to like the isolation, even welcome it. Well, he was a surly, taciturn man. The nobles and gentry who lived in London and its environs did not welcome those qualities in an overseer, just as Ireland and its environs did not welcome Matthew Forrest, the *bought-me-a-title-earl*. In his mad search for the Cochrans and his horses, his questions brought naught but snickers and side glances which told him the Cochrans and what they had done to him were to blame for making him the object of scorn. For two years he had felt surrounded by treachery—both here in Donegal and back in London where Parliament had cast a cold eye to see how much it could wring out of the Irish gentry to help shore up the treasury. Once again he found himself at the mercy of men who had not wanted to make him equal to them in the first place.

Damnation, would it never end?

Aye, he had been scorned. But he was his father's son. He would not be defeated. He had thrown himself into developing his farm and his stables, managing to buy up good stock from breeders as far away as Lyon and the Rhineland. His first two-year-olds were in competition today. He did not expect more than a third place from them because they were untried and not as well trained as the Cochran horses had been. But they were an Arabian cross breed like Black Turk's progeny; and should eventually prove excellent racers.

Eventually.

He shouldn't have had to wait until *eventually*. He should be entering Cuchulain or Emir or Firebrand.

Damn! Why could his agents not find those

horses? How had the Cochrans disappeared so completely?

The trump sounded and he forced himself to watch the first race. He had no entrants but had bet on a two-year-old called Dromahair, a part Arabian mare bred out of the Sidhe Stables high in the mountain peaks in the roughest part of Donegal. He had heard good things about this stable. It had produced four winners at the first spring races, two at the second. Mayhap he could interest the trainers into a more lucrative position in Dunswell Stables—or at the least, a chance to breed his mares with their Arabian. There were other entrants from the same stables, two in each of the eight races. If Dromahair ran as he expected, he would put money on all of them.

The women took to camp seats at an enclosed area but the men crowded the fence as the horses lined up behind the rope at the end of the field. Today's was a flat out race. The horses started at one end of the field, raced to the other end and then back again. The turn was the dangerous part. Many horses were jostled, some riders thrown, some horses hurt badly enough to be put to death. For that reason, these flats were quickly being replaced by the oval track that would be used for the Donegal Stakes in two weeks. He had seen plans for an oval track here at the Rood Running, which would give Ireland seventeen oval tracks to England's fourteen.

These Irish did like a wager with their pints of ale.

The trump sounded three notes, indicating the horses were ready. Dromahair was on the far outside, two horses down from her competition from the Sidhe Stables. Matthew consulted a list of entrants and saw that this horse was named Red Branch Rose. Both jockeys wore a green and white striped pennant affixed to their sleeves. Dromahair's had the number five affixed to that and Rose, a number seven. Two trump notes and Matthew leaned expectantly forward, along with the fellows to left and right of him. One trump note. Then the gun, and they were off.

Dromahair's jockey rode high in the saddle, leaning out over the mare's neck, urging her on without whip or cord. And a word in the ear was all the horse seemed to need, for she streaked out ahead of the pack. Her long black legs seemed to eat up the turf, sending great chunks of grass flying back in the faces of the other steeds. She was first to the end of the track, first to turn. And with a graceful flip of the reins the jockey brought her to the far outside, away from the bunched up pack, away from possible collision, to an open area where the roan mare ran for all she was worth.

Her companion, Red Branch Rose, came in third.

Fenwick, who had also put money on her, did all but dance. "Did you see that, sire? She was at least five lengths ahead of the rest. By God, she's a winner, indeed!"

The jockey dismounted to cheers and some mutterings from those who had not had money on the horse. Red Branch Rose's jockey nudged his third place winner over to the payout circle on the other side of the field. He hopped off Rose and the two Sidhe Stables' jockeys pounded each other on the back. A short, stout man presented the winning jockey with a small silver cup and a large red wool purse. Then he handed two very small black purses to the other two winners. The two Sidhe Stables' jockeys led their horses away, side-by-side. The crowd which had gathered around the payout circle dispersed, and the next race was called.

Matthew went to collect his winnings and put money on the next Sidhe Stables' entrants. Then he put a little money on his own horses, which would come up in the fourth and fifth races.

It was during the second and third races that he realized Dromahair's jockey was once again atop Sidhe Stables' mounts. And twice again the horses made the turn first and ran towards the outside to avoid the pack. Another two cups for Sidhe Stables. Another four purses. After absorbing that information, he went to the paddock assigned to him to tell his own trainer William Bonney, the little trick the winner had used.

"You want the jock to bring Mandrake round to the outside?" William Bonney asked. "That'll eat up seconds we canna afford to lose."

"It may save the horse a collision. Do it."

"Aye, sire. They be your horses."

The race ran almost a duplicate of the first two. With one exception. Matthew had his first winner. Mandrake came in third.

"Well I'll be damned," Fenwick said. "You used that Sidhe sidle."

"Made all the difference," Matthew said. He left his place and called back to Fenwick, "Congratulations are in order for William and the jockey. They carried out my orders to the letter."

With his height, Matthew knew he projected confidence and power, because with a mere nudge the crowd opened up before him and he had a clear route to the payout circle. But before he made it, a voice which could shatter glass sliced through his musings and made the hair at the back of his neck stand on end.

"My dear Matthew, how did you, of all people, produce a winner in such a short time?"

"Ah, Melody," he said to the misnamed eighteen-year-old who wrapped her stubby fingers around his wrist and would not let go. "You and your family have come early to Ireland."

"Papa is quite cross with me."

She pouted in what she thought was a pretty moue; but Matthew wanted to shake her and tell her to be herself. He didn't, however, because she probably had no self to be. She was a product of a marriage made by the court jester. Her father, Josiah Redfern, was a seventy-year-old king's minister of war and finances, an Earl else he would never have won her mother who was the daughter of an Viscount and only thirty-five, now. They had been advancing this featherhead for two years, and their object was an entailed title, full money bags which would last a lifetime and beyond, lands worthy of the daughter of the King's minister, and—God help the man who got

Melody—plenty of room for the impoverished septuagenarian and his wife to take up residence.

Melody snapped her fan against Matthew's hand. "Do you not wish to know why Papa is cross with me?"

"Why?"

"Because I would not accept the Earl of Nuttley's offer. He's too fat and too old and has five children. One only two years my junior. I am not meant to mother quite yet. Besides . . . I have my eye on another Earl. He's not at all fat nor bound up with mewling children. Though he is getting old and had best get himself a wife before he's too spent to get her with child."

Her smile was guile and determination, and Matthew knew one moment of pure terror. He was in her sights. By God, he now knew what the poor fox felt when the dogs yapped at his heels.

"Well, do your best, Melody. Though if your Earl is as tired as you say, he's probably too old—or too wily—to be trapped into a marriage he does not initiate."

"Oh, pooh!" This time she snapped his cheek with her fan and ground her gloved nails into the back of his hand. "You are no fun at all. I suppose you're going to allow me to waste away in this godforsaken country, when I could be persuaded to be most accommodating and most solicitous of your comfort . . . should you seek me out."

Why the coquette offered herself, did she? Did she think to trap him that way? Hardly likely. No woman had yet, and several had attempted it in the past two years. He had sampled a few; but his sojourn in the Haj and Arabia to retrieve his breeding stallions had brought him knowledge not only of how to impregnate horses, but also how to prevent impregnation of women. Well, Melody could be a tasty morsel, but not for him.

There was only one woman for him.

"You had best not expect much from me, Melody. I am working very hard every day to build up my stables and will not even be at Dunswell Manor for more than a day or two at a time."

"Oh, these races! They are such a bore."

He left her at the women's enclosure and strode purposefully towards the nearby payout circle. He nodded and smiled to his own jockey, who was leading Mandrake up to the payout table. Matthew tipped his hat, then shifted his eyes to the two mounts preceding Mandrake. The horse which had come in second—Red Branch Rose, again—stopped at the table behind the winner, Knocknarea. The Sidhe jockeys slid to the ground and put their heads together. Then the winning jockey led Knocknarea out of the payout circle.

By the time the official time keeper and steward knew the horse and jockey had left, Matthew was close enough to hear the confrontation between them and the other Sidhe jockey.

"This has ne'er happened before, boyo. Ye'd best have a good explanation, now."

"Cat had a nature call and with another mount in

the next race, couldn't afford to stop to collect the winnings. Said I should take them, sire."

"Most unusual. But," he shrugged, " 'tis the same stables, so 'twill be the same thing, I suppose. You will see that John gets this?"

"Oh, aye. He and Cat'll skin me alive, if else."

The crowd laughed and the young man disappeared with the cup and the two purses, leading his mount back towards the paddocks.

Matthew heaped all sorts of praises on William and his son Joe, who had ridden Mandrake. "Fenwick calls it the Sidhe sidle. We shall use it on each flat-out race."

"Aye, sire," William said, handing over the purse.

He eyed the bulge greedily; and Matthew wondered if the man could be trusted. Hell, he probably couldn't be; but Matthew had no choice. William Bonney was the only trainer who had accepted Matthew's offer. There was one way to forestall any stealing . . .

Matthew opened the purse and took out two of the sterling pieces. "A bonus each time you bring in a winner, regardless of position," he said, and offered one silver piece to William, the other to Joe.

William's eyes twinkled and he bit down on the coin. "For good luck in the next race."

He and his son won another coin each that day.

And Sidhe Stables ran eight winners for purses totaling over a hundred pounds.

He was in the paddock area, watching while Fenwick, William and Joe loaded the horses into the

special coach William had commissioned for safe
travel. It looked like any ordinary overland coach but
it had reinforced springs. It also had oversized wheels
because it was two feet wider, a foot longer and two
feet taller. It had been stripped of all the interior fin-
ishings, including seats and lanterns. Two half doors
in the back opened outward and a detachable ramp
allowed the horses to enter and exit their temporary
home away from home. Inside, the walls were pad-
ded with special quilting made of colonial cotton bat-
ting and wool felt. The floor was drilled in several
places to allow for easy cleaning.

Already, other stable owners had expressed an interest in acquiring such a conveyance and Matthew
had taken orders and had a blacksmith and carriage-
maker working exclusively on this new design. The
profits from their sales would come in handy; taxes
had gone up alarmingly in the past two years. His entailed estate in the wilds of Ireland now cost him
more in taxes than his entire London mercantile oper-
ation and his townhouse and factory put together. He
could well understand how the original owners of
Dunswell Manor had lost it to the same greedy ministers of finance, probably Melody's father. The old
goat.

"Good race, Matthew," Josiah Redfern said. He
leaned over the rail of his carriage and watched the
process of cajoling Mandrake and the stallion's sister,
Morgana, into the coach. "Two good thoroughbred
English-Arabian winners, I see. Not many did that
well this day."

"Except the Sidhe Stables," Melody maliciously added. "Why that Cat person must have collected twenty purses."

"You should have minded your school lessons, Melody," Matthew gave back in kind. " 'Twas only eight."

"Mayhap they have a titled son who will make a good match for me. Do go and seek them out, father."

"I already have," the old badger said. "The Cochrans may have the best Irish-Arabian strain in the world but their two sons are untitled and under-bred. You deserve far better than they." He tipped his tricorn to Matthew and tapped his driver on the shoulder.

Their carriage drove away leaving Matthew standing stock-still at the edge of the paddock, staring sightlessly after it, building with a rage so deep, so all-consuming, he felt as if his innards were being burned away.

Cat, was it? For Cathleen, mayhap?

"By God, I have them now!"

"Sire? May I be of assistance?" Fenwick asked.

"You may, indeed!" He grabbed the man by the arm and practically dragged him away from the paddock. "They are here."

"Who?"

"The Cochrans."

"Are you sure?"

"Aye. She saw me, obviously. That's why she had a sudden call of nature . . ."

"Are you in need of a physician, my lord?"

"No, I am not in need of a physician. Man, think! We have been hunting these thieves for two years and all the time they have been right here under our noses. Racing! The Sidhe Stables are filled with *my* horses. Those were *my* winners out there today. And those conniving bastards stole *my* purses."

"By God, sire! Shall I call the magistrate?"

"And lose the horses again? Not on your life. I want to know where they've remained hidden all these years. And when I know . . ."

"We'll write out a writ of arrest and you will have the finest stables in all of England, sire." Fenwick rubbed his hands together. "William will make of them what the stables of an Earl deserve. We could take them to the continent. To the colonies. Why stud fees would be astronomical. . . ."

While Fenwick had dreams of races and money bags, Matthew had visions of something entirely different. Mahogany hair. Green eyes. Full breasts. Tiny waist. Slender hips. And legs which wound themselves around him like silken bonds.

He stopped short as they passed the last paddock and still had caught no sight of their quarry. "Where the hell are they?" He raced towards a group of men, some of whom he recognized as bookmakers, and demanded to know where the Sidhe Stables had been paddocked.

"They set by themselves o'er thataways," a gap-toothed boy said. "Set themselves high, they does."

"They should. They win," his double said and the men roared their approval.

Matthew turned in the direction the young lad had indicated—a wooden area behind the racing flat. There he saw a ring of carriages like his own, enclosing an area much like a paddock. "Keep to the trees," he ordered Fenwick. "I do not want to be observed."

"Aye, sire."

They managed to get close enough to hear snatches of conversations.

"Sit here, Mama. And put on your shawl. You don't want to catch a cold, now, love."

". . . two hundred and twenty pounds to add to the building fund . . ."

". . . Dunswell is ours . . ."

"Do you think he saw her? He was that close, I near lost my ploughman's lunch."

". . . the colonies, for sure and forever . . ."

"Well, time to go, Maeve, my darling. Paul, help your mother into the carriage. And mind she doesn't trip like last time."

It was the longest conversation Matthew had ever heard John Cochran say. But it portended no good. "Fenwick," he ordered in a whisper, "bring up our horses."

"Are we to follow?"

"Aye. All the way to hell, if that is where they be headed."

* * *

It wasn't hell, but the location came damn near to
it—if hell was cold as ice, that is. They climbed high
into the hills, putting the towns far behind them.
Night came over them thrice and the Cochrans took
to humble inns and farms which welcomed them so
heartily Matthew was certain they had done this very
thing many times previous. He and Fenwick took to
sleeping on the rough under blanket and cape, taking
watches round the night to be certain the Cochran en-
tourage did not slip out of their accommodations
without being seen. But they kept to a straight route;
and Matthew wondered how many times it had taken
for them to be comfortable enough to know they had
eluded whatever or whomever Matthew had sent to
track them.

On the fifth day the carriages drove boldly through
stone gateposts which had a sign attached, into which
a name had been carved. *Sidhe Stables*.

"They have no shame," he muttered.

He and Fenwick gave them two hours before
stealthily approaching the house and stables far beyond the gate. He stopped and stared at an enclosure
much like Dunswell Manor, only on a smaller scale.
The house looked as if it had been there all along and
they had simply moved in and enlarged it. With *Earl
of Dunswell* money, from *Earl of Dunswell* racing
stock, of course.

"We shall camp here tonight, Fenwick. I want to
be certain they are going to ground for a spell."

"Aye, sire."

Acrid smoke burned their gullets and the fragrance

of Meave's stew gave them both the most uncomfortable night of the trip. They had provisions; but they were hard cheese and harder bread. Coffee, tea, or ale would have been welcome. As it was, they made do with water from a nearby stream. But Matthew was bound it would never happen again. The next day, when he saw that John and the boys—including the she-devil Cathleen—were putting the horses through the arduous three-week training schedule he knew they kept, he and Fenwick rode as quickly as they could to the first town they came to. They commandeered two rooms in an inn and slept and ate until they were themselves again.

The moment he rushed into Dunswell Manor, he threw his cape into his butler's hands and demanded brandy and soda be brought to his library. There, Matthew sank into his desk chair and pulled out paper, ink, and quill. He had had two hellish weeks on the trail. Two hellish weeks in which to see that justice be done this time.

They were thieves.

They would pay.

He would have his horses back.

And his woman.

He dipped the quill into the ink and made the first mark on the paper, then stopped. Ah, damn her eyes! He could not get her out of his mind.

I, Matthew Forrest, the Earl of Dunswell . . .

Her breath was sweet. It lingered in his brain, overpowering the rage he felt. Why did his memory refuse to credit the fact that she was a thief?

. . . hereby proclaim that John Cochran, his heirs, and assigns . . . Perspiration made his palms clammy and he put down the pen to wipe them. Her skin was never cold nor clammy. It was translucent. He remembered how her temple would throb when he approached; but he quickly turned the smile into a frown when his body heated and hardened. She was a thief, damn it!

. . . have willfully stolen goods and materials which are the lawful property . . . But thief or no, her nose was small and straight and lightly dusted with cinnamon-colored specks, as if the fairies which peopled her land wanted her to forever remain young.

. . . of the Earl of Dunswell. To whit . . . a full-sized harp of the worth of eighty pounds . . . In all the world . . . no harp compared to her voice. Nor any smile to her smile. Not only because of her full, generous lips and straight, white teeth, but because she smiled often and joyously. Certainly she did. She had the world, and him, fooled into believing she was more and less than she was—a thief.

. . . and upwards of fifteen horses, which included an Arabian stallion, several Irish stallions, one gelding, four mares, and recent foals . . . One of which he had helped birth.

By God! They had played false with him. Yet he thought of naught but Cathleen, and the wonders of her, at that.

He gritted his teeth and gripped the arms of his chair to will away these contradictory thoughts. By all that was holy, because of all she had done to him, he should be over her! Why then could he not think of anything other than what was wonderful about her? Most wonderful in his memory—she had the strangest, most beautiful eyes in the world. Eyes as changling as her temperament. Green or brown, grey or amber according to her mood, the climate, or what she wore. Flashes of brilliance. Sparks of fire. The darkness of a desire even he had fought. They had all been there, at one time or another—even as she was stealing him blind.

He paused, looked around his huge library and sighed. Though there were priceless portraits adorning the walls, none drew his gaze more than a few seconds, none held appeal like her damnable, delightful, devil's eyes.

His fingers curled round the arms of his chair and he brought them up to look at them. The finger pads tingled. His very body—even the smallest portion of it—knew her. And these . . . these tiny pads knew the best part of her, her long, silky hair. Darker than the strongest tea, it was; yet when the sun glinted off it, it sparkled with red highlights that took his breath away. The English language could not well describe it, though auburn came close.

Beautiful did not describe her, and did not come close.

Her body was tall, lithe, sleek, yet rounded where a woman's should be, and delighted the eye as well as the touch. He had not enjoyed enough touches, more's the pity. And certainly he had not seen enough of her—clothed or unclothed. Although . . .

he had imagined often enough what she looked like under those wild mismatched clothes she did wear. Wild.

Yes, that was descriptive of her. Wild and free and filled with life and hope. Like those horses of hers. No! Of *his*.

The scheming scamp. The angel was the devil. The devil deserved her due.

He slammed his hand on the desk top, sending the inkpot into the books and rattling the glass stopper so it clanged, and jarred, and matched his new mood. Bah! This traipse through memory lane led nowhere, to naught but confusion. He must keep that in mind, else he would lose far more than Cathleen Cochran's family had taken from him already.

So Matthew Forrest, the Earl of Dunswell, picked up his quill pen and with a flourish appended his new title to a complaint which would produce a writ and send the magistrate's guards to arrest those responsible for looting Dunswell Manor and Dunswell Stables.

The damnable thing was, she would not be one of them!

The point bent and broke, and Matthew swore loudly and long. But he sanded the ink nonetheless, blew it off, folded the paper, held a mahogany-colored candle over the edge until there dripped down sufficient sealing wax to hold the flap securely. Then, using his new signet for the first time, he pressed it firmly into the wax.

Done.

He called for Fenwick and ordered him to deliver
it to the magistrate, "Posthaste, Fenwick. Before they
know we know where they are."

"Aye, my lord. And about time, I do say, sire. Terrible lot, these Irish. Terrible lazy louts. And cunning.
All of them. Cunning and sly."

"Aye, aye, man. Now be off with you."

Fenwick returned quickly from his errand and reported that the magistrate would serve the writ immediately.

Matthew calculated it would take the magistrate's
men seven days to arrive at the hidden stables. Each
night he tossed and turned in his bed, disturbed by his
nightly dream of her. He heard later that it was on the
seventh day—when God had rested—that the magistrate's guards swooped down on the Cochran enclave,
confiscated the property delineated in the writ of seizure, and—after tying their arms behind them with
leather thongs—arrested all the Cochrans who had been
responsible for stealing property which was claimed by
Matthew Forrest, the Earl of Dunswell.

He also heard how Cathleen—the paragon of virtue, the angel, the devil—had screamed the house
down and cursed the land the Earl walked upon, the
very air he breathed.

Chapter Seven

Three weeks later, as Matthew Forrest gave over
the reins of his horse to Fenwick, to be tethered, Matthew searched the crowd. *Had she come?* He had
been notified that the writ had been served on her father and brothers. She had no legal standing in the
court. But would she come, defiant as these Irish had
recently proven themselves to be? Half of him hoped
she would. The other half prayed she would. He
wanted to see her, itched to see her. And the damned
itch needed to be scratched—as soon as possible or
he would for certain live up to the title The Mad Earl.

Though he tried to appear nonchalant, uncon-
cerned, as if this were only another day, merely another annoyance in his busy schedule, Matthew must
have given away the uniqueness of his woman-
centered hope, because the magistrate's sergeant-at-
arms snapped to attention and said, "They *all* be
inside, me lord. Good and proper."

Luckily, Matthew was saved from the quick rush

of heat which threatened to unleash his anger—for he was always angry when embarrassed and hated it when he was. But this day one of the locals gave him time to breathe deeply, and calm his roiling temper. There would be time and enough to give into all the damnable feelings which whirled around *her* in the courtroom, where *she* might give evidence.

Matthew's savior was a plump matron with a huge head and equally huge bare feet. She splayed her work-roughened hands on her hips and glowered at the sergeant-at-arms. "And are you not ashamed of yourself, Billy Weeks? Servin' papers on your own cousins an' hustlin' 'em here to the court! You'd best confess that to Father Flynn, you had."

"And why should I, Margaret Mayer? Only doing my job, and all, you know."

"Job, pah!" She tossed her head and flicked her skirts in a comical parody of a young wench. "Only took the job because o' the uniform, Billy Weeks. Thought it would bring the lassies flocking, I ken." Her eyes blazed and her feet stomped. "But you never should have taken a job the likes o'this. No good comes from the King or his toadies. And you'd best not be forgetting that, Billy Weeks, or you be fallin' flatter than dung off a fluxin' cow, and smellin' as bad, too."

As if they had only been waiting for Margaret Mayer to provide them with an energetic entry line, the crowd roared its approval, and laughing, surged forward into the forequarters of the magistrate's house—where his office and court room were situ-

ated. Their conversation buzzed with a vehemence
which surprised Matthew. At first he thought they
echoed Margaret Mayer's estimation of Billy Weeks;
but he was soon disabused of that notion by a small
boy who perched on the shoulders of a short, thin,
tired-looking man.

"There he be, Da. The bought-me-a-title Earl. You
see him?" the lad asked in a loud whisper.

Matthew cringed inside, but kept his countenance
stern, his carriage tall and commanding.

Bought-me-a-title! Yes, he had bought himself a title. An Earl, he was, and he was *not* ashamed of it.
It set him apart. It gave him what was his right and
due—an estate, though in the wild reaches of Ireland,
not the pleasant hills of England.

But an estate was an estate. And a title was a title.

He would make the best of it. He always had done.
He always would do—when once this damned suit
was settled and he got his property back. *All* of it.

As soon as he got inside, Matthew sized up the assemblage. It looked as if every last one of his new
neighbors jammed the public half of Chief Magistrate
Royce's brick and thatched house, where the trial
would be held. In their everyday work clothes spattered with offal and stained by the land, they stood
behind the rope which had been strung from one side
of the room to the other, separating them from the
land owners. He could smell the cologne the English
landed gentry had lavishly splashed on their pocket
squares and were now waving in the air to disguise
odors which had lingered too long on unwashed skin.

Why did they do it? It only made matters worse. And, it seemed to delight the Irish. They pointed fingers at each pinched nose and snapped waft of white square.

Yes, defiant, the Irish were. And, defiantly, there in court the Irish men wore their knitted caps on their heads. The women—grandmothers, mothers, and daughters, whose hair should have been bound and covered—had left it wild and uncapped. They may be fenced in by the laws of the British King, but these people proclaimed a freedom they had in their souls, a freedom Matthew had not known since those carefree early days with Cathleen.

As he and Fenwick began to make their way through the crowd, Matthew wondered if he would ever come to know these people more than he did that moment, and that was not at all. They talked openly about him, as if he were not there, could not hear, did not care.

"He's tall, he is. Dinna think he'd be so tall."

"Handsome rascal. Almost looks like one o' the kindly folk, 'ceptin' for his height. Fool, he be, for doin' what he's doin'."

"The devil take him," said a woman as he nudged past her.

The blond young man with her, guffawed. "Hell and back, Pegeen, the devil himself don't want him."

"Think he'll win, this day?" Pegeen persisted, as if Matthew were not at her elbow.

"And when, I ask, has a gentleman not won gainst one of ours?" the young man sneered.

"Never," another man—older, but much like him in stature, build and coloring—growled. "Damn them all."

The last was accompanied by a dark spat which plopped on the floor only a hair's width from Matthew's boot. He ignored it, as he ignored the comments which were envy, speculation, excitement, and something else . . . something he'd noticed on his circuit of the estate he had spent half his capital and all his time on restoring . . . something unusual in so poor a people.

Pride.

These, his neighbors, though they were hard put to make a good appearance, still held deep pride in themselves and their "own," as they called them.

And Matthew Forrest, the bought-me-a-title-Earl of Dunswell, had that day come to the magistrate's court to accuse one of their own of theft on a grand scale. Not an auspicious way to continue his tenure as the principal landowner in their district. But what had been auspicious about any of his Irish adventure? Misadventure more like it, he thought with a wry grin.

Suddenly, everything he had done since demanding and receiving the King's grant took on new meaning. As he picked up the spark of speculation in each eye, Matthew's skin began to prickle. Jesus! They were warning him by raised eyebrows, sneers, whispers and giggles—warning him that he, the new bought-me-a-title Earl, was in for a surprise.

Hell and damn!

That skin prickle had served him well in business. It had averted disasters, brought him a fortune five times larger than the one his father had left. And Matthew always heeded that prickle.

He looked across at the man whom he had had arrested. John Cochran looked back, a tilt to his mouth, a speculative gleam in his eye. Hell and damn! Matthew assessed the man's relaxed body, and Matthew began to sweat. He had brought his suit in passion—and in passion, pursued it. He never made decisions on passion. Why now? Why, when he needed a clear head and clearer vision?

And the answer slammed so forcefully into him that Matthew knew—for the first time since he had taken possession of Dunswell Manor two years ago, only two days shy of the very day, now. Aye, he knew without doubt that he had made a dreadful mistake. The answer was the spitfire who glared across the room at him, then turned to her father who sat beside her. That glance, and the head toss which accompanied it, was enough to show Matthew exactly where he stood in Cathleen Cochran's estimation. Unlike her father's amusement and her family and friends' disdain which had begun his unease, *her* unconcealed contempt burned straight into his gut ... and a bit higher and lower, though he refused to credit it now.

Too late. The die was cast. He was here. So was she. The circus maximus would go on.

So, preceding Fenwick, he squared his shoulders, pushed past the curious villagers and made his way to the front of the chambers, past the landed gentry, straight to the seat behind the petitioner's table. Directly opposite him sat the defendants—Cathleen's father and her brothers. And Cathleen next to her father.

God, how had this happened?

How was it that he had been forced to put on the defensive the woman he wanted?

He stole a glance at her. Her long auburn tresses— soft as the underbelly of a new foal, he knew—were today caught up on the top of her head by a green riband. A cloud of flyaway wispy curls framed her delicate oval face. He bit his cheeks in a futile attempt to stifle a smile. Hell, she could not tame her hair no matter how hard she brushed it or how many ribands she tied in it. That hair too closely matched her spirit—as wild and as free as this land was green.

Maddening to be thinking like this. Maddening to be here at all! Worse to be so filled with her, that he could not stop assessing Cathleen.

Where was her usual costume of coarse homespun linen shirt and pieced-together man-style chamois trouser-skirt? Today she rivaled any of the ladies seated behind him. Today she rivaled the Queen of England and the Queen of Heaven.

She had donned a finely woven white linen dress with long, elbow-length sleeves. The square neckline and ruffled cuffs were overlaid with small handstitched roses and clover. A green, gold, and black figured shawl was draped from shoulder to hip, across her full breasts, and caught up to her right shoulder by a large, seemingly endless knot of gold which was centered with a green agate stone. A smaller figured square, similar in color and pattern to the shawl, lay across her hands, which were on the table top beside a folded piece of parchment.

He recognized the local magistrate's seal emblazoned on the parchment, so Matthew supposed it was the official arrest writ which had brought them here. The writ which accused her father and brothers of stealing the Earl of Dunswell's property. His— Matthew Forrest's—property. His horses.

Hell, a whole stable full, the Cochrans had taken. Madness! That was it. They had to be mad to think he would let them get away with it merely because he and Cathleen . . .

He shook off the images and cloaked himself in his self-righteousness.

No one stole from Matthew Forrest, the Earl of Dunswell. Not the King's ministers—who had done it once too often to his father, but with Matthew had tried and failed. Not the local tax collectors—who were still insisting he owned more than he knew he did. Certainly not these Cochrans, who were, after all, only stablemaster and handlers!

Today he would get back every last stallion, mare and foal John Cochran and his sons had stolen. And the damned harp. He would get that back too, or the value thereof.

But he would not get all of what Cathleen had stolen.

What were the horses and a harp after all but

things? And to Matthew Forrest *things* did not portend. He had more than enough things. What he did not have was a woman who sucked up his breath the way Cathleen's scent did, who stirred his blood until it boiled with longing, who was so damned infuriating . . .

"Order!" A bewigged and bespectacled man banged the magistrate's staff of office on the floor. "We shall have order!" The curtain behind the raised chair rustled. "Be all upstanding! This magistrate's court is in session. Be all upstanding!"

Cathleen poured all her contempt into one furious glance at the Earl of Dunswell, or Matthew Dunn, or Forrest, or whatever he called himself these days. As soon as she looked into those melted chocolate eyes, however, she was more furious at herself than at him. How could she feel like this! How dare she allow it to happen again. Oh, the contempt was there; but not in isolation from the other feelings—the feelings he had always engendered in her, from the very beginning, that first time he had strolled into the stable, seen her astride Firebrand, smiled crookedly, and then with one long, sweeping, heart-pounding look, unabashedly taken as thorough an inventory of her as he had of the horses.

She shivered, remembering.

"What is it, daughter?" John Cochran asked.

Cathleen hesitated to voice her true feelings. A handsome man in his fifties, her father had not weathered the vicissitudes of their present fate as well as he liked to think he had done. Where previous his thick dark brown hair had been sprinkled with a fine salting of grey, now it was more white than grey, more sparse than thick. And the fine lines in his face had deepened, etched into his forehead and the corners of his eyes and mouth like gouges from a plough in a sun-baked field. But it was his voice which gave away the aging process more than his physical appearance; its deep bass tremored, rising at times to a high tenor, giving away the underlining fear and erasing the bravado he had always shown, and was attempting to show now.

"Afraid, are you, of the like of *him?*" John asked, as if the magistrate's sergeant-at-arms was not standing stiff behind, his rifle held purposefully in his hand. John gave him only a surly glance, then thrust out his chest proudly, ignoring the implied threat of force. "You need not be afraid of any militia man or any bought-me-a-title Earl, darlin'; especially not this one. He cannot hurt us. Do you not know that?"

"Aye, Da, I do know. Up here." She raised her eyes to indicate her brain. "But down here. . ." Her eyes glanced towards her stomach, and she shrugged. "I sense terrible trouble."

"Ah, not the second sight now, Cathleen," her younger brother Donal scoffed.

Like his father, from which his mold had been cast, Donal scowled at the sergeant-at-arms, but Cathleen noticed he and her elder brother Paul immediately sat straighter in their chairs. Donal ran his leather-bound hands down and around to his tied-back queue, then back again to fidget with his unaccustomed lace jabot. Paul bent to unrecognizable shape the starched woolen felt of his new blue and white tricorn.

Even tethered like lambs, oh, how they did try to be the gentleman's sons, the heirs to the kingdom— the kingdom lost, their chances gambled away on a venture which had resulted in this law suit. God, had they not learned? Was there to be another generation built on John Cochran's cock-o'-the-walk attitude? Were she and her mother never to know a day's peace?

Not if those identical gleams in father and sons' eyes was any indication of the Cochran men's intentions, they would not.

And suddenly Cathleen knew why Maeve Cochran—her sainted, beloved mother—sat at home this day. Not only because Maeve could not bear to see her husband hauled before the magistrate, branded as thief for all the village to see. Nay, Maeve's soul could no longer bear to see the play-acting her husband and sons would put on, could no longer bear one more time to hear sweet-talking nothings travel from father to son to son, always saying much and meaning little. They had broken her spirit and their dreams.

"Folderol," her mother called it. "Mere flights of fancy from the fey folk, and don't you pay it no mind, Cathleen. Keep yer eye on the real things o' this world; build on yer strengths; work hard to protect what is yours; and do not take chances. 'Tis chances what get you scorn and misery. 'Tis work and diligence what get you a good life in God's sight."

Donal knocked his elbow into Cathleen's arm. "No second sight for you this day, girl. 'Tis time and enough you put away that childish prattling, that silly game."

John snarled at his eldest son. " 'Tis no game she plays, you silly pup. She has the gift." At Donal's snort, John sighed. "Well-and-a-day, mayhap it has not proved true every time; but often enough to fear knockin' it about." Awkwardly, using both hands, he pulled a yellow-stained folded paper from his leather rucksack and put it atop the writ which had brought them here to what they and their kith and kin considered enemy territory. He jet his jaw grimly, ignoring the occasional snicker and stare from a few people—luckily only a few—who had been his equals only a few years previous; and now, because he had fallen, had aligned themselves on the side of the crown, if not the side of the Earl. "We shall prevail, child. Fear not."

He sounded so sure, Cathleen wished she could believe him. But John Cochran had produced in her a bent to realism which was unshakable because she had a long, jaundiced memory. *Fear not* was her father's favorite admonition. It was what John had said so often to Maeve, that now Cathleen feared worse than she had imagined these many nights since the

writ had been served. Feared, and remembered . . .
and, therefore, feared more.

She wished she could shut out the sounds of her
da's eternal, infernal optimism; but even the reading
of the writ was drowned out by the remembered cadences.

"*Fear not,* Maeve, the mortgage is only temporary.
Yes, me darlin', we risk much. But we shall get much
in return when the Black Turk sires a brood. Each of
the foals will run like Sidhe, the fairie queen of the
sea winds, herself. She came to me in a dream and
sprinkled us with fairie dust, don't you know?" The
fairie queen of the sea winds! John Cochran had
risked everything they had on a sprinkling of fairie
dust from a dream! He had risked all in an attempt to
bring a string of Turkistan horses to Ireland to aug-
ment and build up the blood lines of their Irish race
horses. The best *Irish*-bred, the Cochrans had, already; but the best in Ireland had never been enough
for Da. And what had it brought them all?

"Ah, Maeve, stop up your hand-wringing. *Fear
not,* the ship from Turkistan will not founder in the
terrible squalls where George Pike lost everything. It
will arrive very soon and then won't you feel foolish
when all that hand-wringing will be for naught?" But
Mama's hand-wringing and fairie dust from a dream
had not saved the whole bloody fleet, with its com-
pliment of drowned sailors and its lost-at-sea
Turkistan stallions. Nor had hand-wringing and fairie
dust staved off the bankers and their call for the

mortgage money they were owed on a cargo which never came.

"There has been some mistake, Maeve, me darlin'. *Fear not.* The mortgage bankers are friends from way back. They will not take away our home and livelihood. They will give me time and enough to raise the taxes and mortgage payment." Time and enough to turn over the keys to Dunswell Manor, had been all they gave him. Time enough to move out the Cochran's personal belongings, leaving every stick of furniture behind. For her da had not been content to merely mortgage the house and land. Nay, he had given a bond for the contents as well. Damn men and their risk-taking, their dreams, ambitions, and fairie dust! He had even included a mortgage on all her mother's dowry. As if Maeve were his possession and not her own. As if she had no say, no standing in his eyes, was not a person to consult when rushing ahead to achieve whatever it was *he* wished to achieve. Of course, with a mad rush to destruction such as his had been, he had also mortgaged some of their best horses. They had lost all save the harp which had been in her mother's family for four generations. That, no one had had the wisdom to take. It was Maeve's salvation, now; for she did naught else all the day but cook her stews and pluck on the tough strings. Cathleen's heart felt broken. Her mother had been such a strong, working woman, bolstered by hope, when there was little hope to go round.

"Ah, Maeve, lass, stop up those tears, me darlin'. We've had a stroke of luck, we have. And now we

can start again. *Fear not*. We still have the yearlings
at Paddy's stables, don't you know? 'Tis only a matter of time before they and our new breed start bringing in winners' purses." Aye, they had had one stroke
of luck. But the matter of time to bring in earnings
became two years of backbreaking hours and weeks
and months without let-up, to bring those stallions,
geldings, and mares to winning form. Swift, they
were; but not always swift enough. While they
waited for the new breed to mature and start winning,
the Cochrans had, in order to eat, become laborers in
the very house and paddocks in which they had once
been masters.

"*Fear not*, me love; there has been no buyer for
Dunswell Manor or Stables. We shall soon have con-
sistent winners. Then, I shall buy back our home."

Instead, Matthew had come inspecting, touring Ireland to claim one of the homesteads lost for nonpay-
ment of taxes and confiscated for the English by the
King's ministers—the only way, Cathleen's kith and
kin knew, that the damned British could get their
hands on the rich, lush green lands they coveted. And
wasn't that a laugh and a half crown. For the land
was lush and green only because it rained more than
the sun shone. And it was far from rich. In fact, far
too much of it could produce not much more than in-
termittent moldy patches of scrawny rye; poor,
bumpy hillocks which grew more stones than potatoes; broods of hungry children; and swift, small
horses. Yet many British had come to take country
houses with grand expanses of land which had once

been grazing pastures for Irish-bred race horses. And they had turned those pastures into gardens or potato and corn fields, hiring back the very families who had formerly owned the estates, selling off the produce in its entirety to merchants "back home" in England.

Matthew Forrest, the Earl of Dunswell had been one of the petitioners.

What would have happened had she not been in the stables when he came to Dunswell? What if it had been Da? Or Donal? Or Paul? Or their muck-out, Silent Sean, with his broad, vacant smile, crooked teeth and rheumy eyes? Would Matthew have taken one look at the scrawny horses left in the paddocks while Da and her brothers exercised the best of the lot—and sneered? Would he have inspected the waist-high rye which had taken over the front lawns, the crumbling bricks of the front portico—and blanched? Would he have turned right round to find for himself another, more suitable, country estate?

She wished he had! She wished to God she had not been there, not seen him, not fallen head over heels as if a bolt of lightening had struck her dumb.

That damnable day!

He introduced himself as Matthew Dunn, a field hand in search of work. His first lie. And though she had doubted him, she had half-hoped it was true because Matthew was what other men in her life had not been: courteous, fun, jovial, adventurous, and attentive. They rode, went swimming, fished for trout and salmon, picked berries, dug up potatoes, attended church services together.

Little more than that until that night in the river. Until the birthing of Chuchulain. Until the quiet joy in the deep, dark woods.

She was dumb, had been dumb—to believe in him even as he had told her he had lied, had explained what he was going to do with the manor house, had promised her his station in life would not change the way he felt about her. She had been dumber to hope for one moment that his title meant naught to what they had only a moment before, shared together. Dumb to think that a man four years older than herself could have seen anything more in her than a Garden of Eden tryst in *her* woods, or an "arrangement" such as Matthew Forrest, the Earl of Dunswell, had made plain he was offering her.

" 'Tis a good arrangement, Cathleen. I shall set aside accommodations for you . . . or build you a little cottage on the estate, where we may love each other in secret when I am in Ireland. You will never have to be a stable hand again, Cathleen. And when we are together you can wear silks and laces instead of those awful homespun linens and leathers."

As if she had not had her fill of silks and laces in her life. As if she did not prefer her stable wear, had not made it of her own design, from her own hands, for a use which was comfortable for *her.* As if, because of what had happened in the woods, he had the power and right to tell her what to wear, where to live, whom to sneak away to see, to take to her bed.

As if she were a mere possession, to be bought along with the rest of her former home.

But even then she had refused to allow him to see what he had done, how he had denigrated her by not knowing her, not trying to determine who she was, what she had come from, where she owed her allegiance. Most of all, however, he did not seem to care how she felt. Well, if he did not care, he did not deserve more than a shade of a woman. If shade was what he wanted, then shade was what she would give him.

Nonchalantly, she had asked, "You have bought Dunswell, then?"

"Aye. Because of you. Because of how you looked that day atop Firebrand. And how the wind whips through those dark red curls and the sun bronzes your skin. Such skin! Soft and dangerous. I shall always want to touch that skin, feel the softest parts of you . . ."

Holy Mary and the Blessed Infant, he might as well have been born Irish, he had such a gift of gab. Enough to turn a girl's head, if she weren't careful. Or toss her skirts.

Well-a-day, Cathleen had tossed her petticoats for Matthew for she was a maid and he, a man, after all. And the devil of a man, so handsome and fine-talking, she had thought . . .

Ah, what *had* she thought?

But with that bloody offer for a bloody arrangement, Matthew had broken her heart.

For one moment she faltered but thankfully it

lasted only a heart beat. She straightened, frowned, and with the rest of the assembled villagers, listened to the clerk as the indictment was read. She paid no attention to the words for she knew what they portended. She paid attention only to the mutterings of displeasure around her, the murmurings of surprise, the ripple of fear which eclipsed friend and foe alike.

"... *that the property of Matthew Forrest, the Earl of Dunswell, was willfully and purposefully stolen in the dead of night by John Cochran, his sons Paul and Donal, and his daughter Cathleen. That they did take these possessions of their own free will, knowing the penalty of such crimes. That should they be found guilty, their punishment is fixed by law. And such punishment is that they forfeit all lands and property to the petitioner, be bound over to the magistrate's gaoler, and will, at a time set by the magistrate for the district of Dunswell, be taken to a place specified by him, where they will be hanged by their necks until dead.*"

Chapter Eight

The words roared in Matthew's head with gale force, like the waves at Dover crashing against the white cliffs. Whooshing up, then receding, then back again, but worse. A noise in his head so loud, it was white hot. *Cathleen, hanging by the neck until dead. Cathleen, hanging by the neck until dead.* Nay, he had not intended such.

"I did not name her in the complaint . . ."

The words were whispered, broken; and he was thankful that in the tumult which erupted at the reading of them, none heard.

Aye, he had not named her. Not specifically. What had he done? Think, damn it! He had made the accusation that the Dunswell stables had been looted. *By those left in full charge of them by the estate agents.* The word *those!* The damned fool magistrate had included Cathleen among *those.* Matthew had not. No, not he. He would not cause harm to any woman, regardless of whether she were guilty or innocent.

Of course, Cathleen was not innocent. He wouldn't be surprised if she had been the instigator. To save the horses which were her life, she would think aught of riding them off in the dead of night. Her father was a dreamer like the rest of these Irish, with no room in his head—nor talent—for careful planning. Her brothers were not far behind. The three men in the family would have run the horses in every race until they dropped down dead, as long as the poor beasts brought them winnings. Only Cathleen worried about their health, their stamina. Only she cautioned that rest brought better results and had proved it with that gorgeous roan of hers, Firebrand.

"Raised him myself, I did," she had said the second time Firebrand had won a dead heat two years ago.

Cathleen had been so jubilant, there at the track laid out at Murdoch's Field. She had laughed her musical laugh, tossing her green homespun skirts—that day they were intact, not split and sewed up the middle so she could mount and ride easier. She had pulled him into the fray around the winner and the young lad she had allowed the privilege of jockey. She had handed Matthew a comb, brush, and sack towels, awarding him the honor of currying the panting, damp two-year-old.

As he worked, she chattered on. "When once we started racing these breeds it took me almost six months to convince Da, it did, that resting them would do them all a world of good and make them hungry for a good fast run. But did he listen? Nay, not he. So I had to watch that first awful six months. Six months of seeing the others withering away from too much racing. Six months until Da finally gave in and let me have my way—but only with Firebrand— until I proved my method worked. And look how right I was!" She held up the winner's purse and jingled the coins inside. "Enough to pay his entry fee, put food on the table for a whole month, *and* pay the dratted fish monger. Wouldn't have to pay him at all, if Donal and Paul would only learn there's more to fishing than drowning the poor wee worms." She caught her older brother, Paul, and snapped her changeling eyes at him. "Time for fishing lessons, boyo! Meet me at Dunswell Draw at five in the morning and we'll have a passel of fish by noon."

Paul had looked beseechingly at his father, who chuckled and shook his head. Then he looked to his mother, who raised her eyebrows and winked at her daughter. "Can't get out of it, lad. She'll hound you and hound you 'til you give in. When our Cathleen wants fish, 'tis fish you'll get her."

"God grant mercy," Paul had said. "I hate putting my boots into cold water. I hate gutting the things. And the scales! They cling to cloth and leather for a week 'til Thursday. I'll never get used to it."

"You'd best do," Cathleen answered. "We can't just snap our fingers and order someone else to fish for us, you know."

"I know." Paul glared at his father, then at the matted, mucked ground and kicked at a clod that was softer underneath than it appeared. His boots sank in and he fought to clear them of the muck. "Damn it and all!"

The bitter fury in his voice had been more than the situation warranted and Matthew wondered what had occasioned it. He wondered more when Cathleen pinched her elder brother's elbow and hissed, "Mind who you are, Paul Cochran. You have a mother here who depends on us to keep up appearances. And damn you, you had best remember that."

Paul, older by four years than Cathleen, had jumped a mile, yet capitulated quickly. "Aye, lass. I'll do penance for the slip."

"Aye. You'll supervise Silent Sean while he mucks out the stables—*after* you and me get our passel of fish."

Paul had groaned but nodded.

More than two years had passed, yet Matthew could still see it, still hear it. God, when Cathleen put her foot down all the men in her family trembled. Hell, all the men in the valley!

And now Matthew trembled for her, because he could not imagine how she was going to extricate herself from this.

Was he to blame? Was it his fault?

Nay.

When he had made the offer to purchase Dunswell Manor, he had made certain that the purchase included the entire stables which had belonged to the former owners, contents and all. He had it in the bill of sale, right here in his mail pouch. *Contents and all*, spelled out clear as the sky in autumn. And, as expected, when he arrived at Dunswell Stables to take possession, the stables were intact, with fresh straw in each stall. And each stall was completely empty.

The horses—that wonderful breed which was a combination of aristocratic Turkistan and hell-bent Irish mongrel—were what had convinced him to take Dunswell Manor. They were perfection, itself. Smaller than the Arabians, larger than their Irish cousins, they were sleek and fast and unflagging in their quest to be out in front of the pack. Like Cathleen's Firebrand, all of them had a inbred, uncanny ability to find that small open space which they streaked through until they were running wild, their black tails streaming out behind, like pennants, challenging the others in the race to catch them if they could. Few came close.

And they—by law and contract and bill of sale— were his.

He had paid more than he had intended, more than the estate was worth, because of the breed. He would have them back.

He would have their mistress back, too; but it was impossible, now. Now, because of what the bloody male Cochrans had done, she—as part of the conspiracy to defraud him—would swing.

"Damned fool," he spat at Fenwick. "Why did you not make it understood that I wanted only those who had taken part in it to be arrested . . ."

"But I did, my lord," Fenwick returned. "I told the magistrate when I delivered your complaint that you wished to have charged each and every Cochran who had worked on the estate. The magistrate must have ascertained that all the young Cochrans were involved, my lord. All but the mother. And as they were, they should, by all that's right in this godforsaken land, pay the full penalty the law allows."

Fenwick brushed at his sleeve, dislodging imaginary lint. It was a gesture taken up by so many lately that Matthew detested it because it showed such arrogance. Why, the man beside him was not much more advanced in rank and position than the family—the woman—who was here at trial. But as all those who affected that gesture, Fenwick was English, not Irish.

And therein lay the difference to the steward. The Cochrans and those in the district were to him not worth more than the fleas in his hair. And just as bothersome, since the Cochrans and their kind would not work for Matthew. Refused any offer. And it was nigh to impossible to keep good English servants who had to leave their families and their beloved land and come to Ireland. Fenwick, therefore, felt impotent ... useless ... for in those times when the servants fled, he had no estate to steward, no servants to oversee.

What a mess of potage all this was!

Matthew glanced at Cathleen and his breath caught in his throat. There was no fear in her eyes.

Before it could register, the magistrate cleared his own throat and the ceremony began.

"John Cochran, how do you plead?"

John struggled to stand and only then did Matthew

notice that his feet were also bound with leather, like
his hands. But the grey-haired man stood proudly,
eyed the assembled villagers, and with a clear voice,
said, "Not guilty, sire."

He plopped into his seat as the magistrate scribbled
on a sheet of paper in front of him. "Not guilty John
Cochran says. Paul Cochran, how do you plead?"

And one by one the Cochrans lads stood and just
as loudly, just as defiantly announced, "Not guilty."

When Cathleen's turn came she did not struggle to
her feet as her brothers had. Instead, she rose in a
manner so regal, so commanding, that Matthew was
astounded when the green, black, and gold patterned
square dropped away from her hands and he discovered that her wrists were bound as tightly and as securely as her father's and brother's were. She turned
slightly and raising her hands to brush the knotted pin
on her left shoulder, she glanced around the room and
then pinned her eyes on Matthew.

"I am not guilty of stealing from the Earl of
Dunswell, my lord. Nor have I stolen anything *at all*
in my entire life. 'Tis calumny to infer such of honest
and righteous folk such as we. And I challenge any
man to say different."

"Yet you have been charged by the Earl of empty-
ing his stables of horses."

"Oh, aye," Cathleen said. "That we did, and I most
of all."

Master Royce slid his spectacles onto his nose and
peered over their rims at the young girl who stood
there so proudly. He picked up a paper and read from

it. "I do not understand," Master Royce said, stabbing at the complaint. "It says here that the Earl of Dunswell is rightful owner of the contents of the stables." Master Royce turned to Matthew. "That is correct, my lord?"

"Absolutely," Matthew said. He, too, rose; and produced the bill of sale, which he passed over to the sergeant-at-arms, who passed it to Master Royce. "You will see . . . on page three . . . I don't remember the exact words . . ."

"I see it now," the magistrate said. ". . . the sale to include the entire stables as part of the estate of the former owners, contents and all. To ascertain such, the Dunswell estate and its contents to be adjudged as of in the possession of the owners on the date of default of mortgage, April 11, 1765." He pushed his spectacles to the bridge of his nose and adjusted his wig. "That seems quite clear to me, Mistress Cochran. The entire stables, contents and all." Turning, he addressed Matthew. "And when you took ownership—as was your right and due, since they had been awarded you by the crown—the stables had no contents, I presume . . . else you would not have had to seek redress from this court?"

"That is correct, Master Royce. The stables were quite empty."

"That is not true," Cathleen countered. "There was one set of tack and two tools there, cleaned and hanging in their places. We even put fresh straw in every horse stall, awaiting the arrival of the Earl's own string of horses and his own tack and tools."

"Well, yes . . ." Magistrate Royce cleared his throat. "That seems right and proper, my lord."

"But there were no horses, Master Royce."

Royce took off his spectacles and looked from Cathleen to John to Paul to Donal. "No horses? You took the Earl's horses?"

Just as John was about to respond, Cathleen laid her bound hands on his arm. "Nay, Da . . . Mama said . . ."

"Aye, child."

He settled in his chair and smiled at his daughter. It had been a long, hard battle, but his darling Maeve had won. Paul had wanted to be the spokesman for the family, as had Donal; but Maeve had stared her husband and sons down.

"Cathleen'll speak for the Cochrans. And I'll brook no naysaying, now, John. She's the gift of argument, she has; and none can best her. 'Tis her, or I'll be leaving here this night."

His good wife did not threaten else she was willing to do. The boys might have grumbled a bit; but they were good lads and they knew their mother was right. Cathleen would speak for them all this day. John chuckled softly. Oh, the Earl and the Magistrate were in for it now.

"Go to it, girl," John told his daughter.

And with eyes flashing her father's pride and confidence in her, Cathleen announced to the assemblage, "We did *not* take the Earl's horses."

"Then who did?" Master Royce asked.

"No one," Cathleen affirmed.

"But you will agree that the stables were empty of horses when you left?"

"Aye."

"And they were not empty of horses prior to your leaving?"

"Aye. They were not empty of horses."

"There were horses in them prior to your leaving, then?"

"Oh, aye. Seventeen in all. And why would they not be? For what are stables for, if not to house horses?"

As if knowing what this would engender, Cathleen grinned and her neighbors laughed long and loudly, until the sergeant-at-arms banged his staff on the floor for silence.

"All right, young woman, that is entirely enough. I will not have sport made in this, my court," Master Royce ordered. "Perhaps John Cochran, you would do best at answering my questions."

"Ah, no, my lord. The lass knows the lay of the land, she does, and she's a grand fine speaker of the truth, she is. When she gets to a spot where she needs help, she knows but to tap my shoulder and I will step into the breech, as it were."

The magistrate appealed to the brothers. "Paul . . ."

"I stand with my da."

"Donal . . ."

"Cathleen'll do for me."

Master Royce sighed. "Women . . ." He muttered and Matthew thought he caught, *damned if I do and damned if I don't*. Aren't all men, Matthew thought.

Damned if he hadn't brought this suit because he would *not* be owner of an empty stable; and damned that he had brought this suit because Cathleen was so cunning she was showing signs of making mince of them all.

"We shall start at the middle, then," Royce pronounced, shifting his attention to Matthew. "Mistress Cochran admits there were horses ..." He peered at the number he had written on his court record. "... seventeen, she says ."

"Aye, my lord," Matthew ventured, hoping the truth would make her see the ridiculousness of attempting to ensnare them in talk which was nay more than talk. "The estate agent counted them. They are listed on the last page of the estate contents. Seventeen horses of mixed breeding."

"Aye ... aye, I see it. Right there, Mistress Cochran." He stabbed the paper. "Right there. Seventeen horses of mixed breeding."

"I don't doubt there is writing there on the page, Master Royce. But I dispute what is written."

"What do you dispute?"

"There were only sixteen horses of mixed breeding. And one thoroughbred Turkistan stallion." Awkwardly, because she had to use her two bound hands, she reached into her skirt pocket and produced a buff-colored paper, which she gingerly unfolded. "Those who were in with the stallion when Matthew Dunn ..."

"And who is Matthew Dunn? There is no Matthew Dunn listed in this writ ..."

"I beg your pardon for confusing you, my lord magistrate; but the Earl represented himself as other than he was and it is difficult to remember his correct name."

"Represented himself as other than he was?"

"Aye, sire."

"Now, how did he do that? He is an Earl."

"Aye. But for almost two months he was our field hand by name of Matthew Dunn. I believe he was there taking the lay of the land, as it were, before bidding on the estate."

"Oh, I see . . . a subterfuge taken for reasons of his own."

He looked over his spectacles at Matthew and tut-tutted, then very carefully wrote down what Cathleen had said. And the clever minx glared triumphantly at Matthew, raising her eyebrows in a patrician manner. Well, she had done it. There were enough titters and shocked mutterings to carve in stone his already tarnished reputation. He should have expected it; but so many years had gone by he had not remembered how willful and quick-witted she was. He stiffened with discomfort, trying to get back some of his own pride. And then he smiled grimly. By God, she was magnificent. Even down to the last moment she would momentarily put aside the danger to herself simply to make him eat crow for lying to her.

"May I continue, sire?"

"Oh, aye," the magistrate said. "Please, please do. I would like to get to my supper . . . *today*.

"As I said, sire, when Matthew Dunn . . . beg

pardon . . . Matthew Forrest, the Earl of . . . what was it, now? Ah, yes . . . the Earl of Dunswell . . . when he last inspected the stables there were in it one thoroughbred Arabian and sixteen mix breeds. Black Turk, the Turkistan stallion, of eight years, has won purses totaling more than six thousand Spanish doubloons. Emer, an Irish bred mare, of ten years, has purses totaling nine hundred pounds. Sidhe, an Irish bred mare, of eight years, has winnings which have brought in more than a thousand pounds. The last two mares have been bred the most so their totals are lower. Innis, an Irish bred mare, of eleven years, has won a wee bit more than five hundred pounds. And Niahm, an Irish bred mare, of nine years, counts for only two hundred crowns, but that is because she only raced two years."

As the assemblage leaned forward, and more than one of them counted off on his fingers, Cathleen snapped the paper and took a deep breath. "Now, for the breeding statistics. You won't need to write this down, sire. You may have my copy when I have finished."

"Ah, very good, Mistress Cochran. Very good, indeed."

Well, if the magistrate thought he no longer had to write what Cathleen said, others did. Matthew saw several scribbling on paper with everything from pens to quills to sharpened pieces of coal. Margaret Mayer was most rapt; and had a small board which she leaned on the back of the man in front of her to keep her paper from crumbling.

"We bred each year after the thoroughbred came to us. The combination of Black Turk with Emer produced a four-year-old Turkistan-Irish gelding—he had a terrible accident in the training track and there was naught to do but geld him otherwise he might have produced his own winning line. Very sad, it was."

"Oh, I should say . . ."

The magistrate looked stricken. But from the way she spoke directly across the table towards Matthew, he had suspicions that a good gelding was precisely what Cathleen had in mind for him. He narrowed his eyes and raised himself in his chair to show her he would not be cowed by any foolish byplay. She might have the assemblage wrapped up in her dialogue; but when this was over the facts would speak for themselves and he would have what was due him.

She narrowed her eyes back at him, and continued, "The gelding goes by name of Fergus. He has won more than one hundred pounds in two years. Black Turk and Emer also produced Caoilte, a three-year-old Turkistan-Irish stallion, who won fifty pounds in his first race and seventeen pounds in his second. And Dromahair, a two-year-old Turkistan-Irish mare, who took the Rood Running at her first race this spring and a purse of thirty pounds. 'Tis a good beginning."

" 'Tis a great beginning," Margaret Mayer said. "Won five pound on Dromahair, meself, I did."

Cathleen grinned. "Then, from breeding the Black

Turk with Sidhe, we got four-year-old Countess Cathleen, a Turkistan-Irish mare, who has accumulated purses worth seventy pounds. And three-year-old Knocknarea, a Turkistan-Irish stallion, who has won thirty pounds. And two-year-old Cuchulain, a Turkistan-Irish stallion, who took a third for twelve pounds . . ."

With this, she glared anew at Matthew, reminding him of that day he had helped birth the stallion . . . and reminding him, too, of the way he had told her who he was and what he wanted for her and him. He now understood the reason for her fury. It was damned foolish of him, making love with her, then offering her an arrangement no decent woman could accept. He had handled it badly. If he were to do it now, he would have two years of regret to show him a better way.

If there were a better way. For how could he, an Earl, marry Cathleen Cochran, a stablemaster's daughter? It was absurd.

But, ah, God, how he wanted her.

He listened closely as she continued the litany which was the ammunition the crown needed to judge her guilty. Why was she doing this? Did she not know that she was hanging herself with every word? Or had she too much pride, like the rest of her race?

Pride goeth before a fall, Cathleen.

But Cathleen went blithely on, her voice loudly proclaiming the way it was.

"And there was Eithne, a Turkistan-Irish mare, who has taken three thirds her first year."

"As good as her brothers and sister," Margaret Mayer said.

"Aye," Cathleen acknowledged. "Then, from the coupling of the Black Turk and Innis, we bred out a two-year-old mare, Red Branch Rose, who took a third and a second at this spring's Rood Running, for a total of sixteen pounds. And three-year-old Innisfire, a Turkistan-Irish stallion, whose total is fifty-eight pounds. And four-year-old Firebrand, a Turkistan-Irish stallion, who has brought in one hundred and forty pounds. The total of the purses from the horses which were housed at the Dunswell stables—not counting the purses from horses bred since the herd was moved to Sidhe Stables—is . . ." She hesitated, then quickly said, ". . . five hundred and twenty-three pounds." She folded up the paper. "Because of our success on the track, we have had many offers to breed the mares with other Turkistan stallions. We chose the Black Turk's brother, Black Fire, who is owned by Carleton Stewart of Dublin. The mares were bred each season and dropped more foals the past two springs. We have also had inquiries about stud fees from other race horse owners. All the stallions from the Black Turk's lineage will be out for stud and their fees in their first year should bring in another five hundred pounds."

Cathleen passed the folded paper to the sergeant-at-arms, who handed it to the magistrate. Then Cathleen laced her fingers together, holding them still against her skirt. She smiled benignly. Matthew's fingers curled under. If she did not already have a date with a choke rope, he'd do it himself. What kind of mind . . . and nerve . . . gave her license to mock him, *openly*, here in court? What kind of fire fueled her? Derision, aye. Contempt, surely. He had expected none less. But righteousness? From a thief?

No, he did not understand these Irish.

He certainly did not understand Cathleen Cochran.

Magistrate Royce went to the heart of the matter. He was a horseman, himself. "You neglected to add the purses of the sires and dames. I get a total of more than three thousand pounds these horses have won."

"I did not neglect to add the purses, my lord. I did not include them deliberately."

"Whyso, Mistress Cochran?"

"Because they do not account in this proceeding."

"Of course they account! They were part of what you stole from the Earl."

"We stole nothing from the Earl."

"The horses . . ."

"Are not his."

Margaret Mayer's laughing voice ripped over the heads of the assembled villagers. "You tell 'im, Cathleen, me darlin'. You tell 'im he canna come in and take over, fast as ye please. You tell 'im where he belongs, good and proper."

"Back in bloody-hearted London," a man answered, sneering. "Where the other powdered and laced *not-quite-English-not-quite-Irish* belong."

"Order! I will have order or you will all be evicted from this court," Royce roared.

But order was reluctant and did not come until Cathleen held up her bound hands and smiled at her neighbors. Then they calmed as if quieted by a queen.

By God, Matthew thought, she was impressive. No one he had seen at court had such an impact on an audience as she did.

Audience.

Yes, that was what it was, here in court today. She was playing to an audience, putting on a show. And she had them rapt, their eyes on her alone, their ears tuned to her voice, her bidding, her fire, her truth.

Thank God she was not the jury or he was doomed.

Obviously, Fenwick thought the same, because he leaned closer and hissed, "She's besting you, my lord. And the others are eating it up. They're already a rowdy and unruly lot. If she wins, they'll be impossible and you will have lost your position."

He needn't say, *before you achieve it.* Matthew knew that—and more—was what Fenwick meant. Matthew might have a title but he did not have the power and influence that title should have commanded. He would have to wrest it from these people, or he would have naught. He gritted his teeth, ready to do battle with Cathleen.

He raised his hand. "Master Royce . . . I demand that my property be returned this day."

Cathleen shook her head and her red-black curls

bobbed against her cheeks. "You have all your property. There is naught to return."

"I want the horses."

"Want all you want. You cannot have what is not yours!" She turned to the tall, skinny sergeant-at-arms who had had the altercation with Margaret Mayer. "Billy Weeks, tell this court who owns Emer, the dame of Fergus and Caoilte and Dromahair."

Billy looked strangely uncomfortable. His uniform looked two sizes too small and he snaked a finger around the top of his coat collar, then swallowed. "Well . . . uh . . . she's me pa's, she is. Has been since she was foaled in April of sixty-three."

"And Innis?"

"Well, she belongs to me uncle Willis."

"And Niamh?"

"To Charley Monahan, cousin to us both."

"And Sidhe, for whom the stables are named?"

"She's your uncle Francis's, o' course. Ever and all knows that."

"Thank you, Billy Weeks," Cathleen said. She turned back to the magistrate. "You see, my lord, the mares were borrowed from our family, good friends and neighbors, so we could start our new line by breeding them to the Black Turk. Billy, there, is our first cousin, he is. His ma is sister to mine. In fact, most of us here in this room are Cochrans of one kind or another . . . at least, those on the nether side of the rope."

"So none of the dames were part of the Dunswell estate?"

"No, my lord."

"And the new breed were obtained from borrowed lineage?"

"Aye, my lord."

"To whom do they belong?"

"To us, my lord. My da, my brothers, and myself. We just after paying off the damming fees, we have. They are ours, every last hair and hoof."

"Well . . . that does complicate matters a bit."

"It does not explain the Black Turk," Fenwick muttered.

No, it did not. And if what Cathleen had said were true, the Turk was worth six thousand doubloons. Five thousand English pounds. Obviously, the Turk did not belong to any of Cathleen's relatives or she would have mentioned it from the outset. That she had not, gave him reason to believe she had tried to slip his ownership past the magistrate's nose. She could try it out on him; but she could not try it out on Matthew. He would have what was his. And the Turk must have been in the stables, else why borrow mares to breed with him?

His head snapped up. So . . .

"Sire," he called to Magistrate Royce.

"Aye, my lord?"

"The complications can be cleared quickly and easily. Since the Black Turk was part of the Dunswell estate, then his issue belongs not to the Cochrans but to the estate. Regardless of the lineage or ownership of the mares, it is the stallion which produced them.

Therefore, they are now property of the estate and belong to me."

"Well by Jove! So they are and so they do."

But Cathleen seemed undisturbed. She held out her hand and her father placed in it the folded, soiled parchment he had taken out of his pouch when they had first been seated at the table. Carefully, Cathleen opened the paper and read from it.

"I have here a bill of lading and a port of entry form. The bill of lading is for six Turkistan horses which were being transported from Constaninople aboard three vessels. The ships went down, my lord, and five of the horses were drowned. But . . . one was rescued. Not in time for us to stop the bankruptcy proceedings, nor in time to accumulate enough money to buy back our ancestral home which had been in our family for two hundred years . . ."

Matthew groaned as guilt ripped through him. He knew without a doubt that she meant Dunswell Manor and the estates. Cathleen and her family had owned that huge tract of land and the wonderful house and stables. They had been lords and ladies of the manor when he was a mere dockhand and clerk. Why, by all that was holy, had she not told him?

Bugger it! Why had he not thought to ask?

He had recognized that she and her family were . . . different . . . from her neighbors. More cultured. More intelligent. More astute. More . . . just more! And he had known it and not understood from whence it came.

Fool.

He had bought the surface appearance of the family and had thought her naught but a stablehand, a servant. Yet she was his equal in rank if not in material wealth. No wonder she could stand there and face down Magistrate Royce with such dignity.

And treat him, Matthew Forest, the Earl of Dunswell, with such contempt.

She had been the lady of Dunswell long before Matthew had taken possession of it.

Yet just because the Black Turk had been rescued from sea did not mean it was not part of the estate. She was all but admitting it was, was she not?

"We did, however, have time to breed the Black Turk and raise enough of his offspring to bring in purses better than any ever we had won before. We were saving the purses, hoping to buy back the estate. Since none had come to claim it from the crown in over four years, we expected we would have the time. Everyone here knows now what happened."

"But what happened means naught to these proceedings. We are here to establish ownership of the new breed. And since the Black Turk was part of the estate, he belongs to the new owner of the estate," Matthew insisted.

"Nay, sire," Cathleen answered, but she spoke to the magistrate, not to Matthew. "By law, only the contents of the manor at the time of foreclosure are considered part of the estate. As you read in the Earl's bill of sale, foreclosure on Dunswell Manor and grounds took effect on April 11, 1765, can't you see?"

"Aye. I see," Magistrate Royce said.

"But that bill of lading and the port of entry document, now ... they list the date of entry of the Black Turk into Ireland as September 19, 1765. That's a full five months following foreclosure, it is."

Matthew knew what was coming but had to hear it regardless.

"So ... my lord," Cathleen preened, "though the Earl obtained all our other possessions, including the kitchen cat and all her kits, he does not now, nor never has, owned the Black Turk, nor any of the offspring."

Chapter Nine

"Well-a-day," Magistrate Royce said.

He looked to Matthew for aid, but Matthew was as dumbstruck as he. The Queen of the May had bested him. She had done it without blinking an eye, or losing her composure in the face of the worst punishment anyone could be facing. And, she had done it fair and square. Not like he, who had come to her unmanned by lies and evasions. Truth, he had not known that Dunswell Manor was the Cochran home—or had been until financial setbacks forced them out. But she and her family had stayed to keep the place in repair, and had been paid hardly more than subsistence wages as servants in their own home. Would he or any of the other gentry here have done the same, in the same conditions? He thought not.

He had bought himself a title.

He had bought himself an estate.

He had lost . . . all.

What did a title and an estate matter when Cathleen hated him with a fury unmistakable.

The courtroom quieted while Magistrate Royce carefully inspected the port of entry document and the foreclosure notice. The only sound was a clock ticking in the outer hall and papers rustling as Fenwick ploughed through every document pertaining to the sale of the property and the employment of the Cochrans as caretakers of the estate. In the quiet, Matthew wrestled with what to do next. He could withdraw his writ; but from the looks of Cathleen, her brothers and father, he would face a countersuit for false arrest and deprivations. He would end up owing them.

And he would end up without Cathleen.

For the first time, Matthew realized that as soon as he had seen her in the courtroom he had not truly cared about the horses, and the loss thereof. He thought of and felt only the loss of Cathleen. He had sat under the sword of Damocles and the single hair holding it up had broken. She had neatly cut him in twain with his own pride, resentment, and rage.

Royce cleared his throat. "From my limited French, it appears that the Black Turk did, indeed, enter England on the date so cited here. Long after the foreclosure, I am afeared, my lord. It appears the Black Turk was and is the property of the Cochran family."

"If that be so," Cathleen said in a voice only slightly raised to be heard above the roaring, laughing, back-slapping audience, "do we Cochrans then still stand accused of theft, sire?"

"Nay!" Margaret Mayer shouted. "Billy, remove them bonds, you pea-brain!"

"Weeks, remove that woman," Royce demanded.

"Oh, sire . . . must I? She's me aunt and all, ya see."

Cathleen grinned, raised her bound hands together in victory, and gracefully took her seat as if she were taking a throne. At her startling display of aplomb and decorum, twinlike, Matthew and Royce slumped back in their chairs. Royce looked as deflated as Matthew felt. This was one bloody mess, witnessed by the entire village and all.

Matthew's head swiveled as a chair scraped against the plank floor. "Fenwick! Sit down. We have lost."

"Nay, sire. We have only just begun." The steward held up a paper on which he had been madly scribbling during Cathleen's long explanation. "My lord Magistrate! My lord, may I be heard?"

"Order! There will be order in this enquiry."

"Order there shall be, since we've won and all," Margaret said.

Fenwick stared her down; but she stuck out her tongue and the man flushed angrily. "You shall pay for that," he said under the laughter so that only Matthew heard. When order was restored, Fenwick peered at the paper in his hand and glanced once at the Cochrans. "We will stipulate that the horses . . . all of them . . . are not the property of the Earl of Dunswell . . . correct, my lords?"

Matthew and Royce both nodded.

"Then, if they are not the property of the Earl . . . what recompense will you, as magistrate for the district, assign as a fair price for stabling, training, watering, and housing fees?"

"Recompense? What trickery is this?" Cathleen shouted. Her fists balled up and Matthew saw white spots on her forehead and cheek—a sure sign, he knew from experience, that Cathleen was either furious or terrified. She choked, but managed to get out, "The only recompense here is what is due us. We were hired to maintain the property."

"But you did more than that," Fenwick pointed out. "You used the property for your own purposes, without permission of the mortgage holders. To whit, in your own words, in the Earl's stables you housed seventeen horses which belonged to you, not the Earl. That means there was wear and tear on the buildings. It also means you used extraordinary amounts of water to maintain these horses which were not the Earl's. Water which came from the Dunswell wells and the river which runs through the estate. You planted the fields to provide feed for the horses. You trained the horses in pasture land, and even turned some of the pasture land into a regulation sized race course. Nowhere among the mortgage papers or your employment contract do I find a document giving you permission to do any of these things. Therefore, my lord magistrate, the Earl has been defrauded and the Cochrans—and quite possibly most of the villagers here in this court room who profited by what the Cochrans did—all of them owe the Earl of Dunswell recompense for the unauthorized use and abuse of his property."

The magistrate had had enough. He called a recess

"for noon vittals" and the courtroom cleared out; but not before Cathleen and her family had petitioned and been allowed to remove the damnable leather shackles and bonds and walk freely—with a militiaman as escort. With everyone released, as it were, they repaired to the public coffee house, which was such in name only since its primary function was to serve the dark ale the populace preferred. It was crowded to the outer doors and Fenwick managed only to procure a bucket of ale and two cold mutton slabs. He and Matthew sat under a spreading oak and ate in silence for a time. Knowing Fenwick, the man was probably busy scheming to bring down the poor little dairy maid, he had such animosity towards these people.

If it were up to Matthew, he could tell Fenwick they were not going on with the suit, that Fenwick's position was no longer available and the man would have to go on the tramp. If it were up to Matthew, he would take himself back to his mercantile business in London, and list the manor house with estate agents. It would put paid to this monstrous affair once and for all. But it was no longer up to him. Magistrate Royce had made it perfectly clear that he would render a verdict directly following the noon vittals recess. Matthew Forrest, the Earl of Dunswell, had brought a suit against the Cochrans and the suit had a life of its own. Its tentacles pulled in not only Cathleen and her menfolk, but the townspeople who had profited from the breeding venture, the touters who rated the horses, the bookmakers who took the wagers ... and himself. He was caught as surely as they were. Though he fervently wished to do so, he could not extricate himself from the machinations of the law.

A good lesson to keep in mind should ever he believe he could win in court what he could not win simply by virtue of being in the right.

There were other lessons Matthew was learning. Lessons about women. Lessons about lust and love and the difference between the two. Lust had begun his relationship with Cathleen. It had carried him along for weeks, building inside him a fire which consumed rather than nurtured. Their lust had been born in a stable and fire had flashed through both of them until they could do naught but surrender to its torturous call. But in that surrender had been a peace he had not recognized . . . not welcomed . . . until it was too late. Something had flowered that day in the dark woods. And he, dunce that he was, had not treated it with half as much care as he had given Maeve's rye or hillocks of potatoes.

God, he was weary of this battle. Weary of thinking. Weary of not thinking and acting too hastily. He had other battles to fight. The tax collector had sent a new bill. Five times the original one. And he had only four months to pay it in full. They would bankrupt him, these scheming King's ministers. Gave him a title and then made him pay "just recompense" for his lands until his purse was threadbare because of it, and still they asked for more, over and over again.

Just recompense.

The phrase haunted him.

But today, the haunting lasted only until a rough

crowd exited the coffee house and tussled for a moment in the roadway.

Matthew was not surprised to find that Cathleen was smack in the middle of the fracas. When she spied him and Fenwick, she hung back for a moment. But a second look and a deep breath seemed to make up her mind for her. She took a regal enough stance and marched directly toward Matthew. He would have scrambled to his feet but she clomped her foot on his coattails and he had no choice but to look up into her face. An adorable face, even in its anger. A frowning face, even with the twinkle in her eye that he loved so much. An enemy's face, he realized when she held her arms out for him to see and drew up the sleeves.

"Have you no horse liniment for the likes of these?" she demanded, showing the rough, raw places where the leather had cut through the skin, and blood had dried dark and crusty. "Ah, nay . . . I clean forgot. That was Matthew Dunn who cared about people. This man thing on the ground is Matthew Forrest, the Earl of . . . what was it again . . . the title you stole?"

Her voice had a sarcastic bite to it that made Matthew wince, she had changed so much from the last time he had seen her, there in the grotto in the woods in his arms.

"You know what it is," he said, resigned to hear her out since he could hardly push her away, nor did he want to. "The Earl of Dunswell."

"And do you know how it got that name, Matthew Forrest, or do you not care?"

"You mean to tell me anyway, so why prolong it?"

"Ah . . . you have learned much in the past two years. Learn more, Matthew. Know that Dunswell is named such because one hundred years ago my father's father's father was what you purported to be . . . a Dunn . . . Phillip Dunn . . . Phillip the dunker, that is. You see, the estate began because Phillip dug a well and charged a half pence to dunk a pail way down into it and draw up water for travelers' horses and the travelers themselves. Dunn's Well, it was called. Fancy that, now."

Were those tears in her eyes? Matthew could not credit it, the bitterness was so terrible to hear. More likely the sun, which was high and hot that late May noon, flashed off her ire and made tears appear where no tears were. He wished there were tears. It would unman her, make her more the woman he had loved in those woods of hers.

Those woods of *hers.*

An awful beauty it was, those memories; for they would never have back what they had held so close for so little time. She would forever bear the scars— both on her wrists and in her heart—of his halftruths, evasions, and terrible scrabblings for a justice which did naught but destroy.

"Cathleen, I offer you my sincerest . . ."

"Nay! I will not have it! There are no words which you could say that I will accept. I am Irish, and I know words are words. You have wronged us, sire. Wronged all of us . . . including yourself. And from the looks of that man beside you, you intend to go on

wronging us. Well, tell me no words. I have not ears
to hear them nor heart to hold them."

And with a swish of her skirts she was gone,
melted back into the villagers, who threw a protective
shield around her with their bodies and their epithets
directed at him. He would not listen. She would not
listen. There, they were alike. Somewhere, somehow,
their hearts had turned to stone. For him, the Kings'
ministers had done it; and he had been suspicious of
everyone ever since they had, in effect, killed his father. For her, he had been the instrument; and in her
mind's eye he was the embodiment of the King.

How bloody ironic!

They would hold this deep enmity forevermore because of some damned fancy-dressed man in London
who cared not a whit for the two of them, who knew
not who they were, who would laugh at the story of
the star-crossed lovers who could not bridge the gap
of time, place, or class.

Maeve braved the retelling of the morning's activities; but when Cathleen quickly ran over the events
surrounding Fenwick, Maeve wrapped her arms
around her middle, pulled her legs up to her chest,
and keened for the dead.

"Mama, 'twill work out in the end, you shall see,"
Cathleen said.

She dropped to her knees and tried to pry her
mother's hands loose. But the cadence of the keen
brought tears to her own eyes . . . and a deep sadness

at what had become of her mother. Maeve was the
personification of one of the Greek Furies. Her shining dark hair had turned white and clumps of it hung
loose in untidy rat tails. The immaculate woman of
the house was now dressed in a patched and torn
wrapper which she wore until Cathleen forced her to
take it off for laundering. Knitted wool stockings
covered her legs and feet. Both had become so swollen she could no longer force shoes on. But it was her
face which frightened Cathleen the most. For the first
time in her life Maeve Cochran had taken to powder,
kohl, and rouge. But she did not know how to use the
courtly camouflage. Red circles clung to sunken
white cheeks. Thick, black lines outlined rheumy,
sleep-deprived eyes. Each day more white powder
went on over the old and perspiration gathered old
and new into a crust which flaked off onto Maeve's
wrapper and dripped onto the floor, the chair, the bed.
Luckily, she had stopped cooking, else they would
have found it in their food.

Cathleen was sorely afraid Maeve's mind was slipping away along with the flaking powder. Losing the
manor house had begun the process; but she had
girded herself for battle and gone on, planning for the
day when they would have enough and more to buy
back the manse. And then the awful news about
Matthew . . . news which Cathleen had been loathe to
tell, but knew she must . . . had been the gale which
Maeve's mind could not weather. The overnight
flight into the mountains—away from friends and
family—had nearly undone her. She was just begin-

ning to come around when the magistrate's guard had
swooped down. One more setback and Cathleen did
not know what they would do . . . or could do . . . to
ease her suffering.

She had such pride of place, pride of person. And
she had lost it all. Cathleen vowed that no place . . .
no person . . . no *thing* . . . would be so important that
her whole sense of herself would disappear if she lost
it. She was Cathleen Cochran. Lady of the manor,
jockey, horsebreeder, or scullery maid, it made no
difference. She was who she was. Change would
come. She would bend with it, not break.

"Mama? Can you hear me?"

Maeve nodded, but the keening did not abate.

"We have to return to the magistrate's court. To
hear what he has decided. It can't be much, what he
will want us to pay, because we did most of the work,
and he must see that what we did was more improve-
ment of the land than destruction. So fear not. . . ."

Maeve clamped her hands over her ears. "Do *not*
use those words! There is much to fear; and I shall
fear it until all is back to what it was." She waved her
daughter, husband, and sons away. "Go. Go. I will remain here at Margaret's, waiting . . . always
waiting . . ."

When the door closed behind them and they heard
Maeve take up her keen again, Cathleen shook her
fist at the sun. "Saints and angels, hear my vow. Matthew Forrest shall pay for what he has done to her."

She almost said, "and to me," but she kept that secret locked deep inside herself. If her father ever dis-

covered that Matthew had offered to make her his mistress, the men of Dunswell would rise up and storm his manor house, drag the man out, and stone him—or worse. It had been done before, to other Englishmen who, like Matthew, had sullied a maid and tried to buy her off with trinkets, or throw her aside as soon as they used her. They had thought they were safe behind title, family, and money. But the men of Dunswell always protected their women; and they did it in the dead of night. Though Matthew deserved her enmity—for had he not brought it on himself with all his lies?—he did not deserve that kind of punishment.

Assembled once more behind the rope and in front of it, the suit went one. Magistrate Royce made his formal entrance and what had become a farce to Matthew began its final phase. In front of Royce was a stack of papers with neat rows of figures. Beside him sat Joshua Holmes of Holmesby Manor, the nearest neighbor Matthew had, and a man of finance in the city.

"During our recess," Royce said, "the Viscount Loring agreed to help me determine the just recompense owed to the Earl of Dunswell by his stablemaster and servants, the Cochran family. I will allow the Viscount to explain how he arrived at his figures."

Matthew tuned out as soon as the man began to speak in an affected, nasal voice which sounded like a cat in heat. From shuffling feet, whispers, snorts, and coughs, Matthew was not the only one lost in the monetary muck. Tenant rents, church tithes or widow's mites . . . what was owed, was owed and all that mattered was the final figure.

". . . bringing the total to seven hundred and twenty British pounds sterling."

As the assemblage gasped and the Cochrans blanched, Matthew consulted the figure Cathleen had given for the total of the purses her horses had collected. Aye, he thought he remembered correctly. Five hundred and twenty-three pounds—out of which they had had to live for the past two years.

Was the Viscount mad? Or merely malicious? The latter, Matthew decided when his eyes swiveled to take in the self-satisfied smirk of Fenwick and found the same mirrored in the faces of the gentry. They did not care that it would be nearly impossible—nay, truly impossible—for the Cochrans to pay such a ridiculous sum. They were out to prove who was master, who was servant. They would grind the Irish into the ground and walk away with all the land if given the chance. This suit had played into their hands and they, in the person of the Viscount, had called the suit and fashioned the rules to suit themselves.

And he was part of their conspiracy.

Fenwick jumped to his feet. "My lord, the Earl demands immediate payment."

"But that's six years' income," Cathleen choked out. "We cannot pay immediately. We do not have it." She appealed to the magistrate. "My lord, has the Viscount taken our labors into account in his calculations? We improved the land, maintained the buildings . . ."

"For which you were paid a yearly stipend," Royce said. "And whether you improved the land or no, must be the decision of the Earl." He turned to Matthew. "What say you, my lord? Was the land improved by the labors of these people?"

The man had been out to the manor house. He had seen with his own eyes the sturdiness of the buildings, the symmetry of the training oval. But he had put the onus on Matthew for a reason—to see where Matthew stood. With the gentry, or with the Cochrans.

"The land has been much improved, my lord magistrate," Matthew announced. Royce flushed and the Viscount glowered, but Matthew did not care. "I would request that the court take that into account."

"What would be the value of these improvements," the magistrate prodded.

"Fifty pounds," Fenwick shouted.

"Three hundred," Matthew said. He leaned over and hissed into Fenwick's ear, "One more word from you and you may take your wages and clear out of Dunswell. Do you understand?"

"Aye, my lord. I was only doing what my position demands . . . what you declared was my duty . . . to protect your interests in all things."

"I shall protect my interests in this courtroom. Your purview is on the estate and only on the estate."

"Well, my lord . . . what shall it be," Royce asked, "fifty or three hundred?"

"Three hundred," Matthew said. "Or more . . ."

"We shall leave it at three hundred," Royce declared. "Which leaves four hundred and twenty pounds owed to the Earl of Dunswell. So do I order." He turned to the Cochrans. "You will have forty-eight hours to procure the amount. It must be in the hands of the Earl by the evening of the third day following these procedures."

"But, my lord, we do not have that much," John said.

"Raise it," the magistrate said.

"How?" Paul asked.

The Viscount shrugged his shoulders, then smiled with such glee that Matthew felt that telltale shiver which heralded trouble. "I would suggest that since the Earl is so anxious to get his hands on those halfbreeds of yours, an equitable exchange could be made. Turn over your herd to him and the magistrate would consider it a complete settlement of his judgment against you."

"Done! I shall have the militia collect the herd immediately." Magistrate Royce banged his gavel on the table. "This court is ..."

Matthew jumped to his feet. The stallion was worth more than that. "My lord ... I wish to be heard!"

Royce glared at him and banged the gavel once more. "... adjourned!"

As the crowd surged around the shaken, decimated Cochrans, Matthew fought to get to the magistrate. But the coward took one look at Matthew's furious face and streaked for his door and the privacy of his

own home. The door banged closed and a militiaman
took up position outside it, his rifle at the ready. The
defeated victor plodded slowly out into a day turned
cloudy and threatening to rain. He hoped the oncom-
ing storm was a foul one. It would match his mood.

Fenwick went to fetch the carriage and Matthew
had to endure the congratulations of the gentry, the
curses of the villagers. He was about to stomp off
himself when Billy Weeks approached, took off his
tricorn and handed Matthew a folded note.

> *My lord Matthew. To ensure safe delivery*
> *of the Sidhe Stables' herd into your hands, you*
> *shall accompany my representative, the Viscount*
> *Loring, and the militia when they journey into*
> *the hills. Once you have affected the retrieval of*
> *the horses—and have made certain that each*
> *and every horse you cited in your complaint are*
> *in the herd delivered to you—the Viscount will*
> *have papers for you to sign acquitting this court*
> *of further action. Be ready to leave on the mor-*
> *row at dawn.*

Matthew stewed. Such arrangements could not
have been made in less than three minutes. Hell, it
would have taken thrice that to write the damned
note. Nay . . . the magistrate knew what the judgment
would be and had prepared this well in advance. Matthew wanted the horses, did he? Then Matthew—as
an Earl and Englishman—would get the horses. Regardless of the right of the situation. And the Vis-

count must have been in league with the magistrate, else how had he come up with the kind of figures he knew would bankrupt the Cochrans . . . again. Matthew wondered who had held the mortgage on Dunswell Manor in the first place. Would it not have been usual for John to have appealed to his neighbor, a learned man of finance in the city, to arrange the details? Was Matthew imaging it or were there carefully hidden and orchestrated wheels within wheels, plots within plots? And always the English landowners pitted against the native Irish. It was beginning to turn his stomach.

Startled to have the object of his conjectures sidle up to him, Matthew was even more surprised when Joshua said, "It seems we are to be travel companions."

"Aye, it does seem that way."

"I was wondering . . . would you accompany me in my carriage? I have a proposition for you which might be of immense interest."

Though he disliked the man, Matthew thought it prudent to keep his back from being exposed. "Of course."

He was prepared for a diatribe about the lazy, good for naught Irish and knew if he wanted to learn what he had to deal with among his neighbors that he would have to swallow his bile and listen without comment. The day might come when he could affect some revenge against this man for what he had done to Cathleen and her family. Nay, what he had helped Matthew do. Without his own greed, ambition, and false pride none of this could have happened.

"Pay that scurrilous lot no mind. My driver has orders to run them down if they get in our way."

The scurrilious lot was Cathleen and a few villagers. They did naught but stand silently along the roadway as pricks for his conscience.

Cathleen stood out like a shining beacon in a roiling sea. In that white dress with its green, black, and gold Cochran-patterned shawl, she was the embodiment of all he had ever wanted in a woman.

What was it she had named one of the horses?

Countless Cathleen.

Aye. That was what she was. A countess. She could have been his countess. What an ass he was, not to have considered it!

". . . and please consider my offer in the manner in which it is given, my lord."

"I beg pardon. I'm afraid I did not hear you correctly. What and how much did you say?"

"I repeat. I heard you had enquired of the estate agents whether or no Dunswell Manor would be easily sold if offered now. Whatever they told you, set it aside. I represent an interested party who would be willing to take it off your hands for one thousand pounds more than you paid for it. He has stipulated, however, that one third of the halfbreed horses must be considered part of the estate or there is no offer. Will you think on it and give me your answer on the morrow? He wishes to have the papers signed before you retrieve the herd."

"I will think on it, Joshua. I fear I am inclined to accept. I grow weary of . . ." *Of dealing with tax col-*

*lectors and magistrates who circumvent justice for
their own ends.* ". . . of making that arduous journey
to oversee my mercantile in London."

It was a good offer. He could get rid of a property,
the ownership of which had given him naught but
heartache and still keep two-thirds of the halfbreeds.
At this point he did not wish to keep any—and would
have turned the entire herd back to the Cochrans—
but the magistrate had foreseen such a possibility by
sending the militia and Joshua as his assigns. So Matthew had to hold on to the herd, biding his time until
he could surreptitiously slip them back to their rightful owners.

Consequently, on the morrow he signed the papers
which Joshua brought to the house. The new owner
would take possession within two months, allowing
Matthew sufficient time to move his establishment
back to London. Now all they had to do was ride into
the hills and retrieve the damned horses.

When they rode into the stable yard Matthew
thought he was walking through a recurring living
nightmare. The French had a phrase for it—as the
French always did, he thought bitterly—*dejá vu*. He
had lived this before.

Doors swinging back and forth on creaking hinges
as the wind whipped through empty rooms.

Varmints swarming over spilled grain and drowning in untended troughs.

Feral cats feasting on the varmints. Feral sheep munching on pasture land.

Empty pasture land.

Empty outbuildings.

Empty house.

Empty stalls.

And a note pinned to a bedroom wall.

He took it down, walked out to the stable, where the odor of horse was long gone, and realized that this land had been empty for as long as the Cochrans had been in custody. Cathleen confirmed it in her words to him.

Well, my lord but not my master . . . we come to the end of our journey. We walked together for a time. Laughed together. Played together. Came together in the most intimate way of men and women. Or rather I should say our bodies did all those things. Never were our minds intimate, else you would not have lied to me, you would not have dishonored me, you would not have attempted to defeat me and all those I love. You have no honor, Matthew Forrest. And once again you have no horses. Did you think me and my people would not know what the result of your suit would do to us? Do you think we would not have prepared to outwit you? We Irish, we only have our wits with which to survive the avarice and calumny of you English. Know this, Matthew Forrest, I intend to triumph. I have what you do

*not, what you will never have: and I will hold to
it until I die.*

He knew she meant more than the horses.

From paid informants Matthew discovered that the
Cochrans had made elaborate plans to get out of Ireland. A pirate ship awaited them off the coast with
the herd aboard. Two days following the judgment
against them—when Matthew and Joshua were only
beginning their wasted journey to retrieve what had
already been hidden away, they boarded the ship,
bound for the American colonies along the Chesapeake Bay.

"They shall not get away with this, Matthew,"
Joshua said. "I shall petition the King to alert the colonial guard. They will track down these fugitives.
And when they do, I shall have. my horses
returned . . . ah . . . I mean . . . my client shall have
his . . ."

Matthew laughed in Joshua's face until the tire-
some man harrumphed and had the good grace to
look shame-faced. "It matters not, sir. I care little for
an estate and a manor house which never felt comfortable over my head. I only regret that the Cochrans
will ne'er have the satisfaction of seeing your face
when the next tax bill comes due."

"I shouldn't worry yourself on that matter. I have
always been able to afford the sorry taxes on the land
in Ireland."

"You can afford ten thousand pounds in taxes?"

The Viscount's mouth worked furiously, like a fish trying to slip the hook. "Ten thousand pounds! You cannot be serious."

"Ah, but I am. That was the last assessment, sir. And it is due and payable within the month. It seems our good friends in parliament think to make the Sheriff of Nottingham look like a generous fool."

"My God! I thought to gull you and you have . . ."

"Gotten myself out of a sorry mess and bested the Cochrans' enemies in the process. It was you who held his mortgage the first time, thus bankrupting him . . . was it not?" By the abashed look on Joshua's face Matthew knew he had scored one on the greedy bastard. "Without trying, John may have given back what he received from you. I wish him and his brood well in their new endeavor."

On the long trip back Joshua never said a word, and Matthew was glad of it. He had thoughts which would have made him look ridiculous in Joshua's and any gentleman's eye. But they were not ridiculous to Matthew. Parliament had eyes for gold and more gold to pay for their excesses and mistakes in the colonies. Ireland had been their first target. The American colonies, their second. Were his and his fellow merchants' businesses close behind? He had shipyards, townhouses, a mercantile, and a merchant line. Each was taxable. And for men who were willing to impoverish a whole country to get the gold they needed, impoverishing a small segment of the population would be child's play. They could do it over toast and tea.

The Earl of Dunswell he would always be; but what good would it do him if he ended up being the Earl of Naught?

He had been done in by the gentry, done in by the KIng, done in by his own greed and injustice. He would not be done in again.

As they drove through the gate to Dunswell Manor, Matthew put his scheme to Joshua. "I hold no grudge, sir. In fact, I would be grateful if you would act as agent for me in the city. I have two shipyards, a townhouse, and a row of shops I wish to sell. Find me a buyer and I will double your commission."

Ever ready to enrich his own pockets, and facing a tax bill which would choke him, Joshua eagerly agreed. "Are you also selling the contents of the shops?"

"Nay. Those I take with me on my new venture. I will need the stores to set up business in the colonies. I believe I will start in Baltimore."

Joshua's mouth pursed, holding back a grin; but when Matthew's grin exploded into laughter, the taciturn man joined in. "So . . . you chase after your horses . . ."

Matthew did not care what Joshua Holmes thought. He only cared what he knew. "I go to collect what is mine."

He knew he meant more than the horses.

1773

Pursuit

Chapter Ten

Baltimore.

The American Colonies were naught if not color-ful. Red brick houses. Blue skies. Dun-colored sand which blew in with the tidal winds and made every-one's teeth grind together. Hardy grasses struggling to green up from the burnt umber brown the blasting yellow sun had produced. Wide-topped trees sprout-ing huge green–black waxy leaves and large white fragrant blossoms. Black-skinned people with red squares tied on their heads, bright white shirts with sleeves rolled above their elbows, and trousers or skirts of every hue imaginable. Brown-skinned Indi-ans wearing mantles of indigo-colored homespun—which tinted their skin a startling blue. The mantles were draped over their shoulders and they cradled at least one rifle in their arms. And each of them had tucked jaunty blue or red feathers into beaded bands wound around their foreheads.

Colorful was one thing; but the noise on the docks

was quite another. In Ireland Matthew had been able to hear crickets call to their mates, and the gentle buzz of flies. Here on the docks, as he disembarked for the third time—and he hoped the last—he could not hear himself think. Runabouts pushed carts overflowing with merchandise. They screamed their wares, each trying to attract the attention of passengers such as he. And each runabout hoped he could foist off inferior goods or barely cooked food to people who were starved for more than the sight of water and sky, the taste of wormy hardtack and bitter brew.

On his first voyage, when he had come to scout out a good location for his merchant stores and inexpensive space to warehouse his goods, Matthew had noticed how like the docks of Liverpool or London, these series of piers in Baltimore were. With one notable exception. Americans, it seemed, talked louder than their English cousins. And their accents were broader, more Scots English than London English. There were far more Continental languages spoken here, also. German settlers—Mennonites from the way they dressed so plainly—were bound for farms along the Maryland and Pennsylvania borders. French trappers outfitted themselves for the trek inland. Italian glassblowers and musicians headed for the great cities to ply their trades. Russian fur traders and goldsmiths set up shops close to the docks. They hoped to get first choice of valuable pieces from trappers or new settlers who had not realized how expensive their fare and board would be from England or Amsterdam or Marseilles or Verona.

On his second short stay in Baltimore, Matthew had chosen a city house high on a hill in a neighborhood of the monied and sometimes titled inhabitants. It was small for the area, but suited his bachelor tastes. He had stayed two weeks, furnishing it from his stores while Fenwick interviewed and quickly hired servants and shopkeepers.

"I thought you mad when you decided to leave London," Fenwick said after he had hired the last of the lot. "But there are a dozen anxious and very capable servants to every one surly maid in England. Amazing."

More amazing to Matthew was the countryside around the second largest port city in the colonies.

It reminded him of Donegal, it was that green.

From Fells Point, where captains and shipbuilders had their homes, Baltimore and Maryland spread out and sloped up in rolling hills. Swiftly flowing small rivers and streams cascaded in waterfalls over rocks which hid caves, caverns, and deep water pools. These small rivers joined to make mighty rivers named for or by Indian tribes. The Susquehanna. The Potomac. The Shenandoah. The Monocacy. The Patapsco. The land was wooded and dry in some places, marshy and teeming with insect life in others. And everywhere were white-capped boundary stakes, a sure sign that the land was offered for sale at a very low price by Governor Calvert, who wanted his colony settled as far west as safety permitted.

Near Frederick—a good day's journey west from the heart of Baltimore—Matthew had discovered a parcel three times the size of Dunswell. It had a magnificent hill atop which he planned to build his manor house—what Americans called a plantation house. Behind the hill, near a vigorous stream which would provide fresh water until wells could be dug, was a natural flat as large as the Rood Running race course. Matthew could imagine his horses, as well as his neighbors' and business acquaintances', vying for prizes in Maryland's race course circuit.

On his second trip, he had discovered that the people here loved all forms of entertainment; but they especially loved racing. They were, it seemed, as mad for the sport as their cousins in Ireland and England. And for good reason. The new Rebels loved it because the crowds diverted attention from their "undercover" activities. The Loyalists used it to relieve tensions created by the rebels' clandestine affairs. For both sides, the racetrack was an ideal place to meet. It allowed for intermingling of the two opposing groups. Secrets were exchanged, information bought and sold, assignations made, trysts kept. Matthew believed that in such an atmosphere he could begin again in a place where the law was on the side of the landowner and where the colonial militia refused to uphold English tax laws.

And the asking price for this paradise was half what he had been assessed in taxes alone in Ireland.

All-in-all, it was a gorgeous place which appealed to his adventurous spirit. But he did not make an offer for it until he went riding one day on the adjoining property. He had gone but a half mile or so when he discovered a glen in the woods. Smoke curled from a tall chimney of a good-sized cabin behind which some workmen cut down trees, while others hauled dry lumber from a huge pile at the edge of the glen. Already a huge oval had been fenced in and a black-tailed horse gamboled in the pasture land.

"Here! Who be you, there?"

Matthew looked down the barrel of a long rifle to a black-haired settler who looked more like an Indian than the Welshman he sounded. "Mayhap your new neighbor, if the land proves acceptable."

"Depends on why you wants it." He waved the rifle at Matthew. "Get along, now. The mistress don't like no prowling-about strangers at Siddy Station."

Matthew tipped his tricorn and held Mandrake to a steady, fearless trot. He had heard that the new settlers of the region were suspicious. They had reason to be. Indian raids were not unheard of here close to the Iroquois encampments. And Rebel juntas scouted out land to hold surreptitious meetings where they planned raids on Loyalist outposts. He supposed the "mistress" had been bothered by at least one of the menacing groups, else why post a guard who gave every indication that he would shoot if Matthew did not "get along" quickly. As he left the land by a different route, he noticed a small sign tacked to a tree by the new colonial road. An arrow painted on it must direct the workmen to the correct site, he supposed. He was about to turn and head back to the site he had been exploring before wandering on the other

property, when he reined in Mandrake. He looked at
the sign again.

Sidhe Station.

Not Siddy but Sidhe. Sidhe, the Irish fairy which
guided the seawinds. Sidhe, as in Sidhe Stables? Nay,
there could *not* be another of that name in all the
world.

He laughed aloud. He had spent six months of his
first voyage following up leads, searching for her and
her family from one end of the Chesapeake to the
other. Virginia was the biggest damned colony! But
not a soul had heard of her. *Try Maryland,* had been
the suggestion of every man in the racing circuit.

"Racing's taking hold there almost as quickly as it
is here in Virginia. If there are horses to be run and
purses to be won, you'll likely find your quarry in
Maryland. Round Baltimore way or the easternmost
shore lands. Don't bother with Annapolis. Mostly
stately homes where good loyal lawyers, physicians,
and politicians are settling. The rougher elements and
the Catholic crowd are heading west along the Pennsylvania border or on the banks of the Potomac."

Two voyages later and he had found her without
trying. The land next to her now became very suitable. Aye, he would settle here and build his plantation and racing oval.

And the next time he came calling, no one would
chase him away.

* * *

"Who was that, Mapes?"

"Some fancy pants English gent. New to the colonies, I've no doubt." He patted his rifle stock and grinned with a mouth empty of nearly every other tooth. "Old Deadeye, here, sent him along with his tail atwixt his legs, right enough. He'll not be bothering us again, I warrant."

"I hope you're right. But to be certain, I'd best double up the guards, as Pence suggested."

"Aye. The captain, he be a sharp man what knows the ways of evil men. You be abuilding things here what other men would kill to get their hands on. So take no chances, missy. Me and Mutton can get you all the help you need. There's plenty who find it a sport to shoot a man."

"I don't need killing, Mapes. I need good backs, fast hands, and sharp eyes, don't you know. Men who aren't afraid to work for their wages. I want stonemasons, carpenters, farmers, and stablehands. But they have to hit the center of a target at two hundred paces as if the fairy folk were guiding their shots. If they come on with me now they'll be posted as guard for three hours and will work on the house and stables for another four. And when this station is finished, I'll expect them to stay on. So don't bring me any layabouts from the docks who can't even get passage on pirate vessels. I won't have them, I won't."

"Don't you worry about Mapes, missy. Pence give me the word. And if he finds me slacking off on the job or giving you any trouble, he'll have me gizzard on a pole."

"Then go get those men, and be quick about it."

"Aye, missy."

Mapes turned to get Mutton and their horses when Cathleen called, "And take the wagon and Sean with you. While you're doing what you have to do, he can fetch Da, and all. The cabin is cozy enough now."

Ah, the missy sounded sad as the wind just before a storm at sea, or the little brown owl which had taken roost in the rafters of the lean-to. Plaintive. Lonely. Mapes's old, pirate's heart went out to the woman. Twenty-six and not yet husbanded. No justice in this world. Not for the likes of her. Not for the likes of him. Only Pence had seen the worth of both; and he had taken them on as partners in this grand venture of his. This grand design which the missy had planned and Pence had liked from the very first description of it. They owed him allegiance and honor, if not their lives, for trusting them with it.

The old fellow would come quiet, Mapes did not question it. Da, she called him. Now that was a pure shame, what had happened to him. Going half to pieces after the man lost his wife like that and truly lost she was. Lost at sea. What had she been thinking, letting those horses loose in the dark of night? And riding one of them hell-bent-for-glory, as if they was still in Ireland in them rolling hills. Jumped the rail, she did. Right into the deep waters off those isles the Indians called Chincoteague and Asateague. The horse—big with foal—swam valiantly for shore. If she and her foal survived, they would return to the wild, so none went after them. But his poor wife

now ... she did not crest the waves and all those
who could swim volunteered to search for her. Sorry,
Pence was, to have them come back without her.
Gone to her glory, Mutton said. Or wherever they
took in lost souls. 'Course, she was touched in the
head by the devil, some had said. And some said she
even took her own life. But the missy, now, she stood
up to them, denying that Maeve Cochran would do
such a things, and her a good Catholic. Her mind became unhinged that was the whole of it and the end
of it, poor thing. And missy had been right in that.
Mapes remembered how awful it had been. A terrible
tragedy, watching her slip away day by day into a
dark world where even the missy couldn't reach. Ah,
the sea did that to people too gentle to understand the
power of it. And that lady had been too gentle. Gentle enough to break. The father, too. Heavy burdened,
he had been. Guilt, the crew muttered. Aye, mayhap.
But Mapes thought it was also the burden of being
left with three offspring to fare for and no money
with which to do it. 'Tweren't long afore he had begun to slip into the dark world of his lady wife.

But missy, now. She was another kettle of cod. She
was strong as an oak. Supple as a birch. Pretty as a
daisy. She had an instinct for making money as good
as a pirate captain. Hell, as good as Pence, hisself, who
was the best of the bunch. Look how she had shown
him how to become respectable. Pence was all for that.
So were most of his crew, Mapes and Mutton included.
They were too old to continue awastering on the sea.
And aplundering was not what it used to be. Too

damned many English ships, merchant, navy, or revenue cutter. And each fitted out with the best cannon this side of Zanzibar.

Mapes finished tying up the team to the wagon and went to fetch Sean and Mutton. Aye, Pence had done a good thing, taking on that missy and her brothers. Got hisself a merchant store in the best part of Baltimore, where he could sell his pirate booty without fear of revenue cutters' iron balls and blasts. Got hisself a respectable house where he could act the part of the respectable merchant prince. Hee. Hee. Paraded right under the noses of men he'd plundered more than once in their lives, and none the teeniest bit aware of it. Aye, Pence had done a damned good thing.

And no fancy pants English gent was going to foul up Pence's and the missy's plans and the good life him and Mutton had here at Siddy Station. Old Deadeye would see to that.

"It was him, I tell you. That Fenwick. Matthew Dunn's . . . I mean the Earl's steward."

Donal stared at his brother. Though Paul wore the clothes of a Baltimore gentlemen, he had not shaken off all of the last several years in Ireland. His hair might be wigged . . . he might wear a fine lawn shirt with lace at neck and wrists . . . he might sport gold braid-trimmed green velvet coat and matching breeches, a vest covered with *broderie francaise,* black clocked stockings, and silver-buckled shiny shoes . . . but if one looked closely one could see the rough stablehand in Paul. Donal, on the other hand, prided himself in his ability to blend into whatever kind of situation he found himself. His suit might be brown to Paul's green, but he wore it with more finesse . . . and felt more comfortable in it than Paul did in his, judging from how often Paul ran a finger round the neckcloth of his shirt.

Donal shook off the clutching fingers of his brother's hand and strode into the coffee house. "Fenwick? Nonsense. The man's in Ireland with Forrest, living it up on our heritage. Damn it, Paul, you'll be seeing leprechauns next."

" 'Tis leprechauns we need. Pence . . . ah, hell; I never will remember to call him Sterling the way he wants us to do." Paul looked over his shoulder to be certain none was listening to their conversation and hissed, "*Sterling* arrives soon to look over the books and we don't have the money we lost at the last Mount Hope Stakes."

Donal gave their order to the pleasantly plump serving wench, took out his clay pipe and worked for several minutes to get it lit. It was tough going because he had only recently taken up the gentlemen's habit. He puffed to hold it ablaze, then talked. Puffed some more, then talked. "I told you not to bet against Cat's string of ponies. They're . . . getting faster every day. And I also . . . told you . . . not to take money out of Sterling's account."

The coffee came. Laced with brandy and liberally honied, it was sweet and strong, warming the young men from lips to toes. Donal watched Paul drink his down in three gulps. Not the way of a gentleman. Donal sighed. He was sick and tired of giving Paul lessons in how to act. Paul thought by dressing like a gentleman—complete with ruffled shirt, silver buckles on his shoes, and a snuff box tucked up his sleeve—he would be accepted by the gentry, the way Sterling had demanded when he had accepted Cat's wild scheme.

"Seconds, gentlemen?" the wench asked.

Though she didn't add *so soon,* Donal heard the censure and cringed. The room was peopled with merchants, lawyers, military officers, and the king's representatives. There were also rebels among the gentry, no doubt, since these Americans did not need a hole in their pocket to foment rebellion. Already the Newport Junta had burned one revenue cutter and there were rumbles of worse to come. But regardless of which side of the argument a gentleman was on, he was still a gentleman; and coffee house drunkenness would not hold the Cochrans in good stead.

"We shall stand another round in thirty minutes," Donal said. "We are more hungry than thirsty, this night."

"We have savory squirrel stew and mince pasties, a good corn pudding, potatoes in cream sauce, and sorrel, mint, and carrot salads."

"Bring a dish of each," Paul ordered. "And the best house ale."

They were halfway through their meal when they were approached by a tall, thin man with greying hair and gold-rimmed spectacles balanced on the end of his nose. He wore a fashionably tailored blue coat trimmed with silver braid and large tooled pewter buttons. His shirt was plain, no ruffles like the brothers wore, but his vest was patterned like the finest tapestries. Pale cream suede breeches topped blue clocked stockings. Black shoes with very small pewter buckles and a cockaded tricorn the same color as his coat completed his ensemble.

If any man in that coffee house thought Peter *Sterling* a pirate, he must have gone to sea with Pence or been boarded by him. To all eyes Sterling appeared a respectable member of Baltimore society; and to all purposes, he was.

Why, by all that was holy, had Paul and he thought they could steal over a thousand pounds from the likes of him and get away with it?

Donal had slipped the noose once, thanks to Cat. He did not expect Fate or Luck to give him a second chance to slip it again. Sterling—the pirate, Pence— was not Forrest. Nor was he a fat, complacent magistrate. He had plied his trade for almost twenty years and never been arrested nor boarded. Only a very good pirate lasted that long. Though rumor had it that Pence never killed a man except in self defense. He did not have to. Any of his able-bodied pirate band would do it for him, and gladly. Donal had heard that his band had killed for lesser offenses than dipping into the captain's money chests. Ah, Christ! The soft spot in Sterling's heart for Cat would not save her brothers. Sterling had made it perfectly clear from the start that the merchant business and the horse breeding and training station were separate things. He might have bankrolled each enterprise; but Cat and the brothers succeeded or failed on their own.

Suddenly, Donal's neckcloth also felt very, very tight and he had to stifle an urge to run his finger round it.

Sterling pulled up a chair and plunked his tankard of ale on the table. He snapped his fingers at the serving girl and circled them over the bowls of food to indicate he wished another serving. "Well, gentlemen. You do look prosperous. I've come from the stores and the counters are busy. I like to see that, I do."

"Aye," Paul said. "What with talk of insurrection, the populace are girding for a siege. They be stocking up on everything from nails to tobacco."

Sterling leaned closer and whispered, "Push the rum and raisins, gentlemen. We have another shipment being off-loaded at Tolliver's Landing . . . without the revenue stamps, so we have to sell them fast." He looked up and smiled at the girl when she brought his food. "Well, another pretty Maryland sunflower! I do like this colony. It sprouts the best women in the Americas." The rather plain girl blushed and curtsied. As Sterling tucked into his stew with gusto, he withdrew a white square of heavy paper from his vest pocket and handed it to Donal. "Servant boy brought this round while I was in the stores. Charles Carroll the Barrister has invited us to a masked ball on Friday, next, at his home on the banks of the Patapsco."

Wish You Were Here?

You can be, every month, with Zebra Historical Romance Novels.

AND TO GET YOU STARTED, ALLOW US TO SEND YOU

4 Historical Romances Free

AN $18.00 VALUE!
With absolutely no obligation to buy anything.

YOU'RE GOING TO LOVE GETTING
4 FREE BOOKS

These books worth $18, are yours without cost or obligation
when you fill out and mail this certificate.
*If the certificate is missing below, write to: Zebra Home Subscription Service, Inc.,
120 Brighton Road, P.O. Box 5214, Clifton, New Jersey 07015-5214*

Complete and mail this card to receive 4 Free books!

Yes! Please send me 4 Zebra Historical Romances without cost or obligation. I understand that each month thereafter I will be able to preview 4 new Zebra Historical Romances FREE for 10 days. Then, if I should decide to keep them, I will pay the money-saving preferred publisher's price of just $3.75 each...a total of $15. That's $3 less than the publisher's price, and there is no additional charge for shipping and handling. I may return any shipment within 10 days and owe nothing, and I may cancel this subscription at any time. The 4 FREE books will be mine to keep in any case.

Name _____

Address _____ Apt. _____

City _____ State _____ Zip _____

Telephone ( ) _____

Signature _____
(If under 18, parent or guardian must sign.)

LF1094

Terms, offer and prices subject to change without notice. Subscription subject to acceptance by Zebra Books.
Zebra Books reserves the right to reject any order or cancel any subscription.

ZEBRA HOME SUBSCRIPTION SERVICE, INC.

120 BRIGHTON ROAD

P.O. BOX 5214

CLIFTON, NEW JERSEY 07015-5214

AFFIX
STAMP
HERE

"Mount Clare?" Paul asked.

"Aye."

"Beautiful place. High on the hill, the way it stands. I hear he's planning a racing track on the land."

"Mayhap. But I doubt his wife ... what is it, Meg ... Martha?"

"Margaret," Donal offered. "Of the Tilghman's of Annapolis. Old family. Used to be Catholic, but are now Protestant."

"Aren't they all who settled in Annapolis?" Sterling grumbled. He, too, was Catholic, which was why the Catholic colony of Maryland appealed to him as a permanent residence. He tapped the invitation on the table. "It specifically asks that Cathleen attend; so I am off to the station. I can invite her while I inspect the work that has been done. She says we should be ready to race on the oval by September, two months hence. A little late in the season; but it may be very profitable, since there will be no competition for attendance." He paused then smiled at Cathleen's brothers. "Very capable woman, your sister. Very capable, indeed. Very fortunate, I was, to have had you Cochrans board my ship in your haste to leave Ireland ..." He winked and tapped the end of his nose, indicating he could keep a secret and would do. "All's well that end's well ... hey, boyos?"

"How can it end well?" Paul groaned and slumped into his favorite chair in the large drawing room of the townhouse they owned in Fells Point. "When he gets back from Cat's, he'll go through the books and we'll be cooked."

"Not if we put the money back," Donal said.

"And how do we do that? Sell this place? His name is on the deed and I'll be damned if I'll get caught forging documents. The magistrates are examining everything so carefully, we'll be lucky to get a bill of lading across their desk for those raisins and rum. God, why did we agree to do business with a pirate?"

"To make money. And we have. This house is paid for . . . and never mind that Sterling owns a third of it. He doesn't live here and according to the agreement it will be all ours in three years." Donal grinned. "She was a wonder, was she not, our Cathleen?"

"Aye, that she was."

The brothers looked at each other and laughed, their troubles momentarily forgotten in the memory of the bargain Cathleen had struck with the wily pirate . . . and how she had done it.

One day away from Chincoteague and Assateague, and John Cochran had taken to wandering the decks whispering to shadows, talking to his Maeve. It discomforted Donal to know that he had near gone over the edge, too; and that without Cathleen, the family might have collapsed in the face of troubles too numerous and too frightful to contemplate. But when her parents had broken, Cathleen stood tall. She

2272

would not hear of turning back, giving up, indenturing themselves.

"There's a new country here, abuilding. And new lives to be started. And I have plans. Great plans for all of us. All we need is the capital; and I'll find it. Somehow. Because there's a fortune to be had."

When she began to sketch out her plans for a racing line better than even John had thought possible, Sterling—the pirate, Pence—had been nearby. Wily old bugger! He had ruminated only as long as it took them to round the point and head into the Chesapeake before coming to Cathleen with a proposition.

"I heard you say you needed capital. Aye?"

"Aye. We do," Cathleen said; but she held her tongue for once and waited his next move.

Pence grinned so wide that the brothers saw the flash from his gold back tooth. "I'll bankroll your enterprise." The grin got wider. "All of it."

"And what do we have to give?" Cathleen asked.

"Only the usual. A third of the profits for the next forty years."

"But that's magnanimous," Paul had said.

Cathleen glared him into silence. "Seven years, the same as an indentured servant."

Pence's eyebrow shot up and his grin slipped a mite. "Do you think me daft? I put up all the capital and you walk away with my money in only seven years? Anyone else will take my offer and gladly."

"No one else has our halfbreeds."

Aye, there was that and Pence knew it.

"Thirty years," he countered.

"Ten," Cathleen said.

Pence laughed and his eyes twinkled with delight, which had the crew murmuring of good things to come. "Twenty-five," he said and sat back complacently.

The brothers had sucked in their breath when Cathleen narrowed her eyes and shook her head. *"Nine* years. And I warn you that it will go down at each new counter offer."

Most of the crew gasped at her effrontery. But Mapes and Mutton had crowed with laughter. Soon Pence joined them. "I like you, lass," Pence said. "There's not many men who would stand up to me like that, I vow."

"I trusted I had naught to lose. If you wanted the horses without us, you'd have pitched us overboard and taken them. So . . ." she shrugged and plunked herself on a barrel across from Pence, ". . . when you didn't, I realized you knew you had to have us or the plan would not work."

"There are two plans we talk about here. Yours and mine. We'll work them both together or we'll work neither."

Cathleen cocked her head speculatively. "I don't recall your plan."

"Partnership for ten years . . . yes, *ten* . . . but only if *you,* Cathleen Cochran, take control of the stables."

"Here, now . . . we're the men in the family!" Paul shouted.

"Control yourself, you young pup," Mapes said,

putting a pistol to Paul's head. "The captain was talking. Go ahead, Captain."

"I've been watching you boys," Pence said. "You have a heavy hand with the horses. Oh, you do not mistreat them. But it is Cathleen's hand which calms, her voice which commands. Face it, you two. You do not have the skill your sister has, nor the inclination to dirty your hands every day for the rest of your lives. So I will deal only with Cathleen when it comes to the stables and the racing oval. But have no fear. You two do have an important role to play in my plan. A role which will allow you to live a life of ease and power. Now, as the men in the family, does that interest you?"

Cathleen cut off Paul before he could get an *aye* out. "I would have to hear more."

"Simple. I need an outlet for my surplus goods. I'll set up your brothers in Baltimore as merchants. Their merchandise will be composed primarily of my goods, which will have premium position in the stores. But I'll not stop them from augmenting the stock with fast-selling merchandise brought in by other means. Legal means. My men and I have been pirating too long. We need to settle down, live respectable lives. You can do that for us."

"Very gracious, Captain," Paul said. "And very generous."

"Five years," Cathleen said. "We'll owe you our allegiance and make you a fortune; but I'll not be tied down for ten years. Five or naught."

Paul pinched his sister's arm. "Wist, Cathleen! The captain has made his offer."

"And I have made mine." She shook off Paul's probing fingers. "I care not what rope you tie around your necks; but I'll not have one around mine for ten years." She eyed Pence and smiled. "I'll even sweeten my pot. Equal partners for three years. Then I take two-thirds for the final two. Can you live with that, Captain Pence?"

"Equal is it?"

"Aye. For three years, only."

Pence slapped his palm, spat into it, and extended his hand. "Done." Cathleen did not hesitate. She spit into her own hand and shook his. Then Pence turned to the brothers. "Now yours is a more complicated proposition since it means I will have to provide more than mere money. So . . . I suggest we go back to the ten years, and you keep two-thirds. Agreed?"

"Aye," Paul said. He held out his hand but he did not spit into it.

Pence's grin turned into a tight-lipped sneer. "And done."

Two years later and still Donal did not know . . .

"Paul, do you think Cathleen knew Pence was nearby and listening when she outlined her plans to us? Do you think she planned on him hearing? Do you think she knew he was looking for a way to become Peter Sterling instead of Peter Pence?"

"I wouldn't put it past her. Look at her, now. She only has one year and five months left to split the profits half and half with Pence . . . uh . . . Sterling.

And we have more than eight years to go on our agreement."

"We may not live to see the eight years if we don't put that money back."

"Which brings us full circle to my original question. How?"

"Sell half the mercantile."

"Who will buy half of a mercantile which is entailed to a pirate?"

"Who knows the mercantile is entailed to a pirate? Pence is Sterling as soon as he steps onto a Baltimore dock. Truth, Sterling's name appears on the deed to this house, but not to the mercantile. For all anyone in Baltimore knows, we own the stores outright. We could find an eager buyer ... someone who, like Pence–Sterling needs to establish credibility."

"And we sell them half of everything ... including Sterling's half?"

Donal nodded. "I don't see that we have a choice."

He got up and looked out the window to the street which was almost empty, a street of fashionable homes which were almost as good as Dunswell Manor. Almost. But not nearly good enough. He often was short tempered with Paul, who wore his dissatisfaction too openly. But truth to tell, Donal was no more satisfied with their position than was his brother. They had been bred from luxury. To luxury he longed to return. Nay, they had no choice if they wanted to get on. They had to find someone to bail them out of the mess they had gotten into. And then he vowed he would never gamble again. Never.

"We'll look for our new partner at the governor's ball," he said. "Someone hungry. Someone . . ."

"Someone with gold pieces to throw away."

When Peter Sterling presented Cathleen with the hand-lettered invitation, she was working in one of the training paddocks, working with a colt only five months old. He was a grand sight, that colt. Dun colored with black tail, mane, ears, and socks to his knees, he showed the Black Turk's heritage and his sire's, Firebrand. Cathleen had decided this one would be named Fortune's Fire because his long legs and easy gait gave her to believe that he would be the best of the foals born that year.

She looked over the invitation quickly, then took back the lead from a stable lad. "Nay," she said, and shook her head and frowned. "I have too much to do." Looking worriedly toward the stables where her father was digging in a small garden, talking to his Maeve about the flowers he would plant for her— flowers he never allowed to sprout because he always dug in the same place. "I cannot leave Da. He wandered away three days ago and we had the devil of a time finding him. Finally discovered him splashing in the river in the dead of night, trying to catch fish with his bare hands."

"Mapes and Mutton will see to him, Cathleen. They won't let him wander off or harm himself. Besides," he grinned. "I've ordered a special mask for you from Mistress Bromley. 'Twill be delivered in two days."

"Peter . . . I can't . . ."

"You can. You will. You spend entirely too much time at this station. Better you should spend it in society, where you might find yourself a good man to husband."

"I don't need a man to husband. I am perfectly capable of husbanding myself."

Peter's eyebrows shot to his hairline and he pursed his mouth. Did she know what she had implied? The blush creeping slowly up her neck indicated she did.

Ah, the lovely Cat. Maturity had brought curves where he fancied only sinew and muscle had once been. She was still tall, strong, capable, as she said. But she was also womanly and he thought it a shame that her body had not delivered itself of the fruits all women seemed to desire. Hell, he'd marry her himself if he weren't twenty-four years her senior; but it would be like marrying his daughter and he could find naught more distasteful than that picture.

"The women talk, you know."

"Aye," she said gloomily. "And 'tis me they prattle about when they gather round their quilting boards." She flicked a whip at Fortune's Fire and kept him trotting round in a circle.

"He has the gait for it, I vow."

"Aye. He *will* make us a fortune. I know it. I feel it in my bones."

"Cathleen, we've won enough the past two years for you to have paid me triple my investment in this station. I've no need for more." When her head snapped up and a speculative, enterprising look came into her eyes, he laughed. "But I shall hold you to your bargain. One year, three months and you are quit of me."

"I don't want to be quit of *you*, Peter, I don't. Only the stranglehold of a partner. I'm not fit for partnering, Peter. Not in any sense of the word. Which is why I would make a poor wife. So don't you go advancing me as wife material. That poor solicitor from Essex Junction near collapsed when he saw what was truly your . . . how did you describe me to him . . . *quiet, penitent Irish rose?* Really, Peter! You must be truthful!"

"Why? I haven't told the truth to anyone yet; and neither have you, Cat. The truth would not advance us in any venture, including the marriage mart."

"You are wrong, Peter. I have ne'er lied to a single soul here in Baltimore. Lies almost destroyed me. I hate them. I hate that you have to tell them; but I understand your reasons and don't admonish you . . . much."

"And what do you say when people ask about your partner?"

"I say he is a generous, good-hearted man who made a fortune in the fur and lumber trade . . ."

"Quite true but not the whole truth."

". . . In the fur and lumber trade, then became a privateer during the seven year uprising. Now he lives quietly in Barbados, making occasional trips to Baltimore to inspect his investments."

"Clever, my dear. All true. All believable."

"And entirely acceptable."

A bell sounded and Cathleen handed her lead to the stable hand. "Wipe him down and water him, then come in to noon meal," she ordered the lad. "He can rest this afternoon and tomorrow morning."

"Aye."

Peter took Cathleen's hand and tucked it into the crook of his elbow. "I have a sketch of the mask Mistress Bromley is stitching up. Will you at least look at it and then make up your mind?"

He sounded so hopeful, she could not disappoint him. Not only had he supported each and every plan of hers with money and time, he had augmented her staff with his own men, leaving him little more than a skeleton crew when he went on his foraging trips. Luckily, the trips were getting fewer and fewer and further and further apart. She worried about him. He was only fifty years old and still had years ahead of him. She wanted for them to be good ones . . . outside of prison and this side of the rope. "Of course I'll take a peek at your designs, Peter. After noon meal."

Peter hugged Cathleen's arm against his side. A peek she had offered. A peek he would accept. For only a peek was needed. There was not a woman alive who could resist the design he had commissioned. He had no doubts of the outcome of Cat's little peek. Now all he had to do was find a good seamstress who could make a gown to match the mask. In three days. Unless . . . he made a hasty mental inventory of the gowns he had in his booty chests. Aye, there was one . . . oh, but it would make all the women choke with envy, it was that impressive. Fit for a Duchess, for hadn't it been owned by one when he prized it from the lady's French wardrobe, asailing to England only eight months ago?

Ah, Cathleen, elusive they call you. But in that gown you'll be both elusive and sought-after.

Chapter Eleven

When Cathleen and Peter's carriage arrived at the gates of Mount Clare plantation house they were greeted by a liveried servant who directed them in a growing procession of carriages and coaches, inside of which were cloaked figures, their faces hidden either by the folds of their summer cloaks or the masks they already wore. Cathleen giggled at a complicated affair of turkey feathers and silver braid which covered the woman who wore it like a hood on a cape.

"She must be daft. She won't be able to breathe!"

"She does not have to breathe. She has to dazzle."

"With that? She looks like a turkey ready to be plucked, she does. All we need is a vat of boiling water and we can feast for weeks, don't you know . . ."

"Irreverent baggage! Mind your manners this night."

"Oh, I shall mind my manners, I shall. I can't do much else in this gown."

Peter grinned. "Aye. I thought not."

His stratagem had been brilliantly planned, more brilliantly executed. They were where he wanted Cathleen to be, among the very best of Baltimore society, following carriages and coaches carrying Carrolls and Calverts, Tollivers and Peales, Ellicotts and Dulanys, Bealls and Dawsons, Tylers and Brunners, Hagers and Boons. The parade wound through acres of trees on the huge plantation, arriving at the house which sat high on the hill beside the Patapsco River.

"Iron deposits built this, you know," Peter said. "Helped bolster the shipbuilding trade, as well. Baltimore will eclipse Philadelphia within the decade, I don't doubt."

"Aye." Cathleen already knew that. She had met the barrister and been regaled with stories about the founding of the family. It bored her. What excited her was something more down to earth . . . an extension of the sport of kings, she thought. "Will we see the bowling green, do you think?"

"I would hope so. There are candles aglow all over the yard."

Indeed there were. Candles stuck to the trees lining the drive, lit and glowing though it was only dusk. Candles atop the wooden picket fence which enclosed a wide brick entrance. Candles in every window of the three-storied brick house. Candles on the portico, on the portico roof, hanging in lanterns from branches of the tall oak and elm trees which shaded the house.

Cathleen loved the simple lines of Mount Clare. The central portion had twin chimneys at each end.

She could imagine the fires that would warm the rooms in winter. The windows were smaller than those at Dunswell Manor. There were only two on the first floor and their twins directly above on the second. Unlike Dunswell, however, above the central door this mansion had a large room which jutted out and over the columned portico. To either side of the main house was a one-storied, many-windowed gallery ell. And attached to the galleries—and lined up perpendicular to them—were two identical large buildings which faced the rolling front acreage.

"Kitchen to one side, barrister office to the other, I warrant," Cathleen said.

"You have been here afore?"

She shook her head, then pointed to the brightly clad female servants bustling into the door in the side of the building on the right. Each carried some kind of foodstuff in her hands.

"Ah! Observant as usual, Cat." He fingered the ribbon on the box in which Cathleen's mask sat amidst the softest cotton bolls. "Masks on, I think."

And looking round, Cathleen saw that those who were not already masked were struggling to get theirs on without being seen. Oh, why had she agreed to this? Only to please Peter, who took such pride in her? Only to help push him forward to the respectability he craved? Or did it have more to do with a sense she had not known she possessed—a longing to be someone she was not, if only for this one night. A desire to dazzle, as Peter had said. An ache to be thought of as a woman—desirable, delectable, delightsome to the eye. She had not felt that way in far too long a time. Since . . .

She swallowed hard and opened her mask box. She slipped it over her face as the unwanted name jolted through her head.

Since Matthew . . . Matthew . . . Matthew.

The rat.

And then as she was knotting the riband ties behind her head, she began to laugh and found she could not stop.

The rat. And she, the Cat.

It startled Peter, who frowned with concern. Though he had hoped to lighten Cathleen's mood, this laughter had a tinge of sadness and exaggerated levity. He worried what had brought it on. "What occasions such mirth, my dear?"

"I was thinking about a rat I know and what he would do if he saw . . . this!"

"Turn tail and run?"

"Nay. He's the killing kind of rat. The kind that poisons the very air he breathes. He deserves to come face to face with a cat who has more power than he. Once. If God is good."

Charles Carroll the Barrister adjusted his harlequin mask and slapped his guest on the shoulder. " 'Tis time to join our guests, my lord, else my good wife will skin me alive."

"Margaret has such a sweet disposition I cannot imagine . . ."

"Imagine. My good friend Franklin might have been right to avoid the institution of marriage. Lucky for us, we men may indulge in other pleasures when the sweetness is replaced by regular fluctuations in temperament. The contrariness of the species is a sight to behold—and the only thing to be counted on in the fair sex."

The sight to behold that night were the strikingly beautiful—and in some instances, audacious— disguises the Maryland gentry had chosen. Matthew adjusted his own mask and circled the drawing room, drawn to a buzzing excitement from a large group of men jostling one another to get a better view of . . .

Good God! A cat. Unlike the other women, who wore elaborate wigs, she had piled her deep-colored tresses high on her head and allowed wayward curls to cascade down her back. Here and there in the folds of the curls were sparkling single diamonds and pearls. Her mask was a vision in striped black and white fur with long black lashes and longer black whiskers. Her gown was of a delicate watered white silk with black silk tasseled braid trimming the sack back, and a delicate silk tracery of black stitches framing the low-cut bodice. Long black gloves disappeared inside the black lace at the bottom of her elbow-length sleeves. Her only adornment reflected the highlights in her hair and was pinned to her left breast—a solitary blood red ruby shaped like a heart.

Speculative whispers buzzed round the roomful of women.

"Who can it be?"

"I don't recall a new arrival I have not already met. And none, I say, looked at all like that!"

" 'Tis Cat."

"A cat? Of course it's a cat. The mask could be naught else."

"No! Cat. Cathleen Cochran of Sidhe Station."

"Don't be absurd. Cathleen is over her prime. Besides, she would ne'er be seen in public dressed such."

Matthew—who knew Cathleen better than these over-the-hill matrons—observed the way the cat woman moved her head, extended her hand to an admirer, blushed and lowered her head slightly with embarrassment, shifted her weight from one side to the other. He grinned behind his very ordinary painted tortoise shell silk mask. Yes it was Cathleen . . . Cat. He had seen that foot movement previous. Cathleen had never been comfortable in dancing slippers because they did not have room to wiggle her toes.

He could see, now, what she must have been like as the daughter of the lord of the manor. What she would have been like as a Countess. His Countess of Dunswell. "Damned fool," he muttered to himself. He was about to turn away when Cathleen's head came up and her face turned away from the madness of the men around her. Her gaze flicked nervously across the room, passed over him, then snapped back. He watched her watching him. Silently, he urged her not to turn her head, prayed that she would allow him the opportunity . . .

To do what?

"The most beautiful woman in all of Maryland, I vow," a bass voice rumbled in Matthew's ear.

"Aye," Matthew said. "But Maryland does not encompass enough space for the likes of her. The most beautiful in Ireland and Maryland, I would describe her."

Surprise colored the man's voice as he stuck out his hand. "*Most* perspicacious, sire. Peter Sterling, I am . . . or are we not to reveal our identity?"

"Too late, sire." Matthew shook the hand of the man in a pirate mask with costume to match. Yet Matthew's gaze never wavered from Cathleen's. "Matthew Forrest, recently arrived from London. Do you know the lady?"

With a smile, Peter answered. "Oh, aye. I know her."

Peter had heard often from Paul and Donal how the Cochrans had been running from this man and his damnable law suit. But he also knew that Cat had never gotten over the love she had for him. She had not married, had not entertained thoughts of taking a husband. And Peter had too often seen her lost in thought, a haunted look on her face, a melting softness in her eyes that too quickly turned flinty. "I have the honor of being her escort. All the way from a tiny seaside village in Donegal two years ago, as well as Sidhe Station this night."

"Ah." Matthew nodded, realizing the risk Peter Sterling took in admitting that he was the pirate who had spirited Cathleen and her family away from the clutches of the law . . . and him. No wonder the man's costume had the ring of authenticity. "I owe you much for keeping her safe."

"You owe her more."

"Aye." If he strained, Matthew could see the honied hazel hue of Cathleen's eyes. "I would try to repay it, but knowing Cathleen as I do, I vow she would not allow it."

"You may be right. But tonight she does not know who you are. And she would ne'er guess that you have left your precious estate . . ."

"Sold it to the man responsible for bankrupting her father. Sold it for three times its worth, then stayed to see the bugger get hit with taxes so heavy, they bankrupted him."

"You knew the taxes were coming when you sold it?"

"Oh, aye. Took great satisfaction in the selling." Finally, he dropped his gaze from Cathleen's and looked Peter square in the face. "I have been holding in trust the amount John lost. If you are Cathleen's friend, would you help me get it to them without her knowing?"

Peter clapped Matthew on the back. "I like you, my lord. Did not think I would. In fact, before we had this little talk, and if I were in my old profession, I might have considered making you leap o'er the rail. Now, though . . . you are not what I expected. But you are, I believe, exactly what my dear Cat needs." Peter nudged Matthew's elbow. "Come, my lord; I have a proposition for you. We shall take advantage of Carroll's set-up. You ne'er know what will develop when the lady is in the dark, as it were."

Dare he? Matthew's every pore screamed *aye*.

So after careful consultation with Peter Sterling, Matthew left the assembled guests and fetched his carriage, then waited in the darkness for Peter to do his part.

"My gratitude, good friend," Cathleen said to Peter as he drew her into the line for the first dance. "They were pressing me to choose among them; and since I did not wish to choose any, I was a trifle vexed, for a fact."

"What is the matter with you, Cathleen? You are tripping over your feet. Your mind is not on the music, nor are your words on our conversation, nor your eyes on me." Peter laughed heartily when he realized for whom she searched, then bowed them out of the dance. "I will not have the ladies think *me* the iron-footed one." They wandered the rooms, speaking to one group after the other, not one of which captured Cathleen's interest for more than two sentences. After trying to carry the conversation for them both with seven individuals, and failing miserably, Peter felt extremely satisfied with what he and Matthew had brewed. He took Cathleen's elbow and whisked her into the hall. "That is it. We are leaving. You made an entrance worthy of a queen but you are now acting more the stablehand. The effect is lost."

"I'm worried about Da."

And I'm Mutton's parrot. I've seen you searching, searching, searching. But he is not here; though I know where he is and what will do you both good.

"Of course you are." He took her cloak from the serving girl and hustled them out into the courtyard where a carriage awaited them. He was pleased she was so distracted, for she never realized he was handing her into the wrong carriage.

Cathleen sank back against the puffy velvet pillows and closed her eyes. Puffy velvet pillows? But there weren't puffy velvet pillows in Peter's coach.

The carriage doors slammed closed and she jolted as the horses bolted down the drive. "Peter?"

"Enjoy!" Peter called after her.

"Peter!" She swiveled and climbed up onto the seat, hanging over the edge and shaking a gloved fist as his shape disappeared into the darkness. "Damn you, Peter Sterling. I did not want to come and now you've set me packing on home." Strong hands clamped around her waist and she shrieked. "Unhand me, sire!" She looked behind her to find the stranger in the painted tortoise shell mask, who grinned a lopsided grin at her. "Peter Sterling, I will kill you."

The strong hands helped her turn around; but she shied away, tucked herself into a corner, and frowned at the man in the plain brown linen coat, pristine white unruffled shirt, sand-colored vest, brown and sand tweed trousers, and brown suede boots. His dark hair was not powdered, but worn in a queue tied at the nape of his neck with a brown riband. There were no trimmings on his clothes, nor watch nor chain

tucked into his vest. When she had first seen him, his
command of the room had been achieved solely by
his presence—the way he held himself, walked,
moved. Muscles rippled under linen and velvet,
showing the strength and firmness of his body.

He seemed absolutely delighted at the situation Peter had presented to him, as if Cathleen were the
main course at the Carroll's dinner. Well, she would
see about that, she would. "And who, by all the
saints and angels, are you?"

For answer, he reached across and touched one finger to her mouth, then pointed to his mask and hers,
and held his finger against his mouth. Silence. They
were masked, therefore unknown to each other. By
the adventurous glint in his eyes and the speculative
bent to his head, he was asking that she allow to happen what would happen—and have no regrets if anything did—for she would never know who had done
what with whom.

Ah, an adventure. "You do know the way to my
heart, sire."

He brightened and bowed, then took her hand and
held it, running his thumb back and forth against the
inside of her wrist, sending shivers up and down her
spine.

Oh, Peter! What have you done?

It had been so long since a man had paid her court.
So long . . . and she had missed so much. Though she
tried to pull away, something inside her would not allow her more than a mere squeak of indignation. She
could not resist this stranger's appeal and it surprised

her, worried her. He had a way about him which reminded her so much of other times, other places. Happy, exciting times of wonder and fulfillment. Oh, how she wanted to throw her arms out and laugh as she had that night. Throw her arms out and be the woman she was . . . had been . . . wanted to be again. Not a woman like those left behind, who danced slow, painstaking steps which had right feet tangling with left, but a woman who threw herself into the delightful clogs of Donegal, where men and women jumped and whirled, laughed and cried . . . or showed with their feet only, the thunderous joy in their hearts. How she wanted and needed some of that in her life, a life filled with the dreadful worry of both parents gone mad with grief and loneliness.

Ah, saints and angels . . . one night. Give me one night and I will ask for no more, evermore.

Suddenly, she straightened. She must be daft, allowing herself to be whisked away from a friend's house in full view of her brothers and everyone else, and by a masked man, of all things!

"Stop! Where are you taking me?" she asked sternly.

But the man once more put his finger to his lips. He plucked her cloak from her lap and placed it gently on Cathleen's shoulders. His hands lingered to gently knead the tension from them, and she felt her inhibitions drop away as if his fingers brushed them off one by one. She heard the wheels of the carriage as they rode over the rough brick drive and down onto the colonial road.

"A promenade? You want to take a promenade?"

He shrugged and then nodded. She sighed. "We will scandalize the community." He smiled crookedly and cocked his head. "No, I suppose it isn't that important, what they say." She reached up and tied her cloak; and when she let her hands drop to her lap, he leaned over and took them both in his. She would have snatched them away, but the strength—and gentleness—in his touch gave her goose pimples. And about time, Peter would have said. She supposed he was right. It *had* been a long time.

"A short promenade with a masked, mysterious stranger. I must truly be daft."

Matthew held Cathleen's hand lightly, tamping down the urge to do more than caress her palms and wrists. Why had she worn gloves? It would have been wonderful to feel that soft skin where her pulse always beat erratically when they were together. Of course, he would not know that pulse this night since she did not know he was the man holding her hands. If she did, he'd wager she'd squeeze those hands round his neck.

He brought her to the docks and his new Chesapeake schooner. She made no protest when he handed her aboard and made her comfortable on the small stern deck. From a chest near the hatch he brought out a bottle of good vintage French wine and held it up. When she nodded, he removed two solid pewter goblets from a chest and poured the ruby red wine into them. She leaned back against the taffrail and shut her eyes, sipping the soul-satisfying warmth. She heard sounds but since the man did not come near her, she gave herself to the stillness of the night and the gentle breezes blowing off the bay. The tightness in her body slowly eased and she suddenly realized she was swaying in rhythm with the boat. Opening her eyes she saw her masked stranger at the rail, a line wrapped around his shoulders, straining to bring the boat around as the sails filled.

"Saints and angels!" She had duties at the station. A father to care for. Horses to train. Races to set up. She had no time for a moonlight sail. "Take me back. Now!"

He threw her an unreadable glance because of his mask and tacked into the middle of the harbor, catching a breeze that took them far from the dock, far from safety.

"Are you a pirate? Are you stealing me to sell me into slavery in the Arabias?"

Rich, melting laughter erupted from his chest. He shook his head. A gust of wind teased at the edge of his mask, breaking the riband. He grabbed for it. The line shot forward and the boat luffed to a stop. He stood with his back to her, watching the wind pick up his mask and dance it over the waves until it was swallowed up and sank.

"Damn," she heard him say. With a great sigh, he grabbed hold of a line and jerked it towards him. "Damn. Peter and I did not take the wind into consideration."

No! She knew that voice.

All the horror of the short time they had been together came flooding into her head. The horror that had never ended, had taken her home, her mother, and now her father.

No!

Without thinking . . . and feeling too much . . . she picked up the wine bottle and hefted it in her hands, then brought it up. Would she have swung it at him, had he not turned at that moment and lunged to protect himself? She would never know. Instinctively, she ducked and the wine bottle jerked, spilling its contents and smashing against his forearm. The worst sound she had ever heard cracked across the waves. Matthew's knees buckled for a moment and he moaned.

"God, Cathleen. If I ever pour you wine again, remind me to put the bottle out of your reach." He groped for the taffrail and sank down onto the deck. "For the next few moments could you pretend I'm a decent person and help me set this before it punctures the skin?"

What she had done was done unwittingly. Nonetheless, she was responsible. Anger at him gave way to anger at herself, then bounced back again. "Saints and angels! If you had stayed on the other side of the Atlantic where you belonged and had not stolen me away from my friends this would ne'er have happened!"

"Curse at me later, Cathleen."

"Oh, bother it! We can't be together without one of

us ending in a heap or getting hurt. Why do we keep trying?"

"Ask me later, Cathleen. I don't have strength to think at this moment."

Cathleen tore off the beautiful mask Peter had given her—*and may he have boils and bunions for his underhanded work in this affair.* She searched and found a boat hook and an oar hanging against the side of the boat, and some canvas swatches in a chest. She took one look at the crazy angle to Matthew's arm and threw them down. Matthew sucked in his breath when she eased his coat off.

"Have a heart, Cat. I'm trying not to lose consciousness."

"Lose consciousness. You're bearable that way."

She tossed his coat aside, sucked in her breath and did what she, as a stablemaster's daughter, knew had to be done. Taking hold of his hand, and bracing her feet on the deck and her back against the rail, she gave his hand and forearm a hard tug. The bone snapped into place and Matthew groaned, then flopped over against her.

"Let me catch my breath," he croaked, "and I'll help you set the damned thing."

"Some wine would help."

He gave a weak smile. "I don't believe there's any left, Cathleen."

She had neither the time nor the inclination to feel embarrassed. "There's mine." She shifted and retrieved her glass. Holding it to his lips, she tilted his head back and slowly poured the sweet wine down his throat. "Better?"

"Aye. Thank you."

"We'd best set that arm now."

"Aye. I'll be fine, Cathleen. Don't worry."

"About you? Don't be daft. You'll always land on your feet."

"Nay. That's the province of a cat, Cathleen." He looked her up and down and grinned through the pain. "Look at you. You have wine spots on your ball gown but they look as if they belong there."

Cathleen looked down and saw that the red wine had spattered against the white silk, directly under her heart-shaped ruby. "Dripping blood. Oh, aye. That's just the way you'd like to see me." She picked up the oar and swung it back and forth. It was sturdy and had a flat end which would be perfect for the task at hand. "Well, my lord, I have black tidings for you. My heart isn't broken. And you don't make me bleed."

Saints and angels, if only that were true.

She cracked the oar on the taffrail until it broke, then cracked it again until she had three pieces. She positioned the flat piece on the underside of his arm. "Here, hold this steady." While Matthew held the oar, Cathleen wrapped the canvas securely, but not tightly, around the oar and his arm. On the second wrap of the canvas, she tucked a second piece of oar against his arm. The third piece went opposite. To hold it all together, she pulled the riband out of his hair and tied the bundled arm, oars and canvas, all.

They drifted for a time, until Matthew's breathing quieted and he struggled to his feet. "Damned awkward, this thing hanging."

"Better that than *me* hanging!"

They gazed at each other, each aware of all the agony and all the joy behind that cry.

"Ah, Cathleen. Cathleen, the cat." His heart as well as his arm felt torn in two. "You're *my* cat. Mine."

"Just as you are my rat."

The moment she said it she knew it was true. Both were true. Else why had she not found another man to husband? Why had she never wanted another man, never cared, or hoped, or dreamed of anyone except Matthew. Ah, saints and angels, what mischief have you wrought? She swallowed down traitorous tears, hating having them, knowing it made her human . . . and vulnerable. She was not vulnerable. Could not be. Would not be!

"Damn you, Matthew Forrest! I suppose you were taking me to the revenue cutter to be whisked back to England and the noose?"

"I'd never do that, Cat."

"You did it once . . . or near enough."

"I tried to stop it; but the magistrate went on and on with it."

"You should never have started it. If you had only . . ." She stopped. "No. I promised myself I would never waste my time on *if onlys.*"

"Thank God. Then we can move ahead."

"Oh? And how do we do that? You and that devil Fenwick still have a price fixed on our heads."

"I'll never turn you in, Cathleen. I promise."

"Now, is this Matthew Dunn's promise or Matthew Forrest's? Or am I speaking to the Earl of Dunswell?"

"There is no more Earl of Dunswell. At least, I no longer own the manor house." Quickly, holding his arm so it would not move, would not send tearing pain through him, he told her about her father's bankruptcy, how it had been manipulated by her neighbor Joshua Holmes, the Viscount Loring of Holmsby Manor, and how he, Matthew, had manipulated the Viscount in return. "Last I heard both estates were once more on the king's list."

"So much could have been avoided if you had not lied to me, and all."

"Aye, Cathleen. I know. But I had good reasons . . ."

"Not good enough. And never good enough to offer to make me your mistress."

"Forgive me. If you don't, my life will be a waste, an agony. I thought I had achieved my father's dream and had to live the way of the titled. How else to keep you close when we were so ill-matched?"

"Ill-matched? Why? Because you were an Earl and I only a stablehand?"

"Because I was blinded by the ambition which drove me and could not see you for who and what you were. I did not realize that in trying to keep you close in the only way I thought I could, I would kill whatever there was aborning between us. What we had was good, Cathleen. You know it was. So damned good, I did not want to lose it. But I did not know how to keep it. Not properly. Not the way you deserved. God, I was three times a fool. Please forgive me."

A strong gust rocked the boat and Matthew stumbled. He swung his arm up and it cracked against the taffrail. Immediately, sweat broke out on his forehead and his face blanched. "Cat!" She was there in an instant, bearing his weight on her shoulder, her arms tight around his chest.

Aye, it had been good. She, too, had wanted it to continue. And she had missed him. Missed this melt-all-over feeling when their bodies touched, their breaths mingled. Missed talking with him, seeing him. The laugh lines near his eyes had deepened and looked now more like lines of sorrow, for they bent down and not up. Ah, she did not like to think of Matthew in perpetual sorrow. No matter what he had done, he had tried to stop the court proceedings. Her father's gamble to bring the stallions to Ireland was as much to blame for all of it as Matthew's taking advantage of the situation.

"We are here in a new place, a place where lives are rebuilt and pasts are forgotten and forgiven. I could forgive you, Matthew . . . if you can forgive yourself."

He draped his good arm over her shoulder and braced his feet on the deck. "Ah, Cathleen. So good. So beautiful."

He smiled down at her and her stomach flipped, her heart ached, her body warmed with a need so great she wanted to scream, it was so sudden and so complete. She shivered and he pulled her closer.

"Are you cold?"

She shook her head, afraid to lift it, afraid to say anything lest he know how deeply this closeness affected her. She fought to get back her anger, the only thing which had kept her sane on this long journey right back into his arms. But it was no use. She was mad for the want of him. Driven by the need for him.

"Cat."

The way he said that word warmed her even more than he had before. She snuggled into his chest and stroked her cheek against him. She inhaled his pungent aroma, a combination of the mint he liked in his tea, the spices he kept in his stores, and an overriding scent of cedar.

"I love your new name," he said. He used his chin to force her head up. When he spoke, his lips were only a fraction away from hers and their breaths mingled. "I loved the mask. It made you very mysterious, very sleek and lovely, just like a real cat. The way you truly are, Cathleen. The way I remember you from that night. No, don't look away. I want to tell you how you affect me."

"Ah, don't. Please. I don't know what I will do if . . ."

"I must. I want you, Cat. I always have. Always will. I want you now, even with this arm throbbing away worse than other parts of my body. I want to

hold you, feel you warm and soft against me. I want
you the way we were the last time we were together.
You can't have forgotten . . ."

"Forgotten? Saints and angels, every night I remember. Every night I ache with . . ." She groaned.
"No, Matthew. Not again."

"Always, Cat." He bridged the short space between them and his mouth took hers. He tasted the
wine on her tongue and his body exploded. "Always," he said against her lips.

No! Oh, God, no! Cathleen felt betrayed by her
own body, her own mind. She was frantic, torn between the love she had for this man and the betrayal
she had once felt.

And there, as Shakespeare had said, was the rub.
Once she had felt betrayed. Now? Now, she only felt
the warmth of Matthew's embrace, the fire which
heated her blood, and the urgent call of her body to
find completion and fulfillment in Matthew, with
Matthew. She had been so alone, so lonely. Though
she tried to be strong and self reliant, she was so often filled with a deep sorrow that it took her breath
away.

Matthew gave it back. Matthew filled the void in
body, mind, and soul.

She loved him, God help her. He had been her enemy, and she loved him.

What had she asked on the drive to the Carroll's?
Just one night, evermore. One more night. With Matthew. She would ask for no more, evermore; but
wanted and would take no less.

"Can you stand without my help?"

"Aye. But why?"

She smiled and steadied him against the railing. With one hand she removed her cloak and spread it on the deck. Then, swiftly before she changed her mind, she scrabbled at the lacings of her beautiful ball gown. Skirt fell to the deck, followed by underskirt, bodice and sack back.

"Nay, Cat."

"I want to, Matthew. I *have* to."

"Then go slow, love. We have waited this long; let us enjoy the moment and have good memories for later."

Her hands trembled when she tugged on the ribband in her chemise. "I don't know what or how . . ."

"Let me, love."

"Your arm."

"There is one good one left." He tugged and brought her next to him, kissed her forehead, her nose, her chin, and then back to capture her eager mouth. Their tongues danced together and he smiled against her lips. "I've been starving for this."

She moaned and put her hands on his shoulders, then raised them to his hair. It blew like feathers and she wanted to touch it but the gloves prevented her from feeling the texture. She stripped them off and dropped them to the deck, then opened her fingers and threaded them through the thick, soft darkness of his hair. With each stroke her fear dissipated and left only the loving.

He laughed and kissed her. "I'd like to do the same

but taking down your hair will send jewels flying across the waves." His fingers walked across her cheek, down her neck to her collarbone and down to the ties on her chemise. He tugged on one string and the bodice loosened and fell away from her breasts. "Beautiful," he rasped. "Just as I remembered."

Her heart soared when he turned his hand over and brushed the back of it across her breasts. The silk of her gown was not so soft, so warm, so wonderful. From such sweet contact, her nipples hardened and she moaned as tiny flicks of current surged through her. He nibbled at her lips as his hand went further and he untied her petticoat. It dropped to the deck and she kicked it away. He captured one breast and suckled it until she cried out, "Matthew!"

"Could you help . . . ?"

Since he could not do it, she untied his trousers and slipped them off. Only his shirt covered his manhood . . . and not very well, because he was unabashedly ready for her. Cathleen was overwhelmed by the insistent surge of fire which propelled her into him, until she felt him hard against her belly.

She sighed and searched for his mouth. Their kiss was mindless passion, drunken need, seering pleasure. She was breathless, and breathed him into her. She was empty and her body moved until she found him.

"The deck, I think," he croaked. "But my arm."

"Bother the deck."

Arching her back, she brushed against him, wanting, craving this man, and this man only.

All her life ... all her days and nights ... she would feel this way. She knew it. It terrified and thrilled her.

"I can't wait, Cat."

"Nor can I!"

Cathleen sank to the softness of her cloak and held out her hand. Gingerly, Matthew lowered himself to lie beside her. Somehow, instinctively, her urgent need showed her how to move her body until her legs entwined with his and they joined together. They both held their breaths as he entered her and she welcomed him into her warmth.

"This is home," he whispered. "Ah, God, Cat, I love you."

Cathleen's heart soared along with her body. She felt weightless, flying into unknown realms with Matthew as he surged into her. Fulfillment was swift and blinding, complete and breathless. And still he took her higher, loving her with his mouth and manhood, whispering words into her ear that she did not hear because of the roaring in her head. Her heart pounded, her body jolted upward and ever upward. Then an explosion, so intense she knew she would die from it, propelled her into the heavens and she thought she saw the angels smile.

I love you, her heart sang.

I love you, her ears heard.

Her heart slowed, steadied, beat once again. Stars no longer flashed across the sky but twinkled in place. Seagulls lost their halos and became bellowing scavengers. Fish slipped their wings and flapped down through the waves. Magic fireflies turned back into candles on the shore.

And Cathleen's thoughts coalesced as her body cooled.

She was lying beside Matthew, held close to him with his good arm. Her legs were wrapped wantonly about him.

Once more . . . evermore . . . she was doomed to love this man even though she did not trust him.

Chapter Twelve

The night wind cooled his skin and Matthew drew on Cathleen for warmth. Dear God, it was a miracle, her here in his arms ... arm. Cat. Aye, she was that. How she had begun to swing at him with that bottle. He chuckled at the memory of the surprise and fury etched in her face.

"Your Peter Sterling could use you in his pirate crew, lovely Cat."

Cathleen stiffened and the old worry that Peter would somehow be found out washed over her. "How did you ... ?"

"He told me. Well, in truth he hinted ... broadly. And I've ne'er been told I was slow to understand."

Cathleen eased herself away from Matthew and stood up. "Hah! Someone lied. If they had told the truth, we might have been spared these past three years of misery."

She gave him her hand to help him to his feet, then picked up her cloak and wrapped it around her to chase away the chill she suddenly and inexplicably felt. Hurriedly, the way she had done in the winters when the fires had not been lit early enough to warm the rooms, she slipped into her clothes under her cape. Chemise. Petticoat. Underskirt. Skirt. Bodice. The sack back she hung over the rail, then picked up Matthew's trousers and helped him get himself back into them.

How awkward it was. How horribly humiliating.

"Damn," she whispered. "Oh, damn."

She had promised herself never to cry over this man and here she was, dripping away like a leaking roof. They had just shared something beautiful. Why did the aftermath have to be so sordid? Her fingers fumbled with the flaps and ties of Matthew's trousers.

"Damn," she whispered. "Oh, damn."

When she finally finished, Matthew took her two hands in his one and brought them up to his lips. He kissed them, each knuckle, each finger, the palms, the wrists. She sagged against him, loving the way he made her feel, hating the way he had once betrayed her, hating the way her mother had died, hating the way her father was deteriorating. There was so much for which to hate this man ... and still she loved him. He even made this awkward time a joy.

"We have to go back," he said with a sigh which she knew was as much from inheld pain as regret.

"Aye," she said.

"Do you think you could sail this thing if I give you directions?"

Cathleen laughed. "I have been Peter's assistant in several bay crossings. I can sail this and a ship five times this size, and all. I could even outrun the revenue cutters."

"Revenue cutters?" His eyes narrowed. "I liked Sterling. He had best not put you in danger or I'll have to revise my estimation."

"He would never put me in danger." With a toss of her head and an impish grin, she added, "Only you do that." Matthew held out his arm and she blushed. "Aye. You're right and all. We're even, we are."

"Do you know you sound very Irish when you're embarrassed and at other times, more like one of this rough American race?"

She retrieved the lines Matthew had dropped, wound them around her back and arm, and moved the tiller enough to allow the sails to fill with the soft breezes the deep dark had brought. Matthew plopped down onto the deck at her feet and she captained the boat, tacking when necessary to get them back to the dock.

"Peter thought it best for all of us to make the effort to blend in with our new surroundings now that we are making a fresh start. You should think about doing the same. Unless you're planning to go back?"

"Nay. There's naught there for me. I came to the colonies for one purpose and now . . ." He caught her hand and brought it to his lips. "Now," he breathed against her, "I have achieved it."

She waited for the rest but it did not come and she wondered what his *purpose* had been. To bed her again? Was that all he had wanted? Or had he thought to bend her to his will in the one way he knew she would respond—a physical union? Had she once more been blinded to his *purpose,* blind by love and need and desire? Blind and deaf and dumb. Aye, more truly dumb than Sean, who had a brain in his head though he could not talk.

Well-a-day, nor could she speak at this moment.

What had she expected? A proposal of marriage?

Ridiculous. She, a horse trainer, at the most a stablemaster, always and ever. He, an Earl . . . well, at least a man of property and wealth, title, and position. He would have these Americans fawning over him, tossing their daughters at his feet. All she had been able to garner was her neighbors' censure for the way she dressed, spoke, and worked. Only tonight when they had not known who she was had she been welcomed and wooed by the very sons whose mamas, aunts, and sisters had warned them away from her.

What had she expected? A proposal of marriage?

Her eyes clouded again with tears. Aye. She had.

Why, then, did she not sit the horse facing the tail and make her own proposal to him? She was anything but conventional. The community would attest to that, if not Matthew himself. Then what did she wait for? Permission from her blessed saints and angels? They were her constant companions; but they were not—except when Matthew brought her closer to their realm—equal to her. She could not converse with them in other than her dreams or thoughts.

But what if she listened?

She waited. *Well? I've been talking to you all these years. What do you wait for?*

A whisper nibbled at her ear. *For your courage, dolt.*

It would take that . . . courage.

Courage to face the old hatred and tamp it down with love. Courage to face her father and try to make him understand that with Matthew she was not dishonoring her mother's memory. Courage to face her brothers who . . . who had thrown her into Matthew's arms in the first place, and who were partially to blame for the flustering fix she was in. Courage to face her own fears, the old deep-seated distrust of this man.

The man she loved.

"Matthew?"

"Aye, love?"

"Have you ever thought to wed . . . ?"

"Good Lord, what's that on the dock?"

Lanterns. Men. She strained to distinguish one from another and picked out Peter and Mapes, Mutton and Sean. Mapes and Mutton paced the dock side-by-side. Tall and lean. Short and wiry. Battle scarred and weary, both. Their gait was unsure, as it always was on land. Their bodies bent with the pain of time too long spent on the sea in the cold, damp, salt-laden air. Horse liniment helped in the morning, as it had all those years before with her. But now they were bowed, as if from all the cares in the world.

She brought the beat sharply and cleanly into the dock and threw a bowline to Sean, who caught it and tied it to a piling. As she let down the mainsail, Peter, Mapes, and Mutton swarmed aboard. Mapes growled once and made for Matthew, then stopped when he saw the wrapped arm and Cathleen's abashed look.

"You do that, missy?"

"Afraid so."

"Good! Cause if you hadn't, I would." He glared at Matthew, and with a snarling smile withdrew a pistol from his waistband. He held it steady, drawing a bead on Matthew's head. "This here mess of potage ain't good enough for the gulls. What you want me to do with him, Captain?"

Cathleen clutched Peter's arm. "What's wrong? Why have you come here like this? Mapes, point that pistol somewhere else!"

"Nowheres else brings much satisfaction," the old man said, but he lowered the pistol slightly.

Peter took Cathleen's arm and bent to whisper in her ear. "They came for your father."

Oh, saints and angels, it had happened. Someone had discovered John's madness and sent a committee to take him to the house for the insane in Jepperstown. "Who came? How do we get him back?"

"Be glad you decided to settle Sidhe Station on the outskirts of Frederick. One of your neighbors was on his way back from market with a wagon filled with goods when he saw the militia on the move on the colonial road. He only had to ask a few questions to discover they were heading for the station. He almost killed his team driving all over creation alerting the town and outlying farms."

"Hell," Mapes said, "by the time those buzzards arrived to the station we had us a picket fence of armed farmers and merchants to help us hands. Those Frederick folks were something, they were. They put up a fight as strong as the one they give General Braddock back in fifty-five when he tried to take their horses and such. Now they're ringed round the station and done warned the soldiers they ain't leaving, so the militia had best give it up. Don't worry, missy. Old John is safe. Afore the troops arrived Joseph Brunner's son give him sanctuary at Schifferstadt."

Peter took Cathleen's hands in his. "Your father is comfortable in their nursery bedroom. But we will still have to deal with the British militia. Their lieutenant has declared that he will not disperse his men until John has been arrested."

"Arrested? But that's madness. They would not arrest a man merely because his mind has wandered."

"That's not why they wanted him." He walked up to Matthew and thrust out his jaw. Many a man had quaked at the force of Peter Pence's glare; but Matthew did not flinch and Peter Sterling came close to wondering if any of what had happened that night was real. Then he remembered John and how the old man had cried when he had been taken from the station.

"I can't leave my Maeve. She'll be lonely, she will. Can you not see that? I can't leave my Maeve."

He hadn't quieted until they wrapped a pillow in a blanket and put one of Cat's cloaks and bonnets on it. Damn this British Earl and his glib tongue!

"You should take to the stage, my lord. You had me fooled completely; and I thought I knew men and the truth when I heard it." He jerked his thumb in Matthew's face. " 'Twas his name on the bottom of the warrant. An arrest warrant for horse thieving, naming John—and you, Cat—as the primary conspirators."

Cathleen's stomach roiled, her heart contracted until she could not breathe, her mind exploded with all the contrary images it held. She doubled over and Mutton and Sean helped her to the side where she hung over the rail until she could catch a breath, think a thought, feel the tips of her fingers, hear her own blood course through her. An hour ago she had been so hot she melted around Matthew. Now . . . in an instant of betrayal . . . she was cold. Icy. A frozen shell of what she had once been. He had done it again and she had not seen it coming. When would she learn? When would she trust her instincts instead of her heart?

"Cathleen . . . Cat . . . I did not do this."

Matthew's voice was firm and unshakable, suffused with love. And she did not know whether to believe him.

Cathleen whirled to confront Peter. "Did you see the warrant?"

"Aye."

"Was *his* name on the bottom?"

"Aye," Peter sighed. "Written bold and black as a knave's heart. Matthew Forrest, the Earl of Dunswell."

"God, no!" She raced to Matthew and beat her fists against *his* chest. "Liar! Liar! Liar!"

He let her vent her rage. What else could he do? She thought what was not so; but he had no way to force her to believe him. She either did or she didn't. And with her next words he knew she did not ... probably never would. She fairly spat her fury; her wounded pride; her deep, awful sorrow. He was sure even her own men heard all the nuances and understood the reason for them. He was a knave in their eyes and he could do naught else but listen to condemnation from the woman he loved.

"You and your lust for those damned halfbreeds!" she blazed. "It destroyed my mother's peace and drove her into the sea where she drowned. Because she had had all she could take, and still you piled on more. She was a lady, with presence and position and great faith in the goodness of men. She held that faith through times which would have destroyed giants. And then you came along and took away her hope, stole her home, smashed the only thing she had left ... her good name, her honor, her pride, her faith. You destroyed her as surely as if you had taken a knife and plunged it into her heart. Was not one Cochran's life enough? Did you have to destroy my father's as well? For something that is not yours. Never was. Never will be, evermore."

With a sinking heart, Matthew knew that once

again she did not mean only the horses. And this time . . . this time he was afraid he could not cut through the hatred which burned in her eyes, the despair which vibrated in every word.

"I did not do this," he said.

But she stared defiantly at him and announced, "I do not believe you."

Broken arm or no, they left him there on the dock to batten down the boat and try to get back to town in a carriage without a driver. After three false starts he left the damn thing tied to a tree and walked the fourteen blocks to the house into which he had hoped to bring Cathleen. All the way he went over the events in his mind. He believed Peter. The man had no reason to lie. As a pirate, he was probably wanted himself and had taken a chance facing down the militia. If Peter said Matthew's name was scrawled on the warrant, then it was.

And there was only one man who would have the effrontery to do such a thing. Fenwick. The steward of an estate that he treated as if it were his own. An estate he considered incomplete without the halfbreeds. Fenwick. The avenger of wrongs committed by Irish against English. Fenwick. Who had permission to sign Matthew's name to bills of lading and mercantile orders. And who could sign in such a way that even Matthew himself had trouble telling the difference.

He was so weary by the time he reached his house,

he could do naught but bang on the door for admittance. Teasedale, Matthew's butler, took one look at his master's arm and called for the stable boy. "Fetch Doctor Shaw." He helped his master up the stairs and into his bedroom.

"Is Fenwick here?"

"Nay, my lord. He said we could contact him at Hopkins House if we needed him."

Indeed. Matthew had urged the man to get rooms of his own; he had not thought they would be in the best inn in Baltimore. "Send for him."

"Now? 'Tis near ten, my lord."

"Now. And if he is not there, send to every damned tavern in town until you find him. He has much to answer for this night. Much to answer for . . . but I do not think he has the answers I require."

"And how much do they want for this half portion they are offering in partnership?" Fenwick asked Matthew's land agent, who had helped find the parcel for the horse breeding plantation. The two men sat in a small parlor in one of the larger taverns in Fells Point. Card playing and gambling held the attention of captains and ship builders, merchants, and barristers, officers in the King's army and a few Rebels of note. Though it was still early, Fenwick had long since tired of watching other men raking in silver pieces.

Besides, he had other fish to fry.

A boy he had paid to search for the Cochrans had come with the announcement that they were owners of a mercantile and horse breeding station near Frederick, called Sidhe Station. The boy got half a crown for his labors, enough to keep his miserable family alive for four months. Fenwick was about to turn the Cochrans over to the militia when the land agent—Henry Fielding—took him aside and asked if he or Matthew would be interested in taking over half the Cochrans' mercantile business.

Half? Fenwick would not be satisfied with half. He wanted to control it all; not as he did Matthew's other ventures, but as sole owner himself. Thus, he had not named the brothers in the warrant he had signed. Only the old man and the young wench whose supercilious attitude when dealing with him had allowed them all to slip the noose. From the way she and Matthew had looked at each other there in the courtroom, Fenwick wouldn't be surprised if Matthew had bedded her, or had tried and she turned him down. Which made it all the more exciting to send armed militia against her.

He felt enervated. One troublesome affair completed and another to tie up. Now, he had only to dip into the accounts he had been entrusted with. 'Twould be easy. He had done it before, systematically siphoning a few pence a week until he had accumulated a horde enough to satisfy himself. Now he could satisfy the Cochrans with it and get what he wanted. He would be his own master. But he had to insure his plan from ever being found out. Having been John and Cathleen's instrument of warped justice twice, he valued his own safety because he knew how quickly things could go against you when you were not a member of the established power elite.

Well, once he had what he wanted, that worry would vanish. Here in the colonies, it was money, not birth, which made the man. And when revolution came ... and it would, he was sure ... he would come out of it with all he had ever wanted.

He turned to Fielding and smiled as he lied. "I am very interested in this proposition. But the brothers must not know who it is they will be taking on as partner. For reasons of his own, the Earl wishes to remain in the background. You understand."

"Oh, of course. 'Tis the way of business."

"Aye. That it is. But I'm sure the Earl will wish to conclude this business before someone else can snap it up. 'Tis a good investment. I'm surprised no one already has."

"The Cochran brothers only made up their minds today. As their friend, I have been given first chance to bring them an offer. I could bring them a binder tonight. I'm sure they would be delighted to sign papers on the morrow."

"Why not sign them as soon as the binder is delivered? I'm sure I saw a magistrate somewhere in this crowd. He could draw up the papers, you could deliver the money and the partnership agreement, and we would have it over and done before midnight."

"I like the way you work, sire. Your mind is razor

sharp and you do not hesitate when a good proposition is before you. The Earl is lucky to have you."

Within ten minutes the magistrate—who had indulged in six tankards of ale and could barely read what he was signing—had drawn up partnership papers which would give Fenwick a half share of Donegal Mercantile. The papers did not list Fenwick's name, of course. Nor did they list Matthew's. To all who read the papers, Fenn's Goods and Supplies was tendering a partnership. Fenwick signed as Fenn Rodwick, agent of record; and the inebriated magistrate witnessed his signature though he did not know a Rodwick from a candlewick.

Within an hour the brothers had accepted the tender and signed over the shares Fenwick wanted.

Thus, when Matthew's hired hand came to fetch him, Fenwick went with a soaring heart for having gulled the brothers and bested Matthew. If all went well, he would someday be equal to this bought-me-a-title Earl. For now, however, he would bide his time and hold his tongue, for he had no income other than that which Matthew gave. The time was coming, however, when men would take up arms against those who would stamp on ordinary men, only trying to better themselves. Aye. Time would come . . .

"What were you thinking? Or were you thinking at all?"

Matthew wanted naught more than to shake the satisfied gleam out of his steward's eyes, to see one ounce of guilt ... or at the least, some humility. But Fenwick spread his hands, shrugged his shoulders, held his head high, and stared at Matthew as if his master, and not himself, had lost his mind.

"There was a warrant outstanding and as soon as I discovered their whereabouts, I had it served. I thought that was what you intended with all your chasing about the colonies trying to locate them."

Propped in bed, his arm throbbing like a snare drum in a military drill, Matthew was not in the mood to teach this man his place; but moods were not the harbingers of reality, and Fenwick needed a good lesson. "You are not paid to read my mind. You are paid to carry out my orders. Correction. You *were* paid to carry out my orders. As of now, your services are no longer required. Clear out your things from this house. I don't want to see your face ever again."

"You are making a big mistake, my lord."

"Nay. No mistake. Get out. Now!" He turned to his butler and ordered, "Make sure this snake does not enter my office, or take aught but what is his."

"Aye, my lord," Teasedale said.

Matthew had sent for his solicitor and the commander of the militia. The solicitor arrived first and Matthew ordered him to explunge Fenwick's name from any new papers being drawn up. "He is no longer in my employ. Pass the word, Fairleigh. And do it this night. I no longer trust that man to do the honorable thing."

Captain Roget was horrified to discover that Matthew had not given the order for the Cochrans' arrest.

"But there is a warrant outstanding, my lord. 'Twill take time to vacate it."

"Time you do not have. There are armed farmers and merchants ringed around the Cochran plantation. If one shot is fired you could cause this revolution the King tries his best to avoid. Do you want a *royal* warrant? This time for your arrest for fomenting rebellion?"

"Nay, my lord. I will go at once, my lord."

He waved the man away and was pleased to note the white splotches of fear which eclipsed the man's complexion. White splotches to go with red-rimmed eyes. They would both be sorry spectacles in the morning. A morning he was not looking to with joy, for it—and every morning following it—was devoid of what made his life bearable.

Cathleen.

"Ah, Cat. I would take it all back," he said into the silence of an empty house. A house he had hoped to make their nuptial home. A home he had hoped would be filled with their laughter and their children's laughter. Instead, it was a rectangular box of rooms and furniture. Naught else.

"Damn it to hell!"

He grabbed a pillow from behind his head and threw it across the room. It caught Teasedale on the side of his head as he entered the room, and the tray he carried tilted, spilling some of the contents of a large tankard.

"I should think you would be exhausted from all your troubles."

"I am. But I'm more angry than tired."

Anger fueled him as he downed the toddy Doctor Shaw had ordered. It brought him a restless sleep filled with dreams of things he could not have. Anger woke him to a day of dreary skies and drearier thoughts. It also propelled him out of bed and down to his study, where he summoned architects, carpenters, and racing experts.

She did not believe him? *She* did not believe him?

There was more than one way to skin a cat. He had tried lies and they backfired. He had tried the truth and had no better luck with the woman. Now, he was finished trying. Now, he had a horse breeding business to run, a mercantile to set on its feet, ships and boats to build, and a life to live.

This was a big country. There was room for them both, even if they weren't destined to be beside each other.

With or without her, he was getting on with it.

And he was prepared to fight—her, if necessary —to make all of it happen.

1774

Seige

Chapter Thirteen

To Cathleen's surprise and pleasure Captain Roget attributed the swift removal of his troops to Matthew.

"He's had the warrant vacated, Mistress Cochran. That removes any threat to you or your father."

"And my brothers?"

"I don't recall their names. . . . In any case, 'tis all rectified. His lordship has insisted there is no suit against you. Unless I hear otherwise from a king's minister, that is the way it will read here in the colonies."

Six months had gone by and Cathleen could remember every word, every movement. She could still see in her mind's eye the wart on the end of Roget's nose.

Now, six months later, it was as if Matthew were the wart in her life. His vacating the warrant had come too late to ameliorate the pain the warrant had caused, too late to breach the huge gulf which separated them. She and Matthew existed in the same community. No more.

They saw each other at church services—Catholic Masses held in neighbors' houses because English laws prohibited the building of a Catholic church in any colony, even a Catholic one. They ate across the room from each other at public inns when they went to Baltimore or Frederick to market. They sat opposite each other at the table with other guests at fetes and musicales, for they were liked by the same kind of people. If they did not speak to each other, no one seemed to notice because Cathleen was known to be taciturn to single men and—much to the horror, chagrin, and ire of mothers with marriageable daughters cluttering their houses—Matthew had made it unpleasantly clear that he was a confirmed bachelor.

Quite often Matthew escorted a widow woman or a wife whose husband was out of the colony on business. If he went home with any of these women—and Cathleen too often wondered if he did—he did so discreetly. No tongues wagged. No tales reached her ears.

Less often, but not infrequently, Cathleen accepted invitations from gentlemen of the racing circuit who were trustworthy and reliable. Though she was followed everywhere by Mapes or Mutton, no one saw. From friends who talked, Cathleen knew that speculation about her sexual escapades were not what the women chitter-chattered about when they discussed her over the quilting frame. Her prowess with racing was the sole topic of gossip about her. It was both a scandal and a source of pride with women who hardly had more than a passing acquaintance with the world outside their doors.

Cathleen wore the scandal and pride honorably as she raced her horses against Matthew's in all the flats and all the ovals in Maryland, Virginia, and North Carolina.

And to the delight of Peter, Mapes, and Mutton, Cathleen won more than fifty percent of her races, hands down. From the furious looks thrown her way by the Dunswell contingent, Cathleen knew Howard Bannister, Matthew's new steward, and William Bonney, his trainer from Ireland, were not so delighted. She did not discover how angry Bonney and his son Joe were until it was almost too late.

In fact, Bonney burned, not because Cathleen and Sidhe Stables won so often but because Fenwick cornered Bonney soon after he had taken up his duties. The men knew each other from Ireland, and Fenwick knew the habit Matthew had of rewarding his trainer with bonuses for each win, place, or show.

"You do know the wench at Sidhe jumped a warrant and fled with horses rightfully belonging to the Earl?"

"Course I do. Wasn't I there soon after she did it? I also know the Earl wants naught more to do with the case. The woman walks free."

"Aye. Free to strip your stables of its rightful prizes."

Bonney shrugged. " 'Tis naught to me."

"It will be when you always come up short no matter what you do. And when you're facing the

back end of those halfbreeds time and again,
remember . . . a portion of their winning purses could
have and should have been yours."

The warning did not sink in after the first race that
spring, nor the second, nor the third. But by the time
Cathleen had won every major race in Maryland and
Virginia, Bonney was as boiling mad as Fenwick had
been. He sat at his table one night and calculated the
Sidhe Stables winnings.

"Susan," he said to his wife, "we're being cheated
out of a good living by that Cochran wench, we are.
She should have gone to gaol or been sent back to
England, the way the magistrates wanted to do."

"Not according to the Earl."

"Pah! If she had been, if he had stuck to his guns,
by my count you and me would have pocketed more
than a hundred pounds in bonus money this season
alone."

"A hundred pounds? Are you sure?"

"Aye."

Susan looked at the five faces ringed around the
trestle table. "We could use that money."

"Aye. And I aim to do something about it."

"What can you do? For all purposes, the Earl is
her champion. He won't let you touch her horses, nor
her."

"Short of stealing the horses and having them
boiled for glue, I'm going to cause her so many problems she won't know what's coming next. And don't
purse up your mouth. I will be discreet, I will. I'll
leave no tracks, nor no evidence that it was me what

done it. In fact, when I'm finished, 'twill be that twit Bannister what gets the blame."

Three months later, Cathleen rode into Shifferstadt, Mapes in tow driving a wagon heaped with feed. "Where are they?" she asked. "And are you sure they were mine?"

"Saw some soldiers pulling out of here on their way to Pennsylvania," Joseph Brunner said. "They were your horses they had, sure enough, but the corporal wouldn't take my word for it. Had the signed delivery papers in his hands and insisted the mounts were the ones promised to the army by the Earl." Joseph spit on the ground. "It had to be that Bannister. He's all apple pie and strawberries when he faces you; but he roams these acres by day and far into the night as if he owned them all. Though I've no proof, I warrant he was the one who sold your horses as the Earl's. If we're not careful, 'twill get out of hand, Cat. Then he'll be scooping up anyone's horses soon, whether they carry the Cochran mark, or no. We'll have a local war on our hands, like it or not."

"I don't like it. For me, 'tis already war and I've been stripped clean. Having to go fetch my own horses back! 'Tis an outrage. Well-a-day, two can play at his game. All I need are some of their horses to get back mine."

Joseph's eyes glimmered with expectation of fireworks. Usually he was a God-fearing, quiet, peaceable man; but he and some of the other farmers had already concluded that Bannister was cut from the wool of the cloth which had made Fenwick. Both men would raise the hackles of St. Peter. "Saw a string of work horses over to his Monocacy Ridge pasture land."

"How many did the Army take?"

"Twenty."

"Then twenty will they get. Wish me luck, Joseph."

"Since when does a cat need luck? You have it seven times over."

But she had already used up three . . . or was it four? . . . of her nine lives.

If you counted the bankruptcy of Dunswell, that was one.

Then there was being taken in by Matthew, that was two.

Then barely slipping the noose, that was three.

Then being taken in by Matthew a second time, that was four.

Then the stand-off at the station, that was five.

Saints and angels, she only had two lives left! What a waste.

More wasteful yet, having to gather up Matthew's newest addition to his stables—rough, plain, ungainly, and undisciplined workhorses—the kind the colonies needed most if they were to completely tame the land. She knew why Matthew had begun raising them. She did not know why Bannister had scuppered the English army and her. All she knew was, it took them almost two hours to round and tether twenty horses together. Then she and Mapes had a long, aching trip into Pennsylvania and back.

Cathleen vowed that if one of the Cochran halfbreeds were injured or worked to a lather, she'd sue the breeches off Bannister and Matthew, she would.

After taking a circuitous route into the Mennonite region of Pennsylvania, three days later she faced an irate Captain Vincent Scott of the King's Fusilliers. No matter how much she argued and cajoled to convince him she was telling the truth when she said he had gotten the wrong horses, he did not believe her. Not even when she jammed her hands on her fists and glared defiantly at him.

"Look at them, will you? Those are thoroughbred race horses, those are. Look at their lines, the delicate legs on them, the aristocratic nose, the sheen to their coat. They have been lovingly cared for, they have. And after looking after them, can you rightly think those are workhorses fit only for the military? 'Tis a miscarriage of justice, I tell you!" She revealed the burned-in Sidhe brand on one horse. "Plain as the nose on your face, they are. They're mine! There's none that can claim different."

"The King says the horses are his. He has a bill of sale . . ."

"Not worth the paper 'tis written on, nor is the thief who sold them to the King. And I have proof." She showed him a newspaper article outlining the success of Sidhe Stables and delineating the singularly distinctive mark of the Sidhe horses. " 'Tis an account of the Cochran racing strain and its competitors. And who do you think they be?"

Captain Scott sighed as he read the article. "The Earl of Dunswell, I presume."

"Oh, aye. And there's my mark, the *C* topped with the turban. Right there on that page, you see?"

"I see."

"And there's the damned Earl's right next to it. The one with the crest. They look similar if you don't look close; but they are *not* the same. Now, what do you have on your horses that can tell you which horses are which and whose are whose?"

After careful inspection, the Captain admitted he had aught but her turban and *C* marked horses. "But I cannot give you these, Mistress Cochran. I paid for twenty mounts and twenty mounts I will have. Yours or Dunswell's."

"Ah, but if you own Dunswell horses, then take Dunswell horses."

"And where are we to get Dunswell horses?"

She smiled guilelessly and chuckled. "Well, now, I just happened to have come across twenty of the finest workhorses along the trail, so to speak. And lo and behold, they bear the crested brand of the Dunswells."

"So, Mistress Cochran, it looks as though King George's Army will own the Earl of Dunswell's horses regardless of what we have now."

"I was sure you would see it my way, Captain. 'Tis so simple, after all. I'll just leave the Dunswell horses and take my own back and none will be the wiser."

"Oh, if I'm not mistaken the Earl will be the wiser very soon, Mistress Cochran. What shall I tell him when he or his steward comes galloping in here tracking after you?"

Cathleen winked saucily at the handsome soldier, who was, after all, only doing his duty to his King. "Tell the bloody Earl of Dunswell that he's late to the finish line. As usual."

It was on the way back into Maryland that Cathleen realized this contretemps with the English Army was not an unusual occurrence. Several farmers along the colonial road from Baltimore to Cumberland . . . and through the westward gap . . . had had their horses requisitioned by King George's Army. *Requisitioned,* not sold to the Army by the owner's choice. And now there were rumblings of Rebels in New England and New York acquiring horses in the same way.

When they camped for the night, she walked round the herd and checked each one.

"Not a scratch, missy," Mapes said. "Luck was with us."

"Aye. But will it be with us much longer? War is coming, Mapes. And with war comes dreadful destruction of horse flesh." She shivered at the thought of it. "All of our lives have been wrapped up in one Arabian and his offspring. The feud with Dunswell started over them. I lost my mother trying to bring the herd safe to the colonies. I wouldn't have met Pe-

ter if I hadn't had the horses. None of it . . ." She
snapped a lead against her palm. "I will not see them
go to war, I won't. 'Tis taken six years to build the
strain as they are. I can't start over. I won't."

"Ah, missy. What the King wants, the King gets."

"Not this time."

The meeting she called at Sidhe Station included
all the major horse breeders in Virginia and Maryland. Though she had agonized over it, she also invited Matthew, reasoning that what happened to one
of them affected all of them. But Matthew had not
yet arrived when most of the expected house guests
drove up in their carriages. Four had brought their
wives, as she had requested—women she liked and
had too little time to visit herself. They would stay in
the house in the guest rooms above stairs. The others,
in the cabin where Sidhe Station had had its start.

It was a different cabin now and a new, palatial
house, each designed by her for comfort and peace.
The cabin had been enlarged to three times its original size and was usually Peter's haunt. He stayed
there when he was on the Station. It contained five
bedrooms. One for her father. Four for guests. A
drawing room, study, card room, and kitchen completed the two-level floor plan.

She liked the cabin. But she was more comfortable, more herself, in the house.

To command vast vistas and magnificent views,
and to take advantage of the rising ground to catch

cool breezes, it sat on a rise to the south of the Monocacy River. The simple lines of the two-and-a-half story brick dwelling belied its size because the wings which housed music room and study, library and pedigree room—which Cat used as her office—jutted out like the bottom and top of the letter *C* in a semi-circle in the back. Each of the rooms opened to a central courtyard where a rose garden and small maze took center stage. In the main section of the house were working and visiting areas downstairs and six spacious sleeping quarters with interior dressing areas and comfort stations above. On the first floor, to the right, was a winter kitchen, a dining room which comfortably seated twenty, and a small eating area for her and any guest, usually Peter, where they could be cozy and comfortable. On the left of the central hall were a drawing room, and Cathleen's only bow to domesticity, a sewing room and linen press where she sometimes did terrible needlework and her housemaid mended, sewed, quilted, and ironed. Seven fireplaces—with open hearths both upstairs and down—heated the house in the winter. Large twelve-on-twelve windows, some of which were European-styled doors which opened onto the grounds, lit the interior and cooled the house in the summer. Tonight they were thrown wide to catch the breezes off the river.

Aye, she liked the house. It was larger than Dunswell, but more cheerful, less showy. It was her, and it was a shame it would house no other than she. But that was her life. She had chosen it. Or it had chosen her. She never could reason out which, though it often occupied her mind.

But that night more pressing matters occupied everyone's mind.

She welcomed her guests at the mullion-windowed central front door. May, her Welsh servant girl, took lightweight summer cloaks and coats and hung them on pegs in the large central hall.

"There are refreshments and drinks of your choice in the drawing room, ladies and gentlemen. For those staying in the guest cabin, give your traveling cases to Sean. I'm sure once you get settled you will be very comfortable. But if you need anything tell Mapes or Sean, they will get it for you, they will. Dinner will be served in the dining room in one hour. Meanwhile, we have much to discuss."

While the women sampled the cheeses and corn cakes, cider and dried fruit, the horse breeders gathered at the far end of the drawing room where Cathleen had made a large circle out of armchairs from each room in the house. Though she had not intended it, the gentlemen sat in a pecking order which amused her. She was given center position as befitted not only her role as host for the evening, but also her stature as the owner of stables which produced the most first place winners. To her right and left were the Maryland and Virginia gentlemen who had each taken four firsts and an equal number of seconds and thirds in the twenty-eight races that spring and summer. Luke Masterson of Calvert, Maryland, to her right. George Jepson of Lynchburg, Virginia to her left. An empty chair next to

Luke indicated the man next in order of first place Maryland winners, Matthew. And the circle was completed by Virginians to the left, Marylanders to the right—all the way down to the owner of the newest stables with no horses in first, second, or third places, Frostburg Farms.

And then there was an empty chair for Peter, who was due to return any day from his last "voyage" to the Virgin Isles. He was ready, he said, to retire to respectability. Cathleen thought it had something to do with a young girl from Georgia who was wild and reckless and needed taming if she were ever to find herself a good husband. She smiled. The girl reminded her of herself. *God help Peter.*

God help them all, if they could not agree on a strategy to ward off catastrophe which she believed was coming. She sighed and began, "On my trip back from Pennsylvania, I decided to visit some of the outlying farms and stables, gentlemen, and I'm concerned by what I've discovered."

A knock on the front door made her pause and look expectantly towards the drawing room entrance. She found herself holding her breath until he filled the opening, then the air in her lungs came out with a whisper of relief. She could look at him and not cringe inside. Much.

Oh, saints and angels, who was she fooling? A small cringe was to be expected, was it not? Of course it was. She only then had to get through this evening without stuttering or drooling.

Not drooling was going to be difficult. He looked

magnificent. A trifle older. Some salt and pepper at
his temples which trailed back into his queue. To be
expected, of course. She was almost twenty-eight,
which meant he was heading quickly towards thirty-
three. But his frame did not show his age. He was
still straight as an arrow tall, still broad in the shoulders, narrow in the hips. He yet eschewed fashion for
comfort, wearing his usual brown suit and tan suede
breeches with a shirt much like the one Peter favored.
A pirate in a gentleman's garb. A lone, predatory
animal . . . with breeding.

He smiled at the assembled wives and spoke a few
quiet words to them then ate up the huge room with
only three strides. All the while his heartache-brown
eyes focused on the assembled players . . . and
her . . . aye, on her.

"Accept my apologies, *gentlemen,*" he said, and
she shivered. With such, he was reminding her that
she had not accepted his apologies, nor his excuses,
therefore he would not, did not, offer another. "Problems with a shipment of workhorses to the King's
Army in Pennsylvania."

Oh, dear. Well-a-day, what did he expect? He
should know she would keep or get back what was
hers.

"A mix-up of a sort that has, I am told, been happening too much lately. Luckily, this time it was
straightened out with alacrity. And I want to tell you
all that I will assume control of my stables from this
day forward. It seems my choice in trainers has been
most unfortunate."

Trainers? Not stewards? Good lord, had someone else tried to pull the wool over Matthew's eyes? After all that had happened, anyone who tried it—and she remembered William Bonney and his son Joe—were dolts of the first order. Matthew's eyes had been schooled by better men than them. The dark orbs were far too intelligent and cunning to allow much to slip by.

Since she could do naught to offer more than a weak smile, she was glad when George Jepson rose and clapped Matthew on the shoulder. "We are all well pleased to hear of it, my lord. We all thought Bannister the culprit in things which were not quite right."

"Nay. 'Twas Bonney. Afraid I began a practice he decided was too often too little. A bonus for winning nags. And since mine have had to bow to yours and Mistress Cochran's in most of our meetings together, he decided to even out the competition."

"By removing it," George said. "Ah, the trials and tribulations of horse breeding. Always someone ready to climb over you or bury you in thick dust. But 'tis worth the wear and tear on your hide, 'tis. Never had aught which was more satisfying. Except, of course, for loving my good wife, may she rest."

"Here, here," Masterson said, and raised his pewter tankard of hard cider. "Welcome to the hard times, Lord Matthew. And the good ones, too."

Matthew flipped his coat tails forward and sat in the upholstered horsehair winged chair. Cathleen noted that it did not quite fit his frame. He was far too tall for it. Far too broad. Far too commanding. Why in thunder did she always feel less herself—or more someone else—when he was near? Either she cast down her eyes like a demure maiden or flashed bold glances or stared him down. She could not seem to hold a balance. But she must! She had called this gathering. She knew the dangers. She needed to kindle purpose and action in these men if their livelihoods were to survive the coming conflicts.

"We were about to commence our discussions about what I found on the frontier," she said.

Matthew accepted a tankard of cider from May and nodded. "I camped overnight on Royce Hollister's farm. He had a nice herd of thoroughbreds getting started there."

"Had?" Cathleen asked fearfully.

"Aye. Lost all but five foals to a bunch of no good trappers who called themselves Rebels but will probably take the entire herd into Canada and sell them off for profit. Royce would have put up a fight but the trappers had seventeen Iroquois with them and he had his wife and six children to keep alive. Damn it! He had three placers in the last race. Showed real promise."

Cathleen sat back and studied Matthew as one by one the men told of others who had suffered similar fates, either at the hands of so-called Rebels or from the British Army. Matthew entered into the conversation, interjecting his own outrage, his own interpretation of the events. And slowly—but inevitably—the focus shifted from her as center of the group to him as leader. She wanted to be outraged herself at the turn the meeting had taken; but was it not more important that the men be inspired, regardless of whom inspired them? Besides, she had always known Matthew was a born leader who commanded both from his own energies and inbred knowledge, and from his stature among the men. And though she abhorred it, she also knew she had to bow to the gentlemen, for though they bowed to her ability to breed horses which won race after race, they did not often—in truth, hardly ever—include her in their business meetings. She was and would always remain only a woman in their eyes. An upstart woman, at that, for truth. And for truth, on the surface she knew she appeared to hold her ire; but in truth, she fumed from the unfairness of it. She was as good as they . . . better at what they all did. Why and how could Matthew, who had little more than third-rate horses in his stables, take center place, usurp her own gathering, and do it with such effortlessness?

She folded her hands on her lap so none would see her fingers had curled into fists and stared across the room at the opposite wall, seeing little, hearing it all. And wanting to scream.

Let it go, Cat, a voice murmured in Matthew's head. Lord, she had sat there so silently with those clenched fists that he imagined a volcano ready to erupt. Cathleen was not so docile, nor so equipoised—except on the back of her beloved Firebrand.

Equipoised. Now there was a word for her. *Poised.*
Counterbalanced. *Equis.* Horse. Cathleen, counterbalanced on a horse.

Cathleen, poised in the saddle that day in Ireland.

And not so poised twenty minutes later when she
was wildfire in his arms.

Since Cathleen, he had never known a woman who
made him feel the way Cathleen made him feel. Who
gave everything she had because she did not know it
was dangerous to do, and would not have cared had
she known. Who made him a man loved and cherished. And an hour later snatched it back because of
her suspicions. Suspicions he had planted because
of his damnable, outrageous lies and even more damnable, outrageous offer five years ago. Lies which
had festered, turning whatever they had into wounds
which ne'er seemed to heal. And the wounds produced pain. Awful aches. Terrible tempers. Coruscating countenances.

He tamped down a smile. Her countenance was
certainly coruscating at that moment. Her changing
eyes flashed with withheld anger as she occasionally
peeked up at him. They flashed too at the assembled
guests. Anger there? Aye. By the embarrassed set to
her jaw and the way she bit her lip, or she shook her
head quickly, he knew she was vexed with herself.
He had never thought . . . never imagined . . .

He knew her. Or thought he did. And now she
showed a side of herself he had never seen.

She was jealous.

Cathleen, who never got jealous . . . at least, ne'er showed it. But why?

Cathleen's coruscating countenance crashed with his.

She was jealous of *him?*

She was jealous of him.

Well, hallelujah. At least she was not pretending to be what she had been the past year . . . neutral. He could not stand that. He wanted to see her fire, her fury, her *feelings*. He could work with fury. Hell, he . . . they . . . already had done that. But this aching emptiness . . . this cavern of craving . . . this cipher? Nay, he could not countenance that unemotional living death another day.

Time to play spider to fly. *Come into my parlor.* Her parlor. Drawing room. Meeting. Problem. *Come into it, Cathleen, and set us free.*

Ah, God and her saints and angels, if that were only possible he would give his arm . . .

He rubbed the place where the bone had set perfectly but which now told him when bad weather was coming. 'Twas a constant reminder of that night on the sailboat, that night when he held her gingerly, lay next to her when she slid her bottom over him, tucked one leg between his and arched to take him into her. God! It had been wild and tender, frenetic and gentle. They had loved slowly, deeply, completely.

He wanted that back. He wanted her to finish what she had started to say just before he had seen Peter,

Mapes, and Mutton on the dock and foolishly interrupted her.

Aye, damn it!

They had unfinished business. And he meant to see it finished. His way.

". . . So, I say there must be some way out of this mess. Some way we can protect the strains we have started, protect our investments, and save the horses from destruction by what we are coming to believe is the inevitable upcoming war. Do you agree, Lord Matthew?"

"What? Oh . . . aye, I believe there will be war. Paine's pamphlets have incited too many incidents for King George to ignore. And it is true we will lose our herds to the conflict. Horses have always been the mainstay of an army on the move. King George will not want to import more than he need do. And the Rebels don't have the resources to buy horses, nor do they have enough workhorses or pack horses themselves. We breeders, therefore, are easy targets. Even though I have the least to lose, I don't want to see my small herd or your larger ones decimated. We may never recover if we allow it to happen. I have, therefore, thought of a way to prevent that . . ."

Matthew smiled at George Jepson, who was so old and doddering his body shook. Matthew expected any minute that he would slip off his chair and plop onto Cathleen's blue and gold Turkey rug. But George had looked like that for two years and had always kept his seat. Equipoise. They all had it. Unlike Matthew, they had been born in the saddle and knew

the way to equilibrium of body, mind, and spirit.
Matthew's equilibrium came from that woman at the
apex of the group and the apex of his life. If she
tilted, so did he.

Time to tilt them both upright again.

"When Parliament threatened to tax entertainments, naming horseracing in particular, you had the
good fortune to have an agent in England to squelch
the proposal before it was put to the vote. This is a
different matter. Agents will not help us because we
are bombarded from both sides. Therefore, we must
take matters into our own hands. And there is, as I
said, one possible solution to our mutual dilemma . . .
but it will take careful planning and a good deal of
preparation . . ."

"Anything," Luke Masterson said. "And I think I
speak for all of us, gentlemen?" The men nodded
vigorously. Cathleen unfolded her hands and coughed
very quietly. But effectively. Luke darted a startled
glance at her and actually blushed. "Oh, dear . . .
well, of course I meant you, too, Mistress Cochran."

"Of course. Thank you, Luke."

She looked at Matthew but neither her head nor
her body turned in his direction. He stifled another
smile—something he did often around her—and
tilted his head expectantly. She did not disappoint.
The bite of the serpent was back.

"What *do* you have in mind, my lord? We are
breathless with anticipation."

* * *

I shall kill him. Boil him in oil. Pull out his thick dark hair. Punch that smile off his face.

Cathleen stabbed a needle into her tattered rendition of a sampler and pulled up another broken stitch. She imagined it was Matthew's face, arm, hand . . . any part of his body except the best part, of course. Saints and angels! She stabbed again and this time imagined each and every part. She pulled up the stitch and noted the drop of blood on it. She looked at her finger and the slowly oozing fluid and shivered. She had not felt it, she had been so suffused with images of Matthew's body and its magnificent parts.

She looked up, convinced her thoughts could be read by all the women gathered round the opened doors who each worked on a favorite piece of needlework. But none seemed to notice the quick beat of Cathleen's heart or the heat which seemed to climb from her core to her breasts to her neck. Why did they not gasp? Or chuckle? Or make some comment? She waited. Unable to get Matthew's image out of her mind, she waited for . . . something. But the women merely sat there chattering. Martha Jepson stitched a firescreen of blazing colors to commemorate the burning of the Gaspee in Narraganset Bay— they were fierce Rebels. Susan Masterson put tiny white rosebuds on a fine wool gown for the baby she expected in December. Lorna Polk worked on a unicorn pattern for a vest for her husband Tyler. Jane Fyffe was the only one with knitting; her white cotton threadlike yarn made the sacque she worked on look like dainty homespun. It was a present, she said, for Susan's baby. Her fingers flew as the needles clicked.

Click. Clickety-click. Click. Clickety-click.

Cathleen wanted to clap her hands to her ears and bolt from the room. But she sat there, occasionally taking stitches, but mostly staring into space, wishing Matthew were on the moon. The audaciousness of his suggestion! The nerve of his offering to be their leader! The plan he had made ... well, it was not much unlike hers, and that was what made her so angry, she supposed. That he had usurped her role, had taken the immediacy of the problem and used it for his own purposes. Oh, aye, she did not doubt that he had his own purposes for suggesting ... no, demanding ... that he be sent into the wilds of western Maryland—mayhap all the way through the Cumberland gap—to find a safe place to hide all their thoroughbreds.

I shall kill him. Boil him in oil. Pull out his thick dark hair. Punch that smile off his face.

And all the while she thought these thoughts, she made idle comments which must have suited because none of the women threw her odd looks or gasped in surprise or displeasure. And when the men and women gathered together in the music room to hear a slightly abbreviated rendition of the latest Mozart and Haydn on harpsichord, pianoforte, and harp, Cathleen took her place behind her mother's harp and plucked away as if there were naught but pleasant thoughts in her head, as if God was in his heaven and all was right in the world. Pah!

She knew not what she played but her strumming was lavishly praised. Except by Matthew. He said naught, merely strolled over to the harp and ran his fingers along its strings and down the spine. Oh, dear. He had remembered it, she was certain—that it had been in the manor house. He probably thought she had stolen this, too. She flushed with anger and turned, bumping into Peter, who had drifted in at the end of the recital.

"What's wrong, Cat?"

"I . . . I thought I sounded flat." She evaded his piercing gaze and steadied herself.

"Your music was lilting and rhythmic as usual. 'Tis *you* who is flat, though methinks the lady doth wear a thin veneer. Beware the bubbling beneath, Cat. If you don't let it out slowly, it will burst in one great cataclysm." When she flashed him an exacerbated look, he chuckled, took her arm and tucked it into his. Turning to her guests, he announced, "Ladies and gentlemen, the moon is full and bright this night and the breezes mild and cooling. A stroll in the gardens before we retire, mayhap?"

"The lanterns are not lit."

"Then we will light them," Peter assured Cathleen.

He and Cathleen went before the guests to light the candlewicks in the lanterns atop long straight poles stuck into the ground. The delicate scent of roses mingled with the stronger, headier smell of wisteria vines, which crept o'er nearly the whole of the woods surrounding Sidhe Station. Susan and Lorna found the maze and made a dash for it, at once becoming lost. They giggled and called for someone to find them. All save Cathleen and Peter went to their aid.

"Is the gap full opened?" Peter asked.

"Aye. Fuller than any gap the British have left in the Chesapeake." She snuggled against him. "Baltimore is so loaded with Loyalists and British troops that I worried you would be caught."

"As did I. They increased patrols all over the seas; but the bay was the worst. We had to come in full speed at dead of night. 'Tis luck we didn't ram the three revenue cutters rimmed around the Tangier isles and Wicomico River. We couldn't get near Tolliver's Landing. Luck, too, that we were able to beat a hasty retreat and find another spot to beach our rowboats."

"Peter! You could have been killed."

"Nay, lass. I've more lives than my Cat." He sighed. "My last voyage. But a good one! We finally off-loaded at Miller's Bend on the Choptank and scattered everything over the countryside. The barns are full long before harvest." He chuckled. "Our friends will bring the goods round to the stores in a month or two, when there be no one looking, no one the wiser. Our last voyage was so successful it will take them a good two weeks to get it all to Baltimore unseen. Think of it, Cat. We shall have enough in the warehouses to last the war and make us all rich."

"You and my brothers rich. I only have the station."

Peter's laughter was swallowed up by the thick

hedges of the maze but its tone was nonetheless filled with inordinate glee and affection. "Only? You've made more money with this 'station' than most of the men in this garden. Their wealth comes from plantations and slaves and business ventures. Yours comes from your own labors, your talent with horses, your sense of which of the new foals will be a winner and which should be sold at a great profit merely because of his bloodlines. Lord, Cat, there's not a man in these colonies who achieves the measure of success you have come to expect."

"And he's going to snatch it all away. Damn his eyes!"

Peter assessed the quickly cloaked gleam in Cat's eyes, a gleam he had come to know too well and liked not at all. "I'll bet my share of the profits of this voyage that you're cursing old brown eyes himself. I thought you were through losing time and energy over the man." He studied her face but she gave no indication of what was in her mind and *that* was more intriguing than what she had said, and that she had said it at all. "Now what has brought on this tirade?

"Have you not heard? Oh, aye ... you arrived late." Quickly, she filled him in on the reason for the meeting and the proposition Matthew had made. "He wants the credit. He wants it all."

"Cathleen, regardless of who he is and what he's done in the past, it seems to me that for once the man has a good plan. You must find quarters for the

horses or stand to lose them. And if he wants to scour
the frontier to do it, then you should be grateful . . ."

"Grateful? Are you daft? He has always wanted
my horses. He'll do anything to get them. And now,
he sees the chance and *snap,* I'll lose them sure."

"Cathleen, all he aims to do is find a safe hiding
place."

"Oh, aye? You think that's all, do you, now? And
who, Peter Pence, will be the only one who knows
where this safe hiding place is? And think of the
other men with whom we deal. They are busier than
squirrels in autumn. Do you truly expect any one of
them to drop his busy life, his business or law practice, his political activities, to ferry the thoroughbreds
into the wild? Ah, nay. 'Tis only one man who will
end up taking the bloody horses to the bloody safe
place. Only one man who will have possession of
them for God knows how many months? Or years,
even?"

"Ah, Cat, you have a devious mind."

"Do I, now? Well, if I do, find a flaw in it and I
will take it all back, I will."

"There is one way to insure that none of that happens," Peter said. Lord, what was he thinking? She'd
skin him alive. He'd rather face the bloody British
Navy. He moved away from her and leaned against a
tree, out of harm's way. "You want to protect your
herd?"

"Of course I do."

"Then, 'tis simple. Go with him, Cathleen."

Chapter Fourteen

For the fifth time that morning, Cathleen checked the contents of the traveling cases which hung over Portia's haunches. Journey cakes and dried meats and fruits from Hannah, the cook. A tin of green tea from Mutton. Flint and kindling from Mapes. A ditty bag—Peter's contribution—filled with sewing items and a large slab of sweet-smelling soap. Horse liniment and mint-scented salve from Sean. From Susan and May, a good stock of pledgets and gauze wraps for Cathleen's monthly. Three small wooden plates. One pewter cup. Dried herbs from her garden to flavor their food and brew any medicines they might need. The rest of the supplies were in sacks on the backs of three of Matthew's workhorses. But her rifle and horn filled with dry powder was hung from a sling near the pommel of her saddle. To hand, if they were needed. She only had to remember not to dump the whole blooming horn into the breech the way she had done when she'd first met Matthew.

"Saints and angels," she said to Peter, "how did I let you talk me into this?"

He shrugged and checked the cinch on her saddle. " 'Twasn't me, you know. 'Twas the folderol from those breeder Mughuls."

Right he was. But how had the others had the audacity to demand it of her? Hah! She knew how. They had appealed to her vanity.

"There's none other who can do it, Mistress Cochran." This from George Jepson, who shook with ague or palsy and would not meet her eyes.

"We need someone who loves horses the way you do, who will know the best pastureland, the best water, the safest hiding place." This from Luke Masterson, the solicitor and land speculator, who would have been better suited for the trip.

"The Earl is a good man, but he has little experience in this land. You've been here longer, wrested a good piece of prime land out of the wilderness, traded with the Indians and talked with the French and Germans. I have more confidence in you." This from Benjamin Fyffe who had never met an Indian he didn't shoot.

"Sometimes the Earl can be imperious. If you meet up with the Iroquois, they revere their women. Hell, some of them are sachems and medicine women. Best have a good female negotiator on this trip, in case . . ." This from Tyler Polk who looked at his fingernails the whole time he stumbled through the words his mouth uttered but his eyes denied. And why not? He denigrated every woman in his family, including his mother and wife.

Daft. Fools. Vain and selfish men. Oh, she didn't blame Luke. He had his first baby coming, after all. And George was so frail he could hardly sit a carriage seat, never a saddle. But Benjamin and Tyler were too wrapped up in their politics and pride to make a trip into the wilderness where they might lose their skins. They had not hesitated to send a woman, however. She had analyzed their actions and believed they hoped she'd ride over a gorge and die, then they would no longer have any competition from her stables. She stared off in the distance, to the long weathered building on the top of the hill behind the cabin. The horses, sensitive as ever to changes, neighed and kicked at their stalls. They would have to race with only Mapes and Mutton's help until she came back. Hah! Polk and Fyffe were probably already counting their winnings.

"Why in the hell am I doing this?" Her eyes and Peter's swiveled to Matthew. "Don't you say it, now. I've had quite enough, I have."

Quite enough. The thought which had kept her awake for the past six days intruded again, keeping her wary, honed to a fine edge. The question which did that was: Why had Matthew agreed to let her come?

Aye, he had put up token resistance. Arguing came natural to him, especially when it concerned her. But when the others insisted he take someone and she was the only one available, he had shaken his head, clamped his jaw and folded his arms, mute and un-shakable until they threatened to send her on her own and ignore him in further dealings. He had stood up, towering over her, and stared down in fury.

"You put them up to this."

"Nay, my lord," Benjamin said. "She's only just now heard of it."

Matthew swung round and confronted the men. "Is that the truth?"

Ayes tumbling out of their mouths and hands raised in oath fashion, calmed him down. He turned back to her and nodded. Once. "Be ready at dawn, six days hence. I'll not wait on you."

She'd been ready at eleven the night before, had not slept all the night through, and been up before the rooster crow to visit with her father for a half hour before checking out her mount.

John Cochran was propped in bed, as he was most of the days, now. Mapes slept in a trundle next to him and Sean, in the small room next door. John's mind wandered to his blessed Ireland, his days with Maeve, the early times before the troubles. Twice that summer he had contracted a lung disorder which had made him weak and as trembly as shocks of rye blowing in the wind. His hazel eyes had dimmed to a startling grey, as if a caul had settled over them. She was not sure he saw her, so she always told him she was there. Most times he merely nodded and continued to talk to Maeve. Other times—the worst times—he looked through her as if she were invisi-

ble, shrieked with fright, and flopped back and forth
on the bed until Mapes and Sean quieted him again.

When she left him that morning, he was humming
a song he and Maeve had always liked; but his voice
was so low she could hardly hear it. She worried that
he would not survive until she got back. If that happened, it would be a blessed relief for him; for he
wanted so desperately to be with his love again. And
that, Cathleen knew, could not come until he shed his
mortal body and his soul united once again with his
wife's.

Cathleen prayed to her angels and saints that he
would hold on until she returned. But she did not demand it. She loved him despite the pain he had put
them all through. If he were to go, he would go with
her blessings.

Even if she was not going with his.

She spent a few quiet moments in the stables with
her favorite thoroughbreds, especially Firebrand and
Fortune's Fire. Then she saddled Portia and hurried
to the front drive. She hated hearing the whickering
and neighing of Firebrand and the others. But she
couldn't risk valuable thoroughbred horseflesh on
this trip. She was better off with Portia, the filly she
had chosen. Portia was a heavy crossbreed who was
no racer, but a good, sturdy mount with sure gait and
surer hooves. She had the docile temperament of a
draft horse and the agility of a Turk. She could pick
her way over crumbling rock, and had done . . . more
than once.

When she led Portia to the group awaiting her,

Matthew nodded towards the stables and said, "We'll be back before they miss you."

"That shows you how much you know about horses and why I agreed to make this blasted trip. They already miss me."

"More fools, they," he muttered and walked round to his own mount, Dunston, also not the best in his herd, but surefooted and agile. "Mount up. We have a long way to go."

"Aye, my lord. Ready at your command, my lord."

"I don't like sarcasm, Cat. Don't use it again."

"Then don't give me orders! I'm equal to you on this trip, Matthew; and according to the others, better suited."

He hooted. "You believed them! When they only wanted to get you out of their hair so they could win . . ."

"Enough! I'm going. Accept it and make the most of it."

She turned her back on him so she did not see the flair to Matthew's nostrils, the pursed-lip smile, the cunning flash in his eyes. But Peter did. The men exchanged telling glances filled with questions unanswered, but answers conjectured.

Matthew went to his rucksack and rummaged inside. He had decided long ago to make the most of every meeting with Cathleen. But this trip had only fit into his plans since the night of the great get-together, a week ago, when they were all in the garden. He looked back towards Cathleen, saw Peter watching intently, and smiled. She and he had no idea why she was here, ready to accompany him on his scouting mission . . . but he remembered and thought himself quite clever for what he had done.

On the night of the meeting, he had positioned himself on the other side of the hedgerow in order to hear Peter's and Cathleen's voices and the content of their discussion. Matthew had listened intently to every word and anticipated a quick, violent outburst when Peter suggested she go with Matthew. He had not been disappointed.

Cathleen had sputtered, "Are you daft? He would be weeks on the trail. If there is a trail. In lands uncharted and unexplored by any save Indians and those scurrilous French trappers."

"Weeks in the summer and early fall when the air is clear and vistas breathtaking. Ah, 'twould be hell on earth, 'twould," Peter had said.

"With him? Aye. Did you see how covetously he stroked my mother's harp? Did you, now? He saw it in the manor, I vow. He thinks 'tis *his*. He thinks all I have is *his*."

Aye, Cathleen, love, Matthew had thought at the time. *Now that is the truth you say. All you have is mine. You just do not know it yet. But when you do . . . ah, 'twill be heaven, not hell, on earth. for both of us. This I vow.*

"Go with him, Cathleen," Peter had urged. "How else can you keep him in harness?"

Matthew had heard more sputtering and muffled

stomping, then naught. They must have gone back to the house, he guessed. He rubbed his hands together, smiling like a fool the whole time. He had much to do before the morning. But if all went well, Peter the pirate would be richly rewarded. And to start, he had rounded up old Jepson and young Masterson, then the two others—Polk and Fyffe. Plans were put forth. Stubborn heads became stone heads. Conventions, they declared must be observed. No unmarried woman went into the wilds of the frontier with an unmarried man. Not if she hoped to keep her good reputation.

Conventions and reputations, pah! Mere bagatelle, when business was more important.

After he explained the advantages to his plan, the racing gentlemen had not been difficult to persuade to his side. They did, of course, want Cathleen out of their hair so they could have suzerainty in the racing world. What she feared was true. Hell, most of what she feared in her life was true. The important part, however, the part which forged them—Matthew and Cathleen—together through hate and love, had ne'er been tested as it would if she were with him on the trail.

So another half-lie, half-truth had propelled her into the saddle that morning, ready to brave any number of troubles, simply to find a safe haven for her precious horses.

For Matthew, however, the safe haven he sought

was a respite from the war they had fallen heirs to. A war based on lies. His lies. He shook his head. God help them, he was continuing the damned string of them! But how else to convince Cat to come? She would have laughed in his face, or turned stony, had he approached her straight forward with such a plan. The past always intruded. Misunderstandings became stone walls or great moats which neither could scale or ford. He knew of only one way to destroy both. Blow them up. Give her good reason to trust him again. Then never lie to her. He had the first step in his rucksack. He hoped it began the process of reconciliation. He did not expect it, merely hoped.

He took out the papers which had recently come into his possession and passed them to Peter. "Thought these might be of interest, sir."

Cathleen looked down from her perch atop Portia and said with sarcasm so great it even made Peter scowl, "Were you not anxious two minutes ago to get on the trail? What now, my lord? More warrants?"

"As a matter of fact," Peter said, after a quick perusal, "they are. For Fenwick. Seems he's been dipping his hand into the Earl's accounts. Seems your brothers have been doing the same into mine."

She dismounted quickly. "I don't believe it." She snatched the papers and read through them. There was a warrant, but only for Fenwick, signed by Matthew. The other papers, leaves from ledgers and a bill of sale to someone she did not know, were damning. Her heart felt battered by her brothers as much as it ever had been by Matthew. Reluctantly, sadly, her eyes came up to meet Peter's. "What will you do?"

"To Fenwick? There is naught I can do. He did not steal from me."

"I did not mean Fenwick, and you know it!" Her eyes pleaded for mercy for her silly brothers. "Peter?"

But Peter was not anxious to give her a quick answer, a ready remedy. This was complicated; she must understand that. She might as well stew about it for a few minutes.

"They put the money back with Fenwick's ill-gotten gains. 'Twas the Earl's money, of course. So, the Earl's money found its way into your brothers' accounts. Now . . ." he tapped his front teeth with his index finger, ". . . what would be the best of all possible solutions? Should I give the money back to the Earl? If I do, I would face possible bankruptcy. And after all this trouble we have all had in establishing our mercantile, would that be the best solution? To give it all up and become impoverished because of your brothers?"

Oh, God, no! Not that. That would mean Peter and Mapes and Mutton would be forced back to piracy. Cathleen could not stand that. She swayed, then steadied herself lest one of these men try to help when she felt so helpless. Paul and Donal deserved to be horsewhipped. But the law, if the law were called in, would find another, more deadly punishment.

"I have not asked you for the return of my money," Matthew said to Peter.

"What does that matter?" Cathleen fair shouted. "You have the habit of going to the law for redress, not asking face-to-face."

"Sometimes 'tis impossible to find the faces to ask. They simply melt into the hills and come out only to tease."

"Enough!" Peter said. "There is, here, something more important than your silly feud. There is a cry for justice. Now ... I could exact pirate justice, or the King's justice or ..."

Cathleen was dreadfully sorry she had eaten a large breakfast. It roiled in her stomach and threatened rebellion. "You would not throw them over the taffrail!"

"*Or* there is true justice. What say you, my lord? Shall we call it done and leave it as it is?"

"My very thought, sir. But who will tell Cathleen's brothers?"

"Leave that to me, my lord. I will enjoy this immensely." Peter took a startled, annoyed, sputtering Cat's elbow and helped her back in the saddle. "Goodbye, Cathleen. Have a good trip."

"What are you going to do?"

"Better you should ask the Earl. I believe he had it all worked out before he handed me these papers. And I must say I do not dislike his solution. It will work, my lord. I have no doubts."

Peter did not miss the gleam of pure satisfaction in Matthew's eyes, but did not begrudge the man a moment of triumph. There were far more facets to Matthew Forrest than Cathleen dreamed possible. He had a feeling Matthew had engineered this whole scenario in order to get Cathleen alone, where he might prove to her that her fears concerning him were unfounded. He wished Matthew luck. The Earl had one unpredictable female on his hands. But then, who better than Matthew knew about that already?

Peter chuckled to himself as Matthew mounted and led their lonely pack train out of the station. He laughed aloud when Cathleen turned and glared the fires of hell at him.

"Ah, my lord," he whispered to their backs, "I do not envy you your task."

But he was certainly going to enjoy his. He folded the papers and put them into his vest pocket. He could not wait to unfold them in front of Paul and Donal, and wait for the explosion when they learned who their new partner had become by default, and just how much less of the profits they were going to have to take. 'Twould be a bitter pill to swallow, but a good lesson to learn. They would not soon—if ever—take such chances again.

Chances. Gambles. Risks. He knew personally how men gravitated to them. Hell, he had taken more than his share as a pirate. But he had ne'er cheated his friends, only his sworn enemies or the Crown, and only after giving fair warning. The Cochran brothers had done what they had done in secret, in the dark, to someone who thought them his friends. They had much to learn. He was willing to teach them; but he'd guess they were not expecting the kinds of lessons they were about to receive.

Nor, Peter realized, was Mapes' missy. Oh, what fun it would be for the next month or two, to be a tic on Portia's ear!

Cathleen was oblivious to the passing scene, though she did register that they kept to the colonial road which wound through Frederick and westward towards the Cumberland Gap. She also registered the damp, the quiet, the *silence*. Oh, aye, the silence. From the horses which plodded along behind Mat--thew's lead. From the woods on either side of the road. From the frogs which hopped out, then turned tail and hopped right back to safety. From the birds swooping overhead—hawk, tern, red-breast robin, blue bird, scarlet-coated nutcracker. From *Matthew,* damn his hide.

Portia's ear flicked a fly away and Cathleen wished she could do the same, so easily, to the fly in her molasses.

"Well? Are you going to tell me what you and Peter have decided?"

Matthew laughed so loud the sounds echoed beneath the trees and she heard animals run for cover. She cursed and those sounds were added to his, making a chorus too rhythmic and comic for words. *She would kill him.* She would drop some powdered toadstools into his morning coffee—nay, that was waiting too long. The noon meal would be perfect. Then this trip into the wilds of the frontier would at the least be pleasant!

He looked back and grinned at her and she decided to add sand to his water jug.

"Wondered if we'd get past Frederick before you began your infernal prodding."

" 'Tis not prodding when it concerns my brothers, now."

"Your larcenous brothers."

"Oh, doesn't that give you comfort and all . . . knowing you were correct in your estimation all those years ago."

"And doesn't it give you hives, knowing the same."

Damn his eyes! "Aye," she admitted reluctantly. She held her head proudly, nonetheless. "It may shame me; but that does not mean I do not have feelings for them. It does not mean I do not want to know what you intend to do. If you have not called out the magistrates, then what? Will Peter toss them out without a by-your-leave? What, Matthew? Damn it! Tell me."

The last was so plaintive, Matthew's heart went out to her. He and Peter thought only to play. She bore the brunt of the agony of not knowing. He pulled Dunston out of line and rode up beside her. He put the back of his hand against her cheek and discovered a wet spot. "Cat?"

She jerked her head away. "A speck of dirt, 'tis all."

She swiped at her cheek, then turned to stare straight ahead, a queen on her throne in place once more. Matthew was delighted to see the anger and

pride back in place. It had always gotten her through
the bad times. It would help them through these as
well. "There will be no militia, nor by-your-leave
tossing. I will simply join the firm as a third partner."

"Oh, God," she groaned. "You got your hands on
Cochran goods after all."

"May I remind you that I would not have my
hands on anything had your brothers not had theirs
on it first!"

Oh, aye. He had a point. No bare bodkin, certainly,
with stiletto tip; but it did pierce the heartache and
the thousand natural shocks that flesh is heir to.
Saints and angels, Shakespeare. Hamlet. The cursed
Dane. The bitter gall of bearing whips and scorns of
time, the oppressor's wrong, the proud man's contu-
mely, the pangs of disprized love, the law's delay. . . .
Delay? Not in her case. Too quick, the law. Too
Portia-like. Cathleen patted her mare's neck and
frowned. Now, why did she this day dwell on Shakespeare? Hamlet? Portia?

"The quality of mercy is not strained . . ."

"Was that an apology?" Matthew asked.

"Don't be daft!"

"What? Did I not hear you cry . . . nay, mutter . . .
for mercy?"

"You did not. Nor will you." *Not in this lifetime.*

As he returned to his place, Matthew clicked to
Dunston, a guilty smile giving away his pleasure in
the way his plan was working. She may not have

bent to his will—that would take a miracle or natural catastrophe; and he was not sure he ever wanted her completely at his mercy—but she was at least thinking about their situation. Rather, he *hoped* she was. Else, why had she been quoting the Bard of Avon? Portia's speech. His head whipped round and he stared at the horse on which Cat sat. Portia. Good God! Had she named her that on purpose? It was the only mare which had no Irish name steeped in history wild and warlike. Though, Matthew had never thought the woman Portia had ever displayed the very qualities which she begged from the merchant.

His head jerked up and his heart bammed against his ribs at the connections he had not noticed until now. Did she see those connections? Had she named her mare Portia in jest? Ah, nay. Cathleen was not so devious, so tongue-in-cheek. Or was she?

Portia and the merchant. Portia at the trial in Shakespeare's famous play. Portia—Cathleen—at her own trial as spokesman for her family against the merchant—him.

Well-a-day.

He began to whistle. There was much in Cathleen's nature he was not convinced she knew herself. Much hidden, below the surface, yet pushing, nagging, to get out. And get out, it did, but in convoluted ways which perplexed and surprised at turns. Did they also perplex and surprise Cathleen? He wondered if she ever thought about them, about the ambiguous way she felt, how complex their situation truly was? Or did she ignore it all, merely riding with the vagaries of her nature, never allowing herself to investigate the whys and what-fors of their relationship, only holding onto that awful habit of hating him all the way to her core? Nay, he could not believe that. Not the way she had always responded, even after their dreadful time in Ireland.

She was fair, was Cathleen Cochran. Proud. Wild. Spirited. An unholy terror at times. But always she had been fair. Even now, when she did not want to admit her brothers' faults and crimes, she had accepted the truth. Bitterly. Reluctantly. Finally.

It took her longer to come round than most because she had a character so rich and filled with complicated aspects of herself that a man would ne'er be bored with her as his companion. He expected this trip of theirs to be fraught with calumnies or slings and arrows of outrageous fortune.

Then, if the gods were good . . . if Cat's saints and angels cooperated . . . he might have a chance to show her he was not the devil in this drama the Fates had orchestrated.

Chapter Fifteen

They camped to eat their meager cold noon meal beside a stream which babbled.

They didn't.

Silence reigned once more, since friendship could not; and Matthew was getting damned tired of it. He'd rather she shouted or argued, broke his other arm, or served him poison with his rum. Anything but this cold, contemplative silence. It made him itchy, nervous, and angry. He watched her take little bites of her dried pork sausage and wished he were the damned sausage.

Aye, biting would be perfect.

At his chin. At his ear. At his shoulder. His chest. His thigh.

"Damnation!" He threw down the leavings of his own biscuit and ham and strode away into the woods. "She is the most vexing, most . . . ah, hell."

They had been on the road only six hours and she had already shaken his equilibrium. Merely by eating.

He had been daft to think this would work. By night-
fall, he would be ready for Bedlam, he was so ready
for her. They had to have a truce. There was no other
way they could continue a journey which might take
them one or two months to complete. Certainly, not
three. He did not want to get caught in those mountains when the snows came. He had already spent one
winter in this country and one winter was more than
enough to make anyone respect the power and danger
of the white plague. So they would be together two
months. No more. One month to find a good safe haven and make it ready. One month to return. Then another to buy provisions for the hideaway, take the
horses to it, and . . .

And then what?"

"Damnation, you *are* a dolt!"

He hadn't thought beyond finding shelter for the
horses. But he'd bet his next seven winning races that
she had. She probably even knew which route they
should take through western Maryland to find what
they sought. And he thought he was the leader of this
expedition and the plans he had made for it! Dolt. As
usual when he and Cathleen were together, naught
went as planned. At least, not as *he* planned.

When he got back to the clearing he stopped at the
edge and watched her. She had on her infernal suede
man-skirt; but he was coming to like it on her. It *was*
her. No frills, ruffles, or stays which pinched and
prodded her body into grotesque shape. She had
traded the old ruffled shirt of her mother's for one
which looked as if it had come from Peter. White pi-

rate shirt, with a tie at the neck to allow the neck to
open to cool her chest . . . and breasts. A wide brown
leather belt, from which dangled a small ditty bag.
Sewing or medicine kit, he guessed. Certainly not
powder or rouge. Clocked stockings which were similar to those men wore. Long brown boots. He looked
at them, looked again, and smiled. They were curved
on the outside, the way his were made. She had remembered and copied him. His eyes flicked back to
her face. It was shaded by a large straw shepherdess
hat tied under her chin with a wildly patterned cloth
that trailed down among the dark red curls on her
back.

God, she was still beautiful. Mayhap more beautiful than that day in the stables. She had a maturity
about her, a self-reliance which was arresting. Most
men would hate it. He knew he could not live without it, without her, much longer. Well, there was
naught for it but to go on with his plan and hope to
God it worked.

When he came up behind her, he found that she
was looking over a large piece of parchment which
was yellow with age, grease-spotted, and had three or
four different shades of ink on its surface of meandering lines, shapes of trees, triangular mountain
tops . . .

"A map?" he asked.

"Aye. We should compare this to yours to get the
best idea of what we're looking for."

"Aye. Well, the fact is . . ."

She squinted up into the sun and found his face in

shadow like that day in the stables. Her pulse raced and she had to force it to slow, force herself to push delicious memories down where they belonged and concentrate on what was most important. It certainly wasn't the way he had once made her feel. Oh, bother! Her fingers tingled, the way they always did when she thought about . . .

Nay! Enough of that. They had been talking about the maps. And he had said . . . what he had said, with embarrassment.

"The fact is, what?"

"The fact is . . . I did not bring a map. I thought we would merely explore the region and find what we need."

"Merely explore the region and find what we need? You cannot be serious."

He plopped down next to her. "Sorry. I didn't see the necessity."

"Matthew . . . have you ever been into the interior of this country?"

"Uh . . . nay."

"Have you ever traversed mountains, dropped into valleys, or forded rivers? Here in the colonies or back in England or Ireland?"

"Only when I followed you to Sidhe Stables in Donegal."

"Oh, Matthew." She giggled. "You are either the bravest man I have ever met, or the most foolish. Or the most stubborn. Or the most daft. I can't think, now, which is the way of it and which the worst." She lay back on the grass and laughed up into the heavens, hugging her middle when her sides started to hurt. "So, Moses, which way to the promised land?"

He growled and snatched the map from the ground. He was reading it . . . and a damned good map it was . . . when he heard a commotion coming from the direction of the colonial road.

"Missy! Missy, yo ho!"

Cathleen bolted upright, her eyes wide with terror. "Oh, saints and angels! Let it not be my da."

"We're here," Matthew shouted.

Mapes and Mutton rode their horses into the clearing, horses which were lathered and heaving with exertion. Mapes wasn't in much better condition. The poor man's face was red as a tanager, his chin bobbled like aspic, his hair looked as if it had been raked, and he had trouble catching his breath. And no wonder. He had long ago given off riding horses hellbent-for-lather. Cathleen had to give him a hand down from the saddle. "What is it?" she asked. "Why have you run these horses like this? Is it Da?"

"Nay. The old gent be just as before."

"Then what?"

Mapes wiped his sweaty face with a large pocket square. He spat on the ground, then swallowed a good drink from his water skin. " 'Twere only an hour after ya left when the British come. They inspected the whole damn station, missy. Specially our horses. Said they'd be back, an' you knows what that means."

"Damn!" Matthew had hoped they would have all

the time they needed. "What have you done
with . . . ?" The thundering of more than a hundred
hooves stopped his question. "You brought them
here?"

"Had to. Couldn't let them be taken. Missy would
have skint us all, iffen she came back to an empty
station."

"And what about Matthew's herd?" Cathleen
asked.

"His, too. All the lads worked hard to round 'em
up. They come with us; but they'll have to go back.
We come to go with you, iffen that's what you want."

"And who is with Da?"

"Sean."

"That's all?"

Mapes' face fell. Was she accusing him of not
doin' his duty? Hell, he thought better of missy than
that. "Ah, now, missy . . . we dinna have much time.
The servants from the big house are on duty, and I
sent a note round to the captain. He'll take care o'
things on the station, never you fear."

As Mutton went to help the lads water the mounts
in the stream, Cathleen looked round the clearing. It
wasn't very large. Certainly not big enough to get her
herd and Matthew's in it. They would have to move
on. "Matthew?"

"Aye."

"Bring the map." They spread it on an outcropping. "This," she indicated a broad line which wig-
gled across the whole length of the parchment. "This
is the colonial road. According to the latest reports in

the Baltimore papers, there are workers on it from Frederick all the way to the gap. Here . . ." she stabbed a spot about a third of the way from Frederick to the gap, ". . . is Fort Frederick. Logged walls over a hundred feet long, three man-lengths high, and one man-length thick. Its portals look over the Potomac from a point on Fairview Mountain. It holds over six hundred troops, their families and travelers."

"Bloody hell! And we have to get by it if we're to get through the gap?"

"Aye. Unseen. With my forty-seven horses and your . . ."

"Thirty-six."

"And us and Mapes and Mutton are our pack horses. It won't be easy."

"It will be impossible."

She shook her head and looked up. If Matthew's frown lines got much deeper, they could hide the horses in *them.* "Ah, Matthew . . . there is naught in this wild land which is impossible. Not when you travel with two pirates and fairie dust." Her eyes twinkled and she giggled. "We'll need all the pirate guile and all the Irish luck in the world; but when have Mapes, Mutton, and I not had that?"

Memories flashed from Matthew to Cathleen in sparks from brown eyes to hazel, in gulps from lungs bursting with inheld breaths. Cathleen recovered first and hung her head so she could not see what was all too obvious in Matthew's visage, what called to something deep and dark and demanding inside herself.

She steadied herself and said, "We'll meet up with British outposts, we will, strung all along the colonial road to protect the workers. If we go that way."

"Which means no nights at inns or comfort houses along the way."

"Now I know why I dreamed of tents and camp-fires."

"I don't care if you had nightmares over them. Matthew, tell me you brought tents?"

"Nay."

"Matthew."

"Not tents. Only one tent."

Cathleen looked to Mapes. "Did you . . . ?"

"Nay, missy. We hardly had time to round up vittals. But you needn't mind 'bout Mutton an' me. We'll sleep in the rough the way we always did when we were in strange climes."

Matthew leaned over to whisper in her ear, "My tent is big enough for two."

She ignored him, though his implied invitation stayed warm inside her for the rest of the day. She knew she would have to deal with what it meant, and only a few hours from now; but not then. At the moment they had plans to make and a route to choose.

"I was hoping to make Hager's Town today; but that's impossible, now."

"What, then?"

"There's a new settlement called Boonsboro. Only a few buildings and scattered farms. One British outpost. Ordinarily, we shouldn't go near it. But . . ."

". . . we'll need sacking to muffle the hooves."

Surprised at his quick understanding of their plight, she grinned at him. "Are you certain you were not a frontierman, and all, Matthew Forrest? Aye, you're dead on, you are. Without the sacking, we won't be able to get past sentries or search parties. And we cannot forget the French. They're still hard at work in this land, you know, trapping and trading with the Indians."

Mapes snorted as he sidled up next to Matthew. "Tradin' and terrorizin', more like it; and we pirates know it for a fact. I could tell you stories 'bout that time Pence and us sailed up the biggest river you ever did see. Big as a ocean. Wide and deep and filled with those damned trappers. An' Indians? Whooh! Why does folks gets scared o' pirates when there's wild men more fierce and frightenin'? Specially when they gets drink in them. An' the trappers, they do likes to keep them Indians fired up from rum an' hard cider."

"Ignore him," Cathleen cautioned, "else we'll have no peace, nor time to work."

"Ah, missy . . . you always liked me stories when we was crossin' the Atlantic."

"Around the campfire, old friend. We'll hear them then, we will."

They returned to the map and Cathleen brushed her finger against a long, string-like line which went off the map at both edges. "The Potomac. And these crisscrossed shapes, according to Pence, are dense woods. These flower shapes, cleared acreage, probably tilled and planted. They'll be harvesting soon, they will. We'll have to find shelter for the horses in the woods, near a stream for water. But we'll also need to let them into the fields to graze."

"Not all at once."

"Aye. Only three or four at a time. And that will take us most of every morning we're on the trail."

"At this rate, we'll get to the gap by December."

"Not that long. We could make fifteen miles a day at a steady pace. Since we only have a half day and must find shelter every night, we'll be lucky to do five miles, I fear. Eight at most."

"How far we goin', missy?"

"Straight as the crow flies, almost eighty miles."

"An' we ain't crows."

"A month," Matthew said. "If we knew where we're going; but we don't because we haven't discovered it yet."

"Nor do we know how to gets there away from the colonial road. Whooh! We gots us a mighty long trip."

They decided to put as much distance between them and the station that day as was possible. The horses were dead tired, but Cathleen pushed them more than she thought she would ever push these precious beasts. But her mind was made up and she felt comfortable with it. The horses could recover from overwork and sweats. They could not recover from cannon balls ripping them into shreds.

Using the map, they decided on a route and kept to

it as best they could. They worked hard, keeping the horses in a line four abreast, whenever possible. But in the dense woods, where fallen logs had a covering of years of leaf mold—and disguised rabbit, gopher, squirrel, and raccoon holes and burrows—they had to pick their way slowly. Cat was more frightened for her horses than she was for herself. One false move and a thin, delicate leg could slip on moss or leaves, find a depression, sink into it, and snap in two.

Though he did not know the land, Cathleen thought it best for Matthew to take point; and he did it without assuming the attitude of leader, for which she was grateful. Mutton brought up the rear and Mapes worked to the left. Each rode with rifles loaded and at the ready. She worked mostly to the right; but soon found herself riding all through and around the herd, for she was the best of all of them at calming frightened, pregnant mares; quieting frisky colts; penning in curious fillies; controlling bellicose stallions. Thank all the angels and saints that it was not spring and mating season. She had her hands full enough and all, without that kind of folderol to slow them down.

They were deep into the woods, trying to find a good-sized brook or river when they heard the unmistakable cadences of a French marching song. Matthew held up his hand and rode away toward the noises while she, Mapes, and Mutton quickly herded the horses deeper into the gloom, towards a high outcropping where they hoped for crevasses wide enough to hide at least the younger horses. Cathleen literally stumbled over the cave. It wasn't very large. It wasn't very deep. But with Mapes' and Mutton's help, they got all the foals and most of the mares into the dankness, then dragged as much dead fall of branches and bushes that they could and closed up the opening to the cave. Mapes—groaning at each step, he was that tired and done in—climbed the outcropping which towered at least twenty feet above Cathleen's head. At the top he hesitated, then took to the right, combing the perimeter before venturing further back. Cathleen watched his progress until she lost sight of him. Then she worried.

She worried about Mapes and his "rheumatiz" and how he was going to get down.

She worried about supplies.

She worried that the sun was quickly setting and dark brought other, more deadly predators than French, like wildcats and bears, wolves and snakes.

She worried about her father. Without the friendly visits of Mapes and Mutton, what would he do? How would he fare?

Most of all, she worried about Matthew. Why had he not come back? What was he doing? She had not heard a shot, so he must be in one piece. But the French were known to carry knives and also known to have deadly aim with them. And what if they harbored some of the Iroquois who had broken from the tribe and gone to murder and rape? *Ah, God, saints and angels, keep him safe.*

"Missy! Missy, I found it."

Mapes waved to her from the top of the outcropping and then before she could tell him to wait, like a crab he scurried down the side quicker than she thought she could climb up. By the time he reached her, he was out of breath and his hands oozed from where the sharp granite and shale had cut them. She gave him a water skin and he tipped it up.

"Slowly, Mapes, damn you. It's pouring down your shirt, it is."

"Aye. Aye." He puffed, swiped the back of his hand across his mouth and handed it back to her. "There's a bowl back there, missy."

"We have enough bowls."

"Nay. An earthen bowl." He dropped to the ground, grabbed a stick and drew two circles, one inside the other. "The outcropping goes round the rim. But insides ... ah! There's a small spring, I think. And grazing for the beasties."

"And how do we get them into it?"

"Well, now, that's a mite difficult. I did not see an entrance."

"Horses don't fly, Mapes."

"Mutton an' me'll search round the bottom here. Come on, Mutt. We've work to do."

So did she. Until Matthew got back she was in charge. Not that he would be when he did get back. But 'twas the same thing, and all. He did what he could. She did what she could. Together, if they had that pirate luck and fairie dust, they'd make it.

They had to.

* * *

By the time Mapes and Mutton returned she had a fire going hot, a dried beef stew simmering, and coffee boiled and strained. She did hate the way these colonials drank coffee, grounds and all. The grounds caught in her teeth and she couldn't get the bitter taste out for hours. So, she always strained the coffee through a square of muslin or flannel.

From the way Mapes grinned his gape-toothed grin, she knew they were primed for something. "You found it!"

"Aye. But like the eye of the needle, 'twill be damned hard to get those big stallions through it."

"We'll switch the stallions for the mares and foals in the cave. We'll get the rest of the herd into your bowl."

Mapes looked around. "The Earl not back yet?"

Cathleen shook her head. The more time that passed, the more she envisioned him . . . tortured, maimed, bleeding, helpless . . . and they not knowing where he was. She stood, wiping the visions from her mind, or she would go mad; and now was not the time. Hell, she hardly had time to think; yet think, she must. "We'll get the horses into the bowl and the stallions into the cave. Then we'll eat the stew."

Mapes was right. The opening was so small these horses were bound for glory just by squeezing through. She had to coax so many of them that it took them over an hour to get them into the bowl.

Then they had to herd the stallions into the cave. 'Twas like trying to catch a wet pig. When you thought you had one inside, all nice and comfortable, he heard a noise and bolted. Finally, she decided they had to hobble them, tying weighted ropes around their rear legs. She prayed none would have an accident. If she woke in the morning to sprained equine ligaments, she'd enlist in the Rebel cause and kill every damned British militiaman she could. And then she remembered that if it weren't the British who took the mounts, it would have been the Rebels. She was caught between two opposing forces, neither one of which cared about little things like horses. What were horses, after all, when liberty and justice were at stake? What, indeed? To Cathleen, they were symbols of liberty by the way they ran free and fierce. They were symbols of the justice she hadn't expected and had not gotten in the law suit with Matthew. They were more than home, which she had changed four times to keep them safe. They were more than business, because their safety had cost her her mother and father, and still she loved every cold nose, every rough tongue. They were more than animals, because they were her only family, save Da. They were fiercely protective of her, and she was of them in return. They were loyal, loving, gentle, faithful. And there were none other like them in the whole world. What was a revolution for if it were not to protect those virtues . . . these innocent, helpless beasts?

Helpless.

Aye, that was how she felt as she ladled out the stew and sat next to Mapes and Mutton, eating but not tasting it.

Where, dear God, was Matthew?

Chapter Sixteen

Only minutes after Matthew left Cathleen, the cadences of the French marching song stopped suddenly and Matthew had to ride through the deepest
part of the woods, hoping he was going in the direction he last judged the sounds came from. He prayed
whoever had made the noise had not heard him coming and circled round him. Nay. No prickle at the
back of his neck. He counted on that to keep him safe
until he found the French and saw them on their way,
or at least made damned certain they would not give
him and Cathleen any trouble.

In about an hour he came out beside a covered
wagon, a high, rough pile of logs, and an open campfire on which a spit was being turned by a large, but
handsome woman. She wore a dirty white shirt with
an even dirtier red bodice tied up the middle with a
leather thong. Her skirt was purple—or had been
once. Now it was patched in places with mismatched
squares of gingham and the colors had faded to a

washed-out indigo purple, more violet in some spots. She wore brown shoes, no stockings. Her head was elaborately wrapped with a green and yellow striped shiny cloth, the kind Matthew had only seen used for draperies. She had rolled up her sleeves and her arms were as large and muscular as any man's. She looked as if she could defend herself and the whole world if she needed to. But when he rode into the clearing, she looked up, shrieked, and threw her basting spoon at him, then grabbed for a rifle.

Beside the river behind her, what had appeared to be bushes flew up and men—six of them—jumped from their blinds and came at a full run, rifles aimed at Matthew's head, gut, legs. The oldest of the men stood directly in front of Matthew and tilted his head one way, then the other, assessing the measure of his captive while Matthew assessed him.

Like the woman, this man was as dirty as was possible. His hair was matted, yet tied behind him in a queque. His shirt was yellow with grease spots. His trousers were homespun linen, decorated with tiny animal heads. He wore a vest made of sewn-together snake skins, black boots, and a strange leather hat which sat on his head like a tricorn but had only two sides. In contrast to the nonchalant, even careless way he was dressed, his rifle was shiny and brand new. The other men with him were dressed similarly. They were younger, but of the same general build— square and short with bandy legs and long arms. Their faces were similar, too. Long, full browed, full bearded, with thick lips and thick neck. Seven pair of brown eyes stared at him. Seven mouths worked silently, chewing like cows.

"*Non trappeur*," the oldest one said, then spit a wad of river grass on the ground. He grasped Dunston's halter and jerked his thumb downward. "*Vous! Pied a terre mettant.*"

Hell, the old man didn't even speak good French. Matthew dismounted, allowed one of the younger men to take the reins, and answered the leader in his native tongue. "Have you any food?"

The man stared at Matthew, then raised his busy brows. "What do you call that? There, on the spit? Do we roast horse dung?"

"Any food to spare," Matthew said. "I have been on the trail for three days without food."

The French hunter fingered Matthew's clean shirt and clicked. "*Non.* I do not think so, my friend. You are not saddle weary yet, and you do not stink of the sweat. Whatever you are doing here, you have lied to me. And I do not like lies, my friend. *Non.* Not at all."

He waved his arm at his companions and Matthew found himself grasped from two sides, with a rifle prodding his back. They dragged him to the campfire and pushed him down on a rock. At a movement from their leader, they took up positions around Matthew, several paces away, but rifles ready. The man ignored him and went to the fire. He took a knife from the woman, sliced a piece of meat off the roasting animal, and chewed on it, letting the drippings fall heedlessly on his shirt. When he finished, he wiped his mouth with his sleeve and took a cup from a pile on the ground. He went to the river, dipped the cup into it and drank. He stared off across the river for several minutes, nodding once or twice; and Matthew knew his fate was being decided. Finally, the man approached Matthew, stared at him, then pulled him up from the ground. He pushed Matthew in the direction of the covered wagon.

"Allez."

"Non!" The woman ran up and grabbed the man's arm. *"Non.* She will stay. She will stay."

The man's hand raised as if to strike the woman; but she stood her ground and he sighed, then dropped his arm. "Woman, do not anger me. Return to your fire where you belong. This is a decision only I have the right to make."

She ground her teeth, then like her man, spit on the ground an even bigger wad of river grass. She turned to leave, but apparently thought better of it, because she turned back and put her face up to Matthew's. She sniffed. "Perfume. Pah! How can he help?"

"'Tis not perfume. 'Tis soap."

"Pah!" She grinned maliciously and Matthew felt a her fingers twist around his wrist as she pinched him. "Pah! No meat on him. He will not do."

"He will do," the man said.

"Andre . . ."

"He will do, Celia. Go. Go."

Celia muttered but went, though she kept turning her head to look at them. When she arrived at the spot where Matthew had first seen her, she picked up her spoon, plunked herself down on a flat rock, and began once again to baste the roasting meat by catching the drippings as they fell and ladling them above.

"The woman is protective of her flock," Andre said. "As most women are, I suppose."

Cathleen was. Maeve had been. But the women Matthew knew from Court were not protective of anything but themselves. So he was not convinced that this was a trait passed down from female to female. Nay. He thought it came from something in a particular woman's character which made her more aware of the needs of others than of herself. Something learned, whether from the cradle or from the classroom or from the pulpit. But learned, not inborn. Learned from love, she gave gladly. Learned from being mauled or ordered about, she gave poorly. Celia looked as if her protectiveness had once come from love, but now was given only because the man, Andre, commanded it.

There was something in that for Matthew to ingest and he knew it. But he had not the time to decipher what it was because Andre prodded him into the wagon. They entered single file.

It was dark inside, as dark as night. Matthew blinked but still saw naught until Andre tied up the canvas flaps and the afternoon sun streamed into the interior. Boxes along one side were covered with moldy blankets—obviously where the group slept, or possibly only Andre and Celia. Two trunks divided the wagon in the middle, so there was a division from

front to back. Behind the trunks were piles of old
rags, animal pelts, and food stores.

One of the rag piles moved and popped up. Matthew saw black hair plaited in one long queque. Very
round terrified black eyes. Square face. High cheek-
bones. Suede tunic with fringe and tiny beads sewn
on it in a pattern of pink, blue, white, and black.

A child. A girl.

An Indian girl.

Matthew turned to find Andre's eyes boring into
his with a no-nonsense attitude that made Matthew
know he was in for trouble if he opposed the old,
grizzled man.

"You will buy her," Andre said, emphatically.

"Buy her? *Buy* her?"

"*Oui.* Come," he gestured, "we will bargain."

How in the hell was he going to find Cathleen,
now? It was full dark, he was on foot with a bound
and tethered Indian girl tagging along behind him, he
had a saddle and bridle slung over his back, and he
didn't know where in all of God's country Cathleen
had taken shelter.

Andre had not given him any choice. It was either
bargain for the girl or get a bullet in the back. That
fate, Andre made perfectly clear while they were eating that infernal whatever-it-was that Celia had
roasted. Beaver or groundhog, most likely. But Matthew wouldn't eliminate wildcat or wolf. The bis-
cuits, however, had been light and flavored liberally

with sugar and salt. They had had a tangy taste which Celia said came from the lemon river grass. Settled his stomach well enough. No wonder they chewed it incessantly.

Matthew hoped Andre had forgotten the "bargain" he had offered; but he merely waited until Matthew finished eating before commanding once again, "You buy her, the black-eyed one. Take her with you. She is more trouble than she is worth. My sons fight over her; and she is not yet of an age to satisfy them. Pah. Women. I should never have listened. I should have left her on the trail, even though she was alone. But Celia . . ." He shrugged again and said curtly, "I do not want her. You will pay me for her, then take her to her people."

"Why would I pay you?"

"Enfin. You are not really paying me for her. You are paying me so you may leave here in one piece. *Comprende?"*

"Comprende." So he would have to bargain for his life; and this girl's value was the divining rod. "I will buy her. But I do not think I can take her to her people. I don't know where they are."

Andre shrugged in the way most French of Matthew's acquaintance did. "Leave her in the fort. Me, I cannot go there." *That made two of them.* "The English Army have a . . . what do you call it? . . . where they will pay for my head?"

"Reward."

"Oui." He showed his blackened teeth, what there was of them. "You could refuse, of course, and try to

collect the reward; but I do not think my sons would let you live. Ah, hah!" He sat back, satisfied that he would get his way. "I will take fifty pounds British sterling, your horse, saddle, and rifle."

Two hours and three small tankards of wild whiskey later and Matthew had Andre accepting five pounds sterling and Dunston. He hadn't wanted to lose a horse to the damned British Army, now he had gone and lost one to a damned French trapper. Wouldn't Cat be proud! She'd gloat. Or would she? He thought not. She knew the dangers and wanted them to reach safety without losing their lives and all the horses. They had a damned long way to go, under the most adverse of conditions—thank God it wasn't snowing. They would probably lose more than Dunston before they found good, hidden shelter for horses and men. He hoped not, but he didn't count on anything more than the obvious.

Obviously, he was lost.

He stopped and searched the dark shadows.

An owl . . . several owls . . . hooted. Cries from the feral animals of the forest rang through the night. He listened for a horse neighing and heard leaves rustling over his head. The girl cried out, tugged on her tether, and pulled him into the underbrush. Matthew looked back to see a large brown snake hanging head down from the branch which had been right over his head. Gave him the shivers.

"Certainly glad I brought you."

"Aye. I am glad, also."

"You speak English!"

"Oui . . . uh . . . aye."

She looked up at him with those stark, staring black eyes and Matthew felt his heart flip. She was so sad, so alone. Why had she been with those crazy trappers?

"You will bring me to the fort, please?"

"Is that where you want to go?"

"I would rather go to my people. But that is far from here, for they travel to the winter camp."

"How far? And in what direction?"

"Pardon?"

"North, south, east, west . . . where should I take you?"

"Towards the setting sun. Through the silent passage—what you call a gap, *oui?*—then down into the valleys."

"Well, I'll be damned." He grinned. "We are going in the same direction."

She giggled. "I do not think so. We have gone in circles for a very long time."

Cathleen was certain there were bears clomping through the woods. She knew there were wolves. They howled, damn them. Not that she could sleep, though near the entrance to the cave the horses gave off enough heat to make it comfortable. She couldn't sleep because the moon was high overhead and Matthew had not yet returned. Now . . . why . . . why did it matter so much that Matthew return safely? He was her enemy, was he not? Ah, saints and angels, their friendship ... enmity ... partnership ... call it what you would ... was not easy to understand. But she understood one thing—if he did not come back, she would be desolate for the rest of her life. Because no matter how much she tried to dislike him, no matter how many times they had almost come to blows, no matter how much he had lied, her body, mind, and soul craved him.

She tossed and turned, groaned and pounded the blanket under her head. She fluffed it and turned over. She sat up, propped her head back against a rock, and pulled the blanket to her chin, then closed her eyes. The spots and tiny wormlike things which flashed behind her eyelids drew her attention. She concentrated on them, hoping they would make her sleepy, like counting sheep.

The snapping of branches alerted her that there was a figure moving towards the campfire. She picked up her rifle and horn and prepared to ready it. But the figure was short and moved slowly, painfully. She sighed and gave up the idea of sleeping that night. She folded her blanket and took it with her to the fire. Wordlessly, Mapes poured her a tin cup of coffee from the pot he had put on the hot rocks before they went to bed.

"He's not dead, missy."

"I didn't say he was."

"Ah, but you be thinkin' it. The worried circles under your eyes give you away."

A wolf howled. Then two, then three. "I hate that."

"Aye. Spiders crawlin' up yer back would be better'n that."

The brush crackled and Mapes took Cathleen's rifle, holding it ready should one of the wolves chance taking them. More brush crackled and deadfall sticks and branches snapped like rifle fire.

"Damnation!" a welcome voice said. "Prickers!"

"Matthew!" Cathleen dropped her coffee and ran towards the wild shouts, the wonderful sounds. Raspberry bushes, that was what he was tangled in. "How did you get in here?"

"Walked in. Full face." He heaved his saddle and boots over the bushes. They dropped beside Cathleen. "Stupid, blundering into these damn bushes. But as soon as I saw the campfire and your silhouette, I ran straight as an arrow. And look what happened." He brushed at his cheeks and his hand came away with a small smear of blood. He looked up and grinned sheepishly. "I'm no woodsman."

"You returned in one piece . . . well, almost. That's all that matters." Using the rifle Mapes gave her, Cathleen parted the thorny branches, making it easier for Matthew to get out of his prison. His pristine suit was stained with berry juice and torn in several places. But he was there, alive. "Come, have some coffee. Are you hungry? Where have you been? Did you see the French? Where are they? Will they make trouble for us? And where is Dunston?"

"Hold your questions for a minute," he said. He looked through the berry bushes, squinted and called, "You in there?"

"I do not fight with branches of thorns. I come around."

At the soft sounds coming from behind the barrier, it felt to Cathleen as if her stomach whooshed down to her toes. She had been half sick with worry and all the while Matthew had been . . . had been . . . oooh, she wished she had let a branch snap in his face. "You brought a woman back here?"

"Well . . . not precisely. More like, she brought me." He held his hand out and the Indian girl walked up and took it. "This is Napanna."

"I am called that because I was born after my three brothers and one sister."

"But she's a child!" Cathleen said. She was truly embarrassed at the images she had seen, merely from a voice. Why had it bothered her so much? *As if you didn't know.* She looked at the young girl, her bare feet, her neat suede sack dress, and the way her eyes never left Matthew's. "Oh, Matthew!" She giggled, almost hysterical with relief and love. "You went after the French and came back with an Indian girl. Only you would do that."

Cathleen knelt and took Nappana's other hand in hers. She looked to be about eleven or twelve years old, very thin, with a straight back and long, delicate hands. "How did he find you?"

"He did not find me. He bought me from the wild man."

Cathleen gaped. Her Irish horror at being subject to the gentry rose quickly. "Bought you? Matthew Forrest, I will not allow you to have a slave!"

"Damn it, Cat, it wasn't like that!"

"Missy ... is this the time to be a-yelling? The man's safe. The girl's safe. And we have not much night left to rest in. 'Sides, sound carries right far in these woods. What iffen they was followed?"

Cathleen gasped. "Were you, Matthew?"

Damnation! He didn't know. He had had enough to do trying to find her again. He hadn't had time to worry about what was behind him.

"We were not followed," Napanna said. "I have been with the wild man several moons. He and his sons soon find themselves lost when they wander too far from the river. They are not good hunters. They are slow and plodding, like the beaver they skin and eat. They are not swift and cunning like the wolf ... like this man."

"Matthew?"

"Aye," Napanna said. "He followed the stars, like my people. That is very cunning. And he knew to take his boots off and walk lightly but swiftly. That is very wise. You are lucky to have such a man as your leader."

"Matthew?"

"You sound astonished, Cat. There are some ... even if they are children ... who may know me better than you." With that, Matthew turned his back on Cathleen, picked up his saddle and boots, and walked away. "Where are we bedding down, Mapes? I'm damned tired."

* * *

Having him back wasn't the answer. Cathleen still lay awake, staring at the roof of the cave, listening to the soft whiskering snore sounds of horses sleeping, feeling the warmth of the tiny body curled up next to her. Having him back—and insulting him—had put them at the infernal distance, the one which had shortened considerably when they had had to work together. Why had it astonished her—aye, he was correct, she was astonished—that Matthew could read the stars? Why had she thought the girl had found them, not him? *Ah, Cathleen Cochran, your Irish soul is a warped one.* Warped by time and circumstances, warped by history and enmity, by folklore and fable. To her people, no Englishman was able as an Irishman. Yet Cathleen had scoffed at such nonsense. She had argued often with her da and her brothers that an attitude like that was daft. A man had to be judged by what he did, not by who he was. Aye, by what he did. Which was why she had felt gutted when Matthew Dunn had turned out to be a shadow man of no substance. He had lied. He had played games.

He had hurt her.

Her, Cathleen Cochran, the Cat . . . who had ne'er been hurt by any man because she had ne'er allowed herself to be hurt. Her position in the community had made her remote from them and their customs. She had been one of the few daughters of landed *Irish* gentry. She did not fit into her own family because her father had been more successful than his cousins, brothers, father. And since she did not fit with the villagers, they kept their distance, though they were not unfriendly.

Others were unfriendly, even mean-spirited. Those who had been wealthy for generations saw her and her family as climbing above their station. They acknowledged the wealth of the Cochrans; but Cathleen learned early that wealth did not mean equality. She was not equal to them, and she knew it. Consequently, she had stood aloof from both villagers and the gentry. It gave her an advantage, she thought. She was better able to view the games people played to gain a spouse . . . and Cathleen hated each and every one of them. Hated that a girl or woman had to be someone different for each man who called, or face spinsterhood. Hated that spirit in a woman was abhorred by those who did not have it, and that having it made Cathleen almost untouchable.

She knew those things . . . felt those things . . . before the bankruptcy. During and after it, she was nineteen, twenty, twenty-one—at her prime—and should have been one of the stars of the social scene. Men should have flocked to bid for her hand. Should have. But did not. An impoverished Irish girl could not interest a titled or monied Irish man. An impoverished Irish girl who had once lived in a manor house frightened away ordinary Donegal villagers. God might be in his heaven; but all was not right in her world.

She retaliated in the only way she knew. She became what she wished all women could be—wild and free. She was more than woman, the villagers said.

But that was her protection and her escape. The wonderful thing was that once she began to let go of all the strictures of her life, she began to truly live.

Thus, when Matthew Dunn came to Dunswell, Cathleen was beginning to heal from rejection of all kinds. And when Matthew did not reject her, but encouraged her . . . when he flirted with her, made love to her, he magnified what she had already begun.

She *felt* for the first time in years.

She laughed. She played. She teased. She breathed him in, and loved him.

But she did not know him.

Not because he told her lies. Though she had given him no sign lest he try to take advantage of her vulnerability, over the years she had come to terms with the reasons he had done so. Nay, she did not know him because she . . . saints and angels, what a horrible jest! . . . *she* had not wanted to look beneath the surface. She had had an inkling that something was not quite right about him, but she had forced it to the back of her mind and gone on. Because *she* wanted to. Because she wanted her world, her life, to be what was in her head. She wanted the man she loved to be . . . what he wasn't.

He was not a common field hand. He was not a common horse trainer. He was not a common wayfarer.

He was not common at all.

He was complex, unique.

Peter—who liked Matthew better than he liked most men—had told her about Matthew's father and why Matthew had bought himself a title. She knew about loyalty and family duty. She knew about responsibility. She also knew about subterfuge. She had used it herself for purposes not unlike Matthew's. Yet she had not credited Matthew with any of his best qualities. She had been hurt, and she fought that hurt in the only way she could. Because she was who she was . . . because she would not be a passive victim the way her father had been . . . she struck back, she held on to her rage, she refused to see what was right before her eyes.

Of course Matthew could read the stars. He was a merchant, with a fleet of ships. He sailed his own boat. If he did not know how to read the stars, he would for a fact be a poor, bad merchant and sailor. And of course he had not brought Napanna here as his slave. He would not do such a thing. He was honorable. Kind. Compassionate.

He was loyal.

Though she had made his life miserable, unlike everyone else in her life, he had not distanced himself. He had done exactly the opposite and traveled half around the world to find her. Not to serve a warrant for her arrest, but to make her part of his life.

And she had struck back by ridiculing him as often as possible, in as many ways as possible.

It had to change. This war of theirs was now one-sided and dangerous. It had gone on for so long it was changing her into someone she did not like. Tonight, even Mapes, who thought she could do no wrong, had stepped in and stopped her from mocking Matthew.

A soft waft of warm air tickled Cathleen's hair and she raised up on one arm to find Firebrand nosing her. She reached up and stroked the stallion's black blaze. He curled back his lips, put out his tongue, and horse-kissed her forearm.

"Well, at least you love me, boyo. Even if I don't deserve it."

But would he love her when she took him on the most dangerous journey of his life?

Her sigh was more sob than vexation. Firebrand was not the only "he" she had in mind.

Fall 1774
Alliance

Chapter Seventeen

Firebrand whickered and nudged Cathleen, clicking his teeth forcibly. "Aye, boyo," she whispered. "We'll get you out, we will." Though how she could get herself out of her problem, she did not know.

She eased herself away from Napanna's sleep-limp body and pushed aside the deadfall she and Mapes had used to fill in the cave entrance. It was morning and she had not had one moment's sleep. She sighed. Her bones ached. Her eyes burned. Yet, she did what had to be done to begin their day. One-by-one, she removed the hobbles from the stallions and led each into the woods, finding a good spot with a small brook and some measure of grass. One-by-one, she hobbled them there so they would not roam when she went to get the next of them. Her body screamed from lack of sleep and a cold night on the hard ground; but she kept working because she could hear Matthew, Mapes, and Mutton tending to the two herds inside the bowl.

She had Fortune's Fire almost out of the cave when Napanna stretched, sat up, and squealed with delight. "Oh, missy," she said, and came to pet the stallion's soft nose. "What are they? They are not Indian ponies. And they are not like those fat, scruffy things the old man and his sons rode." She walked round Fortune's Fire as she exclaimed over his attributes. "Thick, black manes. Long, soft black tails. Black stockings. And a black star on his nose. Red coat. So shiny and soft." She threw her arms round him and hugged Fortune's Fire until she was breathless. "He is beautiful, *n'est pas?*"

"Very beautiful, he is, aye, Napanna. That is why we are here, to keep him beautiful." As she led Fortune's Fire towards the brook, Napanna walked beside her, carrying the rock to be used for hobbling. Cathleen told of the way the Irish-Turk breed had begun, all the problems Cat had had keeping them together . . . then she explained that war was coming and the dangers of it.

"You do not have to tell me of war," Napanna said. "My people are always at war. That is why I was alone on the trail when the old man found me. The old ones of my tribe told how the English pushed my people—what they did not kill—from the banks of the three rivers way into the Ohio Valley, close to the land of their enemies. As for me, when my father was forced by the white man to get off the land he had always known, he had to find new winter quarters quickly. Though he did not want to, he took us with him. But the land he found was rich and good for planting. Your people came closer and closer to us. Possibly they were frightened, afraid many more Indians would come to take shelter near us. They were right. My father was already making plans to invite others of my people to come and share the bounty with us. So, to stop that, frontier settlers killed my family, separated me from my brother and sister, and put me to work as a house slave. Then only a year later a Mohawk raiding party killed the settlers. My brother and sister died fighting to save those who had enslaved them. The Mohawks found me and a yellow-haired girl. They took the yellow-hair to sell. And though I pleaded, they refused to take me along. They did not want any Delaware Indian girl because she was not valuable. I had been on the trail four days, trying to find a band of my people, when the old man picked me up. Now . . ."

An expression of defeat clouded her eyes and Cathleen knew how she felt. That same expression had clouded Maeve's eyes . . . and her da's. Cat could not stand to see one so young, so overcome by the tragedies of life. Cathleen could imagine the sorrow of losing one family . . . had she not already lost hers? But to lose family and community and nationhood. To be enslaved, and then shunned by Indians— even though they were not of your nation? Nay, Cat could not imagine that. That was more tragedy than one small body should be forced to endure. She thought of Ruth in the Bible. *Wither thou goest* . . . the child needed a family. They—herself, Matthew,

Mapes, and Mutton—were not much of a family. But they were better than none.

"We shall take care of you until you decide you want to leave us. We will expect you to work, but no more than what we ourselves would do; and no more than a girl your age and size is suited to do. I promise you, too, that no one will pick you up and cart you off, nor will any attack us."

"You cannot promise that," the child said with grave, adult dignity. "This is a dangerous world. But I am happy to be with you now, missy."

They came into the small clearing where Cathleen had taken the horses. Napanna stopped, looked from one to another in the band of stallions, and gasped. She dropped the rock and ran to Black Turk, circled him, then ran to Firebrand and circled him. She did it to each of the stallions—all seventeen of them—then plopped onto the ground, drew her legs up, set her head on her knees, and with the wildest eyes and biggest grin Cathleen had ever seen, watched them munch grass.

"So many. So many," Napanna whispered over and over.

Cathleen chuckled. If she thought this was *so many*, wait until she saw the combined herds. "Will you watch them while I prepare breakfast?"

"You want *me* to take care of them?"

"If you would, please. I will bring you your breakfast when it is ready."

"*Oui!* Aye! I will watch them closely."

When Cathleen got to the campfire, Mapes had already started the coffee and corn cakes. He handed Cat a cup of the beastly strong brew and she sipped it so the grounds wouldn't get into her mouth. She stretched, then looked towards the woods where Mapes had made their comfort station the night before. "I'll be back," she said. When she did return Matthew and Mutton were also at the campfire, drinking coffee and eating corn cakes with slices of fried pork. Embarrassed by what she had done the night before, Cathleen avoided Matthew's gaze, but she could feel it on her. She knew she should apologize. It was only right, and expected. Her heart said, *do it*. Her mind said, *wait*.

Heart and mind warred and her head won. She watched silently as Mapes fried all the fresh meat they had brought so it would not become rancid. They had thought to bargain with it in Hager's Town for more rye or oats. But now, with patrols and French and Indians to keep watch for, they could hardly go easy-as-you-please into a settlement. They would have to keep to the woods, use what supplies and food they had brought, and do it slowly or they would starve. Which was why Mapes cooked all they had. When he finished, Cathleen selected venison for her breakfast. She took corn cakes, two slices of pork and one of venison to Napanna, who ate them with such relish that Cathleen wondered when she had last had a full meal.

Mapes came up behind them. "We have to get going, missy. Can't stay too long in one spot, the captain always said. Makes it too easy to be found."

"Napanna will need a mount. But we don't have a saddle for her."

Napanna's eyes grew even wider, if that were possible. "You want me to ride *them?*" she asked, indicating the stallions.

Mapes chuckled. "She don't know about the others, does she?"

"Not yet," Cathleen admitted.

Mapes appeared to enjoy having this child to tease. He winked at Cat. "Let's you and me just surprise the mite."

Napanna was more than surprised. She was astounded. And entranced. When they urged her to choose one for her own mount, she went up to a small pied black and gray filly from Matthew's stables and put out her hand, then blew into her nose. "So she can learn who I am."

"You may have my saddle."

"Oh, no, missy. I am Delaware. I like to ride without a saddle. A blanket will be all I need."

For the first time that morning, Cathleen addressed Matthew. "Will the filly take Napanna without a saddle?"

"Aye," he said bluntly. "I'll give you a hand up, Napanna."

But the words were not out of his mouth when the girl vaulted onto the filly's back. She patted the neck and asked, "What's her name?"

"Contessa."

Napanna tried it out. "Contessa. Contessa. I like

it." She nudged the filly with her knees and Contessa responded. "Do you have extra bridle?"

"Nay. But Mapes and I should be able to fix you a rope mouth and nose piece, and reins." Matthew went to get some rope from his supplies and came back with a knife and small strips of leather. Within minutes Napanna had a crude but effective bridle and could control Contessa quite easily.

They mounted up—Matthew riding his stallion Mandrake, Cathleen aboard Firebrand, who, she hoped, would help her keep the other stallions in line. Like the day before, each took the place for which they were best suited. They kept to the woods, staying away from the clearings where they would more easily be spotted by British patrols or bands of Rebels intent on mischief making. Cathleen was run ragged by the horses . . . the stallions, most of all . . . because they hated having to trot when they were made to gallop, hated trees which penned them in, hated the slow pace, the jostling bodies around them. They nipped at the mares and foals when they came too close. They broke ranks often and because Cat had had no sleep, she had all she could do to keep them from bolting away through the woods. Her arms felt as though she had hobbles on each wrist and more on her upper arms. Her thighs trembled. Her eyelids refused to stay open, and several times she felt herself slipping from the saddle. She righted herself in time; but Mapes, who watched her, wore a frown grizzling his wee eyes and a guarded expression on his face. So she knew 'twas trouble when he rode hell-bent-for-lather through the trees.

She did not care. She was that dead tired.

Firebrand whickered and flicked his head up and down and her eyes popped open. Had she been asleep in the saddle? Well, it wouldn't be the first time. She patted the stallion, mumbling, "'Tis fine, my boyo. We'll fair just fine."

"Not the way you look," Matthew said. "And not the way you don't look. I rode up and you neither saw nor heard me. Anyone could pluck you up and steal you away."

"Ummm." She did not protest when he lifted her as he had once done and brought her to sit in front of him on Mandrake. He put his left arm around her and tucked her head under his chin. "No sleep," she said.

"Sleep now, Cat."

"The horses . . ."

"Napanna is a wonder. She'll help. We'll manage." He smoothed her hair and kissed her brow. "Sleep."

The lovely rhythm of Mandrake, the warmth of Matthew, the sway of the stallion under her, the scent of horse and Matthew. She loved it all. It lulled her and she wrapped her arms around Matthew, leaned into his body for balance, and slept. Her dreams were filled with the man who held her. Filled with the first time she had seen him, the first time they had made love, the first time she had hated him, the first time she knew she loved him. She dreamed of wide meadows surrounded by mountains, of a black-haired Indian girl bouncing a black haired baby on her knee—a black-haired baby with hazel eyes. She dreamed of black rocks so shiny they gleamed in the dark. Most of all she dreamed of Matthew's hands. How he had raised them in mock horror when she aimed the musket at him. How they had callused from working in her mother's fields. She dreamed of the way they gently withdrew Chuchulain's back legs during his birth. She saw them scything rye in the fields, picking beans in the garden, hilling up the potatoes. She saw how his nails were squared off cleanly, like a gentleman's; but he did not use them like a gentleman ... especially, wondrously, on her. And her heart filled with joy when she relived how his gentle, capable hands worked the soap into her hair, caressed her breasts, explored her fiery moistness.

She was just beginning to remember what his lips had done to her when she dimly heard Matthew's voice. What was he saying?

"Cathleen, do not do that. Stop it, Cat. Wake up, now. God, Cat, please wake up."

Was she not already awake? Touching him, caressing him. As he rode in the saddle, his trousers stretched across his seat. She loved how his taut muscles felt as they rubbed up and down against the leather and her palms. She loved how his thighs bulged as they gripped Mandrake's flanks. His, Matthew's flanks, were like iron; and covered with suede they were almost, but not quite, thank God, like the other part of him with iron inside and softness surrounding. She loved how his middle felt, rippling under her fingers. And she loved his chest, it was so broad and joyously male. But she did not like the shirt. If she could only get it off . . .

"Cat, I tell you what . . . let's save this for tonight, when we're alone . . . when the damned horses aren't bolting for freedom. Can you hear me, Cat? Or am I doomed only to have you love me in your dreams?"

"If I were dreaming, you would be kissing me. Why aren't you kissing me?"

"Ah, God, Cat. You try the patience of a saint."

She raised her head and smiled, though her eyes did not open yet. "You are not a saint, Matthew." Her lips brushed over his chin, up to find his mouth. She tasted it. "Ummm. No saint. But delicious, nevertheless." He pulled her in tighter against him and she felt it once more, that unmistakable mark of a man aroused. "Ah, ummm. Very delicious."

He groaned and with one fierce move, captured her mouth, delving deep inside it, mating with her the only way they could. She lost the will to breathe and did not care. She lost the will to think, and was grateful for the only thing left—feeling. His breath was hot with desire. His tongue, soft and raspy all at once. His teeth smooth and gentle when he nipped her bottom lip. His lips rough, then gentle, then rough again.

He pulled away and gulped a great lungful of air. "Cat, wake up."

"I have been awake."

"Then stop. For God's sake, stop."

"For your sake, I will stop." She opened one eye and peeked at him. "Are you angry?"

"Oh, lord!" He looked down at her and his eyes shone with an emotion so intense Cathleen felt as powerful as Chuchulain when he fought with the sea. "I should spank you."

"Now there's an idea!" She laughed when his eyes rounded. "Remember you offered."

Clouds descended, and not from the sky. "Cathleen, you say that now ... you have said similar things before ... but you always counter them with words and deeds so deadly, they make me wonder whether this is only another form of torture for your enemy."

"You are not my enemy, Matthew Forrest."

"I'm not?"

"Nay. Well, not any more."

"When did it change, Cat? Five years ago? Or three? Or last week, last month, last night? Or mayhap it was five minutes ago? And when will it turn back to the hatred and fury of all those years which have passed us by? Years we could have had together if you hadn't ..."

Irish anger was not easily damped but Cathleen gave it a try—and failed. "'Twas not always me, alone, Matthew Forrest! You contributed your share."

"Aye, Cat. But that was long ago and far away, and still I don't know whether or not you trust me. I don't even know if you like me."

She gulped. Her throat closed up, her mouth went dry. How could he not know? "I love you, Matthew."

"Aye. I do believe that. Because I love you, too. But love and liking are not the same thing, Cathleen."

How could he do it? How could he take her to the heights and the depths in the space of a heartbeat? "You sound as if you have had experience loving and not liking," she said with bitter sadness.

"Sometimes," he admitted. "Sometimes when you will not listen. When you will not see. When you block your ken and all that happens round you. You are stubborn, Cat."

"Aye. As are you, Matthew."

He chuckled. "Aye." He rubbed his chin against the crown of her head. "We are a pair, we are."

"Like oil and water."

"Nay. We mix much better than that. I would say we were thunder and lightening."

"Warm spring breezes and icy winter gusts."

"Oh, not that awful, Cathleen. I prefer stallion and mare. Air and fire. Rain and desert. One does not exist without the other."

He frowned and Cathleen could see in his eyes that he wanted to get the words to say what he meant. She smiled inwardly. They had not talked, thus, in years. She had not given them the chance. But now she wanted to hear what he thought, how he felt. She wanted to know this man whom her body loved, her soul cherished. Only her mind rejected him. If her mind could see him as he truly was, then would not the three parts of herself meld, to hold what was right, truth, need? She thought so. She hoped so.

Matthew brightened as the confusion melted. "Nay, that is not quite right. One could exist without the other. But the mare would not procreate, as she is intended, without the stallion. The fire could not flame bright and hot and high without lots of air. And the desert could not bloom without the rain. It remains parched, unfulfilled. Without its opposite, a thing exists; but it merely moves through a barren life, its existence poor, indeed."

"Is that how you feel about us?"

"Aye." He tipped her head up and kissed her gently. "I only wish it were the way you felt, Cat." He looked round them and found Firebrand trotting nearby. Though he was reluctant to let her go, the others were having a hard time working the herd without her. "Are you ready to help us again?"

She shook her head. "I would like to stay this way forever."

"Not on your life. I have better places for you than in this damn saddle." He nuzzled her forehead as he cut into the herd and trotted up beside Firebrand. "One of these nights, I'd like to see you in a bed, waiting for me."

"Ummm. Nice. But we aren't likely to see a bed for a long time."

He lifted her and with a grace which was all his, he turned her and settled her into Firebrand's saddle. He touched her cheek and it was the breeze of a zephyr, the brush of velvet. "I'll settle for a blanket in my tent."

Before she could answer, he cut through the herd and up to the front, leaving her smiling, with visions of what it would be like on his blanket in his tent.

Chapter Eighteen

It was during noon meal that Mapes presented them with a major problem. "We've been lucky so far. Enough grass and water for them horses. But them racers are used to a mixed feed—oats, rye, corn, molasses, grass. We'll need to get along to a settlement or buy some feed offen a farmer along the way."

"We can't all go," Matthew said. "And we dare not take the herds close enough to be seen."

"We also need to find the Potomac," Cathleen offered. "Since we can't stay close to the colonial road, the only real landmark which cuts across the west to the gap is the river."

"And that will bring us right under the nose of the sentries at Ford Frederick," Matthew said.

"Not if you cross the river and go through the gap on the other side of it," Napanna said.

Cathleen patted her hand. "That won't do, Napanna. We would have to ford the river or use a ferry. We can't take all these animals on a ferry without being found out. And we can't cross any other way because the rapids in the Potomac can carry a man or horse to his death."

Napanna giggled as if Cat were daft. "Oh, how lucky to have this Indian girl with you. She can show you how to cross like an Indian."

"And how is that, little miss?" Mapes asked. "Fly like the great spirit?"

"Nay. Walk across the water."

Mutton chuckled silently, the way he usually did. Cathleen expected him to leave it at that; so when he opened his mouth to speak she was stunned into silence herself.

"This is not the Sea of Galilee and we are not the Christ, nor St. Peter, who walked on its surface," Mutton said in a deep bass voice that sounded as if it should be singing in cathedrals. "If we were, we could multiply our loaves or turn grass into rye and oats. Then we wouldn't need to cross the river or go into town."

"I do not know this Christ," Napanna said. "But if he can do what you say, he is as great a man as our sachems, who taught us that even a small child such as I, can walk across the Potomac. I have walked it many times."

"How many, little miss? You are not old enough to have made that many trips to the frontier."

"Six times, I have crossed, Mapes. My whole family crossed. Our band crossed. Our horses and mules, our wagons and dogs. All crossed. And not once have I seen any man or beast washed away to his death."

Her eyes crinkled with sly humor and Cathleen saw much of herself in the girl. "We are lucky it is late summer and not spring. In spring it is impossible to find the Indian water trail because the river swells from mountain melt. It rises, covering the old Indian magic ... is that the word? ... where we can walk on water."

With a glance, Cathleen and Matthew decided to indulge the girl rather than hurt her feelings by showing they thought she told stories better than Irish folktellers. They also decided to send Mapes and Mutton into Boonsboro for sacks of oats and rye.

"May I go with them, please?" Napanna asked. "I have not been to a village since I was this high," she said, indicating with her hands, half the size she was.

Matthew shook his head. "You will attract attention."

"Not if the little miss slipped in alone. No one pays mind to Indian children," Mapes said. "Let her come."

Which meant they had to find a place of concealment for the night. They finally decided on a valley which had steep sides that showed no signs of worn-down trails—they did not want to be surprised by Indians, settlers, trappers, or British patrols—and was overgrown with bramble bushes. It had an entrance only three horses wide where Matthew could pitch his tent and keep watch, plenty of water from a brook, and several patches of good grazing land.

"We can't stay here more than two nights," Matthew warned Mapes as the three excitedly prepared to leave. He handed the old pirate three gold sovereigns to pay for the feed. "Get in, get out, and get back."

"Aye, your lordship. Just what the captain would say." He took the reins of one of the pack horses— Mutton had the other—and led him out of the valley. He and Mutton had rifles, shot, and powder horns, and long, lethal knives tucked into their belts. Napanna carried a pistol and their foodstuffs in bags slung across her saddle. They looked no different from any other frontier travelers, but Cathleen worried nonetheless.

As Matthew worked to pitch the tent and start a fire, she worried that a curious settler would ask too many questions, the answers to which Mapes would be unable to give. She worried that a child such as Napanna would be overwhelmed by the conveniences and trappings of settlement living and chatter away without thinking. She worried that a purchase such as they were attempting would bring notice. Who bought oats and rye unless they had horses? And if there were British patrols in the area, they could hear about it and . . .

"If that frown gets much worse, your eyebrows will grow together. 'Tis not a pretty sight." Matthew put his arm around her and breathed in her scent. Even though they had worked in the hot sun, Cathleen still smelled of the heather-scented soap she used to wash herself. He loved the combination of her soap and the heady scent of musk and sweat-damp hair and linen. "They'll be fine. Mapes is an old hand at this, else he would not have survived as long as he has. And I'll bet you my next colt against your next filly that Napanna will forget she has a tongue, her eyes will be so wide with awe." Though he would have liked to take Cathleen in his arms and make her eyes wide with awe and her tongue playful and eager, instead he patted her rear. "Come, Cat. These horses need grooming."

"Now? Here? We've weeks ahead of us on the trail. They're going to get dirtier than they are."

"But not matted and scruffy. They deserve better than that, don't you think?"

"Nay. I think 'tis a good camouflage to keep them dirty and scruffy, I do. If they look valuable, and we're found out, then we'll lose them for sure. Besides, there are more important things we have to do and all."

"Such as . . . ?"

"Look for stones wedged into their shoes and remove them. Look for loose nails and replace them. Clean out anything from ears or eyes which could cause irritation or sepsis. Wash cuts. Check for sprains or swelling. They've ridden over the roughest ground any of them have ever seen. And we can't risk losing one of them and all because we neglected ordinary care."

"Cat, we've over a hundred head here."

"Then we'd best begin."

"But I'm no smithy."

"Nor am I. But we shall learn."

They worked hard all the afternoon and found several loose shoes, which they mended together. She calmed the horse and held up the hoof while Matthew dug out crooked or broken nails and replaced them. They found a few swollen fetlocks and knees, which they slathered with ointment and wrapped with gauze strips.

They broke only for a simple late afternoon meal of coffee, cheese, and the last of the cooked meat, then went back to inspect those they had not yet done. Just before dusk they were finished and Cathleen had never felt so tired. She helped Matthew clean the tools, then plunked down beneath an oak to rest.

"Nay, Cat. We are not finished."

"What now, Matthew?"

"We'll need small fires rimming this valley." When she showed her surprise, he shook his head and clicked his tongue. "And here I thought you were the expert on this march. Have you not heard them, Cat? Our companions along the way?"

"Not patrols!"

"Nay. Not two-legged predators. What I have been hearing as we moved among the herd is the far-away sounds of wolves, bears, snakes, and wilder cats than you."

"Snakes? You can hear snakes? You are daft, you are."

"Nay. Just cautious. I almost had one slither down on my head when I visited the Frenchman." He shuddered. "Nasty things. I do not like snakes." He jerked his head to the herd. "Nor will they if one decides to make its way through them. There are poisonous snakes here, Cat. I'd hate to lose one of the yearlings because we were too tired to make a fire to keep them away."

Matthew was right. As usual. He worried about the horses as much as she did, which endeared him more than ever to her. She gave him her hand and he pulled her up. She tucked her arm through his and they walked around the valley as the last of the afternoon sun shone on the backs of the herd. "Look at them, Matthew. Have you ever seen anything so beautiful?"

The horses had intermixed without rancor, and for that she was grateful. Too often stallions became territorial with their mares and fights could escalate into full fledged war, where some came out maimed or dead. The mares who were not pregnant and younger stallions were grouped now in bunches—some grazing, some laying on the ground sleeping, some of the yearlings at play. And rimmed around the herd were the lactating mares and stallions, keeping watch, their ears flicking back and forth, and front to back, listening for danger.

Cat smiled as she helped Matthew gather rocks to pen in their fires. The combined herd was a mismatched group. Though Matthew's had better lines and dispositions than hers since they had been bred from the calmer English and sleeker Arabian stock, she preferred the frisky fighting personalities and slightly stockier stance of the Irish breed. She also preferred the variety of colors Sidhe Stables had achieved. Only Black Turk was a pure color, and that not black. He was the standard Arabian hue— mahogany with black mane, tail, ears, and forelegs.

Firebrand was closest to his color, though more bay than mahogany. And, since some of her brood mares had been Connemara greys, she had several dapple greys with black stockings or socks. There were skewbalds—those with large patches of brown against grey. Pieds, those spotted with dark against light. Chestnuts and browns were rare. As were bays. But she loved the bays most of all because of their contrast between the red of their coats and the black of their tails, manes, and points. Almost all had a mark of one kind or another on their nose. A star set high on the face, a snip of white or grey between the nostrils, a long, narrow stripe running down the full face, or a full wide blaze.

She knew the name of each of her own herd, and some of Matthew's. She wondered if the way she felt about these horses was how other women felt about their children. She knew she would sacrifice everything for their welfare—was that not what they were doing? She knew she would risk her life for theirs—had she not already, when she fled Ireland?

But horses were not children.

Aye, horses were not children.

Suddenly she realized she wanted children. The thought startled her. She thought she had gotten used to being that anomaly in the world, a spinster woman who had chosen that role. But somehow, somewhere deep inside herself was a place which had not accepted her decision, a place which yet saw her sitting holding a baby in her arms. Matthew's baby.

That thought made her gasp.

Her eyes flicked to his; but he was busy setting sticks on the bare earth and piling deadfall on them for a good base for a fire. She studied him. Saints and angels, he was gorgeous in the setting sun! His dark hair had long ago slipped its riband; now it fell across his face as he bent over the fire pit. His wide shoulders, torso, and limbs moved with a muscular grace honed by years of hard work, tempered by the refining fire of English society.

She knew the fire within.

All day she had stolen glimpses of him, evaluating him, wondering if—after what had happened that morning in the saddle—he took the same kind of measure of her. What was he thinking? Did he keep his distance because he did not know how an overture would be received? That was most likely. He had made other overtures recently and she had rebuffed them all. In truth, most of their times together she had rebuffed or ridiculed or reviled him. If he were wary of her, it was for good reason. She could not fault him for that. But she also noticed that he had not set up a separate sleeping area for himself. The tent was there with two blankets rolled in it. Square. Staked. Ready. A blunt reminder of the whispered invitation he had extended that first day on the trail.

What did she want from him? What did she want from herself?

Finishing what she had started on his schooner would do for a start, it would. *Matthew, have you ever thought to wed . . . ?*

Cathleen, have you? For truth, in truth . . . only

with Matthew. She wondered, then, what the night would bring and could not wait for the brilliant oranges of the sky to fade into pinks and purples, and for night to begin.

She was as frisky as a five-week-old foal, as skittery as a squirrel. She chattered like a chicken and made as much sense. Cathleen was on edge and Matthew laughed to himself like a loon.

Ah, the magic of silence.

He had conversed. Analyzed. Pleaded. Cajoled. Ranted. Erupted. He had teased. Deceived. Propositioned. Betrayed. Confessed. He had pursued. Cornered. Challenged. Blockaded. Warred. And wearied.

She had driven him half mad with lust, half crazed with desire, full faithful with love. There wasn't a sane man on the face of the earth who would have her, yet all who knew her reveled in the insanity of loving her. Peter—fierce pirate, with a price on his head from three monarchs—was her even fiercer protector. Mapes would lay down his life for her. Mutton would kill. But none knew her fully. He wondered if she knew herself. Wondered if she cared how each of them felt . . . him, most of all.

He had about run out of patience. Which was why he had kept silent after that little demonstration that morning. Pah! He had kept silent because he was vexed that the only way he got a response from her was in her dreams.

Yet ... it had been a spontaneous response, and she had been full awake when she did it.

He stole a glance at her and his breath stuck in his throat. He couldn't swallow, couldn't breathe.

The last rays of the sun caught her in its embrace, burnishing her with a radiance that seemed to come from within as much as from without. Her hair glowed like flaming pitch. The rays painted her skin a luscious peach and silhouetted her ripe body in a golden haze. As she splashed in the brook and cleaned her face, hands, and arms, water dripped on her shirt and wet it in places which revealed her wondrous breasts, their nipples firm against the fabric, the darkness around them like an eddy, urging him to the center, to the wild endless whorls of desire.

Damnation!

She was innocence and wantonness. Pride and promise. And as stubborn as all her race. He thought she might like to give in, admit the mistakes of the past and embrace a future quite different. He also thought she did not know how to do it without appearing to submit to him, his will and his sway. How could he show her more than he already had, that just as she was, he wanted her. He adored her innocence. Reveled in her wantonness. Took pleasure in her pride, hope in her promises. He understood her stubborn streak. He had one, too. He respected her devotion to her goals because they were his own—at least in business. He was not certain what her personal ones were; she had never hinted that she might want more. But he needed more. And he knew where to start to get it, to convince her that together they could succeed where they warred when apart—the halfbreeds.

Horses were what they had in common. The past was what they had to overcome, triumph over. The future, a mystery. But for now . . . for right now as his eyes filled with the beauty of her and his body hardened in response . . . he would work with what he had, take what she could give, aim for union perfect and indivisible. And never let her think she had surrendered anything to him, else he would lose her. Then all hope of making her his wife and the mother of his children would vanish like the sun as it sank, flashing a warning of doom or delight, depending on the dreams or nightmares of the night.

Since they were out of fresh meat Matthew fished in the brook and caught three small bass which he cleaned, gutted, and steamed under a wet canvas atop hot rocks. Cathleen gathered wild sorrel and mature dandelions, combined them with sliced onions and made a broth which she thickened with corn meal and seasoned with wild parsley, salt, and spicy hot Barbados red pepper—a present from Peter. As they sat eating they could hear the horses splashing into the brook to lap water. The yearlings neighed at each other as they gamboled in the clearing. The mares sighed, lay down, and whickered for their foals. Soon all the sounds of the strangers in the valley settled down and the local inhabitants took over.

Black flies buzzed and landed enough times to send

Cathleen to search for a good strong sassafras leaf, which she used as a fan to ward off the pesky beasts. Frogs chirruped and plopped in the small marshes at the very bottom of the valley. A chorus of tenor-voiced owls vied with the shrill shriek of bats at their nightly forage. A lone wolf howled on top of the mountain and it echoed eerily back and forth until it reached the bottomland in a whisper of its original sound.

Two sounds Cathleen could not identify. A wild cawing overhead and a thrumming noise like a gentle, but loud snore. Both got louder as she and Matthew made the rounds of the campfires to light them and pile them with plenty of wood—enough to last the night and discourage any predators.

"Which watch would you like to take?" Matthew asked, dashing Cathleen's visions of them sharing the tent. She did not know if she was disappointed or relieved.

"The first, if you don't mind," she said.

"Are you certain? You were exhausted this morning."

"Aye." And other things which you dare not point out. Why could she be so decisive in all else but with Matthew be so featherbrained? "But 'tis hell trying to wake me once I'm dead asleep."

"I'll turn in, then." He handed her his rifle. "Keep two primed and ready. I don't expect that animals will skirt those fires; but Indians . . ."

"Aye. I ken." She smiled wanly at Matthew and wished him, "God's peace."

"Wake me when you get tired."

"Aye."

"Promise, Cat. I don't want you waiting, pushing yourself more than you should, and then falling asleep unawares."

"Fear not," she said, and cringed when she heard her father in her words. "I know the danger, Matthew. I will wake you, I promise."

"Aye, then. And God's peace to you, Cathleen."

She prayed they would have it. She knew as well as he that they were damned if they set the fires and damned if they didn't. Aye, the animals feared fire and usually a good circle of it was enough deterrent to stave off an attack. But the circle of fire was a signal to anyone cutting through the valley, for truth. She did not expect British troops, Rebel rabble, or French trappers. But Indians had tread these mountains since time began. They could track and move stealthily. She would not hear them, probably would not see them until it was too late. For Indians were not animals. They might be slowed by the spots of fire which might could blind them for an instant. But with time their eyes would clear and the horses would stand out in relief. Horses. Only rifles were worth more to any tribe.

Her toes and fingers tingled. The tingle became shivers in her feet and hands. Quavers in her legs and arms. Shudders in her belly. Icy tremors in her neck and up her spine. Her whole body shook—not from fear but from a keen knowledge of the terrible struggle they faced in this quest to find safety for beautiful animals.

But did she do it only for the horses?

Was that the only reason she had pushed her family to leave Dunswell in the dead of night? Why she had bullied them into fleeing their beloved Ireland? Why she had plunked herself at the edge of the Maryland frontier? Why she grasped at the first sign of trouble to race into the interior of a country only God knew how wide and wild? Or was there something inside herself that drove her away from the easy way? Drove her from a comfortable "arrangement" with Matthew? Drove her from her mother's beloved home? Drove her from Matthew's suzerainty at Dunswell? From his assurances? From his apologies? From his arms?

Did she fear safety, all the while telling herself that that was what she sought? Was she afraid of love? Afraid of Matthew? Or was it herself she feared?

To the world she appeared self-assured, successful in her endeavors. Saints and angels, she *was* self-assured. But not in all things. She was not her mother. She could not give up the freedom she had fought to gain and subdue her passion for horses the way her mother had subdued her passion for the harp. She could not give way to something she knew was wrong merely because a man wanted to do it. She loved her father; but she saw his flaws and refused to have any like them rule her life.

Yet, she yearned to have Matthew share her passions—physical and emotional, both. She recognized the difference between her and Matthew as a team and Maeve and John as a couple. Maeve had al-

ways curled up in the face of trouble and a part of
her had died with each blow. Cathleen Cochran stuck
out her chin and chest and took the blows, she did,
giving back as much as she got. Where John ruled,
Matthew bargained. Where Maeve grudgingly sub-
mitted, Cathleen joyously warred.

From what, then, was she running? Towards what
was she heading?

And what, dear God, was that sound!?

She sat bolt upright and scanned the darkness of the
mountainsides, using her ears the way the horses did,
turning them in every direction, straining to catch
sounds. There! It sounded again. Oh, dear God, no!

"Matthew," she screamed and primed both rifles.

Black Turk whickered. Firebrand whinnied.
Cuchulain shrieked. The circle of fire kept them contained but the horses milled about in ever mounting
terror.

Matthew bolted from the tent, pulling on his trousers. "What?"

She pointed to the shapes circling the camp.
Shapes so recognizable Matthew swore like a pirate
and dived into the supplies for the five extra rifles
they had had the foresight to pack.

"How good a shot are you?"

"Better than any woman and most men."

"I'll load. You shoot if they break the circle. But
first . . . stay here and keep your rifle pointed at the
biggest one . . ." He scrabbled at dry twigs and began
snapping off branches from brush and small trees.
"Smoke should keep them at bay." He dragged every

plant, bush, and tree from the camp which could burn and scattered them along the ground between the fires, then dumped fallen logs on top of the scrub. "If they look like they're going to break through I'll fire the scrub."

"Matthew! There are others . . ."

He looked where she pointed . . . higher up the mountain. "I'll prime the rifles." He worked quickly, priming them and laying them carefully on a flat rock beside her. "Tell me if you need them."

"Aye." She dare not take her eyes off the shapes circling the camp. "Matthew?"

"Aye?"

"Can you not shoot at all, at all?"

"I can shoot, Cathleen. I'm a damned good shot. But I'll not risk your life." His hands shook but he touched her back and offered her his strength. "Fire is the only thing I know that can keep them away. If they break, I want to keep you safe."

"The herd . . ."

"Damn the herd. We can start again, if need be. You're what's important, Cat. Only you."

"I love you, Matthew."

"Aye. And when we get out of this mess, I'll expect a damned good demonstration of how much."

He set about making straw torches, tying them with tallow string. Tallow. The better to spread the fire quickly, Cathleen thought.

They sat silent. Watchful. Expectant.

The shapes moved, plodding back and forth, their tongues hanging out of their mouths, their eyes dart-ing from one yearling to another. And with each turn they got closer to the fire, as if they tested its strength to see how much they could tolerate.

"I'm not waiting," Matthew said as the shapes made one complete circle and came within three feet of the fires. He bolted, running from one to the other, firing a torch, then dropping it on the piled scrub. He was at the other end of the camp when the first wolf broke through the gap only two fires from Matthew. She screamed, saw him duck behind a huge rock. Then she aimed and fired. The wolf howled, pitching forward.

His howl became the beginning of sounds so terrible Cathleen's soul cringed, it was that other-worldly. The wolves were a grinning death's mask in dozens of shapes. The fires confused them for a moment, but did not stop them. They came. Cathleen shot as quickly as she could, killing the first wave, wounding some of the second. But she could not save one of the yearlings. A huge wolf got it and dragged it away. Most of the others went with him. Those that didn't, she killed.

But she did not leave her post.

She waited for Matthew to fire up the last of the scrub and run to her side to reload and take up a stance beside her.

The killing was not over. On the mountain— moving slowly but steadily closer—there were other shapes more deadly than wolves.

Chapter Nineteen

They stood back to back, with their sides pointing towards the milling, terrified herds, to keep as much of the camp in their sights as was possible. Only a few frightened whickers came from the horses. The departing sounds of the wolves as they dragged the yearling up the mountain became fainter and fainter and then the camp became eerily quiet.

"Will they come, Matthew?"

"Aye. The smell of fresh blood will only spur the others on."

"It was one of yours the wolves got, Matthew. I'm sorry."

"'Twould be a tragedy no matter whose it was, Cat."

"Don't call me that, now," she pleaded. "Not with those things coming down the mountain."

She shuddered and he leaned his back against hers to give her warmth. "Cath-leen, I crave a boon," he whispered.

"Aye, Matthew. Anything."

"Will you finish what you started on my sailboat?"

"I thought we did finish, Matthew."

"Nay. You began to ask a very important question and then I interrupted when I saw Peter on the dock. Do you remember?"

She cocked her head and looked over her shoulder at him. "Aye. I remember."

"Ask now, Cathleen. Though I doubt the answer will surprise you."

Her heart leapt for joy. Joy that in the face of all this madness, Matthew offered his heart, his life, himself. A touch of order returned to the universe, one she needed desperately at that moment. She smiled, warming with the thought of what his answer would mean, what she wanted more than anything in the world this moment; and—she knew with a certainty which only comes when faced with death— what she would always want. Her Matthew, the other half of herself. Her heart. Her love.

"Matthew, have you ever. . . . *Nooo!*"

The small golden cat sprang over a fire which had begun to burn down. She had chosen well, the cat had. A yearling—this time one of Cathleen's—had found the only spot on the rim of the camp not too hot to lay down and rest. Extended in mid flight, the wildcat's claws came down and sliced, catching the yearling's throat. The cat thudded on the carcass, pivoted quickly, picked the yearling up in her mouth, and tried to spring away. But even a great cat such as she was not strong enough to carry the heavy colt over the flames.

Cathleen sighted and aimed. Her finger closed over the trigger. She would have squeezed but a solid black shape streaked over to the predator and its prey. With one mighty scream Black Turk rose on his rear legs and brought his shoed front hooves down on the cat. He trampled her again and again as Cathleen and Matthew held their breaths.

Suddenly, he whirled, whinnying to his band, then circled the herd, nudging pregnant mares and yearlings into the center of the clearing. He whickered at the other stallions. He nudged when he thought they were not moving fast enough.

"Saints and angels, he's taking command."

"And a damned fine job he's doing." Matthew stiffened and raised his rifle as another golden streak came close to the fire barrier and crouched, ready to spring over the smoldering ruin of the deadfall embers. "Nay, you devil. Not another one. Not one more."

He squeezed the trigger and Cathleen exulted in his perfect aim. A larger wildcat lay on its side. Four others paced round it, then looked towards the camp, then towards Matthew and Cathleen. One began to head their way. Matthew dropped his spent rifle and picked up a ready one. He shot it dead.

"Are they on your side, Cathleen?"

"Aye. Three . . . no, four. Higher up the mountain, though. Now they're turning. No, they're coming back. Damn, Matthew, they're fast as the wind!"

* * *

Dawn turned the maelstrom of the camp into a pink haze of shifting fog shapes. Cathleen's legs were numb from standing in one place. Her eyes were weights she could feel, and wasn't that a relief. She hadn't felt anything all the night through except terror. Now, while Matthew finished burying the last of their monster predators and their prey, she had time to allow her heart to return to a normal thu-thump. She had time to survey the wreckage of the herd and found there was little wreckage at all. They had lost four horses. Three yearlings and a pregnant mare. But all the others were safe.

Black Turk walked—nay, pranced, he was so majestic in his movements—through the milling horses. He nosed them one-by-one, smelling to see if they were safe, nudging the younger ones to give them some kind of assurance, rubbing necks with the stallions—even Matthew's—in a kind of truce, whickering or whinnying at the mares until they answered him and bobbed their heads. Cathleen had ne'er seen the like of it, she hadn't. He was keeping order, giving confidence, taking his place as Mughul of his lineage. The Black Turk. Lord of his tribe. He had proven his worth was more than in winning purses. His worth was in giving all he had to protect the weak, kill their enemies, put his own life on the line. The Black Turk. The Black Prince. The Protector.

Her gaze fell on the other protector in that camp.

The Black Englishman. She giggled with relief, fatigue, and love. He was black, indeed. Black from soot and sweat and rich, dark, dirt. But his soul was spotless, magnificent.

Quite simple it was, truly.

She loved him with all her being.

And she had not finished that stupid sentence, that question which needed and answer, though she knew in her heart what the answer would be. Was she prepared for it, and all? Oh, aye. And aye again.

She lowered herself to the ground and let the rifle fall on the pile which had accumulated during the terrible night. She touched them, knowing they and what she had had to do with them last night had filled in the large holes in her thoughts, answered her interminable questions, ended her exhausting quest.

She looked up at the Black Turk and smiled. He, too, had been a part of filling in the gaps, quelling her doubts, illuminating the dark. She knew now, if she had not already known, that life was precious. That love was a gift. That to keep it was the greatest, most important quest in life. That to throw away one or the other was a sin.

Her stubborn Irish pride had almost bought her Hell when she could have achieved heaven with Matthew.

She leaned back and stretched full-length on the cold earth, looking up through the trees to a sky just turning from grey to puce to pink to a soft, silvery blue. Heaven had always been a place up there beyond the clouds—until last night. Last night she had discovered it in something very ordinary—Matthew's back pressing against hers. When the wildcats came, she truly believed that that warm presence was to be the last thing she felt on earth. Now that she was yet here, she knew it was the one thing she wanted to feel every night for the rest of her life, however long God gave her.

What did her pride or fear matter? They had faced death together and survived *because* they were together. No other man would have been so aware of her that words were unnecessary. Any other man— even Peter, who loved her like a father, and therefore treated her like one—would have sent her to a shelter and taken charge. Any other man would have failed. Only Matthew understood her allegiance to her horses and accepted it. Only Matthew valued her judgment and skills and allowed her the right to use them.

God, how she loved him!

She closed her eyes and all she saw on the back of her eyelids was Matthew. She began to giggle as her mind played tricks, and Matthew's clothes began to disappear, leaving only his magnificent body to her view.

"Saints and angels," she whispered.

"Saints and angels," she screeched as two arms picked her up and carried her down a slope. She threw her arms around Matthew's neck, kept her eyes closed and snuggled into the musky-scented man who held her tightly but gently in his arms. As the scent of the horses and the campfires blew in her direction she buried her face against Matthew's neck. "Ummm. I could sleep right here."

He chuckled. "Not on your life."

His arm muscles tensed, then arced, and she was falling free. Her eyes flew open just before her body hit the water. She sank into the cold depths, her clothes a lead weight around her. Those strong arms plucked her up again and stood her on her feet. From his trousers pocket he produced a large piece of soap and presented it with a bow.

"Allow me, my lady," he said, grinning.

She heard a whinny and looked up to see Black Turk leading the herd to the edge of the brook. They did not drink. They watched as Matthew untied her shirt and slipped it from her shoulders. He pulled it free and tossed it towards the bank. Firebrand caught it in his teeth and raced away, the shirt trailing behind him like a pennant. He turned at the edge of the woods and raced back, dropping the shirt on the ground, then taking his position next to his sire, Black Turk.

"Matthew!" She looked down to find him tugging the ties of her split skirt. They floated off and she stepped out of them as daintily as she could. But her boots were filled with water—she did not know how they would fair from this treatment—and she had to throw out a hand for his support. "My boots."

"Aye, my lady."

He stooped to pull up her right leg and she realized he had already removed his own boots, shirt, and trousers. The yearlings were playfully tossing their clothes back and forth to each other. Well, if they could play, so could she and Matthew. Once he pried her boot and stockings off, she balanced on her right foot and gave him her left. But her balance was off and she plopped down into the water. He laughed and came in after her. She opened her eyes to see his wonderful face magnified the way the rest of his body had become. His hair floated out around him like strands of silk. She blew bubbles at him then burst to the surface.

As they had done that night in Donegal, they soaped each other clean. Their ministrations were a balm to the terrors of the previous night and a stimulation to their withheld emotions. Cathleen cried softly—for all she had found, for all she had tossed aside too often.

"Ah, love, don't cry. We've time, now, for everything we want."

She hung her head, humbled by his deep understanding of her, fearful for what came next, fearful for what his response would be to . . .

"Matthew, have you ever thought to wed; and if you have, would you consider me?"

He gave a great shout, picked her up and twirled her around, then carried her up the bank. The horses gave way and Matthew carried her to the tent, laid her down on the blanket and sank to the ground next to her. His hands led. His mouth followed. What he did to her, she did to him.

They loved each other.

Their bodies ached, pulsed, throbbed. Their

mouths kissed, laved, sucked. Their love words mingled with their breaths, enhanced their thoughts, escalated their feelings. She took him inside herself and he filled her with more than his manhood. As his body slid in and out of her, they climbed mountains of pleasure, flowed into valleys of joy. She clung to him, to Matthew, her love, her past and destiny. If there were time and place, she did not know them. So when they crested the highest mountain he took her to another realm, a different plane.

Where love reigned.

For long moments they lay speechless—she, curled in his arms; he, cradling her against him.

"Thank you," he said at last.

Startled, she looked up at him. "What?"

"You can't know—well, mayhap you can." He shifted and crooked his elbow so his head lay in his hand and he could look down at her. He touched her beautiful hair, tangled around her like dark tendrils of fire. He touched her nose and mouth, her neck, her breasts, her belly. He rested his hand against the triangle of curls which had welcomed him so joyously and smiled. "I love you."

"I know."

"Do you know why I love you?"

"Does it have to do with where your hand is?"

"Nay, Cathleen. It has to do with you. You, and what you are."

"Stubborn."

Barbara Cummings

"Aye."

"Mean-spirited."

"Nay."

"Hateful."

"Nay. None of those negative attributes. They are not what drew me to you . . . across mountains and oceans and rivers and continents. And the law. They are not what makes me glad to wake up in the morning." His eyes twinkled and he chuckled. "But that is not to say that you are not sometimes mean-spirited and hateful."

She sniffed. "Then it must be the way we . . . you know . . . come together so well."

He threw back his head and laughed. The sound was picked up by the horses who answered with high-pitched whinnies. "Ah, Cathleen . . . only you would say such things and not know that they have so many different meanings."

"The outspoken, wild thing that I am."

"Aye," he said. "Exactly. The wild, free, wonderful thing that you are." He grasped her hand and put it to his heart. "For that is why I am drawn to you, to soak up that wildness, that freedom. The self-righteous merchant of London, with his penned-in view of the world met a wild thing in Ireland and knew he had no idea what life was about." He kissed the back of her hand then turned it over and kissed her palm. "I had a silly notion that I could experience freedom and real *life* if I had a stable filled with wild, fiery horses who ran like the wind. I thought I could buy freedom, buy life. I had no idea that life for me was wrapped up in a woman who was like no other in the world. A woman who had not bought freedom, but lived free. A woman who had not bought life, but embraced it. Sometimes fought it head on. Always triumphed over adversities which could and did destroy others—including her mother, her father, so many others, even me for a time." He kissed her sweetly, for a long time. "Ah, love. You are my freedom. My life. So I will answer your question. Aye, Matthew Forrest has thought to wed. And, aye, he would consider you. Always has considered you. Always will. Will you wed me, Cathleen Cochran? Can you put all the bitterness behind and join me on the road to God-knows-where?"

She gave him her answer with a kiss so blindingly beautiful he was lost in it. Lost in her arms, ready for her love then and for all time. He took her back to their mountain and loved her with all his heart, all his body, all his soul. And when he once again cuddled her he heard the words which made all the heartache of the past years worth the agony.

"I know where we are going, Matthew. Never fear. 'Tis a wild, wonderful place."

Epilogue

When Mapes, Mutton, and Napanna returned to the camp there was no sign of the terror and turmoil which had occurred. Matthew and Cathleen wished to keep it that way. They had shared grief and death but it had led to joy and commitment. That was what they wished to announce and celebrate.

When Mapes heard, he frowned and doubled his fists. "Don't know, missy. You sure *he's* the one?"

"If it can't be you, Mapes, it must be his lordship," Mutton said. "I offer you congratulations, my lord. And I offer you my best wishes, Cathleen."

"Gratefully accepted," Matthew said. "Now, what do you have to tell?"

"Ah," Mapes grinned. "We have a tasty tale, do we not, young missy?"

"Aye," Napanna said. "We have found what you seek."

Cathleen looked at the restless herd and hoped for their sakes the girl spoke truth. "Tell us."

Mapes cleared his voice and talked about a frontiersman who had settled in Boonsboro after years of surveying the mountains and valleys beyond the gap and across the Potomac. "He says there's hidden canyons—whatever they are—where even Indians have not gone. And narrow, long valleys rich with black soil fit for any crop a man could want. And clear, clean rivers and streams and brooks filled with fish. And trees so thick and tall a hundred houses could be built from but a few. Trees, some of which hang burdened with fruits and nuts in the fall and bushes which bulge with berries in the summer. That's the tales he tells over the campfire at night and in the alehouse in the day. I saw none who did not snicker at him, missy. I do not think they believe him."

"But you did, Mapes?"

"Aye."

Mutton explained, "In our profession, we've had to take the measure of a man quickly, Cathleen. This man did not lie. He did not live in a world of his own making. He spoke clear, clean, honest truth about what he had seen with his own eyes. But I reserved judgment until he told of the loneliness of the place. The winds which howl wild and often, the terrible height of the mountains, and the darkness that descends in the winter. It would take extraordinary people to survive that kind of beauty and agony, he said. To me that meant he did not consider himself extraordinary, because he had turned his back on it and come to the settlement. For companionship. For safety. Mayhap for his peace of mind."

"My people tell of this place, too," Napanna said. "It is across the river, deep in the mountains. I could take you across the river."

"But only if you wish to risk the loneliness of the land," Mutton cautioned.

Matthew and Cathleen exchanged looks pregnant with hope and desire. They had already risked their lives to save the horses. And they knew, each for a different reason, that there would be no loneliness as long as they were together.

When Cathleen nodded, Matthew said, "We shall risk it."

Five days later they sat in the saddle, looking across a Potomac which bubbled with rapids. It was not as wide as Cathleen had expected, but wide enough so she feared what Napanna assured them was no trouble.

"I cannot believe we can simply . . ."

"Do not believe," Napanna said. "Watch."

She dismounted, wound Contessa's reins around her wrist and led her down the river several paces. She scanned the ground, scanned the river, scanned the other bank. She shook her head and moved several yards further south. She scanned the ground, scanned the river, scanned the other bank. Several times she did this until she gave a cry and walked down the bank into the river. She was soon in water up to her knees.

"That's not walking on water, missy," Mapes said. "And if she gets in trouble, I'm not goin' after her."

"Trust, Mapes. We all must learn it."

"Pah! She's touched . . . God almighty!"

For no reason that Cathleen could see Napanna had taken a step forward and upward. Then another step forward. Then another. Though she was twenty paces out into the river the water now lapped her ankles.

"Saints and angels!"

Napanna turned and walked back. "Come," she said, "I will show you where and why."

She took Mapes first, who came back muttering about Indians and magic. Then Matthew, who laughed but would say naught to Cathleen.

"You have to see it, love."

And when she did Cathleen marveled at the wonders laid out before them. "All the way?" she asked.

"Aye. All the way to the other side." Napanna pointed. "See there? That dark shape? And that one?"

"Aye."

"The old ones of the tribe built them in a curve like that to confuse the fish. But they are as wide as the one we stand on. Some, those in the deepest part of the river, are wider. The horses should be able to make it across. Indian ponies always did."

When she returned to the shore, Cathleen saw that Matthew and Mapes had already begun to string the horses one behind the other. They kept the lines short enough to give the animals comfort, long enough to give them room to move.

They knew they had hours of work ahead of them

because they would have to walk back and forth, leading only a few head at a time. But that did not deter any of them. If anything, it spurred them on. Soon, they had groups of four to six horses tied together, milling about the banks of a river which they could not have forded. Cathleen was about to trust her entire life to a young Indian girl, and she did it without hesitation because she had withheld it so often from Matthew. She was a new person, heading for a new life with the man she loved.

Jesus Christ had held out his hand to Peter on the banks of the Sea of Galilee and said, "Fear not. Come to me."

It was as if the world held out its hand to her and soundlessly spoke the same words. And Cathleen Cochran bowed her head, took up the reins of the first group of horses and walked across the Potomac to a new life in the tall dark mountains of a country going to war.

And she had no fear. Matthew was with her.

Author's Afterword

The events around which this novel has been written actually took place. The thoroughbred racehorses of today came from interbreeding of British (or Irish) and Arabian (or Turkish) strains. In fact, every thoroughbred can trace his or her ancestry back to only three famous stallions. First is the Byerly Turk, which was interbred around the turn of the seventeenth century. The Darley Arabian sired his first thoroughbred just into the eighteenth century, about 1705–10. And the Godolphin Arabian, twenty years later. There were thoroughbred racehorses in the colonies (mostly Maryland, Virginia, and North Carolina) by 1743. Horseracing was one of the most popular of colonial entertainments. In fact, one of the favorite topics for church sermons was the sin of gambling, on horse races in particular.

Immediately prior to the beginning of the Revolutionary War, many thoroughbred racehorse owners in Virginia and Maryland hid their prized herds from the

British and Rebel forces by taking them into the Appalachia mountain chain. There they found "hollers" so deep and desolate no self-respecting British or Rebel officer would send his troops into them. There they found safety.

In case you're wondering about that walking on water—that, too, is real. Ruins of Indian fishing traps can be found crisscrossing the Potomac all along its length. The traps were built of huge granite slabs gouged out in the shape of a box with one open end. The open end faced upstream and the Indians stood on the traps, waiting for the fish to blunder into them. When this happened, the Indians scooped the fish out of the water in a woven mat. Their fish traps gave off a dark, ghostly image on the surface of the water. If you knew where to look and what to look for, you could find them. Some can be seen today near White's Ferry in Poolesville, Maryland; but most have crumbled into silt. The traps made it easy to cross a river which had rapids so strong few people would chance it without a boat or ferry; but that was a happenstance, not their intent.

I imagine that every night, Cathleen and Matthew blessed the Potomac Indians for building them, allowing two desperate people to find the safety—and wild freedom—they needed for their horses and their own lives. I like to think that the horse I choose at the Preakness has a little of Black Turk in him.